UNHOLY RETRIBUTION

by

Mary Yungeberg

First published in USA in 2014 by
Mary Yungeberg

ISBN: 978-1495434402

Nicholas Guilak cover photo by Bjoern Kommerell;
Cover design by Matt Christiansen, The Gage Team
nicholasguilak.com and thegageteam.com

ACKNOWLEDGEMENTS

A very special thank you to Nicholas Guilak for once again portraying Rowan Milani on the cover. Nico, in my readers' minds, you have become Rowan. Thank you also for your insight. It took the story to a whole new level and I couldn't have accomplished that without you.

Huge thanks go to Jesse Coleman at NY Book Editors. I wanted an editor who would challenge me to improve as a writer. I received that and much more. It was great to meet you and spend time in my favorite City.

My heartfelt thanks to The Gage Team. From website to bookmarks and everything in between, you kept the project going. Brooke, Matt G. and Matt C. – your expertise, encouragement and friendship are invaluable.

Thank you to Julia Wollman for making the pictures of me look great.

While researching this story I have been privileged to meet, get to know, and call friend, terrific people from the military, counter-terrorism and law enforcement communities. Each and every one of you offered knowledge and expertise without fail. Although you remain anonymous, I know who you are. I appreciate your kind and patient answers to my questions.

To my husband Ernie – thanks honey! A better financier, friend and lover I couldn't imagine. To Becky, my PIP, thanks for all you have done and continue to do. To all the many, many family members and friends who endlessly encourage and support me, THANK YOU. I am most humbly grateful for each and every one of you.

UNHOLY RETRIBUTION

Look not mournfully into the past, it comes not back again.
Wisely improve the present, it is thine.
Go forth to meet the shadowy future without fear,
And with a manly heart.
Henry Wadsworth Longfellow

CHAPTER ONE

Mid-January

Gabriel Hernandez stared at Rowan Milani through the bug-spattered windshield. The hombre acted as though he didn't have a care in the world, his shoulders hunched, his hands thrust deep in the pockets of a worn black leather jacket. Rowan sprinted up the stairs, opened the front door of the mosque and disappeared inside. Gabriel shifted uncomfortably, his stocky, six foot frame cramped in the front seat of the rented Ford Focus. He turned and addressed his colleague. "You know he's got a death wish."

Michael Cristo sat staring at the mosque, tapping his gloved fingers against the steering wheel. "Yeah? What else is new?"

"Well, holy Mother of God, Amigo. Don't you think that might affect what he does – *in there?*" A cold shiver scuttled up his spine, even as he sat sweating in a flannel shirt. "We can't let him run ops this way. It's reckless and he knows better. We could have taken care of that bitch at the hotel."

Michael swept his black hair from his forehead and frowned. "Rowan's on a mission. He's got an endgame and he's hell-bent on making it all go down the way he wants. He won't screw up."

Gabriel shook a gloved finger at Michael. "His lust for retribution has blinded him to everything else. It's like he's gone loco or something."

"If it's bothering you that much, we can talk about it on the way back to Kauai. Right now we've got to finish this."

"Sure, Amigo. Let's get this out of the way." A movement behind the car caught Gabriel's eye and he peered out the side mirror. "Oh shit, someone must have seen us." As the figures passed beneath the nearest street lamp, he saw they were men, carrying pistols that glinted dully in the mellow light. He drew his

Sig P226, keeping it concealed against his knee, invisible in the darkened car interior. The men moved apart and approached the car on opposite sides.

Rowan surveyed the mosque's spacious vestibule, letting his eyes adjust to the light while he got his bearings. Tugging on the baseball cap that made his head itch, he pushed his black rimmed glasses further up his nose and headed down the second hallway on the right. Several men approached, heading toward the vestibule. He kept his head down, murmuring a greeting in Arabic as they walked past. Around a corner and down another branch of the hallway, he found the door he was looking for. He raised his head and smirked at the tiny surveillance camera just below the ceiling.

Entering the room, he noticed a microwave and a coffee maker on a countertop beneath pale wooden cupboards. The scent of garlic, falafel and burned coffee assaulted his nose. He'd found the right room. A rotund man, seated at one of several oval tables, gazed at him over an ample double chin. The man wore a black jacket and matching trousers. A red-checked keffiyeh adorned his head. Falafel balls, along with pita bread and a smearing of hummus, sat on a plate on the table in front of him.

The man looked up, wiped his mouth with a napkin, and addressed him in Arabic. "Can I help you, brother?"

Keeping his eyes lowered, he replied in Arabic. "Are you Brother Mohammad?" When the man nodded, he pushed his glasses up again and smiled. "Master Shemal has requested that I look at the limousine. He is not happy with how it runs."

Mohammad scowled and puffed his chest. "The Caddie? There is nothing wrong with how it runs. I check it myself every day."

The garlic stench burned in Rowan's nose. "I must not disappoint the Master." He wiped his nose and gave the man a conspiratorial wink. "We will both look at the limo. Then I can make a satisfactory report to our Master and keep both our asses safe."

Mohammad chuckled good-naturedly and pushed the plate away. "You speak wisely my brother. Let us do this inspection together. Then we will share some food."

Rowan gestured toward the door he hoped led to the garage. "I'm hungry, let us go now and get it over with."

Mohammad grunted and struggled to his feet. The black uniform strained to cover his chubby figure. Rowan watched the man waddle toward the door, wondering how hard it would be to get him into the trunk of the car. He fingered the Karambit in his jacket pocket and changed his mind, reaching instead for the Glock 18 tucked inside the waistband of his jeans at his left hip. He lifted his jacket and eased the pistol from its holster. Holding it low and slightly behind him, he followed Mohammad into the dank stillness of the garage, his old slip-on leather shoes silent on the spotless cement.

Mohammad sidled between a sedan and an SUV to a sleek, midnight blue Cadillac limousine with darkened windows. While Mohammad fiddled with jingling keys, he placed the barrel of the Glock on his neck. Mohammad froze, dropping the keys in a clanking pile on the floor.

Rowan jabbed the barrel of the pistol hard into the base of Mohammad's skull and spoke in English. "Don't move or I'll kill you." He bent low, snatched the keys and shook them in the man's face. "Open the trunk."

When Mohammad didn't move, Rowan grabbed the man's shoulder and wrenched him around. He pulled off the annoying glasses and shoved them in his pocket. While Mohammad stared at him, he dug in the front pocket of his jeans. He retrieved the suppressor, screwed it onto the barrel and placed the now silenced gun against the man's temple. Holding out the jumble of keys, he glared into Mohammad's frightened brown eyes. "Open the goddamn trunk – right now!"

Mohammad took the keys, fumbling through them with trembling fingers. Choosing one, he pushed a keypad with a stubby forefinger. The trunk of the Cadillac opened with a muted click.

"Get in the trunk." Mohammad took slow, jerky steps to the back of the limo, then stopped. Lifting the gun, Rowan smacked the back of the red-checked keffiyeh. "Get in the trunk – *now.*" The door behind them thudded shut, and he could hear footsteps quickly approaching. Something sharp poked between his shoulders.

A man spoke in Farsi. "Milani, you worthless dog. I couldn't believe it when I saw you on the camera in your silly disguise."

Rowan replied in Farsi. "It wasn't my best effort." Stepping back as he spun to the right, he slammed his elbow into the side of the man's neck. The man fell sideways and bounced off the SUV. A dagger flew from his hand, disappearing beneath the vehicle.

Rowan raised his brows in recognition of his antagonist, sprawled on the cement. "Been a long time, Amir. Who let you into the country?" Not waiting for a response, he stomped on the man's groin, eliciting a shrieking groan. An instinctive reaction raised his choking enemy's head. Rowan rammed the dark face with his knee, banging the man's head against the concrete. Breathing hard, he watched as Amir curled on his side, moaning. He put his full weight behind his foot and stepped down, snapping Amir's neck.

At the sound of scuffling feet, he swung around. Mohammad was almost to the door. "For God's sake, stop, you fat son of a bitch." Raising the Glock, he put a burst of rounds in the broad back and watched Mohammad's body drop to the floor. "At least now I don't have to lift your big ass into the trunk."

* * *

Tensed and ready, Michael lowered the window of the Focus halfway, closing his hand around the Kimber 1911 in his lap. His finger found the trigger as he looked at the man standing outside the car window. He thought the guy must be one of the dozen or so security guards the mosque employed to keep both the curious and potentially malicious off the property.

The guard spoke in accented English. "You must leave. You have no business here."

Wondering what the hell was keeping Rowan, he weighed his options and squinted at the unfriendly face. "Hola. Uh, que pasa Amigo? No Inglés, por favor." He heard Gabriel snort. He stifled a grin and gazed wide-eyed at the guard.

The man frowned at him. Michael saw headlights in the rearview mirror. They blinked bright, then dimmed and went back to bright as a vehicle pulled up behind them and stopped. Beside him, Gabriel stirred and rattled off a few sentences in Spanish to the guard on the passenger side.

He heard a car door slam and then Rowan's voice, barking commands in Arabic. A series of staccato pop-pop's rang out. The guard on Michael's side staggered and crumpled to the ground. The man on the passenger side thudded headfirst against the car door.

One more crack dispatched the street lamp in a mist of shattered glass. The headlights went out, shrouding them in near total darkness. He smacked Gabriel on the shoulder. "Let's go."

Bolting from the car, he saw Rowan wearing a checkered headdress and lugging a body. "Come on, Mike, help me get this piece of shit out of sight. We gotta move."

Michael grabbed the dead man's feet and pulled. "Damn, he's heavier than he looks. Let's just get him to the bushes."

He heard Gabriel on the other side of the car, grunting and swearing. His colleague dragged the body of the other guard from the passenger side, around the front of the car, and over the curb.

After heaving it into the thick shrubs, Gabriel wiped the sweat off his face and then made the sign of the cross. “Let’s get the hell out of here, before the dead come back to life.”

Rowan rushed by, tossing the checkered headdress at him. “Gabriel’s right, let’s roll. We’ve got a date at the Granduca.”

Michael pointed at Gabriel. “I’m driving the limo. You’ve got the Focus.”

Marta Pinella drew the Tanuki fur jacket around her shoulders, clutched her black purse and stepped into the quiet elegance of the Hotel Granduca’s wide hallway. The shimmering, emerald green silk dress fluttered at mid-calf and her three inch heels clacked on the tiled floor. She headed for the lobby, hoping that the car was on time.

A chivalrous porter dashed ahead of her to open the heavy, dark door of the hotel, bowing as she swept past. The limo sat idling beneath the portico, gleaming in the lights. She strode toward the car, fanning pungent exhaust fumes away from her face.

Hesitating when the driver didn’t appear, she wondered if the ugly, fat man who drove for her lover had fallen asleep. If he had, she’d make sure he would pay for the indiscretion. An attendant hurried to open the car door for her. Tossing her luxurious black hair over her shoulder, she slid into the limo’s deep leather seat.

The door closed and locked and the car slid smoothly into gear. She occupied herself by arranging her dress. When a voice addressed her, she jumped. “Hey, Marta.” In the dim light she saw the silhouette of a man seated across from her. The street lamps provided quick flashes of muted light through the darkened windows, but not enough for her to get a good look at him.

Fear gripped her as he spoke again, in a voice she recognized – quiet, sexy and full of contempt. “You look like an expensive whore tonight. That jacket and dress had to cost Muusa a penny or two. It’s gonna be a shame to ruin it.”

Dry-mouthed, she watched as the lights inside the vehicle brightened. Rowan stared at her and ran his fingers through his shaggy black hair. It was a gesture she remembered well. When he stretched his legs, she saw the pistol lying in his lap, a silencer attached.

Panicked, she grabbed her purse, digging frantically for her phone. "You . . ." Fear lodged in her throat, clogging her voice. Unable to look away from his cold, black eyes, she began to tremble.

His quiet laugh unnerved her even more. "What's the matter? Can't find your phone? Want to borrow mine, maybe give Muusa a call? Oh, I know, why don't we call the FBI or CIA, so you can fuck me over again – just for old time's sake."

Unable to control her breathing, she stared at the man who had rejected her – choosing her bitch manager instead. She'd made him suffer for it. "How can you be here? You're supposed to be gone. Muusa will find you."

Rowan laughed out loud. "One day, I'll let Muusa find me. And then, you know what? The two of you can be together again."

While she watched, he raised the pistol almost casually. She heard sharp, snapping sounds and saw a spurt of fire and puffs of smoke. She inhaled the acrid scent of gun powder as pain seared her abdomen. Hunched over, gasping, she clutched her mid-section while warm blood seeped through her fingers. *"Go to hell,"* she whispered.

When Rowan crossed the plush interior to sit beside her, she shrank away. But he wrapped a hand through her hair and yanked her head up. "No worries, I'll be there eventually. But you get to go first."

She cried out. Hundreds of red hot pokers seemed to be jabbing her insides. The pain and the coppery scent of her own blood filled her with terror. "Please, don't."

Head tilted back, she had no choice but to stare at him while he spoke. "You know, I've had a lot of time to think about this."

Something glinted in his hand. She saw the knife as he raised it. The blade curved, like a giant tiger claw. Whimpering, woozy with pain, she tried to speak. "Ohhh . . . no. Please."

Rowan shook his head. "Muusa's people like to behead those they disagree with. I think he'd appreciate it if I upheld the tradition, don't you?"

Moaning as the raw pain wracked her body, she closed her eyes.

He yanked harder on her hair. "Goddamn it, Marta. Hang in there. We're not done yet."

Eyes fluttering open, groaning with each strangled breath, she tried to claw his face, but she was too weak. Her body shook, she cried because she couldn't help it. "Muusa will *kill you . . .* "

The car jerked to a stop and the black tinted glass separating the front and back slid down. The driver turned and spoke. "All right, Rowan, we're ready. End it, so we can head for the airport." The glass went back up.

As her vision clouded, she could barely see the man she hated, but she could still hear him. "OK, it's time." She tried to scream when he tipped her head further back, but could only manage a garbled moan. The pain consumed her as the knife cut deep and sliced across her throat.

Rowan stared out the window of the Gulfstream G650 as the jet's engines roared, vibrating in his chest as the lights of Houston grew small and disappeared. He rubbed his eyes, wincing at their gritty feel. His colleagues wanted to talk and he knew he would need a drink to get through it.

Making his way from mid-cabin to the galley at the front of the aircraft, he observed Gabriel, stretched out on the divan sipping a Coke. Michael looked up from his laptop with a quick grin. Rummaging in the galley cupboard he found a bottle of Jack Daniel's single barrel whiskey and a glass.

Swaying as the jet banked, he poured a generous drink and took the bottle with him. He slumped down in a comfortable leather seat across the aisle from Gabriel and next to Michael. He took a gulp and gestured toward Gabriel with his free hand. "You wanted to talk about this op?" Watching the quick glances between his colleagues, he clenched his jaws and told himself to keep it low-key.

He downed another slug of whiskey and waited for one of them to speak. Gabriel set aside his Coke. It figured. "What's on your mind, Amigo?"

Gabriel looked moody. "What's on my mind is how screwed up this op was, how much cleaner and easier – and safer it would have been to take care of Marta at the hotel."

"Oh, I see." Taking a deep breath and letting it out slowly, he glanced at Michael. "You wanna weigh in?"

Michael shot him an appraising look. "He does have a point. You took some unnecessary risks."

Gabriel pointed an accusing finger. "Si, because you have a hard-on for Shemal, we *all* took risks we shouldn't have."

The whiskey helped to quench his rage. He drained the glass, poured another and took a long swallow. He scowled at Gabriel. "I don't have to justify my actions. *My* plan was to screw with Shemal, cause him as much misery as possible and drive him crazy. I believe I accomplished that."

Gabriel cursed, something in Spanish that Rowan didn't understand and then launched into his critique. "All you can think of is getting even. What would have happened if you'd just skipped smiling for the camera? Or what if you'd listened to us and killed the stupid bitch at the hotel? What if you'd just let her live and concentrated on taking out Shemal and Ainsley instead?"

Rowan tossed back more whiskey and sat the glass in the seat's cup holder. He forced himself to relax and laid his hands on his knees. "I had every right . . ."

Michael reached over and tapped his arm. "Take it easy. Don't pay any attention to Gabriel. I know what you're doing, even if he doesn't, and I'm on board."

Meeting the earnest blue eyes, he raised a brow. "Either of you can say whatever the hell you want, try to kiss my ass or fuck me over, but there's one thing you both need to know." He shifted his gaze to Gabriel's sober visage. "I'm just getting started. This conversation is over."

Retired CIA agent David Harandi stared at Special Presidential Advisor Patricia Hennessey, searching her cold blue eyes, the lines between her aristocratic brows, and then her lips, which were pressed together in a frown. They'd agreed to meet in Potomac, Maryland at what used to be one of their favorite spots, Old Angler's Inn. Over the flickering light of an antique brass lantern, he returned her frown before folding the white cloth napkin and laying it carefully across his plate. "Let me make sure I understand. You . . . well actually the President, would like me to locate Rowan Milani and bring him in."

Patricia sat ramrod straight, hands clutched so tightly together that he could see the tension in the whiteness of her knuckles. "Yes. The President is no longer sure who he can trust. I recommended you."

Thinking about the intricate political chess game he was being drawn into, he stroked his goatee. "No problem, Madam Advisor. I'll get right on it."

Her narrow shoulders remained rigid and he watched as a grimace replaced the frown. "I – I mean *we,* the President and I – need your skill set. Your background and your knowledge of Milani make you invaluable for this operation."

Observing her face in the flickering light, David thought that he would have preferred to relax after dinner and sip cognac on one of the heavy sofas near the fireplace. He sighed. "Anything else, Patti? Would you like me to end Iran's nuclear program if I end up in the neighborhood?"

Patricia sipped the Hennessey X.O. cognac they'd shared many times before, in honor of her ancestors. "This is a serious operation, David. We don't know what kind of damage Milani may be doing to national security."

Noticing how the low light deepened the ochre of the cognac, he murmured, "Soul of the wine." That had been their private mantra – but now wasn't the time for maudlin reminiscing. Lifting his own snifter, he savored the fragrant libation, letting it linger on his tongue before swallowing. "I'm well acquainted with the gravity of this *operation* and how my *background* enhances my prospects for success." Speaking to the President's personal emissary like that should earn him a reprimand, but he didn't give a shit.

Her presumption of Milani's guilt only heightened his angst. "The thing is, Patti, we don't know if Milani betrayed his country. Unlike the FBI, CIA, the media and apparently you and the President, I'm not ready to assume he's guilty simply because he's an American of Middle Eastern descent."

Trying to get hold of his niggling resentment before he went too far, he poured himself some more cognac. He saw the chagrin in Patricia's eyes. Well, *good,* if he'd angered her, so be it. "But of course, being an American of Middle Eastern descent myself, I wouldn't."

As her eyes widened, he knew he'd broken through the superior-to-underling façade. "Oh hell David, you know me better than that. Your *skill* and the fact that you know Milani got you this assignment. And no one is condemning Milani because he's of Middle Eastern descent. The evidence of his wrongdoing comes directly from Muusa Shemal, who's been a good friend to this administration and provided needed assistance to the FBI, and to Director Ainsley in particular."

He sipped cognac and looked at her. "What exactly did Mr. Shemal provide as evidence that implicates Milani? I'm interested in specifics, because that will aid my investigation."

She raised her snifter of cognac, swirled the golden liquid and set it back on the table. "The things Mr. Shemal shared about Milani's activities disgust me. Last winter he approached me with evidence that Milani tried to bring anthrax across our southern border, with the intention of releasing it all around the country. We know he planned a finale in Washington, *specifically* on the lawn of the White House. He was obeying an admonition from a Kuwaiti professor, named Abdallah Nafisi. Milani murdered two men on the U.S.-Mexico border and fled after the anthrax was confiscated by the black ops team he was in charge of. But that's not all."

"That's . . . interesting. Please, continue."

"Mr. Shemal has compiled a wealth of information that shows, among other things, that Milani diverted funds from mosques and several Islamic organizations in the United States and funneled the money to Hamas and al Qaeda. He recorded testimony from people at these mosques and organizations who are willing to testify to Milani's subterfuge."

David drained the snifter of cognac. Patricia's information was disturbing and saddened him. "Has Mr. Shemal shared anything else? The more intel you can give me, the more effectively I can pursue him."

Patricia looked bitter. "The President sought out Milani as a covert assassin, conducting sensitive black ops that only the President was supposed to know about. Instead, Milani ferreted out the informants who'd provided intel to us and tortured them. He killed them, and reported back to the President that he'd eliminated the target he'd been tasked with removing. Mr.

Shemal provided names and dates of execution, as well as how Milani killed each one."

He toyed with the empty snifter. "If this information is ever made public, it will give the FBI a significant black eye. It won't do the administration any favors either."

"This administration is not going to be tainted. In addition to that, I've known Rodney Ainsley for a long time and I won't have his character and commitment to the country besmirched by a man who is almost certainly a terrorist – and a traitor."

When her rigid shoulders slumped, he knew better than to push for any further information. Instead, he tried for a genuine smile. "I'll do my best to make sure that never happens." For a moment he debated pouring more cognac. "Well, it looks like I've got some prep work to do. I'm sure the President expects instant results."

He stood up, keeping his face neutral as he held out his hand. "Madam Advisor, it's been a pleasure. Thank you for your time, and for dinner. Please give the President my regards. I won't let him down."

A glimmer of what they used to have appeared in her eyes and then quickly vanished. "Thank you, and god speed. Keep me informed."

He exited the restaurant and shuttled across the paved parking lot, enjoying the crisp evening air. Sliding into his Mercedes C350, he leaned back in the buttery leather and rubbed his eyes. How in the world had Rowan become so viciously radicalized that he'd even consider spreading anthrax around the country? The kid he'd spent summers growing up with, the smart, cocky young man who'd become a respected FBI special agent would never do that.

Thinking about Rowan's colleagues, the invisible ones who'd helped him escape not once, but twice, brought lingering doubts to his mind. Obviously they believed in Rowan's innocence, so much so that they'd risked capture and prosecution for aiding and abetting a terror suspect. Was it possible that Rowan had been set up? But who would target Rowan? And why? He hit the ignition button on the dash and started the car.

He would find his old friend and figure out whether or not he was innocent or guilty, patriot or traitor. And God help him, because it seemed that every intelligence agency, the President, and as far as he could tell, damn near every American who watched the news, wanted Rowan Milani's ass.

Patricia arranged thick pillows against the headboard of her bed and settled in. A legal pad and pen rested in her lap and a glass of white wine sat on the bedside table. She picked up the pen and started writing. The yellow light from the lamp next to the bed created deep shadows in the room and on the paper in front of her.

Now that she'd enlisted David to find Rowan Milani, she needed to organize her thoughts and begin the final rollout of the plan she'd worked so hard on. David could be trusted to find Milani, she had no doubt of that. Her former lover would be like a dog tussling with a bone. Seeing Milani not just in custody, but headed to Tora Prison under the auspices of Muusa Shemal would be vindication for her, and payback for how the egotistical jerk had treated her.

When Gilford Whitman had won his first presidential election, she'd been right there with him, proud to be his personal advisor and privy to everyone who wanted a piece of him. Controlling access to the President was her domain. Knowing she was considered D.C.'s most powerful woman pleased her. She monitored his inner circle and no one saw the President unless she knew about it.

Rowan Milani had very nearly ruined that for her. Slapping the pen on the legal pad, she grabbed her wine and took a deep swallow. She'd never forget the first and only time she'd met the arrogant man. She'd just started seeing Rodney Ainsley on an occasional basis, while she toyed with whether to pursue him or stay with David. Wanting to impress the FBI director with her level of control and intimacy with the President, she insisted that they drop by his West Wing office one evening, when she knew he'd be there.

To her shock and annoyance, the President was with someone she didn't know; in a private meeting that she, as his personal advisor, had not been apprised of. And he didn't volunteer either the purpose of the meeting or the name of the man he was meeting with. But she'd pressed, while Rodney stood awkwardly beside her, until Whitman reluctantly told her that he was holding a secret briefing with a man who'd been assigned by the previous president to conduct international anti-terrorism black ops. The Commander in Chief, without seeking outside counsel, had decided that it was in the country's best interest to continue the practice. This man's operations were so covert that no one besides the President knew anything about them.

When the President still wouldn't give her a name, she'd confronted the man directly. He'd been observing the exchange between her and the President, lounging in a chair, unconcerned. When she demanded to know his name, he'd remained silent. Then Rodney had spoken up, saying that the man's name was Rowan Milani, and that he was an FBI special agent assigned to a low profile Anti-Terrorism Task Force that conducted specialized operations around the country.

Intent on making sure that the FBI director understood her level of influence and importance, she'd screwed herself into an untenable position. Rodney had not been aware that one of his special agents was doubling as the President's terrorist assassin, but she hadn't known *anything*.

Whitman had been angry with her. He'd told her that she'd overstepped her bounds, coming to his office without notifying him and by bringing Rodney along. While he'd dressed her down in front of both men, Milani had sat there and watched with an amused look on his face. The sordid episode remained as the most embarrassing and humiliating thing that had ever happened to her.

When the President dismissed Milani that evening, she followed him out of the office. She'd gotten right in his face and told him that he must *never again* meet with the President without her knowledge. Milani had stared at her, raised a brow, and said, *I meet with the president when I need to and it's none of your business.*

She had noticed him checking out her body earlier, so she appealed to what she knew about men like him and what they always wanted, especially from women who wielded power. Her face grew hot, even now, when she remembered what happened next. She'd moved closer to him, making sure her breasts touched his chest. When she told him she'd make it worth his while to acknowledge her, he laughed out loud. Then he said, *You are a bitch and I'm not into dogs. Go fuck yourself.* While she stared at him, stunned that he'd dare to speak to her like that, he'd shouldered past her and left.

She'd had a private meeting with the President the following morning. He'd told her that if she did something like that again, he'd dismiss her immediately. She'd tread carefully since that day and she hated Rowan Milani. No one usurped her authority – *no one.* And no one insulted her the way he did without paying a very high price.

After that she conducted her own *covert operation* and found out that Milani received huge, regular payments every month in two offshore accounts. When Muusa Shemal had first contacted Rodney with evidence that Milani was a traitor, she'd relished the thought of bringing him down and confiscating that money. Shemal's offer of payment to both her and Rodney had seemed like suitable recompense for how he'd treated her. Sending

Milani to Tora Prison for interrogation had appealed to her as well.

She jotted notes for a few minutes and sipped more wine. Milani had embarrassed and damaged the country when he managed to escape not once, but twice. One day, she'd make Ralph Johnston and Chad Cantor pay for their role in helping him. At least two other men had helped him escape both times, and she'd see to it that Shemal extracted their names and every bit of pertinent information about them from Milani. Then and only then could she make sure that he was no longer a threat to either the country or her President's administration.

CHAPTER TWO

The Next Day
Rowan thought he'd just closed his eyes, but the sun was shining brightly into the bedroom through floor-to-ceiling windows as he lay flat on his back in the king-size bed. The breeze off the Pacific stirred the coconut palms outside the windows, whispering across the room and raising goose bumps on his arms as he yawned and tried to blink the sleep from his eyes.

Danielle Stratton's body pressed against his. Her head felt heavy on his shoulder and her hair tickled his ribs. His arm beneath her prickled with pins and needles, and when he moved it she woke up. Her hand slid down his chest, over his ribs and drifted to a stop on his belly, making him shiver.

She gave him a sleepy smile. "Good morning. How did the trip go?" She caressed his arm and touched the stubble on his cheek, but it was her naked body between the cool sheets that held his attention.

He stretched, turned on his side and pulled her close, reveling in the soft feel of her breasts against his chest and the heat between their bodies. God, she felt good. "Let's talk later. I have other plans for today."

Danielle giggled and gave him a shove. He let her push him onto his back and settle herself atop him. She looked down, her hair spilling like dark red curtains on either side of his face. "You seem to be well-rested. What time did you get in? I barely remember you coming to bed."

Running his fingers feather soft along her sides, making her squirm, he snickered at the catch in her breath. He liked the friction of her body moving against his. Cupping his hands around her firm rear end, he shifted his knee and pushed her legs apart. He liked that, even more. “How about we talk later . . .” His voice trailed off as her lips, soft and eager, found his.

Clifton Cantor, III stared from behind the solid, comforting width of his desk at CIA Agent Sal Capello, who perched on an antique armchair in his Georgetown office. Knowing he needed to appear relaxed, he kept a firm grip on the annoyance he felt pushing him toward anger. “We’ve been over this before and frankly, it’s getting tedious. Let me reiterate. I’ve never met Mr. Milani. As far as my son and Mr. Johnston are concerned, whatever they’ve gotten themselves into is certainly none of my affair. As I’ve told you repeatedly, Chad and I have never been close. We’ve conversed infrequently over the last several years. How can I possibly be of help to you?”

The stocky, black-haired man eyed him suspiciously. “Mr. Cantor, any information you can give me concerning the location of your son and Ralph Johnston will help your situation. As former FBI special agents, their involvement in Rowan Milani’s first escape and quite probably his second is particularly egregious. Aiding and abetting a terrorist is a serious crime, as I’m sure you are aware.”

Frustrated with the obdurate man, he replied brusquely. “I don’t have a *situation*. Now if you’ll excuse me, I have a meeting with the President to get to.”

The agent waved a thick hand before lumbering to his feet. “For a lobbyist such as yourself . . . well, I’m sure you understand the legal ramifications of withholding information. It will be better for you if I don’t find out you’ve been involved in Rowan Milani’s escape from Quantico – in any way. Rest assured, Mr. Cantor, I intend to apprehend that traitor, along with whoever orchestrated his escape. Please give my regards to the President.”

He waited in silence for the CIA agent to stride through the open doorway and leave the office. He ran a hand through thick, silvering blonde hair to the back of his neck and rubbed vigorously. He hadn't lied to Agent Capello. It had not been his pleasure to meet Rowan Milani – although he'd like to thank the courageous man in person for his service to the United States. Would the country ever acknowledge the sacrifices made by the son of an Iranian immigrant? He had his doubts.

Rising from the desk, he stretched his six-foot-two inch frame, crossed the room to the window and gazed between the blinds at the tree-lined walkway two stories below. The bare branches, the smattering of snow on the cobbled streets, and the mid-afternoon gloom matched his mood. The grandfather clock against the opposite wall struck three o'clock. Listening to the deep chimes, he considered his next move.

For years he'd cultivated a mutually beneficial relationship with a certain businessman. Returning to his desk, he sat down and retrieved his iPhone from his suit pocket. He found the number he wanted and waited, drumming his fingers on the desktop while the phone connected.

A familiar voice with an Italian-laced Chicago accent answered immediately. "Johnny's Place."

"Hello Johnny. How are things in the Windy City this afternoon?"

The gravelly voice sounded pleased. "Well, if it isn't my favorite friend from the District. What can I do for you on this fine January afternoon? Need some authentic Italian food delivered to that dump you call the capitol? Send your airplane and I'll load it up for you."

He laughed despite the serious nature of his call. "I need a favor, my friend. I'm wondering if you'd be willing to lend me a hand."

"This sounds serious, Cliffie. So what, you got some asshole you want offed? I'm in my private office and there aint no bugs on my phone. Say the word and it's done."

Picturing his friend's calculating brown eyes, Clifton knew the job would be done professionally and promptly. "Thank you, Johnny. How you choose to handle this is certainly of no interest to me. My only concern is that you handle it quickly and discreetly, of course."

"Discretion is my middle name. Trust me, Cliffie, you don't wanna know my last name. Who is the guy?"

Even with the office door closed and the knowledge of a secure phone line, Clifton couldn't resist lowering his voice and casting a surreptitious glance around his office. "The name is Sal Capello. He's CIA, so plan accordingly."

Johnny whistled. "That's an ole Chicago boy you're talkin' about. Motherfucker has a bad name around this neighborhood. I'll probably be canonized as a saint for the job."

It wasn't the first time he'd used his influence to hasten someone's departure from the planet. Playing God bothered him, although he had to admit that in this instance it didn't bother him all that much. "You know how much I appreciate your help. One of these days, I am going to get some of that real Italian food you're always talking about."

"That'll be the day. But, you show up at my place and I'll make sure you get the red carpet treatment."

Muusa Shemal sat on a folding chair in front of a scarred metal table, his mind reeling. He'd spent hours the previous evening with the homicide detective seated across from him now. After answering endless questions, he'd been forced to stand and watch as whole areas of his beloved mosque were placed off-limits to everyone but the interlopers who called themselves law enforcement officers.

Now he knew why the limousine had been stolen. Grief threatened to overwhelm him when he thought about his precious Marta. The Jinn had killed her. It could be no one else, although he would never tell the imbeciles in the Houston Police Department. No, he would never do anything that might allow anyone to catch Rowan Milani before he could.

The police had not discovered that he had altered the video recordings from the cameras in the mosque. It had taken all his discipline to control his anger when he saw the contemptible face staring into the camera. But he'd needed to act quickly to remove all evidence of the Jinn before the police arrived with their Crime Scene Unit. He allowed them access to the recordings when they asked. He knew that if he resisted, the kafirs would get a warrant and take what they wanted anyway. By cooperating from the start, he ensured that their suspicions about who entered his sanctuary would be allayed.

He gazed impassively at the man across from him in the cramped interrogation room. Somehow he must find out whether the Jinn was a suspect. "Detective Matthews, although you say there are no leads, surely the limousine must have some fingerprints."

The detective sat with his knees spread wide, his suit pants draped over tan, lizard skin cowboy boots. Long-fingered hands rested on his thighs and his dark brown suit jacket hung open. "Mr. Shemal, my team went over the car, believe me. Whoever did this knew what they were doing. In addition to there being no prints, the vehicle was riddled with hundreds of nine mm bullet holes. I've never seen anything like it. The interior was shredded."

Subdued voices and occasional thumps made him wonder what was happening in the other rooms down the dingy hallway. Peering across the table he met the detective's calm gaze. "What about witnesses? Surely the sound of hundreds of bullets being fired would make considerable noise?"

Detective Matthews rose from the chair and paced around the tiny room. "They left the car in a desolate area, in a gravel pit on the north edge of the city. A group of first-shift workers found it.

The perpetrators most likely used silencers. As far as witnesses go, if the murder took place at the gravel pit, there are no buildings of any kind except for the company's office, within several miles."

Muusa silently thanked Allah that American law enforcement remained as blind and inept as usual. Unexpected pain constricted his chest and sweat dampened his back and chest. He took shallow breaths, trying to alleviate the discomfort. It was imperative that he maintain the artifice he'd created. "It disappoints me that your police department has been unable to make any progress. You must turn the case over to the FBI."

Detective Matthews leaned against the yellowing wall and crossed his arms. "At this time the crime does not fall under the FBI's jurisdiction. I assure you, the Department is equipped to investigate these murders."

Muusa was satisfied that he'd succeeded in deceiving the younger man. "You leave me no choice but to trust your judgment. I only hope that your people will be successful in discovering who has committed these terrible crimes."

"We will work tirelessly to bring whoever killed your friends to justice," the detective assured him.

He took a deep breath, expecting the pain to return, and relaxed when it didn't. "Thank you. If you do not require my presence for further questioning, I would like to return to the mosque."

The detective reached into his suit pocket and produced a business card, slapping it onto the table with a flourish. "Feel free to contact me at any time if you have further questions."

Welcoming the dismissal, Muusa struggled out of the flimsy chair, scooped up the card and reached for the detective's outstretched hand. The firm grip surprised him. "Please keep me informed of your progress."

Detective Matthews escorted him to the door and opened it. "Thank you for coming in, Mr. Shemal. I will certainly contact you as our investigation proceeds."

Gazing into the detective's no-nonsense face, Muusa nodded. "I look forward to any information you can provide. Good day."

An hour later, he entered his private office deep inside the mosque and breathed in the familiar scent of old books and varnished wood. The ancient lamps he'd imported from his homeland cast warm pools of light into the gloom. He shed his suit coat and sat at his desk, accessing the original video recordings on his laptop. Forwarding through the images of the faithful, he stared with concentration. Some of the faces made him smile – until he saw Mohammad. He switched to the footage from the hall by the lounge area and stopped it at the clear picture of a man at the door.

The face that stared deliberately into the camera brought back his nearly volcanic anger. His body shook as he lurched to his feet and planted his hands on the desktop. His agony returned, squeezing his chest. Beads of sweat appeared on his forehead. He shook his fist and shrieked at the image of Rowan Milani. *"As Allah as my witness, you will be mine. You will pay."*

His heart banged in his chest and he pulled in uneven breaths. It had been six months since the Jinn had been whisked from Quantico's brig. Since then, America's vaunted intelligence agencies had found no trace of Rowan Milani. It was as though the man inhabited a different realm. And yet, he appeared at will, *taunting* him. Muusa sank down, into the leather chair. The pain diminished slowly and his rage turned to moans.

Laying his head in his arms, he welcomed the hatred rising in him like a thick black fog, obscuring everything but the face of the man who continued to elude him. He would not rest until the Jinn was his – to do with as he pleased, for as long as he wished. Calm once more, he raised his head. Allah would see to it. And on that day, he would rejoice.

* * *

Danielle perched on the edge of the sectional sofa and tugged at the thick white towel she'd wrapped around her body after showering. Shaking her damp hair around her shoulders, she looked at Rowan, sprawled on the end of the sofa with the remote in one hand, his favorite Starbucks to-go mug in the other. "It's great to have you back. I was hoping we could hit the beach later."

He pointed the remote at the TV. "Uh huh, sure, that sounds great. But first, I want you to see this."

She followed his gesture to an image of Marta, her former employee from the airport in Sioux Falls, South Dakota. Rowan turned up the volume and her stomach tightened as she listened to the description of how Marta had been killed. Heart pounding, she turned her head slowly. "When did this happen?"

When Rowan propped his bare feet on the coffee table, his unbuttoned shirt fell open. She saw the black pistol tucked in the waistband of his jeans. He met her gaze. "Yesterday. I wanted you to know."

She waited for him to say more. He sipped his coffee and looked relaxed. She alternated her gaze from him to the television. "I don't know what to say. Who would do something like that?"

Goose bumps rose on her arms when he snickered. "It was no more than the bitch deserved."

This was a Rowan she'd never seen before. "Do you mean . . ." Her voice faltered at the coldness in his eyes. "How could you *do* that to another person?"

The immediate, savage anger she saw in his face shocked her. Slamming the mug on the coffee table, he stood up. "Goddamn it, Marta fucked you, she fucked me, and she'd do it again, if she could. She needed to be eliminated and that's exactly what I did."

She stared at him, hands clenched in damp fists. For the first time, she was terrified of him. "Oh my God, it never dawned on me when you left. You must have been planning this."

His laugh unnerved her. "You're a smart woman, Danielle. Why do you think I left Kauai? Hell yes I planned it. And you know what? It feels good to be back in business."

"What does that mean – *back in business?"*

The derision in his voice hurt more than his words. "For God's sake, use your brain. Think about it. For a long time my *business* has been eliminating terrorists – it's what I do, or *did,* for the President. For our country. Don't you get it?"

She was unable to wrap her mind around his words. It felt as though a chasm was opening up between them and she didn't know how to reach across it. "Yes, of course I know about what you used to do, as far as killing terrorists, but I thought all of that was behind us. We've worked so hard . . . *you've* worked so hard to recover from everything that happened to you."

Rowan gave her a blank look. She cast about for something that would make him understand. "We've talked so much. Don't you remember, you told me about how you experienced that special *presence*, about how it surrounded you? You said that it helped you. I guess I thought you'd changed. You told me . . . I mean, it seemed like you had come to terms with God and I thought you wanted a different kind of life."

He looked perplexed. "You think I changed? That I want a different kind of life? What the hell are you trying to get at? And what do you mean, *coming to terms with God?* That . . . that *experience* you're talking about happened months ago. You've been spending too much time with my mother, listening to her religious bullshit. Here's reality for you: I intend to eliminate the people who fucked me and all the rest of us. I'm doing us and the country a favor. Why is all of this so hard for you to figure out?"

She saw the hardness in his eyes and the set of his jaw. "Those people hurt you. I *know* that. What they did was unconscionable.

But that's over. It's in the past and you've recovered. We're together and that's the different kind of life I'm talking about. I thought we wanted the same thing. I thought we were building a life here, on Kauai."

Rowan sat back down on the sofa. "Those bastards didn't just hurt me. They are conspiring with the terrorists who want to bring down the country. They are terrorists, too. And besides that, we're not *building a life here.* We're not building anything. We're hiding, waiting for the FBI or CIA to figure out where we are."

She felt the sickness rise in her stomach. Everything she'd believed about him, about *them* had been turned upside down. "Oh my God, you want to keep going, keep killing? I'm not sure I can handle that."

Rowan shrugged. "I wanted to talk to you about all of this. As soon as Chad figures out where Sal Capello is going to be, Mike and Gabriel and I need to head out again."

She tried to appeal to the man she loved. "What if something goes wrong and they catch you again? I'm not sure I can handle that, either." Her voice sank to a whisper. "All I've ever wanted is to be with you. I love you. Please, just don't go . . . don't do this." When he didn't respond, wouldn't even look at her, she stood up and hurried down the hallway and into the bedroom, closing the door and leaning against it.

With shaking fingers she found the lock and turned it. She closed her eyes, wrestling with clamoring, disturbing thoughts. For the first time since she'd met Rowan, she wanted, *needed* to be away from him. The realization pierced her heart. What had happened to the man who loved her? How had she missed this ugly part of him? Somehow, he'd kept the person he really was hidden from her. Opening her eyes, she faced a bitter possibility. What if she didn't know Rowan Milani at all?

* * *

Sal gazed across the wide, glass-topped desk at the President's Special Advisor. He'd found himself on an increasingly short leash since the "Quantico Catastrophe," as the humiliating loss of Rowan Milani from the brig on his watch had been dubbed. And now, he'd been summoned and told to bring all the intelligence he'd collected on the missing terrorist. Much as he'd wanted to avoid the distraction, his boss had made it clear that he needed to heed this particular summons. Paranoid by nature, he held the pile of documents, carefully sorted into tabbed binders, in his arms. This information was everything he'd gleaned in his search for Milani – and it had never been out of his possession.

Patricia looked relaxed. "Agent Capello, thank you for coming, and for bringing the intel you've gathered."

Not trusting the duplicity he saw in her eyes, he grunted assent and shifted the binders, placing a protective hand on them. "You're welcome."

Patricia patted the surface of the desk with her fingertips. "You can leave it all right here. Your compliance is much appreciated by the President."

Sal didn't move. "Excuse me, Madam Advisor. You see, I don't have anything backed up on disk. These hard copies are my entire investigation. If I leave this material here, I lose everything I've put together on Milani."

The woman's face looked like milky white stone. "That is precisely what I want, Agent Capello. You are losing everything because your handling of the incident was deplorable. The President requested that someone more highly skilled take over. We need your material, such as it is, to pass along to our new investigator. Director Ainsley sought your expertise strictly in the capacity of interrogator – at which, I should mention, you failed as well."

As her words and their implication sunk in, anger flowed from his chest upward through his neck, flushing his entire face. "My material, *such as it is,* is the most complete analysis of this specific terror threat, and I am *not* handing it over to some dumbass to make a mess of."

The anger had his chest heaving, but Patricia was unfazed. In fact, he could tell that he'd pissed her off. She stood up, tapping a manicured index finger on the desk. "That's quite enough, Agent Capello. Leave your material and get out of my office, or I'll have you arrested and brought up on charges. How would you like to spend some time in the brig at Quantico? I can make that happen, if you don't cooperate."

He slammed the stack of binders on the desk. A bottle of Perrier water toppled and rolled off the desk, landing with a thud on the carpet. "With all *due* respect, Madam Advisor, it's best you don't threaten me. I'll leave my intel here because the President requested it. As far as I'm concerned, you can shove it all right up your ass."

Rowan tried to thrust aside his irritation with Danielle as he walked along the brick pathway that edged the house and ran parallel to the beach. What made her bring up the painful memories from last fall? Why had she thrown it all back in his face? And how could she be so naive, to think that all he wanted was to *build a life?* What the fuck did that mean, anyway? She should know by now that he couldn't escape the mess his life had become and that he would deal with it – in his own way.

Still angry, he stared at the ocean. Low, dark clouds that matched his mood had transformed the water from turquoise to slate blue. He smelled rain on the breeze that fluttered through the palms. He'd have to try to reason with Danielle again later. Now he had other things to think about. Ralph had called and told him he wanted to meet *right away* with him and with Chad.

It felt like old times. For almost ten years the three of them had planned and carried out operations in the United States under the auspices of the FBI Anti-Terrorism Task Force that Ralph had led. He'd always thought of their activities as the sanitized version of what he did with Mike and Gabriel outside the country, where he wasn't supposed to operate at all.

That he was an FBI special agent, with no jurisdiction outside the United States, had not been an obstacle for the President. He'd never forget what he'd been told by the nation's Commander in Chief: *You're our ghost agent, Rowan, and you work exclusively for me. There is no conflict with your role as an FBI agent, because you don't exist.* He had trusted the man who'd said those words. That man wasn't the President anymore, but the man who was had restated the promise, and he'd trusted him, too.

Shivering in the damp air, looking up at the squawking sea birds, he tucked his mug next to his elbow and buttoned his shirt. He headed up the steps of the deck, crossed the sand blown redwood and slid the glass door open, entering the communal area of the rambling estate house. He'd never trust again.

His former boss sat at the head of a long, polished oak table, wearing a dark blue sweatshirt with NAVY imprinted in bold yellow. "Morning, Rowan. We've got a pot of that Starbucks crap you like so much. It's already eating my stomach lining."

He glanced at Chad, who was seated next to Ralph, looking grubby in a ragged t-shirt. A look of exhaustion had replaced the sunny demeanor he'd come to expect. If something had Chad down, it must be bad. Ignoring Ralph's testy comment, he pointed at the counter, where a bottle of single barrel Jack Daniel's whiskey waited. "Hey, brother, anytime you want, we can start on that. The old man can have all the coffee."

Chad said, "When we're done, OK?"

Ralph scratched his graying whiskers. "At a more civilized hour, I'll gladly crack a bottle of Glenlivet while the two of you destroy your insides with that rot-gut crap."

Rowan poured steaming coffee into his mug and slid into a chair across from Chad. He took a cautious sip and looked from one to the other. "So, have you seen the news?"

They both nodded. "Ding dong, the bitch is dead. Off-hand, I'd say you made quite a splash with that one," Ralph answered. "We'll be damn lucky if law enforcement doesn't put two and two together and figure out that a G650 took off from Hobby. I'm sure as hell the FBI is already involved."

Chad sipped his coffee and set the cup on the table. "Well, that's the beauty of hacking into the FAA's system. There are no records of a G650 landing or taking off."

Ralph looked concerned. "Are you sure no one can trace your work, son? It would be damn unhandy for all of us if they can."

Irritated with Ralph's grilling, Rowan stepped in. "Come on, no one can trace his work. If they could, we'd all be sitting in the brig at Quantico. Besides, you know the Bureau has no reason to get involved in a couple of local Houston murders. Shemal won't implicate me, although by now he knows it was me. If he had, I would have already been named as a suspect – as *the* suspect."

Ralph's eyes narrowed. "And why is that? I was laboring under the impression that this was a clandestine operation."

Chad replied. "You don't think he'd pass up a chance to leave Shemal some kind of calling card?"

Ralph shot Chad a dark look. "No, I don't suppose he'd be able to resist. What did you do, Rowan, send him a card to let him know you sent the bitch to hell?"

Rain spattered against the double glass doors and the windows. His irritation began the burn toward anger as he eyed Ralph. "I just smiled for a camera, that's all."

Ralph clasped his hands together and gave him a hard stare. "God almighty, Rowan, what were you thinking? Now they know you were there. You could have had a neat, tidy operation. What happened to the M.O. you were always lecturing me about? Let's see, how did that go? Oh yeah – *You know how it works, boss. I like to get in and out.* Why didn't you follow your own instructions and keep things clean?"

Rowan tapped impatient fingers on the smooth oak tabletop. "This isn't an FBI assignment you're debriefing me on. I wanted Shemal to know it was me – I wanted to fuck with him and piss him off, so that's what I did. End of discussion." He gestured at Chad. "Have you found out anything more about Capello? I think it's time we go after him."

Chad's blue eyes lit up. "My father called. He contacted a Mafia friend of his, a guy named Johnny Giacopino. He agreed to take out Capello."

Rowan could see that Ralph was ready to launch into a tirade that he didn't want to hear. Shoving away from the table, he stood up and winked at Chad. "I'll talk to Mike and Gabriel and get it set up. I'm not letting some Mafia asshole have Capello. That son of a bitch is mine. I'm game for some Jack, if you're ready."

Ralph blustered in. "Hold on just a damn minute, both of you. Rowan, you need to lay low for a while. And Chad, what's this about your father asking a Mafia hit man to murder a CIA agent?"

His friend's comments deepened his roiling anger. He held up three fingers, ticking each one as he rebutted the criticism. "That bitch was first on my list. Capello is next and then Ainsley. After that, I'll figure out the best way to get Shemal. I'm not your goddamn *special agent* anymore, remember?"

Ralph looked irate. "You got one part right. You're sure as hell not my special agent anymore. I know, because that man wouldn't even think about what you've done and what you're planning to do. You used to have a moral compass. What the hell happened to it?"

"For God's sake, you have to ask what happened to my *moral compass?* You of all people should know I lost that a long time ago."

Ralph didn't let up. "How can you forget that we operate by the rule of law in this country? If you start murdering federal agents – particularly the Director of the FBI – you're as bad as those jihadists you're so fond of killing."

He glared at Ralph. "It's funny you'd mention the *rule of law.* Explain something for me, would you? How exactly did our rule of law country justify sending me to sovereign nations to *murder* their citizens?"

Ralph jabbed an index finger at him. "I'm not getting into a pissing match with you over semantics. You know damn well what I mean. Ainsley and Capello are guilty as hell, but we don't execute people, we try them in a court of law."

Rowan sneered. "That concept didn't seem to apply to me, did it?"

His former boss looked smug. "In case you've forgotten, you were declared an enemy combatant. But *if* you had bothered to consult me, we could have had a conversation about how to handle Marta *and* about why we're here in the first place. But instead, you ran off on your own little *jihad."*

"My own little jihad? Why we're here in the first place? What's all this shit about?"

Ralph looked at him, his blue eyes hard. "Your life was destroyed. But the rest of us chose to support you. I'll admit that when we first got to Kauai, with you all banged up, I wanted to get even, especially with Marta. But we abide by the rule of law. I would have loved to see Marta pay by spending the rest of her life in prison. She might even have been convicted of treason and executed."

Rowan threw up his hands. "Well, this is news to me. And here's some news for both of you: If I don't eliminate Ainsley and Capello and Shemal, the person most likely to be executed for treason is me." An involuntary shudder rippled through his gut. "If you think I'm going to sit here and wait for that, you're crazy."

Ralph took a slurp of coffee. "Listen, no one's asking you to wait around to be executed. But there is a right way to approach this. I've known President Whitman for a long time. I've also got a good friend, a media type who's proven himself trustworthy in the past. Enough time has gone by now and the hubbub over *you* has started to die down. If we can get your story out, then instead of murdering Ainsley or Capello, you can have the satisfaction of seeing them brought to justice."

Rowan shot his older friend a disbelieving look. "We used to be on the same page with this operation. When did you start living in a dream world? Don't you understand that the Muslim Brotherhood has made what you're suggesting *impossible?* Shemal is their front man, you know that. Through him, they've managed to turn Ainsley and the President into their puppets. They pull the strings at the Bureau. Maybe at CIA, too, for all I know."

Ralph looked determined. "You are – were a decorated FBI special agent. That has to count for something. Let me reach out to Whitman and this particular media contact and see if I can't help change the direction of this whole mess."

"Didn't you hear what I said? It's too late for all that. Besides, the President chose to believe Ainsley instead of you last spring. You calling and telling him that he's wrong isn't going to make any difference. Even if he believes you, the damage has been done. If nothing else, the President has to save face. And a couple of media people aren't going to undo the Brotherhood's influence. The time for that is long past. It's *years* past undoing. For God's sake, Ralph, you know all this."

Hurt mixed with defeat in Ralph's face. "As usual, all this . . . well *you,* are out of my control. You'll do exactly what you want, no matter what alternatives any of us point out. But that doesn't mean I can't try."

Rowan sank into a chair. "I'm doing what I have to do, for myself and for the country. Am I the only one who hasn't forgotten what's at stake here? Capello is complicit with Ainsley in collaborating with Shemal. Goddamn it, they're traitors. Once they're gone, then maybe the President will listen to you – or maybe even me."

Ralph's shoulders slumped and his face looked haggard. "No one's forgotten anything. But you run off and commit murder to get even. You leave a string of bodies behind you. You're reckless, or arrogant, or hell, I don't know, both. You're going to slip up and you're going to get caught. None of us has forgotten what that's like, either."

Rowan stood up again, refilled his mug and drifted to the windows to watch the rain. "I'm not going to get caught. Everything I do has a reason and both of you know that every plan has the potential for screw ups. I wanted to send a message to Shemal, let him know I'm not afraid to poke him where it hurts. I want Ainsley and Capello to keep looking over their shoulders, wondering if they're next. And here's something else you both need to know: One of those bodies I left behind was an Iranian operative I've run into before. Shemal must have recruited him. God only knows how he got into the country."

Swinging around, he saw that both of his friends had twisted in their chairs to watch him. Chad spoke first. "I'm with you, brother. I'll do anything I can. Anywhere. Anytime."

Ralph shoved his chair back. "Son, you've got your own problems to deal with."

Looking from one to the other, Rowan came back to the table, but didn't sit down. "What are you talking about?"

Ralph's face softened, he could tell that the older man's fire was gone. "You boys can discuss that between yourselves. Knock yourself out, Rowan. And Chad, you help him. Have a ball. Hell, kill every one of the bastards." His friend finished his coffee, then stood up and reached out to give his shoulder a light squeeze. "Just be careful. I'll let you know what a common sense approach accomplishes after I talk to the President and my contact in D.C." Ralph turned on his heel and strode across the room, opened the door and left.

There was a knock at the door. Derek Norris struggled to his feet. Since it was raining, he'd left the blinds closed and turned on the TV. He had nothing else to do. As a former member of the airline industry and a firm believer in the axiom that it was happy hour somewhere, he'd mixed a Bacardi and Coke. The knocking got louder. He grabbed the remote and shut off the TV. "Give it a rest, I'm coming."

The door to his suite opened and Danielle stepped inside. "I need to talk to you. Have you seen what happened to Marta?"

Surprised, he looked behind her expecting to see Rowan. Before the jerk had entered their lives and wrecked everything, he'd hoped that one day she'd fall in love with him. When she waved a hand in front of his face, he blinked. "Uh no, I've been watching Showtime. What happened to Marta?"

Danielle closed the door and went past him to perch on the edge of the sofa. "Oh my God, it's so awful. Rowan *killed* her, to get even for what she did to him – to us."

He switched on a lamp to dispel the gloom and sat down beside her, trying to pull his eyes away from the snug white t-shirt she wore beneath a light jacket. Touching her shoulder, he felt her trembling. "Dani, are you sure? Try to take a deep breath and calm down. Tell me what happened." He put his arm around her shoulders and gave her a gentle hug. Marta had been one of their best friends.

Danielle took a deep breath and let it out in a rush. "I'm sure. He was gone with Mike and Gabriel for a week. They just got back. It's on the news. No one knows it was him, but he told me."

Derek remembered the day he'd tried to visit Danielle, to talk some sense into her. Rowan had incapacitated him so easily. He'd never forget the look in the man's eyes. *You can be glad I don't have my knife, dumb fuck, because I'd love to slit your throat. But I might break your neck instead.* He glanced at the door, hoping the terrifying man wouldn't know where Danielle had gone. Giving her another quick hug, he stood up, headed for the door, and turned the deadbolt. "You want a drink to help you settle down?"

Danielle watched him from the sofa. "I don't want anything to drink. I don't mean to put all this on you; it's just all of a sudden I'm wondering what in the world I'm doing here."

Was it possible that she had figured out how crazy she'd been to abandon her entire life for Rowan? "What do you mean? Are you talking about what happened to Marta, or how you ended up here, with him?"

"Everything. I can't believe that the man I loved – *still love* – could murder someone just for revenge. What am I going to do? Nothing makes sense to me anymore."

When he heard the heartbreak in her voice, he went to sit beside her again. He took her in his arms and closed his eyes. Her body felt good, so warm and close. But resentment overcame desire when he remembered the other times he'd sat with her while she cried, brokenhearted over Rowan. "Don't talk, just stay here with me for a while."

Danielle sniffled against his shoulder and he held her tight. It had been a lonely six months. The estate on Kauai was like a prison, only he hadn't done anything wrong. Maybe now there was hope, of leaving Kauai, of letting the FBI or CIA know about Rowan, and for both of them to get their lives back – *together.*

Danielle stirred and pulled away from his embrace. "Thanks, Derek. I knew you would listen."

He looked into her worried blue eyes and nodded slowly. "Maybe it's time to think about getting out of here. I'd love to get my life back." He waited to see her reaction.

"I don't know if I can think about leaving. I love Rowan, it's just . . ."

He grasped her hand. "I know, I understand. Let's wait and see what happens. I can't believe Marta's gone. How about we hang out for a while and talk about the good old days?"

"That sounds good. Maybe I will have that drink. It's happy hour somewhere, right?"

He wanted so badly to fix the sadness and make her happy. "That's what I decided earlier. It's what Marta would want us to do. I know that for a fact."

Ralph closed the door of his office and locked it. The last thing he needed was Marion wandering in with a question about the dinner she was planning, while he was on the phone with his media contact. He settled into his office chair and closed his eyes. He'd never seen Rowan so hell-bent on doing things his own way, with no regard for the consequences.

The man he'd only had glimpses of before, the covert assassin who operated outside the rule of law, had come back full force. And now, since their boss-subordinate relationship no longer existed, Rowan had become a law unto himself. He opened his eyes. The hard-headed idiot was headed for certain disaster. There wasn't one damn thing he could do to stop him and he didn't know if he could help him. But he had to try.

He dug his phone from his pocket. It had been nearly ten months since he'd last spoken to his friend Jack McKenzie at FOX News. A trial attorney before turning investigative reporter, razor sharp and unafraid to ask the hard, embarrassing questions, McKenzie had cultivated a reputation as being interested in the unvarnished truth, period. The walls of his friend's office were covered with journalistic awards that attested to the truth behind the reputation.

The wily newsman picked up on the first ring. "This is Jack McKenzie. Who's calling me from a blocked number?"

"Jack, this is Ralph Johnston. How are things in D.C. this afternoon?"

"Holy shit. Ralph Johnston? Give me a sec, I gotta pull over before I wreck my car."

Ralph pictured the angular man with round wire rimmed glasses and a shiny bald head. "I've got all the time you need."

McKenzie muttered. "Why does it have to be so goddamn hard to get around in this effing town? Jesus, Ralph, what's going on? You disappeared with that special agent turned terrorist in quite a spectacular fashion. Why are you calling me, and why *now?"*

"I've been thinking about speaking out for some time. You have a reputation for reporting the truth, as opposed to your *version* of the truth. That's why we need your help. Rowan was set up by the Muslim Brotherhood, specifically by one of their operatives, a man named Muusa Shemal."

"That's quite the accusation you're putting out there. Are you certain Milani is innocent?"

The reporter's words ticked him off. "Hell yes, I'm certain. You think I'd trash my career and my reputation, not to mention the pension I was damn close to drawing on, and go into quasi-permanent hiding on a hunch? Do you think I'm an idiot?"

"Easy, Ralph. You have to understand, other people have done worse. And as far as the media is concerned, you and that youngster Chad Cantor are dog shit for aiding and abetting America's most wanted home grown terrorist."

"Look Jack, you've known me for a long time. Have I ever blown smoke up your ass? About anything?"

His friend sounded somewhat mollified. "No, I've always known you to be a straight shooter. How would you and Cantor and Milani want to handle this? I'd need to do a lot of research. I would want to do videotaped interviews, in person if possible. It will take some time to plan. I need to do some snooping around, gather as much info as possible so I can ask pertinent questions. Shit Ralph, you've got me juiced. This could be the story of the effing century, you know what I mean? Like I said, I'll do some snooping around. We'll talk soon, all right?"

The reporter's rambling enthusiasm sent a wave of relief rolling through him. "Of all the news guys I know, *you* are the one I trust to get at the truth. I'll check back with you in a week or so."

"That'll work. I don't suppose you'd like to give me your number?"

"Good-bye Jack. I'll talk to you next week." Ralph ended the call and stared out the window at the neatly trimmed lawn that bordered the thick underbrush and canopy of trees. He thought about calling the President. He shared a long friendship with Gilford Whitman that had started when his friend's political career was in its infancy. Something held him back, so he decided to wait and see what Jack turned up. He stuffed the phone in his pocket and stood up. The aroma of something sweet caught his attention and his stomach growled. Marion was baking monster cookies for Rowan and he wanted one while they were still warm.

Chad looked up from the recliner and gazed at Rowan lounging on a matching chocolate colored sofa, his bare feet propped up on the low table between them. They'd taken the bottle of Jack Daniel's and moved from the conference room to the study. The only room in the house with no windows, its walls were lined with book-filled shelves. Lit by a couple table lamps, it was cozy, especially after a few hefty shots of Jack on a rainy afternoon.

Surprised that Rowan would actually talk to him after their acrimonious conversation with Ralph, he raised his glass of Jack Daniel's and contemplated the newest disaster. The one he'd created. He wondered how long it would take his volatile friend to explode.

Rowan grabbed the bottle of whiskey and poured some in his mug. "What's up? You said you wanted to talk. So – here I am. Talk."

He hated the sick feeling in the pit of his stomach. "Well, uh there's something . . ."

Rowan gulped whiskey and wiped his mouth with the back of his hand. "What the hell is going on now?"

He swallowed hard. "Bettina's pregnant. I . . . we, uh, it's not like we don't want a baby, but . . ."

The look on his friend's face stopped him cold. For a quick second he wondered if Rowan might pull the Glock and shoot him. "What the . . . *you* . . . with *Bettina?* Goddamn it, Chad. What were you thinking?"

He sat the drink down and wiped his sweaty palms on his jeans. "Oh come on. Shit, how many times could I have asked you the same thing? What the hell were you ever *thinking* with Danielle?"

Rowan raised a brow. "Point taken. That was a stupid question. It's just, Bettina's my sister. And you . . . OK. Whatever. Now what are you going to do?"

Chad grabbed his drink in one hand, gesturing around the room with the other. "I thought we could live happily out here on this island paradise. What about a doctor for check-ups? What about a hospital for – you know, giving birth? I can't believe how irresponsible I was, but I can't undo what's done, so I'm looking for ideas on how to proceed."

Uneasy, waiting for the infamous rage, Chad watched his friend. Rowan tipped his head back and finished the whiskey, held the mug in his lap with both hands and stared at it, appearing lost in thought. "A baby, for God's sake." Rowan looked up, a momentary sadness in his dark eyes before the familiar coldness reasserted itself. "OK, I've got an idea. Why don't you have your father get a hold of Johnny Giacopino and explain the situation?

Maybe he can help. Otherwise, I do know a doctor – and a nurse, who can handle Bettina's, uh, whatever she needs. They run a medical clinic . . ."

Confused, he raised a hand. "What? We don't have access to a medical clinic. Last time I checked, no one here is a nurse. The only *doctor* I know about is Angelo and he's a psychiatrist."

Rowan absently rubbed his shoulder. "I thought you knew. Talk to Mike, he can explain everything."

Chad shook his head. "I don't have any idea what you're talking about, but all right, I'll ask Mike. I haven't had time to think about anything except our security. That's been my main priority, until now."

Rowan gazed at him for a long moment. "Well, taking care of your family is part of that."

Surprised by the absence of anger, Chad snagged the bottle of Jack Daniel's, poured into his glass and tossed back a shot. The fumes made him cough and left his voice rasping. "You're right." He rubbed at the tension in his forehead. Just for a while, he needed to set aside the crushing responsibility he felt to keep everyone safe from the ever-searching, ever-prying cyber-eyes of the FBI, CIA and Shemal.

Rowan looked impatient. "Tell me whatever you know about your father's Chicago connection. I meant what I said – Capello is mine."

The whiskey had begun to take effect. He took another swig. "Ah, that's good shit."

Rowan's fingers tapped restlessly on the mug of whiskey. "Just fill me in on your father's Mafia contact. Then I can get going."

"Can't we just sit and drink – you and me? Damn, I get so sick of the constant battles. All I know is that the Mafia guy is a long-time friend of my father's. C'mon Rowan – just for today, let's drink."

Expecting his friend to tell him to go and fuck himself, he was surprised when instead Rowan hunkered down on the sofa and raised the mug. “All right. Here’s to you and me, brother. Just for today, we drink. And if you’re up for it, I could use your expertise.”

CHAPTER THREE

The Next Day

David stared at the notebook Patricia held out to him. It had to be at least four inches thick and it was crammed full of papers. He took it from her and tucked it under his arm. “This looks like a tremendous amount of information.”

“I tried to organize it. Most of it is in longhand. Agent Capello is old-fashioned that way – and paranoid about leaks. I hope it aids your investigation.” She angled her head. “Let’s walk and talk. It’s not a bad day, for January.”

Standing in front of her at the corner of 15th and Constitution, near the National Monument, he looked around. The temperature had topped out at thirty-five degrees, but there was no wind and the sky was a bright, robin-egg blue. “A walk sounds great.” In another time, before her ambition got in the way, they’d have skipped walking and gone to the Round Robin at the Willard and then to the Occidental for dinner. After that, they’d have spent the night together. But she had no time for him now.

Surprising him, Patricia tucked her arm in his as they strolled along the Mall toward the Monument. “As you might suspect, Agent Capello wasn’t happy about giving up his intel. However, I . . .” She had the grace to look slightly embarrassed. “However, the President didn’t want him creating problems for your investigation. Besides that, he was never tasked with finding Milani. He took that on himself and he needed to be made to stand down. He acquiesced, but took it hard.”

He noted the smug look on her face and marveled at how much she enjoyed her power. Bringing a big dog like Capello to heel must have given her quite a rush. He hoped she never tried that with him. He didn’t relish the thought of a confrontation with her. "Well, I'm sure Agent Capello was anxious to acquit himself for Milani's disappearance from Quantico."

Patricia scoffed. "That was unacceptable on every count – and a major embarrassment for the administration."

Wondering where her loyalties lay and whether she might turn on him if he took a misstep, he kept his annoyance at her tone to himself. "Does that apply to Rodney Ainsley as well? The transfer forms Milani's cohorts used to get him out of Quantico were hacked from the FBI and he is the Director, after all."

She pulled away from him. "Don't be ridiculous. Agent Capello was in charge of Milani at Quantico – that was his responsibility. Rodney has overseen the complete restructuring of cyber-security at the FBI."

Thinking her incredibly naive about Ainsley's capabilities, he curbed the animus he felt. "You're right. Rodney has always been on top of the important things."

Her eyes widened, almost imperceptibly. "Rodney is a smart man. He recognizes who's in power and he knows whose ass to kiss."

What the hell had he said? Oh no, her and *Rodney Ainsley?* She'd dumped him for Ainsley? He was saddened by the ever eroding respect he felt not just for her but for the President who allowed her to play God. He stopped walking and held out his hand. "Thanks for the intel. I'm looking forward to diving into it."

Patricia gave his hand a quick shake. "Stay in touch, David. Don't let me down. I – the *country* needs Rowan Milani to pay for what he's done. Every day that he remains free is a black mark on this administration."

Shivering in the light breeze that had sprung up while they were walking, he zipped up his leather jacket. "I'll be sure to keep you apprised, Madam Advisor."

* * *

Seated behind the ancient steel desk that occupied the majority of his office, Johnny Giacopino sucked on a cigar and stared at Gino, his most trusted crew chief and his younger brother's son. "It's time to call in Sal Capello. And get a hold of Roberto. I've got some work for him that'll make him happy."

Gino grunted. "No problem, Boss."

He laid the cigar in a filthy, round ceramic ashtray. "All right, you're a good boy."

Surprisingly agile, the husky young man pivoted and left the office, closing the door quietly behind him. Johnny leaned back in the creaky chair, reclaimed his cigar from the ashtray and puffed on it until fragrant smoke wafted around his head. The tiny room in the back end of his restaurant served as his inner sanctum. When he needed to have a meeting, he made the parties cram into this office. It reminded them, he liked to think, of why they called him Boss.

He also liked to think that the pictures on the wall behind his desk helped drive home the point. One of them, a personal favorite, was of John Kennedy, flanked on either side by him, at eighteen, and his father. His gaze slid to a similar image, this one of his father and him with Pope Paul VI at the Vatican, not long before both men died. Next to it was a photograph of him, posing with a recent president.

Plucking the phone from the desk, he squinted at the screen and poked the buttons with a stout forefinger. He put the phone on speaker and puffed while he waited. Clifton answered on the second ring. "Hello, Johnny. It's good to hear from you. Do you need something regarding our latest transaction?"

He held the cigar between his thumb and forefinger, tapping it on the ashtray. "Greetings Cliffie. We're in good shape with our transaction, but I'd like to offer my resources. It seems that the morons in our intelligence agencies have things ass-backwards, as usual."

Clifton sounded surprised. "You've certainly done your research, my friend, but I'm not sure if you want to jump on this bandwagon. Some powerful entities are involved."

Johnny puffed on the cigar. "That's my point exactly. Let's get down to business. It didn't take much thinkin' to determine that you must have stashed the principal players on that estate of yours on Kauai. Next, let's chat about Rowan Milani. From what I've heard, he sounds like a stand-up kinda guy. Has he recovered from Capello's version of interrogation?"

"I'm not sure where to start. You're right about the estate. We've got a dozen people hidden there. According to Chad, Rowan is active again and apparently wasn't happy about our arrangement regarding Capello. As a matter of fact, I believe he's determined to take Capello out himself."

Johnny blew a smoke ring. "Is that right? Now that's a man I could take a liking to. I believe I'd like to meet with Mr. Milani. Can you arrange that for me?"

"Of course, I'll ask Chad to put you in touch with him right away. What's your interest in Rowan, if you don't mind my asking?"

Johnny pulled the cigar from his mouth. "Friends of mine in the Middle East jibber-jabbered my ear off about how Milani's been the muscle for our country over there, whackin' the shit out of terrorists. So I can't figure out why he's on the carpet. What the hell is up with the President? I'm curious – do you still trust the guy?"

"I'm losing faith. He's being courted by domestic and foreign sources that seem to have undue influence."

Johnny tapped the cigar on the ashtray. "That's why I want to converse with Mr. Milani. He needs some help. It was good chattin' with you. I'll stay in touch."

* * *

Rowan leaned against the counter and watched Gabriel and Michael nurse cups of coffee. The conference room was the best place to meet with his two colleagues, but he didn't feel like drinking coffee with them. He wanted to finalize their game plan for the Chicago operation and then he needed to find Danielle. "According to Chad's intel, Capello will arrive in Chicago in three days. I've talked to Jerry and Bryan. They prefer to fly into the private side of O'Hare."

Gabriel paced around the table, muttering in Spanish. Watching him, Rowan felt the stir of anger. Gabriel caught his eye and gestured with the cup, sending coffee splattering onto the tiled floor. "Listen, Amigo, this shit is getting out of control. It's gone loco."

Michael muttered "Fuck me," and slouched into a chair at the table.

Rowan stepped in front of Gabriel, forcing his muscular friend to stop walking and face him. "Nothing is out of control or *loco*. We've planned, and will continue to monitor and adjust whatever we need to until we leave – like we always do."

Michael shook his head. "Stop being a bitch, Gabriel. For crying out loud, what's eating at you?"

The stocky Hispanic stared at Rowan, but replied to Michael. "This is bad timing. Law enforcement is going to be on high alert."

Rowan crossed his arms. "Law enforcement is always going to be on high alert. But their focus right now is Houston."

Michael leaned forward. "This is a straightforward operation, Gabriel. We rent a car, watch for Capello to exit O'Hare and follow him. Wherever he ends up, we weigh our options and take him out – before he meets with Mr. Mafia."

Rowan hardened his jaw when Gabriel poked him in the chest. "It's always a simple, easy operation to start with, until you find extra hombres to execute. Then it's a fucking disaster."

Rowan gave Gabriel a shove. "Come on. What's this really about?"

Gabriel stumbled backward, away from him and found a chair. "You want to know what this is about, Amigo? We're dealing with your death wish. I don't want this op to fall apart because of you."

Stunned, Rowan clenched his fists. "What the hell are you talking about? Goddamn it, you think I've got a *death wish?"* Reaching beneath his faded blue FBI sweat shirt, he pulled the Glock 36 from its holster and pushed the barrel against his own temple.

Michael gasped and Gabriel started cursing in Spanish. Holding the pistol steadily against his head with his left hand, finger on the trigger, Rowan glared from one colleague to the other. "I've always got a round in the chamber. If I had a death wish, I'd fix it right now."

Gabriel gave him a baleful stare. "Something is wrong with you. Who gives a shit about justice, when you can stay here with a beautiful woman who loves you? We got rid of Marta and we can take out Shemal. Why not let go of the rest of it? No, because of you, you crazy motherfucker, we have to risk our asses to get rid of everyone."

Lowering the pistol, Rowan shoved it back in the holster and put his hands on his hips. "I don't have a death wish. Justice is the *only* thing I'm interested in and I don't understand why the two of you don't know that by now."

Michael shoved out of his chair and came to stand next to him, waving both arms. "Hell Gabriel, why don't you sit this one out? Better yet, why don't you go home for a while? Sherie's got to be missing you and your kids aren't going to remember who you are if you don't see them soon."

Rowan blinked at his colleagues. Between clandestine ops Gabriel retreated to his wife and kids in San Diego, but not once in the past months of pain and the destruction of his life had he thought about his friend's family. "Mike's right. Take a break and go home. Be with your family."

Michael turned to stare at him. *"What?* I was kidding, trying to piss him off and get him thinking. We can't run this op alone, Rowan."

Gabriel rolled his dark eyes. "Both of you, shut up! I'm not going to sit this one out. But, when it's finished, when that prick Capello is dead, *then* I'm going home to see if I still have a family left."

Rowan decided he'd had enough. "Well, I'm glad we got this all settled." He turned and left the conference room.

Muusa drank in the splendor of the Oval Office with greedy eyes. His access to the brain center of the beast was just recompense for the decades he and the Brotherhood had toiled. But he had to remember why he had entered the enclave of the most powerful man on earth. Rowan Milani stood in the way of all they had accomplished and threatened to expose their deception. While the Jinn remained out of his grasp, it was still possible that he would speak the truth and that the President and the country would listen.

His voice must be silenced – permanently. Only then could *The Project* continue toward its ultimate goal. The fire of longing burned in his heart, for the day when the star and crescent of Islam would be raised over this White House, replacing the loathsome Stars and Stripes. While masking his contempt at the dhimmis who would one day bow, he repeated the Brotherhood's credo in his mind. *Allah is our objective. The Prophet is our leader. Qur'an is our law. Jihad is our way. Dying in the way of Allah is our highest hope.*

The mantra comforted him as much as it guided him. "Mr. President, Madam Advisor, I am honored to meet with you here. It is kind of you to update me personally. My commitments to the

Council of American-Islamic Relations have made this a busy trip to your capitol."

President Gilford Whitman nodded gravely and spread his hands in an expansive gesture. "Mr. Shemal, it is my pleasure to welcome you. My administration and our entire country are grateful for the role you've played in exposing Rowan Milani as a traitor. I am also deeply sorry for the loss of Ms. Pinella and your employees. It galls me that these savage murders were committed without detection. That Milani was able to travel freely to Houston and enter your mosque is simply not acceptable. But I will tell you this. Milani's actions have only hardened my resolve to apprehend him."

The fawning man was a weak dog. He turned to the woman advisor. The President's leashed bitch was more to his liking, even though she dared to leave her head uncovered in his presence. He sensed in her rigid body and clenched fists a shared hatred for the Jinn. "Madam Advisor, I wish to express my appreciation for your assistance in Rowan Milani's first capture. Unfortunately for all of us, the three CIA agents you procured for our mission were perhaps inadequate."

Ah yes, the humiliation she suffered at the Jinn's first and second escape had carved enmity in her face and even as he watched her, it deepened. "Mr. Shemal, you have my most profound apology for the performance of the men I appropriated to arrest, interrogate and transport Milani. Their zeal to see him punished overcame their good sense, I'm afraid."

President Whitman rose from the chair and paced the room. "The mistakes made in our first efforts have been reviewed ad nausea. It is imperative to ensure that when Rowan Milani is apprehended for the *third* time, he remain in custody. Patricia, please tell Mr. Shemal about the newest member of our team."

The President's advisor looked pleased. "David Harandi is replacing Sal Capello. He's a talented intelligence agent who recently retired from the CIA. I've known him for a number of years. He is one of our most highly skilled operators and comes to this mission with impeccable credentials."

Muusa leaned back on the brocade sofa and crossed one leg over the other. He needed time to consider the newest obstacle the infidels had placed in his path. Another so-called intelligence agent would only impede him. But first he must ascertain their commitment to relinquishing the Jinn to his control. "I wish to reiterate my promise to you and the people of the United States, Mr. President. When Milani is captured, Tora Prison awaits him. Incarcerating your country's traitor there will prevent access to saboteurs who would attempt another escape."

The President returned to his seat near the fireplace and clasped his hands together. "My administration cannot afford to let Rowan Milani make a mockery of our security measures. Our efforts at Quantico fell woefully short. I am officially accepting your offer now, on behalf of my administration and the people of the United States."

Muusa returned his focus to the President's bitch. His deception must continue. It was essential that he sow doubt in her fertile mind. "Am I correct in connecting your new agent with Sa-id Harandi, the man I interrogated to gather the intelligence needed to expose the traitor?"

Patricia replied. "Yes, Sa-id was David's uncle. He was murdered soon after your interrogation. The local authorities have never solved the case."

He chose his words with care. "It gives me no pleasure to inform you that Rowan Milani murdered Sa-id Harandi when he learned of his betrayal. Sa-id was involved in Milani's deception, as he revealed under my interrogation. Sometimes, how shall I put it? Blood loyalty trumps allegiance to country. If David Harandi is as skilled as you say, then trickery and deceit would be second nature to him. Although you trust him, have you considered that he may be involved in Milani's deception and using this opportunity to further his jihad against the United States?"

Patricia's face looked like cold marble. "As I stated before, I have known David for a number of years, though I thank you for expressing your concern."

The President shook his head. "Every day I am surprised and dismayed at the repugnancy of some of the people who have been entrusted with the protection of this country. Rest assured, we will bring Milani in."

Muusa suppressed his pleasure and allowed a commiserating frown. "Finding and retaining loyalty is the bane of modern-day leaders around the globe. Have you considered sending your new agent to Houston since that is where Milani was most recently? I would like the opportunity to meet with him myself."

Whitman looked thoughtful. "Yes, I believe we can send Harandi to Houston. Do I understand correctly that you have not revealed Milani's involvement to local law enforcement there?"

He nodded. "I did not wish to reveal his presence. Although I do not understand your legal system completely, I would not like to see Milani detained for those murders in Houston and offered what I believe you call *due process*. He is guilty of much larger crimes against the country."

The President responded. "You don't have to worry about that. Milani has been declared an enemy combatant. As such, he forfeits his right to due process. He will be dealt with appropriately."

Muusa turned to the woman. "If I am to help you as much as possible, it is most important that you notify me immediately when Milani is apprehended. Arrangements for transport must be in place as well. May I trust that you will see to these things, Madam Advisor?"

The bitch retained her imperious tone. "I intend to personally oversee Rowan Milani's detention and transport."

Muusa stood up, satisfied with what he had accomplished. With the Americans, the seeds of deception required careful planting and patient nurturing. Correctly applied, they would produce the desired results. "Thank you. Now, I must attend to my duties at CAIR. Please keep me informed, Madam Advisor. Mr. President, thank you again for meeting with me."

Rowan stalked along the hallway that bisected the labyrinthine house. He'd wanted to hit the beach with Danielle at their favorite spot. But she wouldn't answer her phone. Remembering the fear and distrust in her eyes when he'd told her about Marta, he slammed a fist into his open hand. Did she think he was going to kill her too? Fuming, he rounded the final corner and stopped short. Angelo Blevins stood at the door. "Hey Doc, what's going on?"

Angelo's slender face creased in genuine pleasure. "Rowan, I thought I'd missed you."

"Nope, here I am. What do you want?"

Angelo tucked graying strands of shoulder length hair behind his ears. "I just want a few minutes of your time. I heard you were back and hoped we could talk."

Rowan shrugged, wondering which one of his friends had been concerned enough about him to send the canny psychiatrist to his door. Fifteen minutes later, situated in the middle of the sofa in the living room, a half glass of whiskey clasped in both hands, he stared at Angelo. "What did you want to talk about?"

The doctor sipped a steaming cup of coffee and looked up from where he lounged on a love seat. "Ah, you make a great cup of coffee."

He took a gulp of whiskey. "I'm not in the mood for small talk. Get to it, would you?"

"If I've chosen a bad time, just say so. We can postpone, if you'd like. You did say you had plenty of time, and I confess that I took you at your word."

Wishing he'd gone to the beach by himself instead of coming back to the suite, he stared at the doctor. "You win. Take your time. Hell, let's talk all afternoon."

Angelo gazed calmly at him. "Have I upset you?"

Rowan tossed back more whiskey and put his feet up on the table. "For God's sake, start talking."

Angelo took a cautious swallow of coffee and gave him a shrewd look. "You and I have talked many times about the restlessness you feel being here. About how important justice is to you – and about how you plan to achieve it. You are a smart man, so I am sure you know that some of your friends approached me and asked if I would talk with you."

"Yeah, I figured. Let me sum it up for you. Danielle thinks she's next on my hit list. I don't have a moral compass, though I apparently do have a death wish. Did I miss anything?"

A fleeting smile lifted Angelo's thin lips. "I had not heard about the death wish. I know that everything you have done for your country has been at significant personal risk, and conducted with honor and courage, for a specific cause. You are much more of a *man* than those who pursue you."

He contemplated the doctor's lean, sober face. "I'm pretty sure you didn't come over here at the request of my friends to tell me what a great man I am."

The psychiatrist drank more coffee, cradling the cup in both hands. "My reasons for being here are varied. First, I am interested in how you are doing. That is always my primary concern and of course, the basic reason I am here with you, on the island. Second, if you are willing, I would like to talk about the future. Essentially, I think it would be beneficial for you to consider where you have come from and then, where you are headed."

He drained the glass of whiskey. "I'm fine. Couldn't be better. As far as the future is concerned, I'm ready for phase two. Any more questions?"

"To what do you attribute your edginess?"

Rowan eyed the bottle of Jack Daniel's. "I feel edgy because I'm not interested in you digging into my goddamn head anymore. No matter what you or anyone else *thinks,* I'm going to eliminate all the people who ruined my life."

"Did it ever occur to you that your sense of honor and commitment might have become twisted into a need for retribution – and that by indulging that need, you could be driving away the people who care the most for you? Would losing those relationships be an acceptable cost for the opportunity to get even with the people who hurt you? Have you ever thought that, with so many who care about you, your life is not actually as ruined as you think it is?"

Frustration rose, and, right behind it, bitter rage. He hadn't asked for the doctor's learned opinion in the first place, and he didn't need a fucking psych evaluation. He poured more whiskey, clanking the neck of the bottle against the squat glass. "You know what, Doc? I'm done talking."

"Rowan, you have made great strides since last fall. I remember how wounded you were. But you displayed great courage. You faced the past and all the painful things it held for you. I know that coming to terms with what you have lost was a deeply emotional and hopefully, a healing experience."

"Why is it that you and everyone else keep bringing up *my past?* Goddamn it, I've dealt with my past and I wish you and everyone else would too, because I am sick to death of rehashing it."

Angelo swallowed more coffee. "I apologize for mentioning what is obviously still painful for you. Concern for how the past may be coloring the decisions you are making now is why I brought it up. Take some time and consider the direction you are heading. Search your heart. The stakes are extremely high in this game you are playing."

Rowan stood up and walked to the door. "My decisions are not colored by what's happened to me. They're based on what I need to do. I'm not playing a game. And in case you don't remember, I've had plenty of time to consider the direction I'm heading."

Angelo followed him. "I do understand your rationale. But I am your doctor, and it is my responsibility to point out what might be missing in your thought processes. I would be remiss not to make you aware of ways in which you may be endangering yourself."

He yanked the door open and waited until Angelo stepped through. "Hey, Doc."

Angelo turned to face him, a hopeful look on his kind face. "Yes?"

"I don't have a heart. I thought you knew that." He slammed the door as hard as he could in the doctor's surprised face.

David assessed the deadbolt, chose the tools he wanted, and quickly picked the lock. Stashing the small, leather pouch of tools in his jacket pocket, he drew his compact Beretta forty-five and opened the door. He stepped inside the townhouse and was struck immediately by the absence of personal effects. The elegant Georgetown address had been Rowan Milani's residence whenever he was in D.C., but the man had obviously never considered it a home.

A fine layer of dust covered the glass and metal end tables in the living room, and there was no TV. Between FBI anti-terrorism assignments and whatever else he was up to, Milani probably hadn't spent much time in the townhouse. The sofa, done in rich, burgundy leather with fat cushions, looked comfy. The walls were bereft of pictures, adding to the empty feeling.

Wandering into the kitchen, he noted that the fridge was bare, except for an expired six-pack of Coke. A case of Jack Daniel's single barrel whiskey sat on the counter.

As he followed the floor plan to a spacious bedroom, a kaleidoscope of long forgotten memories surfaced. They didn't square with what he'd been told in his interviews with Milani's former FBI associates. Those conversations had revealed a man who was aloof, confrontational if prodded, and universally pegged as an arrogant jerk.

Shoving aside his feelings of nostalgia, he looked around the bedroom, hoping for clues to the transformation of his carefree friend. A simple dresser stood beyond the end of the bed, topped by a ruined mirror. Something had shattered the mirror. He began a search of the dresser drawers. They contained boxers, undershirts, belts, and only two pairs of dress socks. The closet held black, navy blue and steel-gray suits by Armani, Ralph Lauren and Gucci, along with crisp white shirts and a collection of ties that made him envious. The shelves held jeans, sweaters, and a few t-shirts. He muttered, "Where the hell are the socks?"

Stepping into a second bedroom, he looked around the nearly barren room. A desk sat against one wall with a pen, stapler and a blank yellow legal pad lying on its dusty surface. He checked the legal pad, but there were no impressions, nothing to indicate what had been written on a previous page. A laser printer occupied a matching table next to the desk.

When he opened the closet door he stopped and stared, then whistled. From floor to ceiling, forty-five caliber and nine mm defensive ammunition stood stacked in cases. Mouth open, he tried to count the cases. Finally he gave up. He'd never seen that much ammo in a personal residence before. Milani was nothing if not prepared, or paranoid, or both.

He holstered the Beretta, took pictures of every room's contents with his phone and then plopped down on the sofa to ponder what he'd seen and more importantly, what he hadn't.

After a few minutes, he stared blindly out the bay window that let light into the living area. His old friend liked booze, guns and fancy suits, but apparently not socks. Frustrated, he stood up. As he did, his phone rang. He dug it out of his jacket pocket, glanced at the caller ID and answered. "Hello Madam Advisor. How may I help you?"

Patricia spoke with deliberate authority. "You need to shift the focus of your search. The President and I met with Mr. Shemal while he was in the capitol on a speaking engagement. He specifically requested your help in Houston."

"I've just gotten off to a good start here. Capello's notes are thorough and I'm working my way through the notebook you gave me. Based on his information, I've already got several possible leads."

Impatience colored her response. "My purpose for giving you Capello's mess was not so you could conduct the same investigation. I'm counting on your creativity and your knowledge of Milani to guide you. Mr. Shemal has a video clearly showing that Milani was in the mosque in Houston. He has played an invaluable role in uncovering Milani's treason. We will try to accommodate him with whatever he requests."

"Have you or anyone else seen the video? If not, we only have Shemal's belief that it's Rowan. Has he ever met the man?"

"No, of course I haven't seen the video, and I don't know if Shemal has met Milani. Get on a plane. See that video for yourself and confirm that it's Milani. For all we know, he's still in Houston waiting for an opportunity to take out Shemal. Do what I brought you in to do and find my traitor."

Burgeoning anger had him breathing hard, but he kept his voice neutral. "I'll head for Houston right away. But it's my opinion that if Milani was indeed in the mosque and wanted to kill Shemal, he'd be dead. If he committed these murders and didn't go after Shemal, he has another plan in mind. He's not a stupid man."

Her disapproval came across clearly. "Do your job, David. Contact me after you've seen that video." Then she was gone.

He glared for a moment at the phone and stuffed it back in his pocket. "Oh, I'll do my job, Madam Advisor, don't you worry. And all this time, I thought it was the President who hired me." He gazed around the living room one last time and left. As he headed down the walkway to his car, he noticed snowflakes falling in the afternoon gloom. He'd go to Houston when he was damn good and ready.

CHAPTER FOUR

Angelo tried to relax. The waves slapping the hull of Ralph's cruiser, and the knowledge that they were in water thousands of feet deep didn't help. He touched the bright yellow, padded life jacket cinched around his chest and focused on the shoreline. Kauai's towering green cliffs painted a breathtaking picture against the variegated blues of sky and ocean.

The motor droned on and he looked at Ralph standing at the wheel, his legs spread, back straight. The former SEAL looked the part of a crusty sailor in a tattered, flapping shirt, faded brown cargo shorts and canvas deck shoes. His friend had topped off the ensemble with mirrored sunglasses and a floppy camo hat.

The motor slowed and then died. The eighteen foot cruiser rose and fell in the heaving waves. This was nothing like puttering around on the Missouri River in his father's rust bucket fishing boat. Ralph sank into a deck chair opposite him, popped open a perspiring can of Coke and grinned. "Is this private enough for you, Doc?"

His friend's obvious enjoyment made him smile. "It is." The smile faded. "I am extremely concerned about the direction Rowan's plans for revenge are taking. Do you think there is any way to stop him?"

Ralph gazed across the water. "Short of catching him off-guard long enough to slap cuffs on him and lock him in a room somewhere, the answer is no."

"After working with Rowan for four months, I was confident I knew him well enough to offer a direct, honest appraisal of his actions. I fully expected the two of us to have a reasonable discussion."

Ralph chuckled. "How did that go?"

Angelo grabbed a bottle of iced tea from the styrofoam cooler between them. "He kicked me out. Slammed the door in my face, so hard I'm surprised it didn't come apart."

Ralph pulled the sunglasses off and rubbed his eyes. "I'm not surprised. When he gets something in his head, it's damn hard to dissuade him. I used to have some leverage as his boss, but those days are gone."

A pod of breaching dolphins caught Angelo's attention and he watched the glistening, gray mammals for a moment. "When Chad and Michael approached me last summer about coming here, my intent was to help Rowan heal. I was confident that I could address the post-traumatic stress I thought he was dealing with. Now I find myself questioning whether he has been honest with me at all or whether he is even suffering from PTSD. It is difficult for me to accept that I could have been so easily deceived."

"Take it easy on yourself, Doc. I've known Rowan for over ten years and the main thing I've figured out is that his mulish nature causes most of his problems. And believe me, he's well-schooled in duplicity. You have to remember that he spent a number of years lying his way around the world on our country's behalf."

Realizing he was still holding the bottle of tea, Angelo unscrewed the top and met Ralph's gaze. "It seems that I have taken too many things for granted. I feel like a fool."

"You've helped Rowan more than he'll ever admit to or even understand. And I know the rest of us could benefit from your expertise, especially when the inevitable happens."

Foreboding gripped him and he screwed the cap back on the tea and laid it in his lap. "What will happen to him if he's caught? Is there any hope of the truth coming out?"

Ralph sounded resigned. "Rowan's so far out of control and has already caused such embarrassment that if one of our intelligence agencies nabs him, they'll put the screws to him, big-time. Not to mention the fact that Muusa Shemal wants him worse than anyone."

"If Rowan's apprehended by the FBI or CIA, Shemal won't be able to touch him, will he?"

The lines on Ralph's face deepened. "I think that no matter who catches Rowan, he'll eventually be handed off to Shemal. Too much money has changed hands and too many corrupting influences are involved."

His friend looked so bereft he wanted to reach out, but instead he wiped condensation off the bottle of tea and stared at the undulating turquoise waves. A cloud crossed the sun and the breeze chilled him. "That does not sound like due process to me. They can't just do that, can they?"

"If there's one thing I've discovered, it's that the organization that wants Rowan – the Muslim Brotherhood – has tentacles everywhere and will stop at nothing to get him. Sometimes I think he knows that and he's determined to cause as much destruction as possible before his time runs out."

"Rowan told me he has had plenty of time to think about the direction he is headed and that no one is going to stop him."

Ralph chugged the Coke and belched. "I know. And God almighty, I hope he can pull it off. Last fall Michael told Chad and me that once Rowan recovered we'd have a hell of a time keeping him here. He was right. Maybe Michael knows Rowan better than I ever did."

Angelo looked at his friend, saddened by the desolation in his kind face. "I am beginning to think that no one knows Rowan very well. I have helped many combat veterans over the years, grievously wounded men suffering from PTSD. I confess that Rowan has me stymied. I don't know how to connect with him and I am beginning to think that I never had a clue of what is really going on in his head."

Ralph pulled his hat off, scratched his head and put it back on. "I don't think anyone knows the sort of demons that haunt him. It will kill me if . . ." Ralph's voice caught. "Hell, Angelo. I'm sorry. It's just, we both know he'll go and do what he thinks he has too. All I – all *we* – can do is pick up the pieces. Speaking from experience, it's damn ugly and it sure as hell isn't much fun."

Angelo stared at the bottle of iced tea and then caught Ralph's gaze. "We'll deal with it together. I'll do everything I can to help each of you, if or when the time comes."

Ralph nodded and shoved the sunglasses back on his head. "We better head back. Marion decided to invite Derek over for dinner and I promised to be there. That was another bad decision, bringing him out here. He's a lot more of a liability now than if we'd let the CIA take him in and interrogate him."

Puzzled, Angelo tossed the bottle of tea back in the cooler. "I've often wondered about that, given how much Rowan despises Derek."

Ralph spoke over his shoulder as he headed for the front of the cruiser. "I think hate is a more accurate word. One thing I know for sure, Rowan sees Derek as the complete antithesis of what a man should be. And we're stuck with the lousy shit, because I can guarantee you that the first thing he'd do if given the opportunity is tell anybody who'd listen where Rowan and the rest of us are."

Angelo felt more disquieted than when they started. Remembering the intensity of the anger and pain in Rowan's eyes, he couldn't help feeling that he'd let him down.

Rowan strode restlessly around the living room, stopping only to stare out the big window, across the lawn to the ribbon of sand and the ocean beyond. He glimpsed the sun, hovering over the Pacific like a fat, red ball on the horizon. Right now, he and Danielle should be out there, on the beach. He scowled, wondering where the hell she was. When he woke up that morning and reached for her, his hands found an empty bed.

Maybe she had stayed with Ralph and Marion. Or hell, for all he knew, she might have camped out with Derek. He sneered. Gabriel had stopped him from eliminating the dumb fuck once, but he'd never lost interest in completing the task. He scratched the irritating stubble on his jaw and gazed around the room. It felt like a home. Danielle had placed plants, pillows and pictures throughout the suite.

Spotting the bottle of Jack and the squat crystal tumbler he'd left on coffee table after escorting Angelo out, he grabbed them and poured some in the semi-darkness. He slumped down on one end of the sofa and took a hefty swallow, coughing as the pungent liquid burned in his throat.

The door opened and he waited for Danielle to figure out that he was there. She came around the corner and turned toward the sofa, startled. "Rowan, is that you?"

When she switched on a lamp, he blinked and put a hand above his eyes. "Hey, Danielle." She looked uneasy, so he lowered his hand and smiled. "Whatcha been up to?"

Danielle looked at the bottle of whiskey and the glass in his hand. "Oh nothing, just talking to Marion. Then I went for a walk on the beach by myself."

Seeing her standing there in a snug t-shirt and shorts, with pink cheeks and windblown hair, he wanted her so goddamn bad. He patted the sofa next to him. "Why don't we watch a movie or something? C'mon, grab some wine and hang out for a while."

Danielle met his eyes and he saw naked fear. She opened her mouth, closed it, and for an instant, he thought she might bolt from the room. "Um, just give me a minute."

How could she be afraid of him? Not wanting to ruin the evening, he hesitated, not sure how to respond. "OK." She gave him a quick nod and headed down the hallway to their bedroom.

Realizing he had a death grip on the glass of whiskey, he downed it. Pouring more, he waited.

Danielle reappeared, rummaged around in the kitchen and plopped down beside him, wine bottle and glass in hand. She sat the bottle on the coffee table. Staying apart, not touching him, she sipped her wine. "This is great wine. I've always loved it."

He swallowed more whiskey. Being close to her was hard. "So, what do you want to watch?"

Danielle stared into the glass of wine. "Do you . . . if you don't mind, can we just talk?"

Oh hell, he should have known. She always wanted to talk. "Sure." He spread his arm along the upper part of the sofa, inviting her to move closer to him.

Danielle met his gaze before sliding close. He took a deep breath and let it out slowly. She laid her head on his shoulder and murmured, "This is nice. I've missed being with you."

Raising a brow, he thought of what he'd like to say, decided he'd better not, and tossed back more whiskey. "Same here." Stroking her hair, pulling it through his fingers, he waited.

Surprising him, she snuggled closer, twining her legs with his. "I wish we could stay here, just like this. Forever."

He yawned and squeezed her shoulder. "We can stay here all night." But he didn't mean that. The king-size bed was where they belonged.

Danielle looked up at him. He stared at her lips, hungry for the feel of them against his. She reached up and caressed his cheek, running gentle fingers along his whiskered jaw. "But after tonight, in a couple days you'll be gone again and . . ." Her voice softened to a whisper. "Oh my God."

She couldn't seem to resist pissing him off. "Danielle, what exactly are you trying to say? What do you want? Enlighten me, OK? Because I don't have a fucking clue anymore."

Danielle pushed away from him. "Ever since we met, I've wanted to be with you, no matter what. But now, you've changed everything. It's like you've become a different person. I'm not sure I can be a part of what you're doing, of what you *are.*" She pointed at his left side and gave him an accusing stare.

He finished the whiskey and pitched the glass, listened to it thud and roll on the hardwood floor. Yanking up his sweatshirt, he revealed the subcompact pistol, holstered inside the waistband of his jeans. "Yep, there it is."

Disgust filled her face. "Is that the gun you used to shoot Marta and all those other people?"

He pulled the Glock. "No, this is my forty-five." Laying the black pistol in his lap, he kept going, eager to hurt her, the way she kept hurting him. "The gun I used to get rid of that bitch was a nine mm. You know what? It was the same Glock I taught you to shoot with last fall. You didn't seem to mind shooting that gun. In fact I think you rather enjoyed yourself."

"I did enjoy it. But I was shooting targets, not people."

He holstered the gun, yanking his sweatshirt down over it. "Well, I don't always have the same luxury. But hey, that nine is a great little gun. When I flip a switch, it becomes fully automatic." Closing one eye, aiming with his hand and fingers, he pointed at her face, wanting to shock her. *"Boom-boom-boom."* He lowered his hands and winked at her. "It's quick and super effective. Hell, I can mow down *dozens* of people."

Danielle stared, a horrified look on her face. "I *hate* this part of you. I keep asking myself, how can you be the same man I fell in love with?"

Her words only stoked his simmering rage. "After everything that's happened, I mean *everything* – and I'm the one you *hate?* That *part* of me that you *hate* – that's who I am. The same man you fell in love with, the same man who risked his ass in more countries than you'll ever know so that those bastards couldn't come over here and make another 9/11."

She swung her arm, caught the glass of wine and sent it crashing to the floor. "I'm not stupid. I get it about eliminating terrorists. But Marta wasn't a terrorist. She used to be my friend, and Derek's. I know she did some bad things. I haven't forgotten being detained."

Breathing hard, he raised his fist, blinked at it through a fog of rage and whiskey, lowered it and glared at her. *"Goddamn it.* You haven't forgotten being detained? That's nice. I haven't forgotten those five days in Quantico, either. But hell, I'm so *fucking* sorry that you and Derek lost such a great friend."

He saw the flat of her hand coming and jerked his head back. She missed his face, but the breeze lifted the hair on his forehead. The force of the swing sent her tumbling into his arms. She fought, struggling to pull away, but he held onto her. "Look at me, Danielle. Are you afraid of me? Do you honestly think I could hurt you?"

She flung her head back. "Let go of me. Yes, I'm afraid, I can't help it . . ." Her voice trailed off and then she whispered. "I look at you and I get this picture of Marta and I can't imagine. And you want to keep killing people."

Gripping her arms tight, he gave her a shake, tried to get through to her one last time. "For God's sake, there are people in this world who need killing and Marta was one of them. I did what *needed* to be done."

She twisted back and forth in his grip. "I thought we loved each other. But now, sometimes I wonder if you just wanted a challenge or someone new to sleep with."

His mouth dropped open. *"What?* Maybe you don't remember when we met, but I sure as hell do. If anyone was looking for someone new to sleep with, it was you. And with Derek as a housemate, I don't blame you."

Danielle looked like she might spit on him. "Oh my God – it's taken me a long time to figure this out, but Derek is the smart one. He tried to warn me. He told me you were dangerous and that you'd hurt me." She shot him a vindictive look. "I should have listened, because you are a *monster."*

Her words cut deep, exacerbating the wounds she'd already inflicted. He let go of her. "It's not too late. You can still listen. Don't let me stop you. He's probably more your speed anyway."

She stared at him and rubbed her arms. "You know what Rowan, you're right. Derek is more my speed. He's kind, gentle, and *sane."*

"Touché, Danielle. Like I said, don't let me stop you." Hardening his gaze, he waved an arm. "Go on – I'm sure your kind, gentle, *sane* friend is waiting."

Uncertainty flickered in her eyes, but she didn't say anything. Without waiting for a reply he grabbed the bottle of Jack Daniel's and stepped across the broken glass and the spilled wine. Right now, he needed to numb the ache in his chest and he only knew one way to do that.

Chad felt like a sixteen year old as he and Bettina stood outside the door of the Milani's suite of rooms. His sweaty palms matched the quiver in his knees. This was ridiculous. Getting Rowan out of Quantico hadn't freaked him out this badly. But the thought of facing Khalil and Janice Milani scared the hell out of him. *Yeah, I knocked your daughter up, but hey, we're getting married, so no big deal – right?*

Bettina clung to his arm and he looked down at her. "We better knock, sweetheart, or we'll be standing here all night, which would actually be OK with me."

Bettina giggled nervously. "Oh Chad, it'll be all right. What can they say? Dani says she thinks they've mellowed and Marion told me that the whole idea of a grandchild will pave the way . . ." She wrinkled her nose. ". . . Or something like that."

He knocked briskly and held his breath. The door opened instantly and his gut tightened. He wondered if Janice had been hovering on the other side. “Bettina, Chad, come in, come in.”

Khalil stood behind Janice, looking enthused. “Chad, it’s so good to see you. We have been looking forward to this. Please come with me. You want a beer? I’ve developed a fondness for Primo. They say the flavor is special because of raw cane sugar.” Khalil winked at him and he couldn’t help thinking, *just like Rowan.*

Two beers and a sumptuous meal later, he leaned back in the patio chair, glancing from Khalil to Janice to Bettina. The sun, low on the horizon, cast a glow over the deck and a light breeze carried the scent of flowers. “Thanks for the great meal. It was fantastic.” No one had commented that Bettina had only picked at her food, and the Milani’s had kept his plate full until he was stuffed. For a fleeting moment he felt sad for Rowan. His friend was missing out, but Rowan was so damned stubborn.

Right now he’d give anything for a shot of Jack Daniel’s. Opening his mouth to begin the conversation he had come to have, he caught Bettina’s gaze. Her look reassured him and he grasped her hand beneath the table. “We uh, we wanted to talk to you both.” God, he wished his voice didn’t crack like a kid’s when he got nervous. Irritated, he cleared his throat and decided to get it over with.

Khalil spoke before he could. “Chad, relax. Janice and I are so pleased that you could join us. Whatever you want to tell us, we’re looking forward to hearing it, believe me.”

The kindness and expectant happiness in both their faces made him want to puke. But he forged ahead, figuring he could always drink whiskey later, to put an end to his misery. Gripping Bettina’s hand even more tightly, he took a breath and rushed on. “Uh, well thanks. We feel the same way. See, we wanted to tell you, we’re planning to get married. Angelo is a Justice of the Peace and . . .”

Janice interrupted, and he closed his eyes for a moment, waiting. "Oh my, that's the best news." Opening his eyes, seeing the euphoria in her face, he cringed.

Khalil stood up. "This calls for a real celebration. Janice, where is that special bottle of champagne, the Dom?"

Clearing his throat again, he raised a hand. "Wait, there's more. Uh, we are, well, Bettina is pregnant. But that's not why, I mean, ever since the first time I saw her, I wanted to marry her. It was the first thing I thought of when we met. We shook hands and I . . ." He stopped. He'd really blown it.

Mortified, he watched while Janice covered her mouth with her hands, tears springing into her eyes. Khalil clapped his hands and reached across the table to grasp his in a firm handshake, his voice breaking with emotion. "Bettina, Chad, congratulations! You've made us happier than you'll ever know." Khalil turned to Janice, wrapping an arm around her shoulder, almost pulling her out of the chair. "Honey, could we have better news tonight?"

Janice wiped her eyes. "Oh Bettina, I wondered why you barely touched your food. How are you feeling? Has it been bad, with the morning sickness? How far along are you? What will you do about a doctor? Oh dear, you need check-ups and a hospital."

Meeting his future mother in-law's wide-eyed stare, Chad jumped in, wanting to reassure her, even though he didn't know what the hell he was talking about. "We, uh, well the details will have to be worked out, but I'll make sure Bettina has everything she needs."

An hour later, he walked with Bettina through the early evening darkness along the brick walkway that led to the beach. Keeping an arm protectively around her, he took a deep breath and blew out a relieved sigh. He heard her giggle and stopped, turning toward her before stepping onto the sand. It had cooled off and he shivered in his short-sleeved shirt. "Are you laughing at me?"

Running his hands up and down her arms, he felt goose bumps. She'd worn a red and yellow sundress and she looked so sexy, but he didn't want her to be cold. That couldn't be good for the baby. She looked up at him, her delicious lips parting in a grin. "No, silly, I'm just thinking of how you looked when my mom started crying. I thought you were going to throw up."

He gave her a quick hug, then grabbed her hand and led her onto the sand. The restless blackness of the waves heaved rhythmically up and down and stars sprinkled the sky. He could barely make out the slim crescent of the moon. A headache throbbed behind his eyes and he wanted to down a shot of whiskey and go to bed. "Ya know, I thought I might, but they handled things way better than I expected. Thank God."

Bettina swung his hand back and forth while they walked. "Mm, Dani was right, they've mellowed *a lot.* I'm glad, but it makes me feel bad for Rowan. You wouldn't believe the things my mom said to him. It was awful, so ugly."

Puzzled, he stopped walking and turned to face her. "What are you talking about? Rowan's never been married, has he?" Surely his closest friend would have told him, if he'd been married?

Biting her lower lip, looking embarrassed, Bettina gave a tiny shrug. "No, he's never been married, but he was engaged. His fiancée died on 9/11. You know about that, don't you? Her name was Michelle, and she was pregnant. Rowan doesn't know that I know. Michelle told me. I've never been able to talk to him about it."

He shook his head in disbelief. "I had no idea. But it explains a lot." Shivering again in the breeze that had sprung up while they walked, he felt weary, unable to deal with any more revelations – or more sadness – concerning Rowan. He already spent way too many hours each day worrying about his troubled friend. Just for one night, he needed to escape that ever-present responsibility.

Struggling to ignore the feeling that he was being selfish, he turned. “C’mon honey, let’s go back. I feel like an old man tonight – your old man. I need a shot of whiskey and then *you,* in bed.”

CHAPTER FIVE

The Next Day

David stepped from his suite onto the balcony overlooking the tranquil pool and gardens of the Hotel Granduca. He leaned on the wrought iron railing and yawned. United's 7:20 p.m. direct from Reagan to George Bush Intercontinental the night before had been delayed by several hours. Hearing a knock, he reentered the suite. Muusa Shemal had agreed to meet with him before lunch at the hotel, where the Egyptian maintained a residence.

A thickset man with dark, shrewd eyes stared at him when he opened the door. "Mr. Shemal, I presume? I'm David Harandi. Please come in."

The man stepped into the room. A neatly trimmed beard and carefully groomed black hair gave his visitor's face a cosmopolitan cast. A well-tailored suit added to the urbane image, which was completed by black patent leather loafers.

He held out his hand. "Thank you for meeting with me on such short notice."

Muusa offered his hand in a light grip and let go. "Mr. Harandi, it is a pleasure to meet with you, although my time is limited."

David ushered his guest to the suite's opulent sitting area. "I appreciate your time. Later today, if your schedule permits, I would like to see the video images of Rowan Milani. May I join you at the House of Allah?"

Muusa sat down, crossing one leg over the other, his foot swaying gently back and forth. "You may join me later this afternoon at my residence here. I am pleased to do whatever I can to assist American law enforcement and intelligence agencies in bringing this man to justice."

David sat on a chair opposite his visitor. "Mr. Shemal, I'd like you to know that Rowan was a childhood friend of mine. We spent summers together in California growing up. My dear uncle, Sa-id Harandi, who is now deceased, was a very close friend of the Milani family. That connection, along with my investigative skills, is the main reason the President chose me to search for him."

Muusa's foot went still. Clasping his manicured hands together, the man gave him a grave look. "Mr. Harandi, you have my condolences on the loss of your uncle. It gives me no pleasure to inform you that Sa-id lost his life at the hands of Rowan Milani."

Clenching his hands into fists, David met Muusa's somber gaze. "Excuse me, please. This is a shock. Why haven't you informed the authorities in D.C.? Or do they know this?"

"An extensive part of my work in the United States is through the Council of American-Islamic Relations. Sa-id was employed there, as I'm sure you know. Through his sources, he discovered that Rowan Milani was funneling money to terrorist organizations in the Middle East. He told me he planned to confront him." Muusa spread his hands and looked uncomfortable. "That was shortly before the new year. I cautioned him, but he seemed certain that he would not be in any danger."

Mulling over the new information, his mind racing through the implications, he still couldn't comprehend why CAIR wouldn't have reported their suspicions. "Mr. Shemal, I don't understand why this information wasn't passed along to the D.C. police by you or CAIR."

"It was decided by the national board, when I brought it to their attention, that bringing my concerns to the authorities would only cause problems. It was not my wish to withhold vital information, but oftentimes the reaction of your intelligence organizations and law enforcement community to CAIR's efforts at integrating Islam into American culture is neither appreciated nor properly understood."

"Forgive my reaction. I loved my uncle very much. Sa-id practically raised me after my parents passed . . . and I was a difficult teenager."

Muusa pushed back the sleeve of the black suit to consult a heavy gold watch. "I too, have suffered much loss at the hands of Rowan Milani. It is my fervent hope that you will have success apprehending him where others have failed. But now I must go. We can speak more this afternoon."

David escorted his guest to the door of the suite. "Rest assured, Mr. Shemal, I will succeed."

Muusa gazed at him from the hallway, his look unreadable. "I believe you will. I look forward to that day, Mr. Harandi."

Closing and locking the door, David was drawn back to the patio. He flung open the doors and stepped out, inhaling the scent of flowers, chlorine and warming earth. Pieces of remembered conversations floated in his memory. Sa-id had told him many times about meeting Rowan for dinner or being with Rowan on a holiday, while he'd been on assignment . . . *always* on assignment. Guilt mingled with his sad thoughts. If he'd been available, if he'd paid more attention, could he have averted the tragedy? He headed back into the suite. He would never know.

Rowan sat on the edge of the bed and gazed blearily at the empty Jack Daniel's bottle on the floor. He winced at the light flooding the bedroom from the big windows and closed his eyes. His head throbbed and his mouth felt like someone had stuffed it with cotton. Rubbing his forehead, trying for coherent thought, he remembered the last time he'd been this hung over. Danielle had been the reason for that time, too.

Eyes still closed, he lay back, scratched himself and groaned. Last night, the whiskey had numbed the pain, obliterated the bitter thoughts and doused the rage, allowing him to pass out. But now, Chad had called with new information, which was why he was lying in bed, awake and suffering.

His friend wanted him to come over for breakfast and to talk. Trying to swallow past the dryness, he coughed, which made his head hurt worse. Breakfast was not on his agenda. Maybe coffee. Maybe another drink. But definitely *not* food. Sitting up, he grabbed the edge of the bed as a wave of dizziness rolled over him. "Goddamn it Danielle."

Staggering down the hallway to the bathroom, he thought about what he'd told Angelo. *I don't have a heart.* He'd lied about that, although maybe not that much. It was just that his heart had been shattered and he'd never been able to put it back together. The broken pieces had just lain there, until he met Danielle. Against his better judgment, he'd given in and let himself fall in love. She was everything he wanted, and needed.

He continued to the shower, muttering to himself. "I loved you, I thought you loved me." But her words rang in his mind. *You are a monster.* His stomach rolled. She had no idea. The death he'd given Marta was humane, compared to what the *real* monsters would have done to the stupid bitch.

Stepping into the hot spray, he let it cover his face. Water dripped off his nose and chin. Droplets hovered on his eyelashes while steam rose around him. Behind tightly closed eyes, the images rose and he clenched his jaws. He saw the mutilated, often headless bodies of women, old men, and even children. The jihadists didn't care what they did in their mindless pursuit of Islamic domination of the entire world.

He turned and let the water scald his back while he tried to shove the ugly memories aside. If he took six or eight Ibuprofen, it might take the edge off the jackhammer behind his eyes. Later, in the afternoon, he could drink again.

Finished with his shower, he wrapped a towel around his waist and headed to the kitchen. Water dripped from his hair and trickled down his neck. He shivered as he limped across the living room. Glancing at the sofa, he stopped. Danielle lay sound asleep, wrapped in a blanket. He scowled. She could take care of mess she'd made the night before when she woke up.

Deciding that coffee could wait until he saw Chad, he shook a handful of Ibuprofen capsules into his hand and tossed them back with a mouthful of water. Heading for the bedroom, he didn't even look at the sofa.

Chad opened the door and stared at Rowan, taking in the bloodshot eyes, uncombed hair and what looked like a couple days' worth of whiskers. "Tough night, huh?" His friend didn't answer, just shouldered past him with the distinct aroma of Jack Daniel's trailing after him. Shutting the door, he watched as Rowan made a beeline for the coffee pot.

After pouring, his colleague eyed him over the steaming cup. "So, you've got new information? I'm listening."

Chad grabbed his own cup and leaned against the counter. "Good morning to you, too. And yes, I've got some interesting news. But . . ."

Rowan yawned, scratched his belly beneath the wrinkled shirt he wore unbuttoned, and interrupted him. "Does it change the Chicago op in some way? I've got a few questions about the other deal we talked about, too."

At the sound of animated conversation, Rowan shot him a dark look. Bettina came into the kitchen, with Janice and Khalil Milani behind her. Janice laughed and started to say something to Bettina, until she saw Rowan. "Oh my goodness. Hello, Rowan. You look . . . how are you this morning? Is Danielle with you?" Janice gave her son a timid look.

Observing the Milani family in action fascinated Chad. Rowan barely tolerated his parents while they tripped all over themselves, trying their damnedest to make him like them. Bettina paid no attention to either her brother's animosity or her parents' obsequious attitude. "Hey Row, can you stay for breakfast? Dad's cooking and you know how fabulous that will be."

He had to give Rowan's father credit. While Janice and Bettina bubbled, Khalil hadn't said a word, just looked from him to Rowan. Now the older man stepped in, putting an arm around Janice. "It looks to me like Chad and Rowan need some privacy." Khalil gave his son a once over. "It's always nice to see you Rowan. We'll take this party back to the deck."

Knowing how Rowan hated surprises, Chad stole a glance at his recalcitrant friend and clamped his lips together to keep from grinning. Rowan had produced a smile that was more of a sneer. "Thanks Dad. Chad and I need to talk."

Instant hurt appeared in Janice's kind face, but Khalil nodded, his face a stoic mask as he steered his wife away. "Have a good day."

Bettina stood next to Rowan and punched his shoulder. "Hey grouch, where's Dani? Maybe I'll call her and tell her to get her butt over here."

Gazing at the vivacious woman he loved so much, Chad marveled at her intrepid nature regarding her brother. "Uh, sweetheart, we do need to chat for a bit, if you don't mind."

Bettina smiled at him and put an arm around Rowan's waist. "Come on, you can at least say good morning." She reached up and patted her brother's cheek.

Rowan surprised him by wrapping an arm around Bettina's shoulder. "OK, good morning. How are you . . . uh, how are you feeling?"

Bettina giggled. "You mean since your buddy here knocked me up?" As Rowan's mouth snapped shut, she continued, her tone lighthearted. "Some mornings I probably feel like you do today, but most of the time, I feel great." Bettina smacked Rowan in the stomach. "It's a good thing Mom didn't get too close. You reek of booze."

While Rowan winced, Bettina slipped from beneath her brother's protective arm. "You boys have a good talk. Bye, Rowan." For a moment she looked serious. "Take care of yourself, OK?"

Rowan looked relieved. "Bye, Bettina. *You* take care."

Glad that the byplay between brother and sister was over, Chad replied. "Thanks, sweetheart."

Bettina gave him the sexy smile that always sent his heart rate into triple digits. Facing him, she tipped her head back so she could look him in the eye. "Oh yes, I'll catch up with *you* later." Bending down, he gave her a quick kiss. She was almost a foot shorter than he was and he wanted to wrap her in his arms. But not while Rowan stood there watching.

Rowan stared at Bettina leaving the kitchen, then swung the dark gaze his way. "Well, that was fun. Can we talk now or are Ralph and Marion going to show up next?"

"They got here after I called. Besides, I figured you'd bring Danielle with you."

Rowan sidled onto a bar stool. "She was still sleeping when I left. Now, what new information do you have?"

Shaking his head at his colleague's single-minded approach to damn near everything, he slid around to the opposite side of the breakfast bar and sat down. "All right – this is good stuff. Last summer I hacked into the Bureau's webmail servers. You know that – it's how we knew about Ainsley's plans to move you to Tora. Maybe you remember, a couple years ago I led the development team that designed a whole new online security suite for the Bureau. When the team finished, I created a back door that no one else knows about. It gives me and only me undetectable access."

Rowan shot him a ghost of a smile and snickered. "That's great."

"It's a beautiful thing. So, long story short, Capello got taken off your case, so to speak. The President's personal advisor, some woman . . . Patricia Hennessey is her name, has been emailing Ainsley. That's how I picked up on her. I hacked her email and it's a treasure chest of intel. She contacted a former CIA guy – his name is David Harandi. She recommended him to replace Capello and the guy accepted the assignment. He's supposed to be quite the hot shot. He owns and operates some kind of security consulting firm, but it sounds like he's going to be devoting all his time to you, and . . . what the hell, are you all right?"

Rowan glowered at him. "I can't believe this. David Harandi and Patricia Hennessey. For God's sake."

"Do you know them? She's got the ear of the President, and it sounds like Harandi got the green light to do whatever it takes to find you."

Rowan smirked. "Yeah, I know David *and* that fucking bitch."

He should have known there'd be no information forthcoming. "Is this going to create problems? Do either of them have inside information about you that makes it too dangerous for you to run the ops you've got planned?"

Anger lingered in Rowan's dark eyes. "Nope."

He spread his hands. "Damn it, you've got to give me something to work with. If I don't know what or *who* we're dealing with, I could miss something and screw everything up."

Rowan sipped coffee and scratched the thickening stubble on his jaw. "No worries. I'll tell you all about David Harandi and Patricia Hennessey. Then, I gotta shave and talk to Marion about getting a haircut before I leave for Chicago."

Muusa stepped into the room his holy warriors referred to as their *cyber-jihad* headquarters. The windowless room was stuffy and the stench of sweaty bodies hung in the air. Here the thirty-odd Iranian men he'd recruited toiled in shifts that kept the search going, twenty-four hours each day, except on Fridays when the men took time off for prayers.

These men were Shia and he was Sunni, but he overlooked that, although some in the Brotherhood took issue with it. He felt that the Ummah had already been weakened by too much strife and he would not add to it. They were all brothers, committed to the task of finding Rowan Milani. They combed the internet, looking for any trace of the Jinn's activities. They'd attempted to hack computer records of Milani and all his associates, but had encountered cleverly constructed firewalls they could not breach.

Pairs of these men had traveled at his direction to South Dakota, Washington, D.C. and Chicago in search of any clues to the Jinn's whereabouts. He'd sent others to major airports across the country, searching for the aircraft he'd paid many American dollars to procure. No trace had ever been found. And yet, Milani had known where to find *him* and his habibti. But while he suffered in long hours of grief and rage, Allah had given him a gift, and a new direction.

Striding to the center of the circle of tables, he surveyed the men. Bent over laptops, they were unaware of his presence. The hubbub of shared conversation died out as one after another they looked up, saw him and averted their eyes. Arms crossed, he addressed the subdued group in Farsi. "My holy warriors, I am pleased with your zeal." The dark heads began to lift. The men watched him, listening with rapt attention. He pounded his chest with his fist. "Although the Jinn has struck at our hearts, we are neither beaten nor broken."

Murmurs of agreement broke out. "This day, my brothers, as the holy Qur'an says, we are fighting in Allah's service. This is piety and a good deed. In Allah's war I do not fear as others should. *For this fighting is righteous, true, and good.*"

The murmuring grew louder, heads bobbed up and down. One of the men raised a fist and shouted, "Allahu Akbar." Another followed and another, until as one voice, the men stood and roared, *"Allahu Akbar."*

He raised his arms and joined them. "Allahu Akbar. Yes, my warriors, we will defeat the Jinn and bring him to judgment." Spreading his arms wide, he gestured for them to sit. "War is deceit. Allah has decreed it and so we must continue to deceive the intelligence agents of the United States."

The men appeared mesmerized by his words, and that pleased him. "A new kafir agent has been designated to search out Rowan Milani and Allah has shown me that this one will succeed. We will follow him, we will be wherever he is and when he finds the Jinn, we will step in. Allahu Akbar."

As the group shouted their assent, he pointed at two men and left with them. They followed him, heads bowed, to his office. Seated behind his desk in the perpetual gloom, he gazed at his subservient warriors. They wore baggy tan pants below matching long, belted robes, as he'd instructed. He'd wanted no corrupting Western influences like jeans and t-shirts to distract them from their purpose. He pointed at two chairs. "Sit." The men obeyed. "Asad, Firouz, I have chosen you to lead. You know the men. Choose your warriors wisely. The kafir who has been assigned by America's President to find the Jinn is here."

The two men glanced at each other and nodded. Firouz, the more outspoken of the two, the natural leader, addressed him. "We will do as you have said, Master. How shall we find this kafir? What is his name?"

"His name is David Harandi. He is staying at the Hotel Granduca. You will follow him wherever he goes. Allah has shown me that he holds the answers we seek. He will lead us to the Jinn."

Asad shoved wire-rimmed glasses up his nose. "Master, we will need more appropriate apparel in order to blend in."

He nodded, satisfied that he had chosen well. Asad was an organizer with an excellent eye for details. "Yes, of course. I will give you necessary funds. Be discreet and tasteful in your purchases, my son."

The young men shifted restlessly on the chairs. Feral lust burned bright in their eyes. Firouz stood up. "Master, if we may be excused, I am anxious to get started."

Eyeing the young upstart, he debated reprimanding him for the disrespect of such impertinence. But he didn't want to dampen the appetites he'd so carefully nurtured. Instead, he stared until Firouz lowered his eyes. "Now, it begins. Allah will grant victory. You may go."

Asad waited until he nodded, then stood up. "Allahu Akbar. We will work tirelessly until we achieve the victory Allah has so graciously shown you, Master."

He watched silently as the two men shuffled out of his office and closed the door. After nearly six months of fruitless work, Allah had granted him a new opportunity. David Harandi and Rowan Milani were contemptible kafirs, betraying Islam by their allegiance to the United States. But he knew that David Harandi would be relentless in his search for the man he thought had killed his uncle.

He murmured, "War is deception." He and the Brotherhood had cleverly misled the entire intelligence apparatus of the mighty United States. And now, he would reap an even bigger reward by setting one kafir to catch the other.

There were days when he could barely contain his anticipation, but he knew that he must be patient. The Brotherhood had worked for decades to infiltrate the West, and the United States would be the ultimate spoils of their secret jihad. The country would stand as an Islamic jewel, the new Caliphate, outshined only by Jerusalem, a prize to be secured in tandem with Washington, D.C.

When Sharia Law was instituted, replacing the vaunted U.S. Constitution, blood would fill the streets until the dhimmis learned their place. They would accept Islamic law and Muslim rule or by Allah, *they would die*. He would find much pleasure in assisting the Brotherhood with enforcing Sharia. Nothing less than absolute and total submission to Islam would suffice. Once their jihad had brought the nation to its knees, his task would be to ensure its acceptance of the fate Allah had assigned.

The world would watch and learn. Women would cover themselves. The infidels would pay the jizyah or they would convert. The Qur'an would replace the useless Constitution the Americans were so proud of. He leaned back in his chair and closed his eyes. The day of victory would come to America, just as it would come to Rowan Milani. Allah had entrusted him with those tasks and he would not disappoint his Master.

The Next Day

Patricia marveled at her good fortune as she sat in the Oval Office with the two men who meant everything to her. One she loved and the other, the most powerful man in the world, she worshipped. She looked at Rodney, sitting at attention on the brocade patterned sofa opposite her. His deep-set eyes and receding hairline gave his angular face a forceful, bulldoggish look that whetted her appetite.

Thrilling at the promise in Rodney's eyes, she turned to Gilford Whitman. Always concerned that he look suitably presidential, she approved of his black and silver pinstriped suit and red tie. The suit set off his thick black hair, which was beginning to gray at the temples. He lounged in the chair he'd chosen near the fireplace.

She'd decided on a red linen suit for their meeting, because she knew it turned Rodney on. That kept him the slightest bit off-balance, which she preferred whenever they worked together. “Mr. President, Director Ainsley, perhaps we should get started.”

The President gestured expansively. “Take the lead Patricia. How’s our new investigator progressing?”

“David has spoken with Mr. Shemal and is still in Houston. If anyone can unravel this mess and find Milani, it’s him. I have complete confidence in his abilities. David is a big believer in due process for American citizens, but I’ll handle his penchant for following the letter of the law.”

Rodney stirred on the sofa. “We made sure that Milani was declared an enemy combatant before he was picked up the first time. His status has not changed. You just be sure that I’m notified as soon as Harandi has the son of a bitch in cuffs.”

The President spoke. “Neither of you have any cause for concern on that score. I’ll make certain the whole country knows we’ve apprehended a bona fide traitor. The press and Congress won’t dare broach that question lest they want to risk my outrage.”

Observing Rodney’s lips curling in a self-satisfied smirk, she hurried to make her next point. “Mr. President, although we’re allowing Mr. Shemal to detain Milani in Egypt, I think we should keep tabs on what happens to him, in order to avoid a problem or embarrassment for the administration at a later date. We all know how brutal the Egyptians can be.”

Rodney supported her, as she had hoped he would. “With all due respect to our Egyptian friends, I believe as well that we need to retain some degree of control. At some point we may want to bring Milani back here to face charges of treason. Trying and executing him would bolster your re-election campaign, by showing backbone and resolve. I’ll talk to the Director at CIA.”

The President responded. “That may bring us political advantage, but we have some time before we have to decide. As we approach the election, the ability to present Milani as an example of my success at stopping terror threats may be valuable.

With that in mind, I believe it's in our best interests to manage his custody."

Patricia saw the opportunity she'd been waiting for. "That won't be a problem, sir. The two CIA agents who first apprehended Milani last March have informed me that they would relish the opportunity to recover their standing with the Agency."

Rodney interjected, "You mean the two imbeciles who nearly beat him to death and then lost him when they tried to transport him? Surely you're not serious."

Casting a frigid stare at her lover, she played her card. "I seem to remember that you fell for Milani's subterfuge yourself, Director."

The President raised his hand. "That's enough, from both of you. Patricia, make sure agents Talbot and Hancock understand that Milani needs to be handled carefully. I don't have any problem with them regaining their creds at the Agency."

Patricia replied. "Thank you, Mr. President. I'll see to it."

The President's gaze shifted to the FBI Director. "Milani's first capture and escape brings some very troubling issues to mind regarding your former special agent, Chad Cantor."

Rodney was still red-faced from her jab. He straightened his suit and tugged on his tie. "Yes sir? The defection of both Johnston and Cantor is a sore spot for me as well."

The President looked troubled. "Ralph Johnston and I go back quite a few years. That's the one sticking point in this whole situation. I can't come to terms with Johnston aiding and abetting a terrorist."

Rodney commiserated. "I've wondered about that myself. The only thing that makes sense to me is that Milani was holding something over him. You have to remember that Milani was recruiting jihadists not only in this country but around the globe. It's possible Johnston or his wife had been threatened."

The mention of the name Cantor reminded Patricia of the other item she'd wanted to bring to her boss' attention. "Sir, you mentioned Special Agent Cantor. I know you and his father are friends. Because of that, Agent Capello didn't push as hard as he might have. I'd like David to put more pressure on Clifton Cantor. We haven't dug into his financial records or monitored his associations in any real depth, which is long overdue, in my opinion."

President Gilford nodded decisively. "The Patriot Act allows us considerable latitude, and I believe this situation warrants its application. Also, I'd like you to contact Clifton and arrange a meeting here, with me."

"I'll put the wheels in motion, sir. However, perhaps you'd like to postpone your meeting with Mr. Cantor until after we've gathered some information. I'll bring David back from Houston and make sure he pursues that angle."

The President looked unhappy. "It seems that there are a dwindling number of friends that I can trust. Milani has left a bad taste in my mouth. Both of you know that he was someone I trusted. We met several times in this very office, as well as the West Wing. That he deceived me, working on behalf of our enemies is a black mark on this administration – and not something I'll soon forget."

Patricia shook her head in agreement with his impassioned words. "Mr. President, we will do everything possible to bring Milani to justice and ensure that nothing he's done will stain your presidency. You have my word."

Danielle stretched out on the beach lounger. The sun's warmth was just what she needed, and the water always calmed her. Gazing to the horizon, where sea-green met sky-blue she wondered how much longer she'd be at the estate. Ralph's petite wife Marion slid into the lounger next to hers. "Dani, I'm so glad you called. I brought encouragement."

Marion handed her a plastic zip-lock bag of Monster cookies. They were Rowan's favorite. Grabbing a still-warm cookie, she nibbled. "Thanks. You always know what I need."

Marion brushed chestnut curls from her forehead and gave her a concerned look. "Desperate times call for desperate measures. You sounded so upset on the phone that I thought it was only appropriate. Honey, did you and Rowan have an argument?"

Not sure where to begin, she took a bigger bite, savoring the heavenly combination of chocolate, peanut butter and oatmeal. "Mm, these cookies are amazing." Marion watched her, but didn't say anything. Danielle licked chocolate from her thumb. "What we had was more than an argument. It's over between us. I'm not sure what to do or where to go from here."

"Oh Dani, it can't be that bad. I know Rowan. He loves you. What happened?"

Bitterness fought with misery and she tipped her head back, staring at a jet streaking overhead, its contrail an ever-expanding white plume against the sky. "It's like I never knew him. I think about him and know I love him. But he's over the top, so ruthless and intimidating. He . . . he scares me. And I just can't come to terms with what he did to Marta." She gave her friend a searching gaze and rubbed her arms, remembering how he'd held onto her.

Marion's eyes widened. "Did Rowan cause those bruises?"

She blushed. "Yes, but it's not entirely his fault. I tried to slap him and more or less fell against him. He was mad and wouldn't let go of me."

"It sounds like things got intense. Can you tell me what happened?"

"I'll try. The reason I wanted to talk to you is because I know Ralph used to be a SEAL. I thought you might understand."

"It takes a lot of guts to love men like Rowan and Ralph. They make commitments that we can't begin to understand. I've always thought Rowan had an exaggerated sense of honor.

Maybe that's how he can do the ugly things that keep the rest of us safe."

Danielle remembered Rowan's words. *There are some people in this world who need killing . . . I did what needed to be done.* "It makes sense to me for him to kill terrorists. But Marta was someone I knew. She worked for me at the airport in Sioux Falls. She and Derek and I were good friends. The way he talked, I could tell he was *happy* about killing her."

Marion responded. "You do understand that Marta was helping Muusa Shemal, who still wants to torture and then kill Rowan? And I'm hoping you understand that if Rowan hadn't surrendered last summer, *you* would be in federal prison?"

She met Marion's sober gaze. "Of course, I know all that, and I'm grateful for what he did for me. It made me sick to know how much that CIA agent hurt him. But he's different now. He's so harsh and cold. It's like killing someone is nothing to him."

"I think part of the problem is that you're seeing a side of Rowan you wouldn't under normal circumstances. If we weren't stuck here, I mean, if he went away for months at a time, to carry out an operation and then came home, you'd see the man you love. This other persona or whatever you want to call it is the mindset he needs to have in order to do his job."

"I guess that makes sense. It never occurred to me that for him it's a job, but that's exactly what it is. When I met him in Sioux Falls, he was on an FBI assignment, not like when he'd go assassinate terrorists for the President." Her breath caught in her throat. "Oh no."

"What now? You look like you just lost your best friend."

Her heart ached, remembering the hurt she'd seen in his face and then the bleakness when he let go of her arms. Looking up, she murmured, "Oh my God, I am so *stupid.* I said some things. We both did."

The older woman fiddled with the collar on her sleeveless blouse. "We all say things we wish we hadn't. But you've both had time to cool down. Rowan came over for a haircut yesterday afternoon. He looked like hell. I bet he can't wait to make up with you."

Sudden hope made her giddy. She grabbed the bag of cookies and stood up. "I need to find him and apologize. Thank you so much."

Marion squinted up at her. "Good luck, honey. Let me know how it goes."

CHAPTER SIX

The Next Day

Rowan headed out the front door of the house, down the cement steps and across the driveway, carrying his briefcase and the carryon bag that held all the clothes he'd accumulated since arriving at the estate. The black Escalade waited in the gloom preceding sunrise. He saw Gabriel hoisting boxes and luggage into the rear compartment of the vehicle. Michael conferred at the passenger side front door with Chad. Angelo sat behind the wheel.

Starting an operation always invigorated him and he grinned at Gabriel's solemn countenance. "Hey, que pasa, Amigo?"

His colleague grabbed his suitcase with a meaty fist and tossed it effortlessly into the SUV. "What the hell are you so happy about this morning?"

"It's a great day for starting another successful op."

Gabriel gave him a sour look. "You never know what could happen. Maybe you should think about that for a change."

Watching while his stocky friend picked up another suitcase with one hand and heaved it into the SUV, he shrugged. "It's not like we've never done this before. We can talk about it en route. You'll just have to stay awake for a while and participate in the discussion. The plan should work." He winked at Gabriel. "It's the essence of simplicity."

Hearing car doors slamming, he turned. Mike had crawled into the front seat opposite Angelo, while Chad walked toward him and Gabriel, holding up a paper bag.

Gabriel muttered something in Spanish, closed the cargo compartment and headed for the passenger side back seat door. Chad threw the bag at him. "You're going to need these."

He caught the crackling brown paper. “What’s this?”

Chad looked smug. “It’s winter in Chicago. You might want to wear socks while you’re there, and gloves. I know you only think in terms of warm weather, so I didn’t want your fingers and toes to freeze.”

His friend’s unfailing kindness touched him. Feeling awkward, he wasn’t sure what to say. Chad had proven over and over to be not only his best friend, but a brother. “Thanks.”

Chad seemed to sense his unease. “Looks like it’s time for you guys to take off. Keep me informed, all right? I’ll do whatever I can to run interference, toy with the airport’s central servers, hack surveillance cameras – you know, the fun stuff.” Placing a hand on his shoulder, his tall friend turned serious. “Look my brother, be careful with this plan of yours.”

Ignoring the concern he saw in Chad’s eyes, Rowan nodded. “I’ll be careful. And you take care of *my sister.*”

“No worries there, brother. See ya.”

As he turned to head for his seat, he heard the house door slam shut. Looking up, he saw Danielle rush down the steps and run toward him. “Oh, hell.”

“Good luck,” was all Chad said.

Reaching the door of the Escalade, he opened it and waited. Danielle stopped in front of him. He stared at her, wishing she didn’t look so goddamned sexy. She flung the dark red hair he loved behind her shoulders. “I’ve been wanting to talk to you since yesterday afternoon. Where were you? I looked for you and tried calling. I didn’t realize you were leaving this morning.”

Drinking in her features – the luscious hair, creamy skin and firm breasts, he swallowed hard, irritated by his increasing heart rate. Drawn in spite of himself he closed the distance between them, pulling her into his arms, trying not to think about how good her body felt pressed against his. “We need to get going. What do you want?”

Her arms went around him. “Well, I wanted to say good-bye, and that I'm sorry for all the things I said. I wish we could talk more, about everything.” She reached up and touched his face.

Opening his mouth to speak, he glanced past her and saw Derek standing on the steps of the house watching them. The sight of the insipid man filled him with rage. But he couldn’t ignore the desire she’d lit for him, like she always did.

Trying hard not to sneer, he lowered his head to hers. She greeted his lips eagerly, opened her mouth to his probing tongue. He tightened his arms around her while her hands caressed his back. Giving in to the rage and desire, he fisted one hand in her hair and deepened the kiss, brutalizing her mouth until she clutched at his sides, whimpering. He took his time, forcing her lips to submit to his.

When he’d had enough, he raised his head and gripped her arms. “Did you forget what a *monster* I am? Remember, Derek warned you and for once the dumb fuck was right. But hell, don’t worry. He’s right back there, waiting for you.”

Looking dazed, touching fingers to swollen lips, she twisted around and gasped. “No, I love *you.*” Her voice broke. “I understand now, about Marta and what you have to do.”

Tamping down the ferocious anger, ignoring her panicked declaration, he yanked her around to face the house, leaned close and whispered in her ear. “What you want – what you *need* is waiting right inside.” He gave her a quick shove, climbed into the back seat of the Escalade and slammed the door. His heart pounded and pain lodged inside like a permanent lead weight. He noted the sepulchral quiet inside the vehicle and scowled. Both his colleagues sat ramrod still, staring straight ahead. Catching Angelo’s somber gaze in the rear view mirror, he raised a brow. “What’s the holdup? C’mon, Doc, let’s go. We’ve got a plane to catch.”

* * *

Grief-stricken, Danielle watched as the Escalade lumbered down the driveway toward the gate and the road beyond. Hands clutched to her chest, she took deep breaths, unable to stop shaking. She heard footsteps and turned. Expecting Derek, she was surprised to see Chad.

The compassion in his eyes had her fighting to keep from breaking down. "Oh my God, Chad. What have I done?" She closed her eyes as he drew her close and patted her back.

The terrible anger and utter coldness she'd seen in Rowan's eyes told her that he didn't love her – not anymore. She moaned and her body trembled so hard that Chad pulled her away and held her at arms' length. "Whoa, hey, Danielle, take it easy. Try to tell me what happened."

Chad looked concerned, but she could never tell him the awful things she'd said. She took a hiccupping breath, remembering the finality in Rowan's voice when he shoved her away. Mortified, she could only whisper. "It's my fault. We had a fight. I didn't understand, about Marta. And now he's gone and I can't explain. When is he coming back?"

Chad's eyes held the unhappy truth. "Rowan's not coming back."

She sagged against him, knowing she had to hang on, keep it together, until she was by herself. "You aren't going to tell me where he's going, are you?"

He looked uncomfortable. "No one knows except for me and that was his choice. I'm sorry. Let me walk you back inside." She trudged with him back inside the house to the door of what was now just her suite. Chad put his arm around her. "Are you sure you want to be by yourself? You can come over if you want. I know Bettina would love to see you."

The thought of being with Rowan's sister was too much. "Thanks, but right now I need to be alone. If, um, if Rowan calls, please tell him that I'm sorry and that I want to talk to him."

Chad gave her a final hug. “I’ll tell him. If you need anything, just call. We’ll check on you later.”

She shut the door, leaned against it and closed her eyes. The desolate stillness was almost more than she could handle. Hating herself for doing it, she walked to the bedroom and pulled open the closet door. All of Rowan’s clothes were gone. In a daze, she wandered down the hall to the bathroom. His toothbrush, shaving kit and the one comb he owned were all gone as well.

She walked mindlessly to the kitchen and spotted a half-empty bottle of Jack Daniel’s whiskey on the counter. When she pulled the stopper and stuck her nose in the bottle the fumes invaded her sinuses and she coughed.

A glass sat on the counter. She poured herself some of the whiskey and took a deep swallow. The biting liquid assaulted her throat. She gasped and choked, before tipping her head back and draining the glass.

Feeling woozy, she grabbed the bottle and headed for the sofa. She stared at the corner, where she’d been so cruel, where she’d lost him, and couldn’t bear it. But she couldn’t stand to be in the bed they’d shared. At the opposite end of the hallway was the spare bedroom they never used. She grabbed a throw from the sofa and made her way to the room.

Blinds darkened the windows and the chilly emptiness matched her frame of mind. She sank down on the floor, sitting cross-legged with the bottle of whiskey in her lap. Who needed a glass? She held the bottle in both hands and gulped more of the vile liquid. Her lips were numb and the feeling in her arms and legs was disappearing. Blinking in the darkness, she mumbled, “No wonder Rowan likes this so much.”

The one thing she could still feel was the horrible, aching emptiness of his absence. With fingers that felt thick and uncoordinated, she gripped the bottle and lifted it. This time her fingers slipped and the whiskey ran in cold rivulets down her neck. She didn’t care. She didn’t want to feel anything. Tipping sideways, she grabbed the throw, tugged it over her head and lay in a heap on the floor.

Derek paced around the spacious interior of his suite, staring moodily out the patio doors at the lawn and the dense tropical forest beyond. But all he saw was Rowan's dark head bending to kiss Danielle. He'd been unable to look away. She'd been so upset afterwards that he'd gone back inside, disgusted.

Would she ever learn? Every time – *every time* the guy seemed to cast a spell over her. Breathing unevenly, he stomped to the kitchen, eyed the bottle of Bacardi on the counter and shook his head. Could he *hate* anyone more than he hated Rowan Milani?

He strode into the living room, wondering if there was any way for him to notify the FBI or CIA or *anybody* who could arrest Rowan. He shoved fingers across his forehead, trying to relieve the tension. What could he do? Chad monitored everything he did on his computer. The phone he'd been given only worked to call people on the estate. Shit. Maybe he could figure out a way to get a message to someone.

He looked around the comfortable quarters and grimaced. It was his prison. "Come on, think." Continuing his restless march through the living area to the bedroom, he spotted his NWA cap and the pack of Camel Wides he'd opened the night before. Shoving the hat onto his head and tugging it low, he decided to go for a walk and a smoke.

Thirty minutes and four cigarettes later, he stood, hands on hips, staring at the water. Walking in the deep sand had worked up a sweat. His t-shirt clung to his body. He pulled the cap from his head and ran his fingers through his mashed down hair, scratching his sweaty scalp.

The walk and smokes had cleared his mind and given him an idea. Maybe there was a way out after all. Gabriel had talked to him months ago and told him he could take some classes to refresh his aircraft mechanic skills so that he could work for Jerry and Bryan, the two pilots who flew the Gulfstream G650 that had brought everyone to Kauai. According to Gabriel, the two guys had an aviation business based in Atlanta. From there they flew rich people all over the world. He frowned. If that was the case, how come they were always available when Rowan needed them? Well, as soon as he showered, he'd find Chad and see if he could get something lined up, for real.

Gazing at his cap, his resentment churned. The airline industry had been his life. It was the biggest thing, other than Danielle, that Rowan had taken from him. He'd met her ten years earlier, when he'd been a mechanic for Legacy Airlines. Danielle had been a hell of an agent, on the fast track to management. He'd moved on to Northwest and followed her to the airport in Sioux Falls.

They'd always been friends, but he'd loved her since that very first day. When Northwest succumbed to Delta, he'd become a supervisor and hoped that made him closer to her league. But then, Rowan Milani had come into their lives and taken her away from him. He ground his teeth and shoved the hat back on his sweaty head.

The climbing sun warmed his back as he trudged along the beach, nullifying the cooling effects of the morning breeze. If they let him work for the two men in Atlanta, he'd find a way, somehow, to let the government know where Rowan was hiding. He'd give anything to blow things wide open and *finally* get the woman he loved out of the reach of the jerk she couldn't seem to walk away from.

Khalil Milani sat disconsolately at the polished oak table in the kitchen. Stirring sugar into his coffee, he tapped the spoon on the edge of the cup and laid it on a napkin. He sipped the hot liquid and stared out the window. It was another picture perfect day.

From his spot at the table he could see across the expanse of green to the strip of white beach and the endlessly rolling turquoise water. The smell of seaweed and flowers wafted through the open window, mingling with the scent of freshly brewed coffee.

Gratitude was what he knew he *should* feel, but a heavy sadness left him conflicted. Of course, he was grateful they were all safe. He was thankful for the generosity of Chad and his own son, which provided the home and anything else he or any of them needed.

Yes, his son had provided everything for them except the only thing that mattered to either him or Janice – the friendship they both longed for. For years the two of them had dreamed of rebuilding their relationship with Rowan. But they'd spoken only briefly with their son in the almost six months Rowan had been with them on the island.

At first he'd understood, knowing that his son had endured horrific treatment. But even as he recovered, Rowan remained distant. Danielle was friendly and polite, but she stayed close to Rowan. Much as he tried to rationalize the reasons, his son's indifference and outright coldness hurt more deeply than he wanted to admit.

He swallowed more coffee. It didn't help that he knew *why* Rowan remained distant or that he remembered *how* he'd lost that special father-son bond. Steeped in regret, he thought glumly that retrospect provided painful clarity if a man had the courage to examine his past.

Would Rowan ever understand or believe how sorry he was? Sorry for not standing up for his son, for not having the fortitude to stop Janice in her endless condemnation. He'd been much too easygoing and tolerant of his wife's passionate nature. Could Rowan ever forgive either of them? Finishing the coffee, he put his head in his hands. He'd give anything for the chance to explain – to tell his son how sorry he was and to beg his forgiveness.

A gentle touch on his shoulder brought his head up. Janice stood next to him with the coffee pot in one hand, concern on her face. "I made fresh coffee. What's the matter?"

Her eyes reminded him of Rowan's, nearly as dark and intense. "I'm all right. Just thinking about how much I'd like to talk to Rowan and explain . . . well, you know. And yes, I would love some more coffee."

Watching while she poured the coffee, he saw her furrowed brow and the wetness in her eyes. He wished he hadn't mentioned Rowan. She returned the pot and sat down across from him with her own steaming cup. He hoped he could put her mind on another, happier track. "This morning when I mowed the grass, I noticed how everything you've planted – the flowers and the shrubs, are flourishing. Soon the whole estate will look like a garden paradise."

"You know, transforming the landscape here is not even like work to me. It's relaxing and gives me time to think. I look forward to it every day. *Oh dear.*"

The thick passion in her voice made him stop, cup halfway to his mouth. "Are you thinking about Rowan, too?"

Tears stood in her eyes and her voice was full of anguish. "It's hopeless. I've tried talking to him, but you saw how he was at Chad and Bettina's that morning. He doesn't even acknowledge me. I don't think he will ever understand how sorry I am. And now he's gone. What if he's captured again? I don't think I could bear it." Tears dripped down her cheeks.

Khalil sat the cup down and reached across the table, taking her hands in his, relishing the smooth warmth as he rubbed his thumbs back and forth. "You've done everything you can to apologize and ask his forgiveness. You cannot be responsible for how he responds. In time his heart may soften. But we have to live our own lives and create our own happiness. Rowan must chart his own course, wherever it may take him."

Gabriel leaned back in the luxurious seat. He heard Michael chuckle over the sustained rumble of the twin turbofan engines. His colleague looked relaxed and comfortable with his feet up on the low table between them. Not wanting to wake Rowan, he tried to keep his voice down. "What's so funny? You know we're probably heading into a disaster."

Michael eyed him from under dark brows. "What happened to make you such a wet blanket? For crying out loud, we've run more ops than we can count, and this one is straightforward. Hell, it'll be a snap."

He angled his head toward Rowan. Stretched out with his hands folded in his lap, snoring softly, the volatile man seemed completely at peace. A bottle of Jack Daniel's whiskey and a squat tumbler sat on the floor next to his chair. "El Diablo here scares the shit out of me and so does this operation."

Michael shot him a sardonic look. "Like I keep telling you, Rowan is focused on a mission. Damn it, you know him as well as I do. He's not going to screw it up. Besides, I think our plan for getting a hold of Capello is brilliant."

Disbelief had his mouth hanging open. "You've got to be kidding, right? This operation has more holes than a sieve."

Michael snagged the bottle of Jack Daniel's and the tumbler. Gabriel watched while his friend poured whiskey, paused when the jet hit rough air, then tossed back a swallow and shuddered. "Fuck me. This is why I drink beer. Damn it, you're driving me to drink. Listen – I guarantee you, Rowan is fine, especially now."

Gabriel shook an index finger at his colleague. "That's the other thing. What he did to Danielle when we left was not right.

She's a good woman. She loves him more than the loco idiot deserves."

Michael raised the glass to his lips, then lowered it. "Hell, that's the plight of every woman, isn't it? I think *your* big problem is guilt. You've been away from your family for damn near a year and I think it's eating you up." His friend's eyes lit up and his voice got louder. "Yeah, so, you're transposing, or transferring – whatever the hell it's called, you're putting *your* problems on Rowan."

He wasn't certain if his smartass colleague was serious or trying to provoke him. Either way, the words struck home. Guilt had plagued him ever since the day Michael told him to sit out the op and go home. He'd realized that for a while he hadn't even thought about Sherie and their two children.

Michael gulped more whiskey and coughed. "Besides that, you don't know what Danielle might have done to Rowan. Neither of us knows that and we sure as hell aren't going to ask him about it."

Feeling sad, Gabriel gazed at his friend and decided he didn't want to talk anymore. This operation had the potential to blow up in their faces. He'd have been less worried if they'd been heading to foreign soil. "I just don't want Sherie to see me arrested, in chains, facing life in prison or worse if this thing goes to hell."

Michael smacked himself on the forehead. "You are the biggest damn drama queen I've ever met. *Sherie's going to see you in chains?* Look, it's going to go smoothly. I know it."

Why Michael couldn't see that Rowan had gone loco was a mystery to him. "Sure, whatever you say. I'm going to try to take a nap."

Jerry stepped down the aisle. At the same time the engine noise shifted to a lower decibel and the jet felt as though it was sinking. "Hey guys, we're starting our descent. We made it to O'Hare in record time. We should be on the ground in about twenty minutes."

“Thanks.” Gabriel cast a sideways glance at Michael. “Fuck you, Doctor Phil.”

Jerry’s brows rose. “All right boys, see you in twenty.”

Gabriel closed his eyes. No matter what Michael said, he knew this op was one of the most foolhardy and dangerous they’d ever attempted.

Rowan yawned as the G650 finished the long taxi to the private side of O’Hare. Beneath bright lights, vehicles hurried across the tarmac. The last time he’d looked out the window of an aircraft at snow was damn near a year earlier, when he’d landed in Sioux Falls. Irritated by his melancholy mood, he glanced at his colleagues. Michael looked alert and ready to go. Gabriel looked sleepy. He turned back to the window.

The jet came to an abrupt stop. While his colleagues busied themselves collecting their things from the overhead bins, he stood up. The brown paper bag from Chad caught his eye and he picked it up, found a pair of black leather gloves inside and put them on. He tossed the paper bag back onto the seat. The flight deck door opened and Jerry and Bryan exited, heading for the cabin door.

He’d been waiting for that. Pulling the nine mm Glock from its holster at his left side, he pointed it as he spoke. “Hey Bryan, leave the door closed for a minute. We need to have a quick chat.” While Bryan and Jerry froze in place, he reached beneath his jacket for the sub-compact forty-five tucked in the small of his back.

Michael glanced up at Rowan’s words. “What the fuck are you doing?”

Gabriel swung around. “Holy Mother of God, I told you. He’s loco.”

Keeping one pistol aimed at Jerry and Bryan, the other pointed in Gabriel and Michael’s direction, he alternated his gaze between the four men. "OK, here's what we're going to do. Jerry and Bryan will take off with you two, as soon as I'm out of here."

Michael's right hand started to move. Raising the forty-five to chest height, Rowan met his friend's eyes and winked. "Don't, Mike. I'm loco, remember? Just relax and let me finish."

Michael's cold blue eyes bored into his for a moment, then his friend blinked. "All right, finish."

Giving Jerry and Bryan a brief look, he shifted his gaze to the stocky Hispanic. "Gabriel, get your ass to San Diego. Your heart isn't in this op and I sure as hell don't need you screwing it up." He turned back to Michael. "I've got this, brother, trust me. Chad needs your help with a few things."

Jerry spoke quietly. "Rowan, airport operations is calling. They want to know why we haven't opened the door."

He stared intently from Michael to Gabriel. "You two stay cool, all right? I'll be in touch eventually. If I need anything, you'll be the first to know. Jerry, tell them you're opening the door now, leaving one passenger and then taking off again."

He heard the aircraft door crack open and then the gentle thud of the air stairs connecting with the tarmac. Holstering the nine mm, he grabbed the paper bag from the seat. Backing away from Michael and Gabriel, he nodded at Jerry and Bryan. "Thanks for the ride, guys. Catch ya later."

Turning toward the door, he tucked the forty-five back beneath the jacket, against his spine. He stood for a moment at the top of the stairs and squinted into the false daylight created by the lights illuminating the tarmac. Errant ice crystals sparkled and swirled in the unruly wind. Inhaling the frigid air, he shivered and zipped up his black leather jacket.

He descended the stairs and headed for the rear of the aircraft. After gathering his suitcase and briefcase, giving quick, shouted instructions to the ramp agents to reload the other bags, he headed across the tarmac, trying with limited success to mask the slight but persistent limp that dogged him.

Once inside, he stood by the windows and tried to warm up. Beneath black dress pants his legs felt like blocks of ice. Thick black socks shielded his feet inside his old slip-on shoes. Still shivering, he touched the paper bag tucked under his arm. As usual, Chad was a godsend.

He stared out the window at the G650. A ramp agent scurried to pull chocks from the nose gear wheel while another stood in front of the jet. Once the agent dragged the chocks away, the other one waved a glowing orange wand. In the captain's chair, Jerry snapped a salute and turned the agile jet away from the building in a precise arc.

He watched the glistening black aircraft rumble across the tarmac, turn onto a taxiway and disappear from his line of sight. Thinking about the shock and anger in Michael's eyes, and the hurt in Gabriel's, he shook his head. They would never have agreed to his plan.

He'd been so goddamned tired of arguing over every point, every idea. Now he could do things his way. He turned away from the window, heading with briefcase and suitcase in tow for the O'Hare Hilton. He couldn't wait to stick it to everyone looking for him.

Thirty minutes later he stood at the check-in counter of the Hilton. The clerk helping him was blonde. Her name tag said *Alicia.* Unable to ignore her body – the kind of athletic build that looked good even in a hotel uniform – he stared, imagining how she would feel beneath him. He was hungry for it, too, because Danielle hadn't been interested in making love to a monster. Had she been willing with that dumb fuck Derek?

Taking a deep breath and letting it out slowly, he handed Alicia the FBI badge and ID Michael had fabricated for him, along with the credit card Chad had set up. His friend had hacked into a local Kauai bank and created a fake profile and a bogus account that they'd stashed several thousand dollars in, specifically for this op.

While the clerk twirled wheat-colored hair between her fingers and examined his ID, he studied her face, admiring the full lips she'd colored a subtle pink. His eyes followed the line of her slim neck to the high, firm breasts beneath a white blouse and burgundy vest. He could almost feel their buoyant fullness in his hands. His eyes wandered along the lines of her slender legs, coming to a perfect apex . . .

He blinked when Alicia spoke. "Thank you, special agent Harandi. Give me just a second and I'll have your keys."

Still indulging his lustful thoughts about her body while he gathered the fake credentials, he replied without thinking. "Thank you and please, call me Row . . . uh, David." Momentary alarm spiked and sizzled through his body. Goddamn it, he'd better get a grip before he blew the op.

Alicia blushed. "You're welcome, David."

He listened to her rendition of hotel and restaurant amenities, replying with a tight-lipped "No thank you," to her offer of a bell boy to take his one suitcase.

An hour later, in his room, sitting in a chair near the window, he gazed at the airport operation eight stories below, where a parade of mostly United and American aircraft made their way to overnight gates. A headache threatened to expand behind his forehead. Since broaching his plan to Chad, he'd spent hours going over the security specs of O'Hare and the Hilton until his eyes burned.

Even as he'd traversed the distance from aircraft to hotel, he'd known when he was under video surveillance. Everything he did was part of a plan to fuck with Ainsley, Shemal and David Harandi. By the time he left Chicago, they'd have a trail so hot that FBI agents would trip over each other to follow his seemingly careless movements. And just when they thought they had him, the trail would disappear. Anxious to get started, he thought about the bottle of Jack Daniel's in his suitcase. The operation came first. But hell, he might as well have a drink.

Chad stared at the waves and dug his feet into the warm sand. It felt good to sit and stare at the water – alone. He'd needed a break. Fixing things so that Rowan could head to Chicago with the necessary ID and funds had taken most of the last forty-eight hours. He cracked his knuckles and looked up. As the sky darkened, stars appeared, scattered across the empty blackness. A cool breeze ruffled his hair and he wished he'd worn jeans and a sweatshirt instead of shorts and the t-shirt he'd pulled on earlier.

Sometimes, when he had a few minutes to consider it, the about-face his life had taken the previous spring still overwhelmed him. Leaving the FBI and helping his best friend left him diametrically opposed to the law enforcement agency he'd been a part of for ten years. He'd gone from upholding the laws of the United States to thwarting the cyber-security of the FBI, CIA and FAA. The simple truth was that the government didn't operate a system he couldn't hack.

He'd always wanted to use his skills on behalf of his country. As far as he was concerned he was doing exactly that, but his former colleagues in the Bureau wouldn't think so. They'd see him as a criminal. All he wanted was for someone, somewhere, to appreciate his hacking ability. Of course, Rowan did. Whatever that was worth.

For the government, the embarrassment over how easily he breached their systems would have every agency lusting for the opportunity to screw him over. He shivered. The other thing that overwhelmed him – scared the hell out of him – was that it was only his skill that kept them hidden from the various entities searching for them.

He bent his head and rubbed his eyes. He could only deal with a few crises at a time. Getting Rowan safely out of Chicago and to his final destination without detection was his first priority. He'd done everything he could, but he wouldn't relax until Rowan called to tell him everything was copacetic. His concern for Bettina had been shoved temporarily to the back of his mind, but came rushing back when he tried to relax.

Johnny Giacopino had offered a surprising lifeline, insisting that *Cliffie's future grandchild would be taken care of.* In a couple days, he and Bettina would step onto the old Don's jet at Lihue and fly to Chicago for a private consultation with a family physician who didn't ask questions. He'd been so relieved. Making sure Bettina and their baby were all right consumed him, kept him lying wide-eyed and awake during the night while she snored next to him.

And now he needed to think about how to help Danielle. Maybe Angelo could talk to her. He was beginning to understand Ralph's point of view. Picking up the pieces after Rowan wasn't much fun. His single-minded friend left more than just dead bodies in his wake. Then he'd have to figure out how to deal with Derek. The guy was an annoyance, a pain in the ass that he didn't need, especially now that he had started harping about working for Jerry and Bryan in Atlanta.

His phone rang. Glancing at the caller ID, he grimaced. Michael's voice reflected what he knew must be incredible anger and frustration. "What the hell is going on? Did you know about this?"

According to the timetable he and Rowan had worked out, the call was right on schedule. "Hi Mike. Yeah, I knew. Where are you?"

"How could you let him do this? He can't handle this on his own. What do you mean, where are we? Fuckin' A! We're on our way to San Diego, as I'm sure you know."

"You know Rowan would have done this whether I agreed to help him or not."

Michael kept hammering him. "Yes, but if you'd brought me in on this . . . this *plan,* I could have talked him out of it, or been there with him."

Chad gazed at the sky. "Yeah, well, whatever. Rowan asked me to help him, so I did. We planned it out. If everything goes well, he'll be on a plane out of Chicago in . . ." He looked at the glowing green numerals on his watch and made quick calculations. "In approximately eighteen hours. He'll be long gone before anyone knows what happened."

Michael couldn't let it go. "That's an eternity when you're on an op, especially for someone in Rowan's state of mind."

"Damn it, listen. You know as well as I do how he is once he's made up his mind."

He heard Michael's heavy breathing on the other end of the connection. "Yes, I know what he's like. But I could have helped him. Capello isn't someone he should screw with on his own. I can't believe he was so fucking devious."

He'd told Rowan the same thing, damn near verbatim, but his friend had been adamant about Michael helping him – helping Bettina. "Here's the thing. Bettina is pregnant. She's going to need medical care. Rowan wanted – *insisted* that you help me with things here. That's why he didn't want you with him."

"What? Bettina is . . . how in God's name can I help you with *that?"*

Chad twisted his shoulders in a futile attempt to alleviate stress. "Hell, I don't know. Rowan told me to talk to you about access to a clinic and a doctor. But when Johnny Giacopino called to talk to Rowan, I arranged for Bettina and me to fly to Chicago for her first check-up. So I need you back here to manage things while we're gone."

"I'll be damned. We can make whatever arrangements you want for Bettina. There's just one thing. I'm not sure if I'm coming back."

Chad panicked. "Look, things are a little unsettled here. It's Derek, and Danielle. Just get your ass back here and I'll fill you in on everything . . ."

Michael interrupted him. "Like I said, I can help you with arrangements for Bettina, if necessary. But I made a decision of my own after Rowan dumped us. As soon as we drop Gabriel off in San Diego, we're taking a detour. Jerry and Bryan don't mind and I need to think a few things through. I'll let you know whether or not I'm coming back to Kauai. Right now, I'm just not sure."

"Look Mike, I can't keep things from unraveling around here without help. And I can't delay the trip to Chicago."

"Let Ralph and Angelo step up to the plate. I'm tired of being jerked around. This is something I need to do."

Chad closed his eyes as the tension gripped his forehead. "All right. Let me know what you decide. Mike, you'll get back to me in a couple days, right?"

"I'll be in touch."

CHAPTER SEVEN

The Next Day

Michael woke up as the G650 stopped with a jerk. He could still hear the muted roar of the engines. He sat up as the flight deck door opened and Jerry stepped out, a black overcoat over one arm. "Hey Mike, it's fifteen degrees out there, with a forty knot crosswind. Didn't you feel it when we were descending? I hope you've got some kind of coat."

He stifled a yawn with his fist. "I grew up around here, remember? Hell, at least it isn't snowing. Asal should be waiting and she'll have the 'burban all warmed up. Thanks for stopping over for a couple days. I really appreciate it."

Jerry stepped to the door and punched buttons. Before the door thumped on the tarmac, an icy wind swirled through the cabin. "It's no problem, brother, you know that. January is a slow month for us."

Bryan peered out the flight deck door. "Shit, that wind is brutal. I hope you've got a stash of booze at this outpost of yours. Any reason we couldn't have taken a couple days off in San Diego instead of Pierre, South Dakota?"

Michael eyed the two pilots. "You boys have turned into a couple of whiny pussies. It's only like this six or seven months out of the year. That's why God made fireplaces and brandy, and buffalo steaks."

Jerry shrugged into his overcoat. "I'll take one of each, starting with the brandy. Bryan, if you want to shut this mother down, I'll do the walk around, and grab our bags and button her up."

Bryan was already turning back into the flight deck. "You got it, Kemosabi."

His friends' camaraderie was a relief after the tension of the past few days with Rowan and Gabriel. The three of them used to have the same easy companionship and trust, but his friend's surprise move in Chicago had blown that all to hell. As far as he was concerned, Rowan could go pound sand.

He couldn't wait to see Asal Tehrani, his *honey,* which was the Farsi translation of her name. It had been way too long since they'd spent any time together. He needed to work through the turmoil in his mind and she always had a perspective he hadn't thought of. A man couldn't ask for a better partner, or lover. He didn't make major decisions without talking them through with her.

Jerry hollered from the air stairs. "I can see Asal. She's standing by the door waiting. You better get your happy ass to the FBO lounge before she decides to leave without us."

A few hours later, Michael sat with Asal close beside him on the sofa in the cozy living room of their home. Jerry and Bryan had taken over the lower level, content with his big screen TV and satellite service. He and Asal had fed them the promised buffalo steaks and offered a full liquor cabinet. Now that his guests were settled, he could concentrate on *his* problems, and *his* woman.

Asal tugged a plush throw over their legs and put her arm across his midsection. She laid her head on his chest. "What's going on, Mikey? You seem so sad. Did something go wrong with the op? I thought you'd be in Chicago until sometime tomorrow."

A log in the fireplace popped and crackled as it sank lower. He squeezed her shoulder, wishing they'd have gone upstairs to bed instead of getting so comfortable in the living room. "The op sort of fell through. Well, what I mean is that Rowan decided to do it on his own. Gabriel has been crying like a little bitch about his family, so Rowan told him to go home. We dropped him off before we flew here."

She raised her head and gave him an understanding look. "The strain of the past year is showing. It was bound to happen, to all three of you."

He thought about that while he messed with her hair. It slid through his fingers like blue-black silk and he liked how it felt. "I guess so, but none of this shit has bothered me. I'm all in, like always. But Rowan scared the hell out of me, and that's *never* happened before."

Asal laid her head back on his chest and snuggled close. "Tell me what our Rowan did. Tell me what's been going on. I've missed you. It's been a long time since you've been home with me."

He couldn't stop the lingering twinges of jealousy he felt when she said *our Rowan.* Irritated with himself, he shoved his doubts aside. Asal had been the love of his life for over five years. But she didn't know that he knew . . . "On the jet, sitting on the tarmac at O'Hare, Rowan pulled both his guns on all four of us. He told us to leave and then he took off on his own."

She murmured into his chest. "Oh my. How dramatic of him. You didn't feel inclined to ignore him and stay anyway? It's not like you to abandon an operation you're committed to. I think the stress has finally gotten to you, too."

"Honestly, from the look in his eyes, I think he'd have shot me. I thought, well *fuck it,* we're done. I let him go. Hell, I'm tired, too. I'm ready to do something different. So, here I am. I want to be with you and forget about all this shit."

She reached up and cupped the side of his face with her hand. "You used to tell me about the wounded animals you brought home when you were a kid, for your father to fix. Remember?"

He leaned into her palm, wondering where she was going with that particular memory. "Yeah, sure, I remember. My dad could have been a veterinary surgeon after he worked on all the hurt animals I dragged home. What's that got to do with Rowan ditching us and damn near shooting me?"

Asal patted his cheek. "What happened to all those wild animals after your father fixed their injuries?"

He stared at the fire. "You know the story, we turned them loose. They were wild. It wouldn't have been right to try to tame them." He stopped, not sure if she was making an analogy about Rowan or him.

She put her arm back around his ribs. "Rowan hurt you deeply, didn't he? I know he needs your help, even though he's too stubborn and damaged to see that. I also know you, Michael Cristo, and you have no intention of leaving Rowan to finish this on his own. You'll go back, because you love Rowan and because it's your nature. Neither of you can be tamed. That's one of the many things I love about you."

Peace settled around him and some of the hurt dissolved. "How do you figure all this shit out?" He pulled Asal onto his lap and planted kisses on the side of her face until she turned and met his lips with hers. He wrapped both arms tight around her and deepened the kiss. When she finally pulled away, his heart was pounding. "God, I've missed you. More than I realized."

Asal untangled her lithe body from his and stood up. "C'mon Mikey, let's go upstairs. I've had the fireplace going in our bedroom since you called and I don't want to make love to you on the couch. I want to take my time in our bed."

He shoved the throw aside and reached for her hand, letting her help him stand up. "I'm all for that."

Heading out of the secure area of O'Hare, Sal dodged flight crews and harried passengers. He pulled his carryon bag close and stopped to consult his watch. It had been a long, screwed up day, starting with the fact that he'd overslept. Rushing to Reagan as fast as he could, he made his flight, but missed the chance to upgrade. Even Economy Plus didn't offer him the room he needed. He'd been miserable for the entire flight.

Still frustrated, he followed the signs guiding him to the underground walkway that connected the main terminal to the Hilton. He'd been dreading the trip to Chicago ever since he'd gotten the call from Johnny Giacopino's flunky. And now, after the humiliation he'd suffered at the hands of the President's Special Advisor, he had to take the time to meet with the old bastard and grovel. He knew better than to ignore the *Boss*, as everyone called Johnny, but why he'd been summoned for a meeting remained a mystery.

Once he'd checked in and gotten settled, he'd head downtown for a proper Italian meal. Later he'd call Johnny and set up a time to see the old Don. As he trudged along the walkway, his phone rang. He dug it out of his pocket. The number was one he didn't know. Thinking it might be another one of Johnny's surrogates, he answered brusquely. "Agent Capello."

The voice that replied had some kind of an accent that he couldn't quite place, yet it seemed vaguely familiar. "Agent Capello, welcome to Chicago."

He stopped walking. He hadn't told anyone about this trip. "Who is this?"

"My name is David Harandi and I must confess, you have my utmost admiration."

Suspicion warred with curiosity, but impatience won out. "I wasn't aware that I had a fan club. Unless you have something to say, I don't have time to talk to you."

"My apologies, Agent Capello. Let me be brief. I have been tasked by the President to find Rowan Milani. I know that you have more insight into this traitor than anyone else, and I'd like to meet with you. You spent five days interrogating Milani and observing him up close. The only thing I know about him is what

I gathered in interviews with his former FBI colleagues. Truth is, Agent Capello, I'd like to pick your brain."

"Surely Patricia Hennessy handed over my entire case folder to you. As you must know, I've been dropped from the operation."

"Oh yes. Ms. Hennessy gave me your information. However, I'm aware of your abilities as an interrogator. I'd like to explore the possibility of teaming up with you."

Something didn't add up. "Mr. Harandi, how did you know that I'd be in Chicago? I didn't tell anyone about this trip."

"I'm an FBI special agent. When I need information, I get it. As soon as I knew you were flying into Chicago, I flew here myself. My room number at the O'Hare Hilton is 858. I've got a bottle of Jack Daniel's single barrel whiskey waiting and I'd very much like to talk with you. I'll even buy you dinner later. Tuscany is one of my favorite restaurants in Chicago."

He made a snap decision. What the hell. He'd meet with David Harandi and keep himself in the game. No one else needed to know. "I prefer the Pompei. Give me an hour to check-in and freshen up."

"Thank you, Agent Capello. I look forward to a mutually beneficial collaboration. I'll see you in an hour."

Muusa rolled off the whore and lay on his back, chest heaving. The cloying odor of sweat and sex invaded his nostrils. Shoving the silk bedding from his legs, he glared at the bruised backside of the young woman, the daughter of one of his followers. "Worthless whore – get up."

The woman shuffled off the bed. Wiping sweat from his forehead, he moaned as pain shot through his chest. The familiar bands of agony wrapped around his upper body and he gasped as he struggled to breathe. The woman stood in the middle of the spacious bedroom, befouling the carpet with her filthy body. She gave him a timid look from the eye that wasn't swollen shut. "Master, what is wrong?"

The pain abated and he laid a hand on his chest. It was her fault. Her hands were awkward and rough, her mouth and tongue inexperienced. He had to teach her what to do. When she had groped, pinched and tugged on his delicate skin, he had lost his erection.

It had taken hours for his flaccid penis to grow large again and when she took him in her mouth she choked and heaved, then spat out his semen. Enraged, he'd grabbed her thick sable hair, ripping out chunks while he wrestled her onto the bed. Then he beat her, as was his right – punching, slapping and kicking her into submission. A woman should know how to please a man. It was her duty.

He sat up and glared at her cowering in the middle of the room. Covering her breasts with her hands, she stared at the floor. Even though he'd closed the heavy drapes, sunlight glowed around the edges. The mirror above the dressing table reflected her hunched back with its rolls of excess flesh.

Anger churned, burning in his chest. He waved an imperious hand. "Cover your ugliness and leave me. *Now!*" He watched her step clumsily out of the room and tried to ignore the pain still radiating from his chest. No one could ever take the place of Marta, his habibti.

Closing his eyes, he saw her smiling face and magnificent breasts, felt her quick, gentle mouth and hands. Like the artwork he'd brought from his homeland, she was priceless. And she had belonged here, with him. He ground his teeth as the picture in his mind shifted and he remembered how she'd died.

Clenching his fists, he cursed Rowan Milani. The horrific pain roared through his chest again and he groaned in agony and rage. "Allah will see that you are delivered to me. You will be *mine*. I will torment you until eternity comes. Fear the affliction and trial that awaits those who do not obey. *Allah is severe."*

He wiped spittle from his chin, rose unsteadily from the bed and pulled on a thick cotton bathrobe. A cup of jasmine tea would soothe him. Walking to the kitchen, he thought about the call he'd received from Rodney Ainsley. He filled the teapot and twisted a knob on the stove to heat the water. For years he had patiently recruited and nurtured the faithful in mosques throughout the infidel nation. And now, a cadre of holy warriors waited to join him.

He plucked a china cup from the cupboard and lifted a teabag from the bowl he kept on the countertop. For now he must continue to practice tawriya in his façade of cooperation with the ingratiating Director of the FBI. As agreed, they would hold a conference in Houston, to show their joint commitment to tolerance and peace. It was Allah's will for the dhimmi country to pay jizya – and this *conference* was but the start.

The whistle blew on the pot and he poured boiling water into the cup. Crooking an index finger through the handle he raised the cup and breathed deeply, inhaling the steam and letting the aroma of jasmine calm his mind. But when he thought once more about Rowan Milani, the cup shook in his hand.

The Jinn knew the truth about the plans and goals of the Brotherhood and would destroy everything they had striven to achieve, if given the opportunity. He must find the elusive man and bring him to Tora Prison. Once that was done, his plan for the United States could move forward. And then he would teach Rowan Milani the true meaning of retribution.

He took a cautious sip of the scalding brew and sat the cup on the counter. A cruel smile raised his lips and bared his teeth as he remembered the comforting words of the Prophet. *He who fears will mind.*

* * *

Sal stepped out of the elevator on the eighth floor of the Hilton and strode purposefully down the carpeted hallway to room 858. Staring for a moment at the door, he squared his broad shoulders and knocked briskly.

The door swung inward immediately. The man that greeted him had black hair and a moustache and goatee. "Agent Capello, please come in."

Observing the man's casual sweater and jeans as he entered the room, he wondered if he'd misunderstood about dinner. "Special Agent Harandi, I presume?"

His host turned from the door and held out a hand. "It's a pleasure to meet you. Please call me David. May I call you Sal?"

Gripping the man's hand, he gazed into inscrutable dark eyes. "It's nice to meet you and yes, please call me Sal. I'm wondering, have we met?"

David gestured toward the windows where a small table held a bottle of Jack Daniel's whiskey and two glasses. "Stranger things have happened. Who knows, we may have crossed paths at some anti-terrorism function. Come, sit, relax and have a drink."

Feeling vaguely uneasy, he followed Special Agent Harandi to the table, noticing that his host walked with a slight limp. Sitting in one of the chairs, he waited while David slid into the chair across from him, poured the potent liquid and grabbed one of the glasses. He picked up the other and raised it. "Here's to finding Rowan Milani and seeing justice served."

David lifted the other glass, clanked it against his and winked at him. "Between the two of us, I believe we can accomplish that, sooner rather than later." The special agent tossed back his whiskey and smacked the glass on the table before leaning back and smiling at him.

The niggling disquiet persisted. "Ah David, would you mind showing me your creds? I've learned to be a cautious man."

The special agent stood up. “Absolutely.” While he waited, the man stepped to the bedside table and returned with his FBI ID and badge.

He took a long swallow of whiskey and wiped his mouth with the back of his hand before picking up the credentials. They looked like legit FBI creds as far as he could tell and he shoved them across the table, nodding as his uneasiness receded. “Thanks.”

“In our line of work, it always pays to be thorough. I’ve learned that there are very few people I can trust.”

Ready to get down to business, Capello settled deeper in the chair. “I agree. Now, let me tell you something. Milani is cagey and he’s got friends. You’ve seen my notes. How do you propose to nail the son of a bitch?”

“He is a slippery bastard, I’ll give him that. But a guy like that can’t stay hidden forever. Besides, I think Milani is after retribution.”

“Milani’s not the one who deserves *retribution.* My whole career has been destroyed because of him. And just when I’d uncovered new leads, I had to hand everything off – to you, as it turns out.”

“I read the transcript of your interrogation of Milani in Quantico. He never admitted to being a terrorist, even in the face of enhanced interrogation techniques, which I noticed you escalated quickly.”

Capello took another swallow of whiskey. “Milani was an obstinate son of a bitch, but that doesn’t make him innocent.”

“True. Tell me about your new leads. I must have missed them in my initial reading of your notes.”

“That’s because they aren’t included. I have every intention of pursuing those leads myself, on my own time. For one thing, Marta Pinella, the woman who was murdered in Houston has a connection to Milani. Here’s some new information for you. If not for her, I'd never have gotten the opportunity to interrogate him. Maybe Milani got some retribution after all."

Harandi gave him an incredulous look. "Are you saying it was *Milani* who murdered her? How in the world did he manage that? You don't really think that he's out there, moving around freely, do you?"

Nodding when the special agent grabbed the bottle of Jack Daniel's and held it over his glass, he watched as the other man poured. His stomach growled and he glanced at his watch. "He obviously has a network of terror cells around the country that helped him escape – *twice."*

"I guess anything's possible. Milani could be anywhere." David looked at him and raised the glass of whiskey.

He followed suit, tossing back another hefty swallow. When the special agent raised his arm, the sleeve of his sweater shifted and he caught a glimpse of peculiar scars on the man's wrist. He frowned, trying to remember where he'd seen scars like that.

His mouth went dry. The scars and the limp . . . It *couldn't* be, and yet that face, with its unrepentant, arrogant smirk could belong to only one man. And that man had been toying with him, leading him on. *"You raghead son of a bitch."*

Fumbling for the forty caliber Ruger P94 holstered beneath his suit jacket, he gasped when Rowan flung whiskey in his eyes and then drew a Glock from beneath the sweater. "OK, Sal. Go ahead and toss that pistol onto the bed. Then put both your hands flat on the table."

He complied. "What do you think you're doing, Milani? What do you want?"

The black pistol never wavered. "I know exactly what I'm doing. And as for what I want, we'll get to that."

The fact that the traitor hadn't shot him meant he had a chance to distract him and make him act carelessly. "You know, if I could have had access to you just one more time in Quantico, with those broken ribs, you'd have told me everything."

"You're such a moron. I tried to get this through your Neanderthal skull when you had me in the brig – *Shemal* is the terrorist. For God's sake, he's been working with the Muslim Brotherhood for *years* to undermine the country."

"Why the hell should I believe you when Shemal presented solid evidence of your treason?"

"Did you ever verify any of Shemal's goddamned *evidence?* Or was the financial reward just too good to pass up? I spent years eliminating terror threats all over the world at the President's request. Shemal and the Brotherhood figured it out. After that, he turned the tables and set me up as a double agent."

After everything he'd subjected him to, Milani's story had never changed. "If you're innocent, why hasn't the President spoken out on your behalf?"

"You know, I've wondered that myself. It's my guess that his special advisor, Patricia Hennessy, has worked over-time to poison his mind. She never liked me."

Maybe he could lull Milani into thinking he was on his side. "That tight ass bitch hates my guts, too. Why don't we both talk to the President – together?"

Rowan snickered. "How would we do that? Oh, wait . . . I know, I could surrender and let you take me in. That would show good faith on my part, right?"

The overt menace in the cold voice sent a wave of panic through his gut. Heaving the table forward with both hands, upending the bottle of Jack Daniel's and the glasses, he lunged for Milani. His opponent twisted away. The whiskey slowed his reactions, but he snagged Milani's sweater and yanked him off-balance. Rowan cursed and fell against his greater bulk. Seizing the opportunity, Capello shoved the man against the wall and grappled for the gun, managing to wrap a massive fist around Milani's left hand.

Legs spread wide to brace himself he leaned hard into Milani, pinning him while he banged the gun against the wall. His other fist found purchase on Milani's ribs. The Glock flew across the room. Hearing Milani grunt and swear, he chuckled. He'd be in control before long. Grabbing the smaller man around the neck with one hand, he squeezed. Rowan took a strangled breath and sneered at him. Reaching with his fist to bash the defiant jerk's head, he staggered as pain enveloped his groin.

His hand loosened involuntarily and Milani coughed. He groaned as the agony rose through his mid-section and into his chest. Sinking to his knees, he saw his bloody insides, spilling out of his ruined suit pants.

He tipped over onto his back. Rowan bent over him, breathing hard. "Goddamn it, I've had *enough* of you pounding on me." Then Capello saw the knife, dripping with his blood. As shock set in, he clutched at his sides with shaking hands. The warm, wet mass sent terror rippling through his body.

Rowan crouched beside him. He saw a line of sweat running through a bloody smear on the man's cheek. "Here's the thing. Unlike you, I don't get any pleasure from causing pain. I've always made my kills as quick as possible. How about this? You answer a few questions for me and I'll end your suffering."

Breathing in painful moans, his eyelids fluttered as he stared at Milani. Even now, killing him, the raghead was still arrogant. He whispered. "Stick your questions . . . up your ass . . . and go to hell." As the pain intensified, encompassing his entire body, he coughed, choking on thick blood in his throat.

Rowan leaned close. He felt warm breath on the side of his face. "OK. But there is one thing you need to know. I'm *innocent*, you dumb fuck. As far as going to hell, *you first.*"

Rowan secured the middle button on the black suit jacket and ran two fingers around the inside of the collar on his dress shirt. It had been a long time since he had worn a suit and the tie was uncomfortable. He walked out of the elevator with his briefcase and carryon bag. His flight to Houston left at 8:46 p.m., giving him three hours to complete the Chicago op, navigate security and head for his gate on the G concourse.

Wanting to avoid the front entrance and any attention from the check-in clerks, he walked through the nearly deserted pedestrian tunnel connecting the hotel to Terminal Two. He reached the exits for ground transportation, stepped through the sliding doors and scanned the crush of taxis, limos, assorted hotel vans and cars.

Gripping the handle of his carryon, he shivered in the frigid air and breathed in the automotive exhaust. Traces of winter pastels lingered in the western sky. Streetlamps and headlights punctured the gloom at street level. A black Lincoln Town Car stopped sharply in front of him with a screech of brakes, eliciting honks from the vehicles behind it.

The passenger door opened and a stocky man wearing an overcoat stepped out, angled a bald head at him and opened the backseat door. Hesitating for only a moment, he walked to the car. The man waited, observing him with arctic blue eyes before gesturing for him to enter the vehicle. Handing off his carryon bag, but keeping his briefcase with him, he slid into the warm, ample interior.

On the opposite side of the back seat, an older man with thick, iron-gray hair puffed on a fat cigar. Grasping the cigar between stout fingers, the man waved it through a haze of fragrant smoke. "Rowan Milani, it's a pleasure. Not often an old man like me gets to meet a true American patriot."

Gazing at the bulky figure, dapper in a navy blue pinstriped suit, he nodded. "It's a pleasure to meet you as well, sir."

The trunk of the Lincoln closed with a thud and the bald-headed man entered the front seat and slammed the door. The Don tapped the burly driver on the shoulder, dislodging ash from the cigar, which tumbled down the arm of the driver's suit. "All right, Gino, let's go." As the Lincoln rolled smoothly into the traffic, the older man leaned back and pointed at him with the cigar. *"You* call me Johnny. So tell me, how'd you clip that rat, Capello?"

He turned to face the Mafioso who'd insisted they meet. "When noise will cause problems, I use my Karambit."

Johnny puffed on the cigar and pointed at the bald-headed man in the front seat. "Roberto here is a friend of mine. He handles contracts from time to time. Judging from the marks on your neck, you maybe coulda' used some help."

Rowan touched the abrasions on his neck. "I appreciated the offer, but this was personal. I owed him, you might say."

Johnny's raspy chuckle made him think of a rattlesnake. "Anytime you want to embrace the Italian side of your heritage, you let me know. Guy like you belongs in an organization that appreciates the kind of skills you bring to the table."

Staring at the lined face, he could hear Ralph's words. *We operate under the rule of law in this country.* Hell, maybe he'd been working for the wrong people all along. "When I'm done with the things I've got planned, I would be interested in pursuing that possibility. If I'm still alive, of course."

The wily Don waved the cigar, which had gone out, then gave him a thoughtful look. "I did my research on you. My contacts in this country and the Middle East confirmed your innocence. Why our intelligence apparatus has so far been incapable of figuring that out is up for debate." Johnny grinned. "Bunch of fucking morons, if you ask me."

Feeling like he was repeating an endless refrain that no one ever listened to, he answered. "Muusa Shemal and the Muslim Brotherhood have been working for years – for the Brothers it's been decades – to worm their way into the highest levels of our government. They've never varied in their goal to make this country their own. I got in the way."

Johnny squinted out the window. "Gino, park in that lot over there to your left." Still gripping the cigar, the Don turned toward him. "I'm not unaware of what they're up to. I got anything to say about it, they're not going to be successful. This is my country, too."

Pressed against the window as the big car swung around and accelerated, he gazed at his newfound ally, wondering if the man had any idea of the far reaching tentacles of the Brotherhood and the inroads Shemal had already made. "Sir, Johnny, you realize the Brotherhood has a global organization. I've been out of the loop for a while, but from what I've observed, they've been gaining acceptance, solidifying their positions of power, both here and abroad."

Johnny gave him an appraising look. "You've got a lot to learn about your Italian forebears. The family has a slightly longer history in the United States. Those ragheads want to start a turf war I got one thing to say: *Bring it on.* They aren't the only ones with a *global organization.*"

"You can count me in, anywhere, anytime. Like I said, I have a few things to finish first."

Johnny replied. "From here on out, you're under my protection. You're part of the family now – my family. Capisce?"

Not sure he understood exactly what the man had in mind, he rubbed his jaw. "I'm not asking for your help. What I've got to do is my responsibility and . . ."

Pointing with the cigar stub, Johnny interrupted him. "Clifton Cantor asked for my help. He brought your situation to my attention. I have great respect for your achievements as well as your performance under what some might call extreme duress."

When he opened his mouth to speak, the older man silenced him with a glare. "I said – *you're part of the family now.* I take care of my family. *Capisce?*"

Realizing that he wasn't going to win the argument, Rowan gave up. "OK. Thank you."

The old patriarch looked smug. "You just remember that. Now, my jet is on its way to Kauai as we speak. Your sister and Clifton's son will be well cared-for and safe while they're in my city. The medical care I have access to is state-of-the-art and my people don't ask questions – period."

The Don leaned forward and tapped the broad-shouldered driver. "Gino, it's time. Head back to O'Hare." The Lincoln lurched into motion and Johnny turned toward him. "Gino will be sure the rooms are clean. Roberto will take care of whatever you need until you reach your final destination."

Feeling like he was caught in a vortex with no way out, Rowan folded his hands in his lap and looked first at the two men in the front seat and then at Johnny. "I checked in for two nights and left *Do Not Disturb* signs on both my door and Capello's. I've got a flight this evening to Houston and then . . ."

Johnny waved him to silence. "Go get on your flight and relax. You won't notice my crew, but they'll be around, keeping an eye on everything. I'll say it once more and you listen this time. I take care of my family."

The car stopped abruptly. He was surprised to see that they'd pulled up in front of the American Airlines departure area. Rowan held out his hand. "Johnny. I don't know how to thank you. It was not my intention to involve you in my activities. All I wanted was the opportunity to eliminate Capello myself."

Johnny grasped his hand. "You need anything, you call me. A man like you deserves some help. So shut up and take it." The old man winked. "I'll stay in touch."

Rowan stashed his bag in the overhead bin and slid into his window seat in First Class. He yawned hard, buckled the seat belt and leaned back. Smiling to himself, he wiped the wetness from his eyes. Neither the pilot nor first officer had ever seen the full-auto version of Glock's nine mm pistol. They'd been like kids over a new toy. He pulled the plastic cover off the blue airline issue blanket. Huddled beneath the blanket, he closed his eyes, ready to doze off. He opened them again when someone slid into the seat next to his. Johnny's friend Roberto gazed at him, his upper lip curled in a faint smirk.

Sensing a challenge, he raised a brow. "Hey Roberto, are you going to be my shadow from now on?"

Surprising him, the stocky man held out his hand. "Lighten up, Special Agent Harandi. Name's Bobbie. I've got my job to do, same as you."

He grasped the thick hand and gave it a firm shake. "OK, call me David. And tell me, what does your job entail, exactly?"

The big man leaned close and spoke in a low voice. "It was supposed to entail offing Capello, but the Boss decided to honor your request, *Rowan,* so instead, I'm going with you to your final destination, making sure you stay safe. I'll set up the crew to keep an eye on your place and stay as long as the Boss wants. Then I'll head home."

"I see, and where's home?"

Bobbie folded his hands in his lap and looked content. "Home is where the heart is, don't you know?"

Rowan settled deeper into the seat. "I wouldn't know. I don't have a heart."

CHAPTER EIGHT

The Next Day

The sedan pulled away from the gated entrance and Rowan looked at the beach house that he, using his alternate identity as businessman James Hawthorne, had rented. Feeling unexpectedly bereft, he dragged his one suitcase to the entrance. Sweat trickled down his chest. The polo shirt and jeans needed to go, along with the socks that had felt so good in Chicago.

Sorting through the keys Bobbie had picked up from the rental agency in Key West, he found the one marked *Front Door* and inserted it. The frosted, paned glass opened to an entryway that had the cool, empty feel of disuse.

An open staircase rose to his left, while straight ahead a hallway ran to what he guessed was the kitchen. He opted for the stairs, lugging the suitcase behind him, anxious to be done with the saga that had started almost thirty-six hours earlier in Kauai. He hadn't slept, just dozed on the flight from O'Hare to Houston.

He'd had almost eight hours to kill in the Houston airport, which had given him the opportunity to shave the moustache and goatee. He'd shed the suit along with his identity as David Harandi and become James Hawthorne. While Bobbie stood watch he'd tried to doze in the airport, but was too wired. He'd been wide awake on the early morning flight to Miami and the connecting flight to Key West. Now he was ready to be left alone to unwind.

He wanted to change clothes, take a quick walk on the beach and then hit the king-size bed he'd ordered delivered to the master bedroom, along with a case of single barrel Jack Daniel's whiskey.

Fishing his favorite cutoffs from the pile of clothes in his suitcase, he ditched the jeans and pulled the polo shirt over his head, wincing at the soreness in his ribs. Capello's pummeling had produced a cluster of bruises on his right side.

He thought about how Capello had lain on the floor, moaning and gurgling for almost an hour after telling him to go to hell. It wasn't his style to let someone suffer, but the stupid bastard had deserved it. Grabbing a bottle of Jack from his new stash, he headed out of the bedroom and down the stairs. He rummaged in the kitchen for a glass and poured a drink.

The ocean beckoned. Stepping out the back door, he heard the waves and inhaled the humid salt air, heavy with the scent of fish and seaweed. He took a long pull on the whiskey and put his sunglasses on. Following the narrow, sandy path between tufts of stringy grass, he reached the private beach.

Wading out a few yards into the water, he dug his toes in the sand. It felt good. He took another deep swallow of whiskey and stared at the turquoise water. For the first time since he'd stepped off the G650 at O'Hare, he could relax and let down his guard for a few minutes. A group of scraggly palms, anchored in a pile of rocks whipped in the wind, while gulls wheeled and squawked. He finished his drink and yawned. Weariness combined with the alcohol to slow his thoughts. He headed back in the house and up the sweeping staircase to the bedroom.

Thinking about Johnny Giacopino's crew – somewhere outside keeping watch – he remembered the older man's words. *A man like you deserves some help. So shut up and take it.* He stretched out on the firm mattress, pulled the holstered Glock nine mm from the waistband of the cutoffs and laid it next to him.

Much as he'd craved solitude, now that he was alone, the emptiness that hovered around the edges of his consciousness threatened to overwhelm him. Danielle's presence had kept the terrible desolation at bay and now he missed her. Heaving a sigh, he got up and lowered the wooden blind to cover the windows. He poured more whiskey and downed a hefty swallow.

His phone rang and he grabbed it from the nightstand where it sat next to the Glock forty-five. He stared at the ID, took deep breaths until it quit ringing and then laid it face down on the bed.

He'd thought, planned on her always being with him. But her words, the look of revulsion on her face and the fear in her eyes had changed all that. She didn't love him. More than that, *she hated what he was*. And now it was too late. His course was set.

He gulped the rest of the whiskey and tossed the glass, watched it bounce off the woven sea grass rug onto the hardwood floor, bang into the wall and crack as it rolled to a stop. *But goddamn it, he still loved her.*

He punched the pillow into shape, grabbed the forty-five and pulled it from the holster. Laying back with his ankles crossed, one pistol resting on his belly, the other lying next to him, he drifted toward unconsciousness. The whiskey had done its job. As his head sagged to one side, his breathing slowed and deepened. Exhausted, wrapped in a whiskey-induced peace, he slept.

Two Days Later

David sat in an overstuffed chair, a silver coffee service on the occasional table next to him. He gazed out the glass doors that opened onto the balcony. A light breeze and sunny warmth made him wish for a reason to stay in Houston. Talking with Muusa Shemal had been productive. Although he hadn't been given permission to enter the mosque, he'd seen the video of Rowan sneering at the camera.

He'd spent the past five days after that *doing his job,* as Patricia had so archly requested. His years as a covert operative for the CIA made it easy for him to blend in with the riffraff, deep in the seedy downtown areas of Houston. But his trolling for information about Rowan hadn't gotten him anywhere. None of

Houston's bottom-feeders knew anything about his old friend. He'd heard some far-out theories about the murders, but none of them involved a wanted terrorist.

While immersed in the city's underbelly, he'd noticed two men following him. Curious, he let them get close so he could study them. They were young Iranians, wearing hooded sweatshirts, jeans and tennis shoes. Could these be Milani's accomplices? If so, his old friend had not chosen wisely. The two men appeared to know nothing about the art of tailing someone and their clothes looked brand new, which told him that they were rank amateurs.

He followed them, hoping they'd take him to a specific location, but instead they wandered aimlessly. It dawned on him that they were looking for him. Unconcerned at that point, he let them find him again and then lost them when he wanted to return to the hotel. No one knew he was in Houston except Patricia and Shemal. He could think of no reason why the Egyptian man would have a couple of bumbling losers follow him. He shrugged. The two men were harmless.

Now Patricia wanted him back in D.C. He glanced at his watch. His flight left at noon, giving him plenty of time for another cup of coffee before heading to the airport. He poured more from the pot and took an appreciative sip. A loud knock on the door made him jump. His eyes widened when he heard a tense voice say, *"Houston SWAT coming in with an arrest warrant."*

Before he could react, the door splintered, crashed open and banged solidly against the wall. A SWAT team swarmed into the room. The men carried pistols at the ready with M4 rifles slung over their shoulders. They wore Kevlar gloves and helmets along with goggles and ballistic vests. Four burly men grabbed him. His coffee cup flew out of his hand, splattering coffee across the table before bouncing to the carpet. He found himself staring at it, his face pressed against the coffee-soaked carpet while his hands were swiftly zip-tied behind his back.

His heart thudded out of control. He raised his head, trying to see something besides the cup and lace-up, black boots. Two pair of hands wrenched him upward and sat him down hard, in a chair. A wave of dizziness had him wobbling. The team leader spoke into a hand-held radio. "The scene is secure. Bring in the detective."

A lanky man in a white dress shirt with the sleeves rolled up to his elbows, black suit pants and lizard skin cowboy boots sauntered into the room. He spoke with a deep, Texas drawl. "FBI Special Agent David Harandi, we have a warrant for your arrest for the murder of CIA Agent Sal Capello in the O'Hare Hilton in Chicago. Two homicide detectives from Chicago are en route as we speak."

He stared, flabbergasted. "You want to tell me who you are and what the hell is going on?" He coughed, unable to say more. The adrenaline rush had dried his mouth and he couldn't swallow.

"I'm Homicide Detective Matthews. We have an Arrest Warrant and you are going to jail, Mr. Harandi. That is what's going on."

He coughed again. "I did not murder Sal Capello. I've never even met him. I have not been in Chicago in over a year. And why are you calling me an FBI special agent?"

The detective ignored him. The four SWAT team members who'd tackled him marched him along the hallway to the elevators, down to the ground floor and paraded him through the elegant lobby and out the front door. A black and white Houston PD car with flashing red and blue lights sat waiting under the hotel's portico.

They shoved him unceremoniously into the back of the squad car. Two police officers were in the front seat. He sat in silence while they drove into downtown Houston. When they arrived at the police station, the two officers hauled him out of the car. Detective Matthews was waiting, along with the four SWAT guys. They surrounded him and moved as a group into the station through the Sally Port, a separate entrance at the back of the police station.

All of them crammed into an overheated elevator. It was a relief when the doors opened. At the end of a hallway, he saw a sign that said HOMICIDE. The two police officers ushered him into an interview room. While one held onto his arm, the other removed the zip-ties. The detective leaned against the wall and watched.

He massaged his wrists and eyed the detective. "You have got to listen to me. I did not kill Sal Capello. I have been in Houston for the better part of the past week. I can verify my whereabouts with witnesses. You can ask the hotel for my check-in date. And let me be clear, I am not, nor have I ever been, an FBI special agent."

Matthews appeared unmoved by his statement. "That's interesting, since I have images of you from surveillance cameras showing you in O'Hare and at the Hilton. Agent Capello was found murdered in your room. I also have an airline reservation that shows you flew here from Chicago two days ago."

"I need to make a phone call. This is a huge mistake or a misunderstanding of some sort. I can *prove* my whereabouts and my innocence. I'm not talking to anyone until I get that phone call."

The detective pulled a cell phone from his pocket. "All right, make your phone call. I'll be back in a few minutes."

The two police officers and the irritating detective left, locking the door behind them. David sat down at the scarred metal table and hoped he could remember Patricia's mobile number. Relieved when she answered, he explained the situation.

She sounded mystified. "David, I saw a report on CNN, moments ago. What in the world happened?"

Slumped in the chair, he gripped the phone. "I don't know, but I need you to call the Chief of Police in Houston and get this straightened out. Then maybe I can figure out how and why this happened. Two Chicago homicide detectives are flying in. We've got to sort this out before they arrive and try to transport me back to Illinois with them."

"Give me a few minutes and I'll have this mess taken care of. Sit tight. You won't be detained for long."

While he waited, pacing the claustrophobic room, he realized that he was going to miss his flight to Reagan. He sat on the edge of the metal chair, but couldn't curb his impatience and got up again. He paced some more and swung around when the door opened. Detective Matthews entered the room, followed by an African American woman. The tall detective closed the door and leaned against it.

The woman pulled out a chair and sat down. She gestured at him. "Mr. Harandi, please have a seat. I'm Captain Lavoe. Of course, you've already met Homicide Detective Matthews. I just finished a conference call with the Chief of Police and Presidential Advisor Patricia Hennessey. Never, in twenty-five years, have I seen a situation like the one we have here. I apologize on behalf of myself, Detective Matthews and the Houston Police Department. Can we get you anything? A cup of coffee?"

David sat in a chair opposite the woman. "It's nice to meet you, Captain Lavoe. Yes, Detective Matthews and I met earlier, at the Granduca. I'm glad you were able to talk with Ms. Hennessey and ascertain my innocence. I don't need anything. I'd like very much to be on my way, so that I can rebook my flight to Washington."

Captain Lavoe gave him an inquisitive look. "Mr. Harandi, you are certainly free to go at any time. We'll give you a ride back to the hotel. First, though, would you mind taking a look at some surveillance photos of the man who impersonated you in

Chicago? It may help our colleagues there. I know they would appreciate any insight you may have."

Relieved, but wondering how someone could have assumed his identity so completely, he spread his hands. "I'm more than willing to cooperate in whatever way I can. I'm as anxious as you are to get to the bottom of this."

A smile barely touched the firm line of her lips. "Ms. Hennessey mentioned that your reason for being in Houston involved national security, although she was reticent about the details. Were you planning to make the Department aware of your investigation, Mr. Harandi?"

Thinking fast, he tried to assess the best way to appease the collective egos bruised by his subterfuge. "The nature of my assignment precluded my making contact, as I'm sure Ms. Hennessey explained. However, if you'd like to share the evidence leading to my arrest, perhaps I can be of assistance in clearing things up. Then I'd like nothing more than to head for D.C."

Detective Matthews shoved off the wall. "Sharing information is a two-way street in Texas, Mr. Harandi."

Captain Lavoe raised an index finger. "That's enough, detective." She opened the portfolio and slid it across the table. "Take a look at these images. Any light you can shed on the identity of this man will be helpful."

He picked up the top photo. His mouth dropped open as shocked recognition hit him. Blown away by the middle finger, in-your-face *fuck you* sent directly to him from Rowan Milani, he muttered, "Son of a bitch. How in God's name . . ."

The captain stirred. "Do you know that man?"

Breathing hard, he laid the photo down and glared at her. "Yes."

Detective Matthews prowled the room before coming to a stop in front of him. "Well, are you planning to make us privy to your knowledge?"

Hearing the steel in the deep voice, David looked at the detective and then the captain. He needed to get a hold of Patricia, so she could inform Rodney Ainsley. And he needed to call Muusa Shemal. Both men were in mortal danger. He turned the photo around. "This is Rowan Milani, our country's most wanted home grown terror suspect."

The Captain gave him an incredulous look. "I've heard all about Rowan Milani. You're certain that's who this is?"

"Yes, but I have no idea how he knew I'd be in Houston."

Matthews propped his rangy body against the wall and crossed his arms. "Are you certain he's not pursuing you?"

Captain Lavoe tapped the table with a red lacquered nail. "My gut tells me that your reason for being here in the first place involves Rowan Milani. Am I correct?"

He chose his words with care, loathe to further expose the details of his assignment. But his old friend Rowan had done that for him. "Five murders in Houston, involving the House of Allah, may be connected to Milani, which is why I am here. In my opinion it is very possible that he is still here. It looks as though I'll be staying on indefinitely. It is imperative that I notify Muusa Shemal. I believe he is one of Milani's targets."

Detective Matthews flung his arms in the air. "This is just great. While you've been here poking around, I've been conducting a multiple murder investigation which Shemal is smack in the middle of."

The captain arched a pencil-thin brow. "I'm sure that national security concerns demanded that your assignment be covert. However, I must tell you, I share my detective's frustration. We need – and would be grateful – for every detail you can provide."

He slouched in the chair and stroked the goatee his old friend had so cleverly copied. Thanks to Rowan, the stern captain and her grouchy detective were now a part of his investigation. "How about the three of us meet for dinner this evening, say seven o'clock at the Granduca? That gives me time to learn everything I can about what happened in Chicago. I'll prepare a report with all the details you are entitled to."

Captain Lavoe looked pleased. "You've got yourself a deal, Mr. Harandi." She glanced at the silver watch peeking from beneath the cuff of her tailored suit jacket. "That gives you most of the afternoon to recover from this ordeal." She stood up and held out her hand. "Again, my apologies. You also have my thanks in advance for any information you can provide us. It's been . . . interesting . . . to meet you."

He gripped her outstretched hand and let it go before standing up. "Thank you, captain."

She stepped to the door and opened it. "You're welcome." She gestured toward her tall detective. "We'll see you at seven."

Gabriel lay flat on his back with one arm around Sherie, his wife of thirteen years. Her head rested on his shoulder, her fingers tapped lightly on his forearm and she had one leg plastered across his legs. He could feel her toes on his calf muscle.

It felt good to be in bed with her. It had been five months since he'd been home and even longer since they'd had any time to themselves. Sherie's mother had taken Jamie and Sophia, their ten-year-old son and seven-year-old daughter, the previous evening so he could be alone with his wife. And much too soon, he had to leave.

The responsibilities waiting at the Kauai estate weighed on his mind, spawning resentment he couldn't ignore. For the first time, he didn't have the zest for completing the operation, for finishing the job. The task of ensuring the safety and security of Rowan and the entire group of people hidden on the island would *never* be over. He reached up and rubbed his forehead with his free hand.

Sherie whispered. "What's the matter Papa Bear? Afraid I'll wear you out?"

Feeling inordinately sad at her use of the pet name their children had dubbed him with, for once he wished he could tell her what he was thinking. *Nah, baby, it's not that. I'm just trying to figure out how to tell you that I have to go again and I don't know when I'll be back.* Instead he rolled onto his side so he could drink in every detail of her luscious body before he had to walk away from it again. "Ah, Mamacita, you can never wear me out."

Her delicate lips looked so good that he bent forward and kissed her. When she responded with a happy sigh from deep in her throat, he gathered her in his arms. Laying her gently on her back, arms planted on either side of her body, he clung to the kiss as long as he could before pulling back. Every heavy breath had his hard muscled abdomen rubbing on her soft belly, cranking up the heat of desire all over again.

Taking in her enticing, full breasts, he couldn't resist bending low and running his tongue between them, reveling in the spicy scent of her perfume. Raising his head, he smacked his lips. "You taste good. You know you're in trouble now, baby."

When she flung her head back on the pillow, swirling thick, wavy black hair around her face, he could only stare, wanting her with a ferocity that bordered on desperation. Sherie put her hand on the back of his head and pulled him down, murmuring into his mouth as it closed over hers. "I'll show you trouble, Mr. Hernandez. Now make me a happy woman."

Ralph took his morning coffee with him to his office and locked the door. He grabbed his phone, punched in his friend's number and waited. "Jack McKenzie here."

"Hello Jack. Have you been able to dig up anything of interest?"

McKenzie didn't waste any time. "Ralph, you have to understand something. The Muslim Brotherhood is very highly thought of in Washington, D.C. It's gone so far that you might say engaging with the Brotherhood has become official policy. Muusa Shemal, the Brotherhood operative you mentioned, has been to the White House and met with the President."

"That doesn't surprise me. Does that mean you're not interested in helping us?"

Jack laughed. "You know me better than that. I'm always interested in a good story and I'm opposed to seeing someone innocent being railroaded. In the short time I've been able to poke around, the main thing I've realized is that this mess goes deep, and it could lead to the exposure of some very troubling issues for the country."

Ralph shifted the phone to his other ear. "If you're game, there's nothing I'd like more than to know you're on our team. I'm limited in what I can do, but I'll help you in any way I can. The main thing is getting the truth out. I have always had great faith in my fellow Americans. If the people of the country know the truth, I believe that in the end, they'll rally around Rowan."

"Don't get your hopes up. There's a lot of dope out there about Milani's supposed wrongdoing. It's the kind of shit that gets a person a lifetime ticket to a supermax somewhere, or maybe even the needle. You know what I mean?"

The words sent a shudder through his body. By God, he wouldn't give in to fear. "I know Rowan and I know the *truth.* You find a way to help me get it out there and it'll speak for itself."

"You have to understand, Ralph. We're going to be fighting the force of the media here, of which I am a fairly entrenched member. That may help you, or it may not. Besides that, like I said, the Brotherhood is very much in vogue, both with the media and the political types."

"Just keep digging and I'll stay in touch. It's possible we could work out some meetings with you. Let me give that some thought. Take care, Jack. I'll contact you again in another week or so."

"You too. Stay safe, wherever you are."

Ralph ended the call and sank lower in his chair. Staring out the window, he wondered if his efforts would make any difference. It all depended on the course Rowan chose to follow. That thought did not comfort him.

Rowan watched the flat screen TV with deep satisfaction. Grabbing the glass of whiskey he'd poured for the occasion, he took a long swallow. Seeing David Harandi hauled off made his day. He hoped the message he wanted to send had been received. And he hoped Ainsley and Shemal got the message, as well. "You're next, assholes."

He got up from the recliner and sat the glass of whiskey on the end table. Wandering into the kitchen, he slapped a peanut butter and jelly sandwich together. He made a second sandwich while he took huge bites of the first one. He stuffed the last bite in his mouth, grabbed the other sandwich and headed for the beach.

Munching through it, he made his way down the narrow sandy path, licking jelly from his fingers and letting his feet sink into the warm, gritty sand. A light breeze cut through the heat of the sun on his face. The sound of the waves rolling in and out, the gulls occasional squawking and the rustle of nearby palms were mesmerizing.

He headed to the edge of the surf, where he could walk and let the water wash over his ankles. His phone rang and he pulled it out of his shirt pocket. He punched talk and pressed it against his ear, his moment of carefree happiness evaporating. "Hey Mike, what's up?"

Danielle answered. "Rowan, it's me. Please – *don't hang up.*"

He could barely resist the urge to toss the phone into the waves. "Put Mike on the phone, right now."

"Rowan, please don't do this. I need to talk to you."

For God's sake, she was the last thing he needed. "Danielle, put Mike on the phone, or I *will* hang up."

She didn't answer, but he heard the phone being handled and then his colleague. "Hello, Rowan."

"Goddamn it. Why did you let her do this? Aren't you supposed to be helping Chad with things at the estate?"

Michael's voice was flat. "That's exactly what I'm doing."

Plodding aimlessly along the beach, he rolled his eyes. Michael had always been such a pushover. "And you're doing a hell of a job. I am not going to talk to her, so deal with it – deal with *her."*

"Look, Amigo. You need to let her explain things to you. You *owe* her that much. Now is not the time for your stubborn shit."

So, he was being stubborn. Hell, all right then. "Listen up, Mike. The next time I see your ID on my phone, it had better be *you* when I answer and it had better be about something important. Comprendé, *Amigo?"*

Not waiting for an answer, he ended the call. *He owed her?* Stuffing the phone back in his shirt pocket, he stared across the water. The undulating turquoise waves and their foaming white caps no longer held any appeal for him.

Walking without seeing or hearing anything, he made his way back inside and slumped into the recliner. He reached down, fumbling until he found the bottle of whiskey and poured the glass full. Staring at the amber liquid, he took a deep breath and let it out in slow increments.

He swallowed as much as he could in one gulp, wincing as the whiskey burned its way down his throat. He tossed back another swallow and then another, impatient for the alcohol to do its job. He pulled the phone from his shirt pocket and turned it off.

Gabriel sat in a chair and watched Sherie. She was tending to the flowers she maintained on their patio overlooking the Pacific. He loved how she fussed over each colorful plant, plucking and digging, sometimes moving a pot to a different location. He loved the house, too, and everything about their property. And now he had to leave again. He didn't want to. But he'd made a commitment, and he always honored his commitments.

She turned toward him. The ocean breeze twirled her hair, blew it across her face. She lifted her hand and brushed it away. "What's the matter, Papa Bear?"

He eyed the bottle of Don Julio Real and gripped his empty shot glass, tapping it on the cedar table. "Baby, we need to talk."

She gave him a puzzled look. "Is something wrong?"

He gave in and pulled the silver stopper from the bottle of tequila and poured himself a shot. He tossed it back and poured another while Sherie ditched her gardening tools and sat down across from him. "No, nothing is wrong. I've got to get back to, you know, the job."

She bent her head and covered her eyes for a moment, then looked up. "How can you leave so soon? Jamie and Sophia will be heartbroken. They need their papa. And I need my husband. You've been gone so long this time. Can't someone else finish this job?"

He couldn't meet her eyes. Instead he stared at the golden liquid in the shot glass. "This is a different kind of job. I don't want to go, but you know how it works. I don't have a choice."

Sherie said, "Last summer, while you were gone on this *job,* a terrorist escaped from Quantico. What was his name? I can't remember. He was a traitor to this country and a real bastard."

Surprise crackled through his body. He downed the tequila and coughed. "Si, I know what you're talking about. It was a mess. I don't recall his name, but he was a bad hombre."

"One thing I do remember. On the news, one of the guards from Quantico was interviewed. You'll never guess what he said about that day."

He tried to look curious. "I never saw any interviews about that. What did he say?"

"The guard told the news reporter that one of the men who helped the terrorist escape was about six feet tall and stocky. He remembered that this agent was Hispanic and had a thin moustache."

His heart pounded and heat prickled across his chest and back. He started sweating in the cool breeze. "You think that was me? I can take you downtown and show you a dozen stocky Hispanic men and more than one will have a moustache like mine."

"Gabriel Alonzo Hernandez. We have been married for more than a few years. Treachery may be part of what you do, and I'm sure you are an accomplished liar on the job, but you cannot fool me."

"Baby, don't be loco. While you are here by yourself, your imagination runs wild. I have been out of the country for a long time. That's why I don't know much about this escape."

She waggled a finger in his face. "Shush. I am not one of your children. This interview intrigued me, so I googled the whole story about that terrorist. Oh – now I remember his name. Rowan Milani. Does that stir your memory?"

Dreading what she might say next, he shook his head. "No, it doesn't ring a bell."

Her look became pitying. "My search taught me so much. I realized that the terrorist – Rowan Milani, had escaped twice. The first time happens to coincide with when you left last spring. Why are you continuing this charade?"

He answered, feeling desperate. "What can I say to change your already made-up mind?"

Sherie looked triumphant. "I love Google. Did you know that when that hombre escaped the first time, his friends were so bold that they stole a jet from the CIA? It was a big, fancy airplane, brand new. A Gulfstream G650."

"What does that have to do with me? I don't know one airplane or jet from another."

Sherie grabbed his shot glass, poured it full, tipped her head back and swallowed. She shivered, but didn't cough. "The jet that dropped you off was impressive. I asked a man at the airport about it and he told me it was a Gulfstream G650."

"You are putting these parts and pieces together because you want to believe that I helped a terrorist escape? I was a Ranger, I took an oath. You know I would never do anything to endanger this country."

"This Rowan Milani, he must be a good man. He must need you desperately if you will leave your family for months and come home only for a few days."

The sadness that welled in her eyes left him floundering in guilt. "I don't want to leave. As soon as I can come home forever, I will. This job . . . it has not been easy."

She reached for his hands, grasped them and held tight. "I can't bear to lose you. Please be careful with what you do for this man. I am trusting that your love for me and your children and your country will guide your decisions."

It was time for him to get out. Rowan's loco plans would end with all of them either incarcerated or dead. He couldn't do that to her and to his precious family. "It is almost finished. This time, I won't be gone too long." He squeezed her hands. "Sherie, I mean what I say, you know that."

"I trust you. But I know how your *jobs* go. I will wait for you as long as I must. But please, I don't want to raise our children alone."

David surveyed his new partner. After dinner with Captain Lavoe, he and Kyle Matthews had found a spot in a corner of *Bar Maletesta* in the Granduca. A tuxedo clad pianist played softly and subdued conversation flowed around them. The intimacy suited his task of getting to know the man who sat brooding across from him. "Tell me how an Irishman like you ended up in Texas. But first, thanks for getting my room back at the Granduca. I wasn't sure they'd take me, considering the way I left this morning. But after your call, the concierge gave me a bottle of their best Scotch."

Kyle crossed long legs and sipped coffee. A ghost of a smile lifted his lips. "You're welcome. My great-grandfather was among the first Irish immigrants to settle here, well actually in West Texas. My father became an attorney and moved our family to Dallas."

He'd noticed the plain gold wedding band. "Married, I presume? Any children?"

The detective pulled a tooled leather wallet from the back pocket of his suit pants. "My wife's name is Erin. We've got two busy rug rats, Casey and Patrick."

David gazed at the image of a black-haired young woman and two happy boys. Red-heads, he thought, but couldn't tell for sure in the low light. He caught the detective's unguarded gaze and saw simple adoration. "How does Erin deal with your profession?"

Kyle took the wallet back. "I'm sure she has her moments, but with me she's cool. She's an ER trauma nurse and just tells me not to ever end up in her 'precinct.'"

"Good for you. Well, I'm guessing that since you're slurping coffee, you still have work to do tonight, so let's talk business. Rowan Milani's *activities* have brought me face to face with some unsettling questions."

Kyle shot him a grim look. "I agree. Such as, how does a wanted terror suspect move freely around the country? How did he know where to find Shemal? And how did he know my dead vic was in town and staying at the Granduca?"

"You've pretty well summed it up. It's a mystery to me how he can move around the country undetected. Forehand knowledge of locations and timing of events has become a hallmark of his operation. It's mind boggling that he knew, somehow, that the President had assigned me to bring him in. And, how did he know Agent Capello would be in Chicago at the O'Hare Hilton? No one else involved in this case, including me, knew that."

Kyle whistled softly. "That implies some serious hacking ability. Not to mention the balls it took to impersonate you. What makes an American citizen become a terrorist?"

David finished the glass of wine and poured more. "I wish I knew. On 9/11 he lost his fiancé in the North Tower of the World Trade Center, which makes this even harder to understand. I just can't get a grasp of how he became radicalized. But I intend to ask him, and believe me, he's going to answer."

The lanky man straightened in the chair, looking concerned. "His trail ends here. We need to assign a couple uniforms to protect you."

"I'm former CIA. If Milani's here, I hope he comes after me. He's not going to like the payback I've got in mind."

The detective rubbed his neck. "Still, I'm going to post a couple undercover guys at the hotel. No point taking unnecessary chances. Here's a thought – if he's got access to your communications, why don't we feed him false information and create a trap?"

"That's interesting, I've been thinking along those same lines. We'd have to craft something convincing. Milani is a smart man. He won't be easy to fool and neither will his cohorts, whoever they are."

Kyle stood up and held out his right hand. "I guess I should apologize for the way we met. And after everything we've been through today, I think we'll do all right as a team."

David grasped the outstretched hand. "No apology necessary. You were doing your job, same as I would have. I'm looking forward to working with you."

The detective stifled a yawn with his fist. “You were right. I’ve got some work to finish up tonight. But tomorrow, I’ll be ready to hit this – hard. Let’s make Rowan Milani face some good old-fashioned Texas justice.”

He wanted to tell detective Matthews that he’d have to get in line, but decided not to. “Let’s do it, detective.”

CHAPTER NINE

A Week Later

Rowan twisted his shoulders. The headache he'd tried to ignore had entrenched itself behind his eyes and for once it had nothing to do with whiskey. He stretched and groaned. Maybe Jack Daniel's was what he needed to relieve the jackhammer in his head and the tension between his shoulders.

For the past eight hours he'd focused on his plan to take out Ainsley and Shemal in the same location. For God's sake, they'd made it so simple. The conference Ainsley was speaking at along with Shemal was perfect and he'd take great advantage of their lack of forethought.

He stared at the laptop screen, contemplating the overt stupidity of the *intelligence* community in creating a venue presenting both men together. Chad's expert hacking skills had given him access to the event details, including information on a private meeting between the two men the day before the conference. That was what he wanted to research further.

Glancing at his phone, he saw that he'd somehow missed a call from his sister. Setting his work aside, he headed outside, across the yard to the sand path leading to the beach.

He inhaled the salt air, enjoying the warm breeze that ruffled his unbuttoned shirt and kept the group of palms at the edge of the property in perpetual motion. His feet sank into the deep sand and he winced at the pain in his left foot as he navigated the path, waiting for Bettina to pick up. "Hi Row, I was wondering when you'd get around to calling me back."

The lighthearted voice left him relieved. "Hey little sister, what's up? Everything OK with the, uh, baby? Are you feeling all right?" Reaching the hard-packed sand of the beach, he stopped walking and stared at the aquamarine waves.

"I'm fine other than the fact that I eat like a horse, all the time. We had a great trip to Chicago and our first check-up went well. Good ole Johnny boy has a super doctor. But that isn't why I called."

Rowan let the waves wash over his bare feet and dug his toes into the thick wetness. "Oh, let me guess, you've been talking to Danielle, right?"

"For heaven's sake, why can't you have an argument with a woman and get over it? This is Danielle we're talking about. I know you love her, you idiot."

He watched the water rushing in, foaming around his ankles. The waves sucked away at the sand beneath his feet as the ocean pulled the restless water inexorably back, the same way his relationship with Danielle threatened to suck him back, into depths he could no longer navigate. "I do love her. I just figured out that she doesn't really love me."

"Oh please, do you know how ridiculous you sound? This is the woman who walked away from everything for you."

"Did she happen to tell you about how she thinks that I'm a monster? Or about how smart her friend Derek is and how he warned her about me?"

Bettina huffed. "You told her about how you killed someone she knew personally the same way you'd describe running over a skunk. Geez Row, for people who aren't deep into the clandestine, assassin shit like you are, the things you do can be a little unsettling."

"Yeah, whatever." He stood for a moment, listening to the raucous calling of the gulls as they swooped and dived. The sun hung on the horizon, turning the mesmerizing waves into rolling, liquid gold, but he couldn't enjoy it. "Danielle deserves a normal, safe life somewhere. I'm done with this. For God's sake, I've got other things on my mind."

"I know how stubborn you are. You get it from Mom. And now you're treating Danielle just like Mom treated you after 9/11."

He stood, feet rooted in the water. "What the fuck did you just say?"

Bettina had no problem repeating the accusing words. "I said *you* are just like Mom – so hell-bent on having everything your way. You should be ashamed of yourself, especially after how badly Mom hurt you."

He rubbed viciously at the pain hammering in his forehead. "I am not like Mom. And I don't have anything to be ashamed about."

"Prove it. Call Danielle and have a reasonable conversation. Maybe you could even bring yourself to forgive her so you both can move on, together."

The sun sank beneath the waves while they argued and the breeze turned chilly. He shivered and turned his back on the pastel streaked sky, heading to the deep sand and the path to the house. Bettina was just as goddamned stubborn as she thought he was. "All right, I'll call Danielle tonight and have as reasonable a conversation as I can."

It pissed him off to give in, but it was the only way to get rid of her. Bettina sounded pleased with herself, which irritated him even more. "That's the first smart thing you've said. Thank you for listening to reason. *Finally.*"

He stepped into the house and made a beeline for the bottle of Jack Daniel's on the kitchen counter. "Yeah, well you take care of yourself and be nice to Chad. I gotta go."

"Come on, I'm always nice to Chad. Be safe, big brother. I love you."

Sinking down into the recliner, he silently cursed her ability to manipulate him. "I love you too. Bye." He tossed the phone to the floor. Retrieving the bottle of Jack and the glass he'd snagged, he poured and drank. Stretching out, he closed his eyes against the pounding headache and folded his hands around the glass of whiskey on his lap.

David stifled his restlessness. Patricia had called him back to D.C. from Houston to work on Clifton Cantor's connection to Milani. He'd been torn about leaving. Collaborating with Detective Matthews was a pleasure. They'd come up with a scenario plausible enough to lure Milani and he was anxious to flesh out the details.

But this evening, his focus was Clifton Cantor, who was sitting across from him in the bustling restaurant. They'd agreed to meet at a hole-in-the-wall Italian joint. A waiter placed steaming plates of spaghetti topped with rich sauce and fat meatballs in front of each of them. Next he deposited a linen-cloaked basket of garlic bread and refilled their wine glasses before gliding away.

For someone who had to know he was under surveillance, Clifton appeared relaxed and confident. "Bon appetite, Mr. Harandi. Thank you for allowing me to choose our meeting place. This restaurant was a long-time favorite of my wife's. I still frequent it as often as I can."

David pulled the linen cloth down and nabbed a slice of fragrant bread. "Please call me David." Thirty minutes later he laid his fork on the empty plate. The simple Italian fare was the best he'd ever tasted.

Clifton gave him a questioning look. "You seem to have enjoyed yourself. Now – what can I help you with? The unfortunate demise of Agent Capello had me hoping that perhaps I'd escape further harassment, but I doubt you just wanted to enjoy a nice dinner and make a new friend."

The waiter appeared one more time, sliding pitch black coffee in white china cups in front of them. David watched as Clifton stirred a heaping teaspoon of sugar into his coffee. "The President has tasked me with apprehending Rowan Milani. My gut tells me you can help me with that."

Clifton finished stirring and sat the spoon aside. "As I told Agent Capello numerous times, I've never met Mr. Milani, and therefore do not understand the ongoing interest in me."

"With all due respect, your son Chad disappeared along with Milani. Also, it's common knowledge within the intelligence community that he helped facilitate Milani's first escape."

Clifton took a sip of coffee before replying. "Yes, that has been a source of embarrassment to me, especially since the President is a personal friend. However, my son's behavior does not qualify me to advise you in any capacity. Nor does it implicate me in his activities."

David marveled at the man's unflappable demeanor. "Since Milani and your son disappeared at the same time, I have this feeling – call it a hunch, that they are together somewhere. If you have any information regarding their location, it may be useful – and it might help to mitigate Chad's culpability."

Still appearing infuriatingly at ease, Clifton gave him a dry smile. "And mine, I presume?"

He wasn't sure whether Clifton was toying with him or trying to provoke him. "If necessary, certainly."

The older man gave him a judicious look. "You appear to be a resourceful investigator and that will benefit you as you move forward. Do you foresee the need for us to meet again, considering the point we've reached this evening?"

He'd never been told to *fuck off* so politely. Knowing he needed to contain his aggravation, he stroked his goatee. "I do believe we've reached an understanding of sorts. For my part, I understand that you feel insulated from my efforts to ascertain your son and Milani's whereabouts. What I hope *you* understand is that I intend to bring Milani and whoever is working with him into custody."

"Be careful and watch your back, David. You're a good man, and it would be a shame to see anything happen to you." Sliding out of the booth, Clifton stood up, holding out his hand. "It was my pleasure to join you this evening. And please – dinner's on me."

Not sure how to take the insinuation-laden comments, he gripped the man's outstretched hand. "The pleasure has been mine. Please enjoy the rest of your evening."

Observing Clifton saunter to the front of the restaurant, he heaved a sigh. The man was a formidable adversary and he'd bet a year's pay that Clifton knew exactly where Rowan Milani and his entourage were hidden. Hopefully, the FBI team Rodney had assembled for him had found something of value in the warrantless search of Clifton's Georgetown condo during dinner. The President had personally approved the search and he couldn't wait to see what it yielded.

Rowan woke with a start when the glass of Jack Daniel's sitting on his belly tipped over, sending a river of whiskey down his side. He wiped it away with his shirttail and struggled to sit up. Moonlight streamed through the windows and he groped for his phone in the semi-darkness. He'd only planned on resting his eyes, but he'd slept until damn near midnight.

Thinking about Danielle filled him with dread. Being far away, unable to sense her presence or catch her scent, the pain was manageable, a dull ache that he could ignore most of the time. He fumbled for the bottle of whiskey and refilled the glass on his lap. Taking a hefty swallow, he grabbed the phone and punched her contact.

She answered on the first ring. "Hi Rowan. Thanks for calling."

"Hey Danielle. I thought maybe we should talk."

"Oh my God, I've been *dying* to talk to you. You have to know, I freaked out over Marta. I didn't get it, but now I do. I always understood about the terrorists. Marta made it personal, you know? You had to . . . to take care of her before she could hurt you or us again. It makes sense to me now. I tried to tell you before you left."

"OK." He laid his head back and closed his eyes. Hearing her voice, seeing her in his mind's eye, he could almost feel her skin. God, she was so soft. He breathed deep, remembering the strawberry scent of her hair. A wave of longing rolled through his body. *This* was why he didn't want to talk to her.

"I miss you so much. I'm sorry for the things I said. No matter what Derek says, I'll always love you."

He opened his eyes and sat up. *"What Derek says?"*

She spoke in a rush. "No, no, I'm sorry. I just remembered what I said to you – before. I don't care about Derek. All I care about is you."

"No matter what, we always end up talking about Derek. Why is that?" Punching the speaker button, he laid the phone on his lap and poured more Jack.

Danielle sounded tinny and distant. "The reason we always talk about him is because you can't figure it out. How many times do I need to tell you that he's just a friend? That's all he's ever been. Why don't you get that?"

Holding the glass of whiskey in both hands, he rolled his eyes. Then he remembered his promise to Bettina. "All right, I get it. Keep talking. I'm listening."

"I hate that I've hurt you. I hope you can forgive me."

He swallowed more whiskey and twisted his tense shoulders. He could still hear Bettina. "Of course I forgive you."

Danielle spoke so softly he had to strain to hear her. "Thank you. It's so sad here without you. I was hoping . . . you know I just want to be with you, no matter where you are."

"That's impossible."

"I don't want to be here without you. Our suite, it's so empty. Everything seems so meaningless. What am I supposed to do?"

He finished the whiskey and refilled the glass. "I don't have any answers. They'll always be looking for me, you know that."

She laughed, sounding halfway hysterical. "It doesn't matter to me when I'm with you. I'd hide with you for the rest of my life."

He cringed. "Look, I've never wanted to hurt you and I'll always be sorry you got stuck in this mess, but . . ."

She interrupted him. "Don't you dare tell me that we're done. I want to be with you. I don't care where."

He gulped the whiskey and touched his lips, realizing they were going numb. For God's sake, he couldn't drink enough to get through it. "How many times do we have to cover this?"

Danielle kept pushing. "You know, I have never met anyone more pig-headed than you. How about if I just leave and start over?"

He snickered at the defiance in her voice, wondering if she was naive enough to think he'd actually buckle. "Now you're talking. How's this – *we're done.* You're free to leave Kauai and start over."

"If that's what you want me to do, I'll leave. I'm sure Derek will want to leave, too."

He downed more whiskey. He'd let Chad tell her that Derek wasn't going anywhere. "Yeah, you be sure to take your *friend* with you. Tomorrow morning I'll talk to Chad and Mike. I've got a house in San Francisco and you've got a new identity as Mrs. James Hawthorne. That comes with a bank account holding over a million dollars. Mike set that up for me – for *you,* last summer."

"I don't want your money or your house. I can take care of myself. My parents live in Seattle. I'll contact them."

God, she made him want to go out and shoot someone. "In case you've forgotten, the FBI and Shemal are still looking for all of us. The last thing *I* need is for you to be detained again. Just take the money and use the goddamned house."

"Fine. I'd hate to cause you any more problems. But I want Gabriel to help me. He's the only one who understands how I feel."

"Work it out however you want. I don't care."

"I understand that now. I don't know what else to say. Good-bye, I guess. Take care."

He grabbed the phone, punched *END* and tossed it to the floor. Lying back, he stared at the shadows flickering on the ceiling. "Good-bye, Danielle." Someday, she might forgive him for being such a jerk. Maybe now he'd be left alone to concentrate on what he needed to do.

A Week Later

Chad stared at the computer screen. Emails between David Harandi, Patricia Hennessey, Rodney Ainsley and Muusa Shemal had all but dried up. Yet, Harandi and a detective named Matthews were corresponding in a flurry of messages about the investigation into Marta's death and whether or not Rowan was still in Houston.

Massaging taut shoulder muscles, he continued staring at the screen. Niggling doubts ate away at his fragile peace of mind. Why had the emails dried up? Did that mean the FBI had figured out he was using a VPN and had managed to trace his real IP? If they had, were special agents even now surveilling the estate, planning to apprehend all of them?

Tension wrapped around his head and squeezed. His heart pounded while he carefully checked the firewall configuration file to make sure there were no possible loopholes. Everything was in order. Breathing heavily, he grabbed his phone and called Rowan.

After a dozen rings, he heard fumbling on the other end of the connection. “Chad? Hey. What the hell’s going on?”

He tried to gather his thoughts. “Oh man, I forgot about the time. Uh, something isn’t right. We need to rethink a few things.”

“Why? What are you talking about?”

Why hadn’t he thought it through and talked to Mike before calling? “It’s about email and the firewalls, but I checked everything. So far I think we’re all right. We need to find an alternative for Kauai, though, just in case.”

Rowan mumbled. “Firewalls? An alternative for what in Kauai?”

“It’s nothing. I’ll call you back tomorrow after I discuss it with Mike. Go back to sleep.”

“It is tomorrow, goddamn it.” The phone went dead.

Despite the stress, he chuckled and punched in another number.

Michael picked up on the first ring. “What’s up, Chad?”

“We need to meet.”

“All right, hot tub on the west deck, in fifteen.”

Twenty minutes later, sitting in roiling bubbles that hit him at mid-chest, Chad clutched a cold Budweiser in one hand and rested his other arm along the curved side of the tub. “This is just what I needed. Thanks. And, thanks for coming back. I haven’t had a chance to tell you how much I appreciate you being here.”

Michael chugged his beer and belched. “You’re welcome. In the end, I couldn’t walk away, from you – or Rowan. Besides, I’m having so much fun giving Gabriel *guidance* on helping Danielle with a new start or whatever you want to call it. Angelo thinks she’s on the ragged edge emotionally, so they’re trying to keep her occupied.”

He stared. “Damn. Well, you aren’t going to like this any better. Something doesn’t feel right to me with regard to communications between our players in D.C. Emails have dried up and that makes me think that they've figured out that they've been hacked, which means they could find us. And . . ."

His colleague raised a hand. "Whoa, wait a minute. Did you check the firewalls you installed?"

"Hell yes. Everything appears intact, but you never know. If they find some kind of loophole and trace my IP far enough, they could find us."

Michael swilled more beer. "First of all, they'd have to be morons not to figure out we're hacking them. How else would we have known about Harandi being hired to find Rowan? Or about Marta and Shemal being in Houston?"

Chad sank lower in the hot tub and tipped his head back, taking a long swallow of beer. "Ah, that hits the spot. What you're saying makes sense. But Ainsley is still sending emails to the Assistant Director in Charge of the Office of Public Affairs, about the conference and his travel arrangements. That concerns me as well, because I found an inconsistency."

Crumpling the beer can and dropping it onto the deck, Michael grabbed another. "Such as?"

Chad finished his beer and flung the can. Michael tossed him another. "According to emails I hacked earlier, Ainsley is traveling to Houston on Saturday morning. That's the day the conference starts and he speaks that afternoon. No changes have been made to his travel requisition, but now he's meeting privately with Shemal on Friday, the day before he's scheduled to arrive."

Michael stared past him for a moment. "It could be a simple thing. Someone may have screwed up the travel requisition or the itinerary hasn't been updated. Or, maybe they're screwing around, trying to create confusion since they know *someone's* hacked them. The other option is that they're getting smart and are trying to set Rowan up by providing a tidy, private meeting that puts Shemal and Ainsley in the same place at the same time."

Unnerved at that possibility, Chad gulped beer. "I hadn't gotten that far. We better let Rowan know. He should abort this plan and wait for a different opportunity."

Michael looked skeptical. "I'm with you, but I wish you luck getting Rowan to go along with that. He's not going to back off because we *suspect* they *might* be trying to set him up. We both know that."

"Yeah, you're right."

Michael brightened. "This is the perfect opportunity for me to step in. You've got things under control here. Danielle is taken care of until Gabriel decides to bolt for home. I can head for Key West and show all this stuff to Rowan. Then the two of us can fly to Houston and run the op together."

Chad couldn't resist a smirk. "I wish *you* luck with that. This time, he will shoot you."

"Oh, hell. I hate it when you're right. Rowan's a scary motherfucker anyway, but with a gun in each hand, he puts the fear of God in me, and *that's* saying something."

"Rowan terrifies anyone with half a brain, including our resident pain in the ass. Any ideas on what we should do with Derek?"

"I know what I'd like to do with that weasel. You know, if it wasn't for that sneaky shit, Danielle would still be here and Rowan would too. It wouldn't be too much trouble to take him out in Ralph's boat and dump him overboard. After shooting him, of course."

Lulled into peaceful relaxation by the combination of the bubbling water and Budweiser, Chad gazed up at the nearly full moon. "I could go for that."

His colleague crumpled his beer can and popped the top on another. "Well. Fuck me. The sharks probably wouldn't even want him."

Chad laughed. "That'd be just our luck. We better keep him here and let Marion keep mothering the dumb fuck – as Rowan would say."

"If we'd been thinking, we could have encouraged Rowan to off the jackass. Now we're stuck with him."

Draining the beer, surprised he'd finished it already, he pitched the can and expertly caught the cold, dripping one Michael sent across the hot tub. He pulled the tab slowly, listening to the fizz. "We should think about an alternative to the estate in case they do figure out where we are. My father said the pressure is increasing after Capello's death. Harandi met with him, and now the President has requested a meeting."

Michael scratched the stubble on his jaw. "We can always go back to South Dakota."

"You mean Sioux Falls? That's one of the first places they'd look for us."

"Didn't Rowan ever tell you? The medical clinic my parents run is adjacent to their ranch and sits on the edge of the Cheyenne River Indian Reservation. The ranch is over 20,000 acres and it's desolate. There are cabins in remote areas that only get used during hunting season. They never would have found Rowan out there, but we couldn't keep him from leaving."

Everything clicked in Chad's mind. "Remember when Rowan told me to ask you about a doctor and nurse for Bettina's pregnancy care? We never got the chance to talk about it, since Bettina and I left for Chicago before you decided about coming back. Now I understand what he meant."

Michael nodded. "If we ever need to leave in a hurry, it's the ideal place. Jerry and Bryan are familiar with flying in and out. My father was an Army surgeon and my mother is an RN. They run a medical clinic for the Native kids on the rez."

He swallowed more beer. "Let's make a contingency plan. You can alert Jerry and Bryan, talk to your parents, and let

Gabriel know as well. I'll talk to Ralph. He can work with Rowan's parents. We should be ready to clear out of this place in a hurry, just in case."

"Consider it done."

Chad laid his head back and closed his eyes. It felt great to relax, even for just a few minutes.

The Next Day

Danielle stood at the bay window, gazing at the rusty-orange spires of the Golden Gate Bridge rising through the fog. She loved its ghostly look and how it changed when the sun burned off the fog and left it standing out against the sky. She loved the house, too, and could *feel* Rowan in every room. He'd loved being here, she could tell. And she'd never known. He'd never told her about the home Gabriel said he'd been to many times over the years.

But then, she hadn't had years with him, like everyone else. And now she'd never have anything with him. He'd made that clear. She thought about what she'd told him about reconnecting with her parents. She'd never felt so alone and needed to be with people who knew her and cared about her. Angelo came into the room. "How are you this morning, Danielle? Enjoying the view, I see. It's magnificent, isn't it?"

She turned. "I'm doing great. Yes, I've always loved that bridge. Living here is a dream come true."

"It's a new adventure for me. Anytime you want to head out and enjoy the city, I'm game."

If she got out of the house, away from the constant reminders of the man who no longer loved her, maybe she could start to think again and plan for her future. "That sounds fantastic. Do you like clam chowder? I know a perfect spot, tucked away in Cow Hollow."

Angelo rubbed his hands together vigorously. "I'd be delighted. Your career with the airline afforded you such wonderful travel opportunities. You'll have to teach me everything I need to know to get the most out of this city."

She knew he meant well. "Sure, I've been here lots of times. I'll take you everywhere. Maybe even to The Stinking Rose."

Genuine pleasure creased his lean face. "Don't say another word. Just take me there. Like I said, I'm game for darn near anything, as long as it's legal."

Gabriel appeared in the doorway. A dish towel lay over one shoulder and a pistol of some kind hung at his right side. "Breakfast is ready, can't you smell it? We're eating on the deck this morning. Come on."

She nibbled on a slice of bacon and tried to ignore the aroma of eggs mingling with the fishy breeze off the Bay. Gabriel stuffed half a slice of bacon in his mouth. He waved the other half at her. "Honey, you gotta eat."

She hadn't been hungry since her last conversation with Rowan. From the corner of her eye she saw Angelo watching her. She laid the bacon on her plate and looked at Gabriel. "I told Rowan that I'd like to get in touch with my parents. Last summer, everything happened so fast. The day the FBI picked me up I'd been planning to call them. After we got to Kauai it wasn't possible. I never had a chance to tell them very much about Rowan and me, or anything."

Gabriel stared at her, the bacon still clutched in his fingers. "Oh honey, we have to be so careful. We don't know where the FBI or Shemal has eyes. Your parents may even have the FBI looking for you."

Angelo wiped his mouth with a napkin. "You know, Chad made arrangements for me to send money to my daughter and ex-wife. He set it up so that I could contact them occasionally. Isn't it possible he could create the same set-up for Danielle? These connections, with family, are so important."

Gabriel looked pained. "Si, I know. Leaving my family this last time damn near killed me."

It seemed that she didn't know anyone she'd been with for the past six months. "You're married? You have children?"

Gabriel looked sad. "I've been married thirteen years. We have two children, a boy and a girl. I miss them, very much."

She pushed back her chair and stood up. "I'm sorry you have to be away from them in order to babysit me. I can't imagine . . . well, I guess I can. What I mean is . . . oh, never mind."

Gabriel looked up at her. "The choices that took me away from my family have nothing to do with you, honey. I'll talk to Chad. We'll work something out so that you can talk to your parents."

Angelo tossed his napkin to the table. "How about we get out of the house? After a week, I think we're all settled, don't you?" The psychiatrist looked at Gabriel. "You'll keep an eye out, make sure no one is following us and all that?"

Gabriel nodded. "We're safe here. Let's go have some fun."

She looked from one kind face to the other. "Thanks, Gabriel, for everything. Let's do the tourist things first. How about Fisherman's Wharf and then Ghirardelli Square? I could use some chocolate. A bottle of wine sounds great, too."

Angelo looked guilty. "I forgot to tell you, a couple cases of that wine you like so much arrived yesterday. It's Bolgheri something or other."

The sharp jab of pain hit her. Rowan had given her a bottle of Bolgheri Sassicaia that first night. Once he knew how much she loved it, he'd made sure she never ran out. "Oh, wow. We can share a bottle tonight. Give me a sec and I'll be ready to go."

Rowan stood in the deep sand facing the water, raised his head to the warmth of the sun and closed his eyes. He listened to the rhythmic push and pull of the waves. The squawking gulls made him smile. The breeze off the gulf filled his nose with its fused scent of seaweed, fish and salt. He breathed in deeply, opened his eyes and squinted at the turquoise water. It shimmered in the sun, so bright his eyes watered. In the short time he'd been at the beach house, he'd loved it.

But it was time. He turned away and trudged back to the house. Grabbing his suitcase and slinging his briefcase over his shoulder, he locked the front door and tossed the keys on the floor. Lingering at the door, he called Roberto. "Hey, I just watched a couple guys in a boat. They came in way too close and I think they had binoculars. I saw a couple men snooping around on the beach earlier. It might have been the same ones that were in the boat. I'm surprised your crew didn't notice anything. OK. Thanks. Let me know what you find out. I'll be in the house."

Johnny's hit man would go into high gear and take the whole crew to check out the bogus threat. The ugly pink taxi pulled up as he walked toward the gated entrance to the property, right on time. He climbed in the back. The driver turned. "Key West airport, right?"

"Yes, please."

CHAPTER TEN

Clifton sat on the brocade sofa in the Oval Office and tried to appear relaxed. The aide who'd called had simply said that the President requested a meeting with him right away. That the summons followed so closely on his dinner with David Harandi made him wary. He clasped his hands loosely in his lap. "It's a pleasure to see you, Gil. How are you weathering the current political storms? What can an old friend do to help?"

President Whitman looked troubled. "Your friendship has meant a lot to me over the years. That makes this especially difficult for me."

He frowned at the man he'd known on a first-name basis since before either of them came to Washington. "That sounds somewhat dire, Gil. Please tell me what's on your mind."

The President crossed one leg over the other and fussed with the crease on his suit pants. "I'll never forget when Chad was recruited by the FBI. His skill with cyber-security has always been exceptional. If I recall, he acquired the reputation of being a hacker extraordinaire at Quantico."

Clifton straightened his tie and unbuttoned his suit jacket. "Yes, Chad started writing code when he was eleven years old. We tried to be proactive to keep him out of trouble when he discovered his special knack for breaching every firewall he ran across."

"Didn't you and Natalie work out projects *with* local law enforcement when he assured you that he could hack into all the local and state government systems and shut things down if he wanted to? How is Natalie, by the way?"

"Being proactive requires quick thinking and creativity. We saved him from juvenile prosecution. Natalie is doing as well as can be expected. The Alzheimer's Unit at the facility in Potomac provides excellent care. I visit, if you can call it that, once a week."

The President replied. "I'm so sorry. Both my wife and I always loved Natalie. Alzheimer's is a horrible affliction. But I didn't ask you to drop by today to catch up. Some things have come to my attention and I've reached some disturbing, but I fear unavoidable, conclusions."

"You've certainly no need to skirt the issues with me. As I said before, please tell me what's on your mind."

A muted knock turned the President's head. "Come in."

Uneasy, Clifton watched David Harandi enter the Oval Office, followed by Patricia Hennessey and two Secret Service agents. David sat down on one of the chairs adjacent to the sofa and clutched a folder. Patricia sat next to the President. The agents stood next to each other in front of the door. "Gil, what exactly is going on?"

The President answered him. "Some disquieting things have come to light. David, if you would present your findings, please."

David opened the folder and gave him a calculating stare. "First, Mr. Cantor, while we were at dinner last week, the FBI conducted a search of your Georgetown home. We found electronic correspondence between you and your son that discredits the statements you made to me. Second, documents held in a safe in your home office revealed that you own property on the island of Kauai. Third, other documents reveal a long-time relationship with Johnny Giacopino, considered by some to be *the* Boss of the entire Mafia organization within the United States. He owns an apartment leased to you in Potomac that is covered with your son's finger prints, as well as those of Ralph Johnston. You also lease a black Mercedes. Coincidentally, the car driven by the fraudulent FBI agents who enabled Rowan Milani's escape from

Quantico last July was a black Mercedes. That car has never been found."

A heavy silence descended. The President cleared his throat. "Thank you, David. Now, Clifton, would you care to address these findings?"

Clifton let his gaze linger on the President. "Gil, you've known about all of this. I've never tried to hide any of these things. As I told Mr. Harandi, my conversations with Chad are infrequent. However, he does occasionally contact me from wherever he is located. It is true that in years past, he used the Potomac apartment when in town visiting his mother. Whether he invited his boss Ralph Johnston there is unknown to me."

"I am hard pressed to find any crime in my association with Mr. Giacopino. I freely admit that I have conducted business with him, as have various government entities. I doubt very much that I am alone in owning island property. Mine is an old family estate, which I haven't visited since my wife succumbed to Alzheimer's. The black Mercedes was a leased vehicle, also courtesy of Mr. Giacopino. I returned it last year because Chad gave me his Shelby GT 500 Mustang."

Patricia stood. He saw only acrimony in her cold eyes. "We're not finished, Clifton. Your financial records show a major investment for a client named James Hawthorne. It's a tremendous amount and curiously, it matches almost to the penny the amount of cash confiscated from Milani's two offshore accounts after he was apprehended the first time. We're running the name *James Hawthorne* through every database available to us as we speak."

Clifton looked from David to Patricia and let his gaze stop at the President. "Well, lady, and gentlemen, I'm guilty as charged. I've been a well-known, sought after financial planner for a number of years. As I recall, Patricia, I've made investments on your behalf several times. Mr. Hawthorne is a businessman. He was referred to me and yes – I invested a major sum of money for him. I'm outraged that any of you would *assume* that it's the money confiscated from Rowan Milani. I'm at a loss as to how, once Milani's funds were seized, they could be appropriated for investment."

Patricia scoffed. "Spare us the clueless routine. Your son's skills are well-known. Someone breached the FBI's servers and has monitored Rodney Ainsley's communications with each of us and in addition . . ."

The President raised a hand. "That'll do, Patricia. I'm afraid all of these things taken together demand that I act. Clifton, until these matters are sorted out, I'm instructing the Secret Service to detain you."

Clifton forced himself to feign calm. "Unless something has changed drastically, as an American citizen, I have the right to due process. Am I mistaken in still believing that I'm innocent until proven guilty? No one has read me my rights. I'd like to call my attorney."

David responded. "This isn't an arrest, Mr. Cantor. It's the legal detention of an American citizen suspected of providing material support to a terrorist and his organization. You lose your rights as a citizen when you participate in that type of activity. Perhaps you'd like to be more forthcoming than you have been. If so, it's possible we can avoid disrupting your life so drastically."

The situation had become surreal. The careful deception he'd helped craft was collapsing. "Gil . . . Mr. President, if you plan to ignore my rights based on flimsy assumptions advanced by your people, I can't imagine that anything I say now will change your mind."

The President looked grim, but he could see ugly triumph in the look Patricia shot his way. "This administration doesn't act on *flimsy assumptions.* The FBI has sent a surveillance team to Kauai. You've been caught in a web of your own creation. I look forward to the day that your son is apprehended. Maybe you'll share a cell for twenty or thirty years. Who will care for Natalie, I wonder?"

The President stood up. "Patricia – *that's enough.*"

David motioned to the Secret Service agents and then looked at him. "Mr. Cantor, please stand up."

He did as he was instructed and waited, heart pounding as the agents approached. When one of them produced handcuffs, he turned to the President. "Is this necessary? I won't resist your armed thugs, Gil. I'll go quietly to whatever gulag you have prepared."

The leader of the free world had the grace to blush, but his Special Advisor seemed to have a bottomless reservoir of malice. "Be careful you're not declared an enemy combatant like Milani. That description fits your son as well. Perhaps you can be present for both their executions."

While the President sputtered, David intervened. "Madam Advisor, shut up. Mr. Cantor, if you'll accompany us without creating an incident, I believe we can hold off on the cuffs until we're out of the White House. Agreed?"

Clifton nodded. Fixing his gaze straight ahead, he ignored the President and Patricia. The Secret Service agents, along with David escorted him to an underground garage. He held his breath as his hands were cuffed. The agents helped him into the back seat of a black Suburban and seated themselves on either side of him. David climbed in the front passenger seat and nodded at the driver.

As they drove out of the garage and stopped at the gated entrance, David turned to stare at him. "Why are you protecting Rowan Milani? I can understand why you don't want to implicate your son. I can help you with that, if you tell me what you know. If Milani has something on Chad or Ralph Johnston, we can prove they didn't have a choice but to help him."

Raw fear clenched his gut. "You've chosen to align yourself with people who have little regard for the Constitutional protections we as citizens are supposed to enjoy. Be careful they don't turn on you as well."

"Stop with the obfuscation and give me an honest answer."

The gate opened and the Suburban glided through. Already weary, knowing the real interrogation hadn't even begun, he met David's earnest gaze. "If you want answers, you have to start with facts and the first one is this: Rowan Milani is not the traitor you think he is."

Rowan sat at the desk in his room at the Hilton Americas-Houston hotel and studied the online schematics of the convention center. Concentrating on the maze of private meeting rooms in the monstrous building, he massaged his aching eyes. He'd hoped for close access to either the parking garage or the hotel for a quick exit after eliminating Ainsley and Shemal. His phone rang. "Hey Bobbie, what's up?"

"You know, I've been wondering the same thing. I'm sure you're surprised as hell to find out that we didn't see a boat or any strange people hanging around your house."

"I'm a firm believer in taking every precaution. Thanks for the effort you made in checking things out for me."

"You fucked me. The Boss isn't pleased, with me or with you. We can't protect you if we don't know where you are. He wants you to get your ass back here."

"This isn't personal. Tell Johnny that I appreciate everything he's done for me. The thing is, I work alone or I choose my own partners. Capisce?" He ended the call and laid the phone on the desk. He stood up and stretched. If he strolled through the convention center connected to the hotel, he could get a better feel for things than simple schematics provided.

He donned his FBI ball cap and tugged it low, rubbed the stubble on his jaw and decided against shaving. He shrugged into his black leather jacket and tucked his forty-five beneath it. The nine mm Glock was holstered at his left side and the lethal Karambit lay nestled in the left pocket of the jacket. He stuffed the bogus FBI ID for Special Agent James Hawthorne in the right pocket of his jacket and found the gloves he'd needed in Chicago.

The Starbucks coffee shop on the second floor was busier than he'd expected for early evening. He stood in line, avoiding eye contact and ordered a tall coffee. The barista handed him the paper cup and he fiddled for a moment with a sleeve before leaving the counter. A rangy man with reddish-brown hair and curious eyes blocked his way. He noticed the glint of a badge at the man's waist and glimpsed a holstered weapon beneath his suit jacket. "Excuse me."

The man didn't move. "I thought I'd met all the special agents assigned to this event. But I don't remember you."

The last goddamn thing he needed was a nosy cop. He raised his head, letting the bill of the cap keep his face shadowed. The guy had probably seen a picture of him. "My flight was delayed. I just got in. Thought I'd scope things out before the Director arrives. Catch you tomorrow morning." Sidestepping the man, he headed toward the skywalk connecting the convention center with the parking garage.

He entered the walkway and sipped the hot brew while he strode along as quickly as the limp he couldn't conquer let him. Headlights gleamed as traffic zipped by on the street below. Reaching the dimly lit interior of the garage, he relaxed and moved deep into the assortment of parked cars. He was certain he'd ditched the cop until he heard quick footsteps behind him. "Excuse me, Special Agent. I didn't get your name."

He stopped, swung around and walked back the way he'd come. The man was damn near as tall as Chad and traipsed along with one hand casually near the holstered pistol he'd glimpsed. Knowing he needed to act fast, he held out his right hand, edging the lid off the paper coffee cup with his left thumb as he closed the distance between them. "I'm Special Agent James Hawthorne."

When the cop held out his hand, he looked him in the eye and kept coming, kicking the man hard, just below the patella. His prey yelped. "Ouch, shit. What the hell?"

The tall man bent double and grabbed for the injury. He flung the steaming coffee in the cop's face, let go of the cup and dug his fingers into the man's thick hair. Using his hands, he propelled his opponent's face into his knee as he raised it. The cop staggered backward. Blood spurted from his nose. He hammered the side of the man's exposed neck with the edge of his forearm. Not waiting when the long-legged man crumpled to the ground, he drove his knee into his victim's quadriceps tendon.

Automatic reflex raised the groaning man up. He caught the jutting chin with the heel of his hand and slammed the cop's bleeding head into the concrete with the full force of his upper body.

The dazed eyes snapped shut and the battered head lolled to one side. He took deep breaths and wiped sweat off his forehead. A stomp to the throat would finish the job, but he wanted to know who the cop was before he read about it online. Glancing back the way they'd come, he didn't see anyone and didn't hear any footsteps. Crouching next to the unconscious body, he remembered the gloves in his pocket and put them on. In the cop's pants pocket he found a tooled leather wallet and opened it. "Homicide Detective Kyle Matthews, you are a fucking idiot. A smart LEO would have called for backup and waited." He scowled. Maybe backup was on the way.

Opposite the Houston Police Department ID, he saw a picture, squinted at it and hung his head. "Goddamn it." He clambered to his feet with the wallet and a cell phone he'd found in the man's suit jacket. He dialed 911 and waited.

An operator answered, “What is the nature of your emergency?”

“Homicide Detective Kyle Matthews has been disabled in the parking garage attached to the convention center downtown. He needs an ambulance.” He left the connection open, tossed the phone and wallet onto the prone body. “It’s your lucky day, detective.”

Heading deeper into the garage, he found his empty coffee cup and lid. He stuffed them into his jacket pocket along with the gloves. They’d figure out it was him when the detective regained consciousness, but there was no point in giving them his fingerprints.

The Next Day

Rodney stared restlessly out the French doors that opened onto the spacious deck of his rural Virginia home. On a normal winter evening, he’d be outside with his jacket on, tending the grill, enjoying the brisk weather. He and Patricia would be discussing local politics with friends, hosting a casual dinner party of steak and potatoes, his specialty on the grill.

Instead, because of Sal Capello’s brutal murder, he was hiding out in his own home, as the Special Agent in Charge of the Washington Field Office had prudently advised. Mindful of the cruel subterfuge of Milani’s cohorts, he’d assigned a special agent to his mother at the assisted living facility in Roanoke as well.

He drew the blinds on the doors. He wouldn’t make himself a target for a well-placed sniper by standing in the doorway or walking through the backyard. Besides, he’d bet that Milani was on his way to Houston, if he wasn’t still there. But the SAC hadn’t wanted him to take any chances. He strode to the bar and perused his selection of spirits. The sixteen year old bottle of A.H. Hirsch bourbon caught his eye.

He grabbed the bottle and then shoved it back. The Hirsch was deserving of a special occasion. He'd wait until Milani was in custody. Instead he poured Maker's Mark into a glass and raised it to his lips, appreciating the subtle caramel aroma before gulping it neat. Gritting his teeth and sucking air, he shuddered as the alcohol made inroads on the tension between his shoulders.

He took another pull on the bourbon and ambled around the family room, turning on table lamps between the sofas and chairs to dispel the darkness. The lamps created pools of soft light and the cozy ambience he usually enjoyed. But tonight he felt uneasy and wondered if he should have stationed one of his special agents in the house. He checked the double oak doors leading into the room to be sure they were locked.

Back at the bar, he perched on a padded leather stool and poured again, contemplating the reddish-gold liquid, thinking about the bogus meeting he and Patricia had set up between him and Shemal. They'd realized that Milani and his cohorts must be hacking their emails. He didn't think the man would be able to resist the possibility of taking out both him and Muusa together.

When Milani took the bait, they'd nail his ass. If everything worked out, he could have America's most wanted home grown terrorist in custody within the next forty-eight hours. That would resurrect his career and help him regain the respect he'd lost in the intelligence community when Milani escaped.

His lips twisted in a leering smile and he sat up straight, cracking his knuckles. Before delivering Milani into the capable hands of Muusa and his Egyptian handlers, he would conduct a private interrogation session with the worthless piece of shit. Movement in the mirror behind the bar caught his eye and his heart leaped when he saw the reflection of an open patio door. He swiveled on the stool, his elbow catching the glass of Maker's Mark. It tipped and rolled, spilling bourbon across the bar and onto the carpeted floor.

The mellow light made it hard to see, but his shoulders slumped in relief when Patricia stepped through the door. "Why are you coming in from the deck?"

She looked annoyed. "I parked in the garage and thought you'd be cooking dinner. Why aren't you grilling tonight? It's beautiful out there."

He crossed the room to take her in his arms. "The SAC told me to be extra careful and not take any chances. Since we don't know what Milani's organization *isn't* capable of doing, I thought it best to pay attention."

Patricia laid her head on his shoulder and wrapped her arms around him. "You can still cook me dinner. And pour me a glass of bourbon, would you? It's been a long day."

Her plentiful breasts took his mind off his plans for Milani. "I'll cook you anything you want, honeybunch."

She answered by pushing tighter against him and sliding her hands from his back, up and into his hair. Drawing his head down, she kissed him. "Call me *honeybunch* again and I'll have your job."

He slid one hand onto her butt and squeezed. Putting his other hand on the back of her head, he guided her lips back to his and made the kiss deep and hard. He never knew for sure if she was serious with her threats. He'd keep her satisfied and give her whatever she wanted because he sure as hell didn't want to find out.

David walked into the hospital room and stopped short, mouth open. Kyle lay on the bed, eyes closed. Bandages covered his nose and most of his face was black and blue. The skin of his neck and jaw on one side was bright red. Below the thin hospital gown his right knee was swathed in bandages. A slender woman with long black hair stood next to him, taking his pulse.

Not sure what to say, he stepped to the edge of the bed. The woman held Kyle's arm and gazed at him through serious blue eyes. "You must be Mr. Harandi. I'm Erin Matthews, Kyle's wife."

"It's nice to meet you, Erin. I'm very sorry it had to be under these circumstances. You're a trauma nurse, right? Were you working when they brought him in?"

"I was. I've told him so many times not to try things on his own, but of course he doesn't listen."

"What do you mean? I was en route from D.C. when I got the message from Captain Lavoe. Do you know what happened? Are there any suspects?"

Erin shook her head. "Someone made an anonymous 911 call with *his* phone. He was lying on the cement in the parking garage of the convention center downtown. The docs want him kept sedated because he sustained a severe concussion and a skull fracture. His head took a beating, as you can see. Brain swelling is a concern, as well as blood clots. In addition, his nose is broken and his quadriceps tendon was ruptured."

"As soon as I can, I'll listen to the 911 call. When he regains consciousness, I need to talk to him."

Erin stared at him, brows knit together. "Nothing was stolen. The paramedics told me his wallet and phone were lying on his chest. Why in God's name he didn't grab another LEO or call for backup is beyond me. Do you think he might know who did this?"

"It's hard to say why he did what he did. My guess is that he was following someone and didn't want to lose visual contact. It obviously wasn't a robbery. But, man, whoever did this knew how to take someone apart. He could easily have died. I'm sorry for saying that, although I guess you know that better than me."

"In this case, I wish I didn't know so much. Once he's out of the woods with the head injury, he's looking at surgery to repair his tendon. After that he'll need a brace and crutches for at least six weeks, plus rehab. He's not going to be a happy guy."

He studied her face, noticed the dark circles under her eyes and thought Detective Matthews was damn lucky to have a woman like this. "How are your kids taking this? Do you have any help at home?"

"Kyle's mother is staying at the house. They're being spoiled to the point that I may have to send them home with her when this is over."

Antsy to hear the 911 recording and confirm his growing suspicions, he held out his hand. "Well, I've got to get going." He hesitated, then tried for a moment of levity. "I don't suppose Kyle told you how we met?"

She gripped his hand. "He did, but I didn't want to bring it up. He told me about how he had SWAT put you on the ground." She giggled. "I'm sorry. That was one of the funniest stories he's told me in a while."

"From my standpoint, the story wasn't quite as humorous. But I was looking forward to working with your husband."

"Well, he's going to be sitting this one out. But at least he's alive."

He dug a business card out of his pocket. "Erin, it's been a pleasure to talk with you. Call me when he's conscious, no matter what time it is, day or night. I'm anxious to get his take on this."

She plucked the card from his fingers. "As soon as he's conscious, I'll call you."

Outside the hospital, walking to his rental car, he mulled over the details she'd given him. How in the hell had Kyle run across Rowan Milani? He wondered why the detective hadn't called for backup. And why had Rowan let him live? *That* was out of character for the ruthless killer. Answers were what he needed and, one way or another, he'd get them.

Rodney stretched out in bed and put his hands behind his head. Patricia rearranged the sheets they'd rumpled making love and curled up with her head on his chest. He put one arm around her and stuffed a pillow behind his head. He enjoyed tracing the curves of her body with his hand. "Your trap in Houston is a stroke of genius. By this time tomorrow evening, we could have Milani in custody."

She wiggled closer, patted his chest and left her hand there. "Mm, I agree, pure genius. We know Milani won't be able to resist coming for both you and Shemal. It worries me, though, that you're acting as bait. We don't know whether or not he's working alone."

Reaching low, he grabbed her leg behind the knee and pulled it across his body. "We've been coordinating for a couple weeks with the Houston Field Office and the local PD. Between special agents and plain clothes cops, Milani has no idea what he'll be walking into. It'll be easy as hell to nail the son of a bitch. My only concern is how Harandi is going to react when we've got Milani back here and your CIA agents arrive to transport him to Egypt."

"I'll handle David. His assignment is to locate Milani and bring him in. What happens after that is not his affair."

He moved his hand back and forth from her hip to her knee. Patricia was a hell of a lover, and a more powerful woman couldn't be found in the Capitol. And she was a real bitch. Tweaking her and watching the sparks fly was more than entertaining. "You never know honeybunch, that man's got some kind of a chip on his shoulder about Milani."

When she yanked on his chest hair, he winced and grabbed her hand. "Hey, what was that for?"

Freeing her hand from his, she tapped his chest with a forefinger. "I told you not to call me *honeybunch.* There's no reason to doubt my control over David. Don't forget, he and I had a long relationship. I know how he thinks and how to twist him to suit our needs."

Intense jealousy made him frown. “As far as I’m concerned, he’s still a wild card and we can’t let anything screw this up.”

She scooted up, rubbing against him and nibbling on his ear. “You don’t have to trouble yourself. I’m more than capable of pulling his strings. He’ll do exactly what I want. Trust me.”

He wondered what she had on the former spook that made her so sure of herself. “I trust you. But Harandi is another matter. He’s too much of a Boy Scout for me. It wouldn’t do for him to find out about the money Muusa paid us in return for access to his uncle Sa-id.”

She propped herself up on an elbow. “My CIA agents told me it took a week of interrogation by Muusa before Sa-id gave up everything he knew about Milani and the terror groups he is involved with.”

He stared. “That must have been incredibly brutal. It’s no wonder he died. God help us if your Boy Scout ever runs across that nugget of information.”

Patricia made lazy circles on his chest with a forefinger. “Muusa extracted enough information in that week to enable us to destroy Milani’s credibility for good. But it wasn’t the interrogation that killed Sa-id, it was Rowan Milani. Muusa shared that with me the last time we met with the President.”

Uneasy, he grasped her hand. “What I don’t understand is why Sa-id didn’t willingly give up the information. Do you suppose Milani had threatened his family?”

“Muusa told me that Sa-id was part of Milani’s organization. When Milani found out that Sa-id had betrayed him, he killed him.”

“Good God. It will be a relief to see this sordid chapter end.”

Patricia cuddled beside him again, her arm draped across his chest. “Yes, it will. And I’m hoping we’ll get our hands on Ralph Johnston and Chad Cantor as well. Those two represent as much potential embarrassment for the administration as Milani does.”

He was still curious about how she intended to curb her spook. "I wish you'd tell me how you plan to keep Harandi quiet."

"It's simple. If David raises a fuss about how we can send an American citizen to Egypt for interrogation with or without his precious *due process* I'll remind him that Milani was declared an enemy combatant. If that isn't enough, I'll tell him that his uncle's associations will be splashed across the media if he goes public. If he still won't back down, I'll get presidential authority to detain *him,* right along with Milani."

His phone rang and he rolled over to pick it up. "This is Director Ainsley. Yes, go ahead, please." He listened and then grinned. "Excellent. I'll be there in an hour. Call Deputy Director Berenger and tell her to meet me. Tell the surveillance team on Kauai to be ready to move. Put a team on the house in San Francisco, right away."

Patricia sat up, eyes wide. "Did we get a hit on something?"

He couldn't stop grinning. "The name James Hawthorne is popping up all over the country, starting with a money market account in a small local bank on the island of Kauai and another at a Wells Fargo branch in San Francisco. We've got an address in San Francisco and a rental in Key West, plus airline tickets from Houston to Key West and back to Houston."

She gripped his arm. "This is the beginning of the end for Milani. I can't wait to make him pay."

He stared at her smooth, long neck, ample breasts and flat stomach. "Everything is coming together. We've got to get to HQ and put it all in motion. Come on, honeybunch, get a move on."

CHAPTER ELEVEN

Two Days Later

Gabriel stared through the binoculars with increasing unease as the dark blue sedan cruised by the house for the third time, turned the corner at the end of the block and disappeared. Lying flat on his belly behind the rail of the fourth floor balcony, he waited. Within a few minutes, two men in shirtsleeves walked down the street, stopping occasionally to look around. He squinted and adjusted the binoculars. "Oh no."

Resisting the urgency to get Danielle and Angelo out of the house, he watched the men as they moved down the street. They stopped and both answered their phones. A moment later the car drew up, the two men climbed in and it sped away. "Holy Mother of God. Shit." He scrambled up, the need for flight taking over as he raced down the hallway and hit the stairs. "Danielle, Angelo, meet me in the kitchen, *now.*"

As he skidded to a stop on the bottom landing, Angelo came around the corner, followed by Danielle. He tried to catch his breath. "We need to leave right now."

Angelo put a hand on his arm. "Slow down. What's happening?"

He grappled with his panic. "The FBI will be here soon. Grab the suitcase you have packed and be in the garage in five minutes."

Angelo headed up the stairs. Danielle stood on the landing, looking guilty. "This is my fault."

He touched her arm. "Honey, don't be silly. It's nobody's fault. Now go and get your things. We need to leave."

She didn't move. "If I hadn't wanted to leave Kauai, if I hadn't been so freaked out over Marta . . . Oh my God, none of this would be happening."

The first inkling of Rowan's frustration with the beautiful woman rose up and bit him in the ass. He grabbed her by the shoulders and shook her. "Danielle. It's *not* your fault. Now go and get your things. *Hurry,* or we'll all be in custody."

Danielle blinked at him. "OK." She rushed down the hallway.

Ten minutes later he sat tapping his fingers on the SUV's steering wheel, waiting for her. For the first time he felt sorry for Rowan. The hombre must have loved her or else he would have shot her months ago. Angelo put a gentle hand on his shoulder from the back seat. "Do you want me to go get her?"

"No, Amigo, I will."

The garage door slammed and Danielle appeared, climbed in the front seat and hoisted a small suitcase after her. "Sorry."

He nodded curtly and hit the door opener. Light filled the garage and he said a silent thank you for the vehicle's darkened windows. "Hopefully the agents haven't had time to set up a road block. If we get out of the neighborhood, we will be all right. I changed the license plates a few days ago. The vehicle will show ownership by my mother in-law. A more law-abiding woman never lived."

Neither Angelo nor Danielle answered him. He drove at normal speed until they reached Geary Blvd. Rolling his shoulders, he lightened his grip on the steering wheel and caught Angelo's gaze in the rear view mirror. "We'll head for the I-5 and drive straight through to my home in San Diego. We can stay there indefinitely, I think. I'd better call Michael."

Chad stared at his phone. "Answer, damn it." The call to his father's phone went to voicemail again, the way it had the last time and the time before that.

Michael tapped his fingers on the arm of the sofa. "Voicemail again? This is the second straight day, right?"

He sat the phone on the low table between them and wiped sweating palms on his shorts. Trying to breathe evenly, he stayed on the edge of the recliner. "Something isn't right. Ever since this whole thing started, he's made a point of getting back to me within several hours."

Michael's phone rang, jangling his fraying nerves. His colleague scowled. "It's Gabriel. Give me a sec."

"I'm going to call Johnny Giacopino. Maybe he's heard from my father."

Michael's voice jolted him. "Amigo, slow down. Speak Inglés, por favor. *What?* Let me know when you arrive. Call Rowan, would you? Thanks."

His gut twisted. "What happened?"

"Well, I guess we know why your father hasn't called. Gabriel spotted FBI agents snooping in the neighborhood. He's headed to San Diego with Danielle and Angelo. If the feds know about the house in San Francisco, they know about us here."

Chad stared unseeing. "James Hawthorne. That's the tie-in. They must have gotten into my father's financial records and that means they'll freeze our assets . . ."

Michael stood up. "If your father hasn't answered his phone in more than a day, they're making preparations. The Bureau's Honolulu Field Office has SWAT capabilities. We've got to leave. *Now.* It may already be too late."

"Johnny told me to call him if anything went wrong. Round everyone up while I talk to him."

His colleague was already heading out the door. "Keep me informed."

An hour and a half later, Chad straggled through the front door, arms loaded with boxes. Sweat and dust caked his body. His t-shirt clung to his back. He felt bereft, isolated and in the dark without the communications systems he'd designed. He sat the boxes down at the back end of the Escalade and wiped his forehead with a grimy hand. “Did Ralph and Marion leave with the Milani’s?”

Michael grabbed a box and sat it on top of the stack of suitcases in the back of the vehicle. “Yes. They’ll moor the cruiser in Nawiliwili Harbor and catch a taxi to the airport. You and Bettina and Derek and I will meet them there. Ralph’s idea about splitting up was excellent. Where’s Bettina? We need to get going.”

“She’s in the bathroom. I’ve got to grab my laptop, too. I’ll go get her and the laptop and be right out.”

His colleague slammed the back doors of the Escalade. “The moron and I will be waiting. Hurry.”

“I’ll be right back.” He jogged back to the house and down the cool hallway. Regret filled him as he navigated the empty home. The six months he’d spent there with Bettina were special, in spite of the stressful circumstances. Rounding the final corner, he slowed to a walk. He went inside their suite and headed for his office. “Bettina, come on sweetheart, we’re ready to leave.” She didn’t answer. Stepping inside the office, he stopped. His laptop was gone. “Did you grab my laptop?” She still didn’t answer. The hair on his arms rose. Oh God. Bettina . . . He grabbed his phone.

Michael sounded stressed. “What now? Why the . . .”

“Get to the boat dock, now. Don’t wait, go, go, go.” He dropped the phone as the barrel of a Glock pistol appeared in the doorway, followed by a muscular body, clad in a Kevlar vest with FBI emblazoned in yellow on the front. The man had an M4 rifle slung over one shoulder, wore mirrored sunglasses and a mic connected to an ear piece.

The special agent spoke into the mic. “All agents to the boat dock, now. I repeat, *boat dock now*. The house is secure.” The barrel of the pistol pointed at his chest. “Special Agent Cantor, you know what to do." He sank to his knees, laid down on the floor, and put his hands behind his head.

Michael stared at his phone and tossed it on the console between the seats. "Fuck me." He started the engine and pounded the steering wheel. Movement caught his eye. Derek sprinted across the driveway, around the house and disappeared. "You rotten little shit. We should have shot you a long time ago." He forced himself to drive slowly to the gate, scanning for a SWAT vehicle, expecting agents to swarm the Escalade and force him out.

The gate was open and he cruised through, turned onto the road and realized he was holding his breath. He started breathing and swallowed hard. "Come on, motherfuckers, where are you?" Turning onto the main road, he gradually increased his speed and squinted at the flashing lights coming his way, still far off. He wiped sweat off his face, set his jaw and kept driving until they were close, then he slowed and stopped on the shoulder.

A parade of police cars and a couple black Suburbans roared by. The Escalade wobbled in their wake while rocks pinged off its side and windshield. He pulled back onto the pavement and hit the gas, sweating and driving as fast as he could without rousing suspicion, until he reached the airport. He parked and loaded the boxes containing Chad's computers into his arms.

Ralph greeted him as he stepped through the wide open doors of the airport's Fixed Base Operator where private jets arrived and departed. "Where the hell are the rest of them? Are they getting the suitcases?"

He shook his head. "Not now. We need to go."

Ralph motioned to Marion and the Milani's. "All right folks, the fun's just starting. Let's head out."

The threesome rose obediently and trooped behind Ralph and him out the door and across the tarmac to the blue and white Lear VII that sat gleaming in the sunlight, its engines roaring. He lurched up the stairs with the boxes, deposited them on a seat and waited while the others moved past him.

Ralph sat down across the aisle. “Well, let’s have it.”

“Chad made a last trip into the house to get his laptop and Bettina. SWAT must have come in from the back side, through the rainforest. He called me, told me to go to the boat dock. Evidently the SWAT geniuses bought it, because I drove out of there and didn’t see a soul, no vehicles – nothing. But down the road, a shitload of cop cars and a couple Bureau ’burbans passed me going like bats out of hell.”

“God almighty. What about Derek?”

“The little shit disappeared. My guess is he’s chattering like a fucking monkey to anybody who’ll listen. Thank God he doesn’t know very much.”

“Sweet Jesus. I can’t believe they’ve got Chad. And Bettina. We’ll be out of reach, we won’t be able to help them.”

Michael rubbed the back of his neck. “I know. I made a split second decision. Chad was giving me an out, telling me to leave. But maybe I should have stayed. I might have been able to distract the bastards long enough to grab them.”

Ralph gripped his arm. “That’s enough. You did the right thing. Chad can handle himself and the Bureau isn’t going to rough up a pregnant woman. When we get to Dubai, we’ll figure something out.”

He stared. “Johnny is sending you to the UAE?”

The older man scowled. “That’s what I surmised when the customer service agent told me to enjoy my stay in Dubai. Chad is the one who talked to him, didn’t he tell you?”

“He just said Johnny arranged a charter flight to where he is on a combination business and vacation trip. But, I’m not going with you.”

“I figured as much. What’s your next move?”

The Captain opened the door to the flight deck. “Gentlemen, we are prepared to depart. Do you require anything further before we close the door and get underway?”

Michael turned to face the rotund, mustached man. “Thank you, sir. I’ll be leaving the aircraft.” He read the dismay in Ralph’s face. “I’ll stay in touch. You do the same.”

Derek couldn’t believe he was still handcuffed. He’d run as fast as he could when Michael got the phone call. After the FBI guys grabbed him, he told them that he’d been a prisoner. They laughed and hauled him to the conference room and made him sit on a chair. Chad and Bettina were there, too. It made him feel good to see Rowan’s friends sitting there humiliated and angry. The three of them had been sitting for a couple hours while the agents ransacked the house. His arms hurt, he needed to take a piss and he craved a smoke.

One of them men came and stood in front of him. “Mr. Norris, I’m Special Agent Anakoni Nawahine, with the FBI’s SWAT division out of Honolulu. Feel free to call me Tony. Please tell me again why you were here with Rowan Milani’s associates.”

The rifle slung over the agent’s shoulder, besides the pistol holstered at his side, scared the crap out of him. He hoped he could talk, now that someone seemed willing to listen. “Uh, see, I was Dani’s roommate. We lived together in Sioux Falls. We worked at the airport. I was a supervisor for Delta. Then Rowan Milani came and . . . and he brainwashed her.”

Special Agent Nawahine held up a hand. “Stop for a second. Who is Dani? We don’t have that name in any of our files.”

“Oh, sorry. I’m talking about Danielle Stratton. Anyway, after *he* got picked up again or whatever, two CIA guys came to the house looking for Dan . . . Danielle. They told me they were coming back to talk to me so I called Chad. After that Michael came to pick me up and we flew out here.”

Tony ran a hand through short, black hair and looked confused. "We'll talk about Ms. Stratton in a minute. Who is Michael?"

"Michael is one of Rowan's friends. He was here, with the Escalade. We were supposed to go to the airport and leave, but I ran when he wasn't looking. Uh, Danielle was here, but she's in San Francisco now."

Staring intently at him, Tony grabbed a chair with one hand, banged it around in front of him and straddled it. "One of Rowan Milani's associates was here but left for the airport and you were supposed to go with him?"

"Yeah, that's right. The others already left by boat."

Special Agent Nawahine fingered the small mic lying against his cheek. "What color is the Escalade? And what is Michael's last name?"

"It's black and practically brand new. I don't know Michael's last name."

Tony spoke into the mic. "Special Agent Pukahi, head to the airport. We need a BOLO on a Black Escalade, new or nearly new model year. Check our name list on all commercial and private flights. Thanks." The agent looked at him. "Back to your story. Who left by boat?"

Glancing at Bettina, he saw indignation replace the worry on her face, but he was glad. It was a relief to think that the nightmare he'd been living was coming to an end. "Uh, well Ralph Johnston and his wife, and Rowan's parents."

Tony looked surprised. "Damn. We were about ten minutes late. Where were you supposed to go? Who was flying you?"

The agent's casual demeanor helped him relax. "I don't know where we were going, but before, when they brought me out here, we took the G650 they stole from the CIA. They painted it black and changed the tail number, but the same two pilots always flew it."

"Do you remember the tail number?"

"No. I'm sorry. I don't remember. Ask Chad, he made a bogus front company and changed all kinds of stuff so no one would be able to trace it. Michael told me that on the way out here. It's about the only thing any of them ever told me. Except, the pilot and first officer who flew the plane were from Atlanta. They have some kind of aviation business and their names are Jerry and Bryan."

The dark-haired man swung toward Chad. "Special Agent Cantor, care to help Mr. Norris out?"

Chad scowled and didn't say anything. Tony turned back to Derek. "He's not nearly as talkative as you are. Tell you what. We're going to get rid of those cuffs. You can get something to eat. Then we'll go to a room down the hall where you can tell me more about Ms. Stratton."

Tears of gratitude flooded his eyes. "Thank you." Tony stepped behind him and unlocked the handcuffs. He rubbed his wrists and stretched. When he looked up and wiped his eyes, he caught Chad glaring at him. The guy looked like he wanted to kill him. Before he looked away, he smirked. He couldn't wait to tell the FBI everything he could remember about all of them.

The Next Day

Rowan slipped out of the parking garage adjacent to the Hilton Americas-Houston and the Convention Center. He headed across the street toward Discovery Green Park. It was dusk and the park offered shadowed areas to walk and to think. Gabriel's phone call the day before had changed his plans. He'd left everything but his weapons in the hotel room and spent the night moving through the seamy alleys and dilapidated buildings downtown. Everything important from his laptop's hard drive was now on a flash drive he'd stuffed into the back pocket of his jeans. An ATM in the hotel had allowed him to withdraw cash, but it wasn't nearly enough, and he knew better than to try again.

He followed the jogging trail, wanting to go deep into the park, thinking he might be able to break into the Lake House or the Alkek Building after the park closed. He wanted to catch some sleep before the scheduled meeting between Ainsley and Shemal. His phone rang. He looked at the ID. “Hey Mike, what’s going on?”

For the first time, he heard defeat in his colleague’s voice. “It’s not good. Chad and Bettina are in custody. Ralph and Marion and your parents are on the way to Dubai.”

He sank down, against a broad tree trunk and tried to absorb the shock. *Not Bettina.* His phone lay on the ground and he sat with his arms wrapped around his knees, head buried. Michael was yelling. He raised his head and picked up the phone. “How did it happen?”

“Fuckin’ A, Rowan. They came from behind, through the rainforest and must have broken in through Angelo or Derek’s suite.”

He shivered. He’d prowled the house in the dark, imagining that exact scenario on too many sleepless nights. “I can’t go back to the hotel. The entire area is crawling with undercover cops and special agents. I don’t even trust the cabs. And besides that, a couple guys have been following me. They have to be Shemal’s guys. Wait, *Dubai?”*

“Yeah, how’d you like to go back? If I remember, we were in a hurry to leave the last time.”

He raised a brow. “Well, it’s smart thinking. No extradition treaty. Hell, maybe we should head there too. I’ve always liked that city.”

“All right. Here’s what you need to do. Take the bus or walk, but get to the airport. I had some stuff to get rid of, but I’ve got a flight out of Lihue tonight. I’ll be in Houston before noon tomorrow. Jerry and Bryan will meet us there. We’ll get the hell out of town and regroup.”

"OK. I can make it to the airport." Movement on the pathway caught his eye. Two figures in hooded sweatshirts approached. They veered from the path to the trees and back as they walked, heads constantly turning. "Hey, I gotta go. The two morons following me are back. I'm going to take care of the problem. I'll see you tomorrow."

His colleague sounded relieved. "Be careful. See you soon."

Scooting back behind the tree, he stood up and stepped casually back toward the path. He fingered the knife in his jacket pocket. He didn't want to deal with them close to the entrance, so he kept going, moving further into the park.

Asad looked at Firouz. "Did you let the Master know we are following the Jinn?"

Firouz jerked his head up and down. "Of course I did."

They stood on the jogging path in Discovery Park. Regularly spaced lamp posts created pools of light among the trees. Milani had disappeared around a curve. "He's gone. I think he saw us. It would be wise for us to call more brothers to join us."

Firouz started walking and motioned him to follow. "I have met the Jinn before. He murdered many of Allah's finest warriors. We are not going to share this victory with anyone else. I want to deliver him to the Master myself."

Asad caught up and grabbed his friend's arm. "We will do this together. But you must not underestimate our enemy. Where did you meet him?"

His friend shoved him away and kept walking. "I do not underestimate him. We met on a battlefield in Afghanistan."

Asad knew that Firouz struggled with pride and he feared it was leading them into needless jeopardy. "If he tricked and murdered the freedom fighters in Afghanistan, he will be difficult for us to deal with. We must alert our brothers to help us before we can have this victory."

Firouz stopped. His voice dropped to a whisper. “Have faith in Allah’s power. He will give us the Jinn. Be still a moment. I believe he is behind us. Are you ready?”

Asad fingered the item in the front pouch of his pullover. “Yes. I am ready.”

His companion’s eyes glinted with excitement in the lamplight as his voice rose. “Excellent. Allahu Akbar.”

“Allahu Akbar indeed.” Startled, Asad turned around. The Jinn stepped out of the darkness behind them. The hair on the back of his neck rose. The sacred words became blasphemous when uttered by the man who stood not more than six feet away.

Firouz elbowed him aside. “At last you come out of the shadows, Milani.”

Death emanated from the Jinn. It swirled around him and flowed toward them like a pitch-black river. Asad saw the glimmer of a knife in the man’s hand. He knew Firouz had a knife too, but his friend would be no match for the Jinn. Firouz stepped in front of Milani. “Firouz, wait, what are you doing? You must stop.”

The Jinn stomped on Firouz’ ankle. His friend buckled over, but slashed the Jinn’s arm with his knife. The man cursed, then stepped quickly behind Firouz and sliced down low across his friend’s kidneys. Firouz screamed and arched back, flailing at the wound.

Asad grasped the syringe in the pouch with sweaty hands. Breathing hard, he pulled off the cap, exposing the needle. Firouz would die if he didn’t act quickly. The Jinn reached forward and brought the curved blade under his friend’s jaw. Asad lunged toward Milani and grabbed his shoulder, pulling the man’s jacket halfway off and jamming home the powerful contents of the syringe in the Jinn’s arm.

Milani cursed again and staggered backwards, dragging Firouz with him. Asad tried to jump out of the way, but his feet tangled with the Jinn's and all three of them crashed to the ground. Asad saw blood pouring from Firouz' opened throat. He crawled to his friend, cradling him in his arms. Milani stood up and swayed unsteadily. Blood dripped from beneath the man's jacket sleeve. Firouz must have wounded him severely. But the Jinn pulled a gun from behind his back. "It's your turn, little fool."

The Jinn fired the gun. Asad heard twin echoing booms, saw flames spurt from the barrel and felt the excruciating pain as he toppled over onto his friend.

Rowan leaned against a tree and slid to the ground. The pathway seemed to rise and fall in waves. Everything blurred. He squeezed his eyes shut and then opened them. The stupid bastard had injected him with something. Rolling his head sideways he saw blood forming a pool beneath his arm. But he didn't have the strength to pull his jacket off to look at the wound or to make a tourniquet.

He heard sirens and knew he needed to move. But he couldn't. He laid his gun down and dragged his phone from his jacket pocket. Squinting at the screen, he punched the contact he wanted and managed to hit speaker before the phone dropped from numb fingers into his lap.

Danielle answered on the first ring, like she always had. "Rowan?"

Hearing her voice brought a painful lump to his throat. "Hey, Danielle."

"Rowan – it's really you. It's been so crazy. I'm in San Diego with Gabriel and his family. Angelo's here too. Are you all right? Can you tell me where you are?"

He closed his eyes, picturing her face. "I'm in Houston and I'm OK." He coughed. "Too bad you had to leave. Did you like the house? The city?"

"I loved the house and the city. I kept thinking about how much fun you must have had picking out that particular spot."

He coughed again. “Love the bridge. Bought that house for the view.”

“That was my favorite thing, too. Um, I’ve been thinking about something. Do you have time?”

He opened his eyes and saw flashing red and blue lights through the trees. “Go ahead, I’m listening. I wanted to hear your voice.”

“I told you this once, but you probably don’t remember. The first time I saw you, standing in the doorway of that jet in Sioux Falls, I knew you were someone special. And then you came to the ticket counter in the airport and I couldn’t believe it.”

Hot tears brimmed in his eyes and slipped down his cheeks. “I remember.”

Her voice softened and he strained to hear. “No matter what stupid stuff I said, I love you. I’ll always be waiting for you if you ever change your mind.”

A chill settled deep inside and set his teeth chattering. The darkness closed around him, making it hard to see. He blinked, trying to keep it at bay. Goddamn it, he wasn’t done talking. “Danielle . . .”

“Rowan? Are you all right? You can tell me anything, you know that.”

The numbness crept throughout his body. He had to get the words out, to tell her, before it was too late. “I’m sorry. I never stopped . . .”

Her voice sounded far away. “Rowan, what’s going on? Are you all right? Talk to me, please.”

His head listed sideways and his body followed. The darkness, always waiting for its opportunity, dragged him away.

CHAPTER TWELVE

The Next Day

Danielle looked at Gabriel's wife, Sherie. She was sure she'd never met a calmer, more tolerant woman. When they'd arrived after midnight, frazzled and exhausted, Sherie had met them with kindness. Whisked off to the lower level and a quiet bedroom with her own private bath, she'd immersed herself in solitude.

She'd gotten settled and thought again about finding a way to contact her parents, just to let them know she was all right. Then Rowan called. She'd been thrilled to hear his voice, to tell him what she needed him to know. But at the end, she'd sat in horrified silence, listening to frantic voices debating whether or not he was still alive. Someone, a man, had spoken into his phone, asked who was there. She'd hung up and sat awake all night, hugging her pillow, burying her face in the down softness.

Sherie patted her hand, rescuing her from the dismal thoughts. "You don't strike me as the kind of woman who wallows in her grief. From what Gabriel tells me, you are a strong person."

"Gabriel has always been kind to me. I used to think I could handle anything. But lately it seems like I can't keep myself together."

Sherie squeezed her hand. "You will recover. Your heart will survive. This hombre that you fell in love with would task the strongest woman in the world."

If only she could believe the well-meaning words. She took a deep breath of ocean air and lifted her face to the sun. "It's so hard for me to think of never seeing him again. He was so fierce, so full of passion. If he's gone . . ." Envisioning him lying dead and all alone – of the man she loved out of reach forever – she covered her face.

Sherie was resolute. "But remember, we don't know that your hombre is gone. Silence means hope. If he had died, it would be all over the news."

She took a shuddering breath. "Thank you. I'm sorry."

"You have no need to apologize for your grief. Whenever Gabriel leaves on one of his missions, I listen to every newscast with two sets of ears. One set for the story being told and one for the story that is not being told. Many nights I have lain awake, wondering if I will get a phone call or if he will simply never return. This last time was the hardest."

"You mean when they had to help Rowan? If I hadn't been detained by the FBI, Rowan wouldn't have surrendered and maybe Gabriel could have come home."

Sherie looked at her, brow furrowed. "Rowan surrendered to the authorities for you? That takes honor and courage. I knew there must be a reason for Gabriel's devotion to this man. He would not admit that he was involved, but I knew."

"I think Gabriel and Rowan and Michael have a commitment to each other that is unshakable."

Sherie grasped the bottle of Don Real Tequila from the middle of the table, pulled the silver stopper and poured a shot. "We need to discuss this. I want you to tell me everything you know about their escapades. And you must tell me about the other one, Michael."

The darkness ebbed from Rowan's consciousness. He felt each pain-filled rise and fall of his chest, heard his harsh breaths. His left arm throbbed with fiery agony and every heartbeat fueled the vicious ache inside his head. His nose itched and he tried to raise his hand to rub it. Cold metal on his wrist stopped him. He felt the chain around his waist. Without thinking, he moved his right foot and nudged the leg iron he found above his left ankle. His heart pounded, threatening to split his head in pieces.

He opened his eyes, saw fluorescent light panels above him and was glad they were turned off. Without moving his head he could see a window cut into the thick wall. Inset iron bars and wire glazed panes filtered the daylight, turning it gloomy. He heard the clunk of a lock and a door opening. The lights above him flickered on and he squeezed his eyes shut. Rough hands dug under his arms and hauled him up while another pair grabbed his feet and swung them to the floor.

He gasped at the raw pain. Hard fingers tapped both cheeks. "Rowan, wake up." He opened his eyes. Unfriendly hands gripped his arms. He realized he was between two sturdy men in police uniforms. One of them reeked of cheap cologne.

His captor, a man he'd called a friend long ago, stepped back and surveyed him. "You don't look so good. The two men you murdered look worse, I'll grant you that. What's going on that you've taken to killing your own colleagues? CIA agents and women weren't enough? According to the ER docs who stitched up your arm last night, if we hadn't found you when we did, the dose of barbiturate they rammed into your system and the artery they nicked in your arm would have killed you."

He swallowed hard, touched his cracked lips with his tongue. He craved water. The pain in his arm and head as well as the remnants of the drug he'd been given left his thoughts muddled. Coherent thinking seemed an impossible task.

David studied him. "I've got a lot of questions for you to answer. Right now, though, someone else has requested a visit. Since you and I have a plane to catch in a couple hours, I'm granting his request."

The two police officers pulled him to his feet. He clenched his jaws to keep from groaning. The fire in his arm intensified and his head pulsed. They moved and he had no choice but to stagger along with them, out the door, down a hallway and around a corner. They stopped in front of a door. David unlocked it, but didn't enter.

Unreasoning anxiety wound through his mind and sweat dampened the scratchy orange jumpsuit, making it stick to his body. He tried to think, but his thoughts meandered from one terrifying possibility to another. He couldn't provide information he didn't have, and he'd never confess to being a traitor to his own country, no matter what they did to him. But what if Shemal was waiting for him in that room? If so, then all hope was already lost.

The officers dragged him inside and shoved him into a chair in front of a heavy wooden table. No one else was in the room. Relieved, he let his head droop. His jumbled thoughts drifted away in a haze of unremitting pain. The door slammed and he jumped. He looked up, surprised to see detective Matthews hopping on crutches to the chair across from him. The man's lean face was mottled purple and blue-black. A bandage covered his nose and an angry red stain streaked his neck, disappearing beneath his open shirt collar.

The detective looked past him. "Guards, please leave us alone. I'm reasonably certain that Mr. Milani is not able to cause me any further harm." The two officers grunted assent and left the room. Matthews glared at him and scooted around on the chair, looking uncomfortable. "So far, you've murdered seven people in my city, and came pretty damn close to making it eight. The federal government seems to think that the crimes you've committed against the United States are more important, but Mr. Harandi has graciously offered me first crack at you, so to speak, before he takes you out of my jurisdiction. I want to know why you killed every damn one of those seven people."

Rowan blinked, trying to clear the fog from his mind. Matthews had to be the most determined cop he'd ever met. And from the look on the bruised face, the man wanted payback. He watched with dread when the detective reached for the crutches. "Listen Milani, I've heard about how you refused to talk, even under enhanced interrogation. But this is Texas and I'm not playing."

His dread turned to panic, which swept the fog away. The guards would come and march him to another room. They'd water board him or string him up and he couldn't stop them. The tall man lurched around the table on one crutch, grasped his wounded arm and squeezed. He closed sweating hands into fists and struggled to control his breathing. The detective dug into the injury with unrelenting strength.

Light-headed, groaning, he gave up. If the son of a bitch wanted the truth so bad, then by God, he'd give it to him. "OK, *Ok.* Ask your goddamn questions."

Matthews wobbled back to the chair. "That's better. Now, start with Marta Pinella. Why did you kill her?"

Rowan slumped in the chair and closed his eyes while waves of nausea rolled through his gut. His arm throbbed with renewed intensity and his nose poured a river of sticky wetness that leeched through the whiskers and onto his lips. He swallowed bile and took a deep breath before opening his eyes. "The bitch . . . needed to be stopped."

The detective arched a brow. "From doing what?"

The waves of nausea kept coming. "In cahoots . . . with the Muslim Brotherhood. Undermining the country . . ."

"The Muslim Brotherhood? You mean Muusa Shemal, the man who exposed you?"

He sneered, but didn't answer.

Matthews scowled. "I wish we had more time. I assume the murder of the guards at the mosque, the limo driver and the security supervisor were what you'd call collateral damage?"

Wanting nothing more than to wipe the snot off his nose and escape the all-consuming agony, he nodded, which started the waves of nausea again. "They got in my way."

The detective snorted. "Of course they did. What about the two men last night? Why would your own colleagues try to drug you?"

He swallowed bile again and looked at his hands. He should have ditched the two men and headed for the airport instead of screwing around with confronting them. When the detective cleared his throat, he looked up. He wished the bastard would leave him alone. "They weren't my colleagues. They were sent to deliver me to Shemal."

"Why does Shemal want you *delivered* to him? I don't understand the connection."

Since he had to answer the fucking question, he'd tell the truth and see what the cop did with it. "Shemal is the terrorist, not me. He needs to get rid of me, which he's going to do . . . now . . ."

Matthews checked the watch he wore beneath rolled up shirtsleeves. "Milani, you're creating way more questions than you're answering, but here's my last one. Why didn't you finish me off the other night? You knew I wasn't dead, otherwise you wouldn't have bothered to call 911."

"I guess you're just lucky."

The detective looked pissed. "Damn it. That's all the time we have. You've been less than forthcoming. Someday you may find yourself extradited back here for these murders. If that day ever comes, I'll find a way to get a few more details from you."

"OK." The gung-ho cop would never know how much he'd prefer that to where he knew he was headed.

The tall man hoisted himself out of the chair, grabbed the crutches and gave him a searching look. "I'm going to think on the things you told me. If you're telling me the truth, then this whole pile of shit adds up to one hell of a set-up. And that's damn hard to believe, coming from a man who's committed numerous murders with no remorse."

He watched the man's awkward progress toward the door. "Hey, detective."

Matthews stopped. "What?"

"It was the picture."

The detective stared at him until recognition dawned in his hazel eyes, then turned and stumped out the door.

David paced the hallway outside the interrogation room. He'd agreed to allow Kyle to question Rowan because he thought the detective and the Houston PD deserved a few minutes with the man they all knew was responsible for the string of murders in the city. Captain Lavoe had expressed her gratitude and also cautioned him about leaving Rowan in the city lock-up. Emotions were running high among the rank and file, especially as to why their suspect was off-limits for questioning. The captain wasn't sure she could guarantee his prisoner's safety.

And now, he had one more phone call to make. Patricia would not be happy that he was transporting Rowan to Quantico He looked at his phone, realizing she was calling him. "Yes Madam Advisor, how can I help you?"

"What's this I hear about the FBI's jet arriving in Houston to transport Rowan Milani this afternoon? That is not what we agreed to, David. You *will* make sure it doesn't happen. I've planned a photo opportunity that will showcase the administration's success in the apprehension of America's most wanted home grown terrorist. When we transport Milani, there will be press coverage. This is huge. Rodney and Mr. Shemal and I have waited a long time for this moment. And besides that, they have a commitment to the conference here in Houston. If you take Milani now, we'll have to cancel their joint appearance."

Bristling at her blithe assumption that he'd come to heel, he decided it was time to test his theory of whether she'd turn on him. "I'm transporting my prisoner this afternoon for his safety, on the advisement of the Houston PD. There's no need to cancel anything. You'll have access to him in Quantico. Have a press conference in a couple days. What difference does it make? If I recall, the *President* tasked me with locating and apprehending him, which I have done. The President also asked me to interrogate him and determine to the best of my ability, whether he is guilty of the charge of aiding and abetting our enemies. I intend to fulfill that assignment."

She was silent for a moment and then replied in a voice that raised the hair on his arms. "You work for *me.* I represent the President and his administration, and *what I say is the law.* You don't want to cross me, David."

He had his answer. "Well, Madam Advisor, until you're the *duly elected* President of the United States, you will have to take second seat and live with it. I'll do what I believe is in the best interests of the President and the country in this matter. I will do my best to ensure success in the assignment I've been given. See you in Washington in a couple days."

"This is the only warning you're going to get. If you defy me and move Milani before we can take advantage of his capture, I'll make sure that the press has full knowledge of the connection between your uncle Sa-id and Rowan Milani's terrorist activities."

"What are you talking about? Sa-id was a loyal citizen. He loved the United States. He was murdered because he confronted Milani about his deception."

"Your uncle fed information to Milani that aided his activities. Sa-id was part of Milani's organization, you idiot. Milani killed him because Muusa Shemal forced him to confess. Do you want your precious uncle's reputation besmirched?"

He was thunderstruck that she'd take that tack with him. "You've gone past the limit with this . . . this slander of my uncle. You are the idiot if you believe my uncle was part of Milani's organization."

"Think about this, David. You may come under scrutiny as well, once your uncle's treachery is publicized. Wouldn't it be a shame, after all you've done for your country, to face investigation and possible detention? After all, in this atmosphere of heightened threat, given your past affiliation with Milani and of course with your uncle, that may be a consideration."

He stared at his phone, trying to process her words. "Don't ever threaten me again. I'm transporting my prisoner this afternoon." He stuffed the phone in his shirt pocket. Patricia had gone beyond the pale and he'd make an appointment with the President as soon as he returned to D.C. He reached the interrogation room as Kyle came through the door, an unreadable expression on the bruised face. "How'd it go? Did you get Rowan to talk?"

"Oh, I got him to talk. The fact that he was still half doped up helped, I'm sure. Not allowing the ER docs to give him any painkillers probably helped, too. If that guy was firing on all cylinders, I don't think he'd give up much, if anything."

David was anxious to get underway before Patricia took action to prevent him from leaving. "Good. I'm hoping those two factors will aid me in my conversation with him during our flight to D.C. We'll get out of your hair as soon as your SWAT team brings me secure transport to the airport."

"Look, Milani didn't bubble over with information, but he said some things that made me wonder about the credibility of the claims against him."

"This is the man who damn near killed you, remember? He is *highly* skilled at lying."

"I know. But he didn't kill me, did he? Just for shits and grins, I'm going to take another look at Muusa Shemal and the mosque he keeps under such tight control. You can attribute it to the smack I took on the head if you want."

* * *

Michael waited in the customer service lounge sipping hot coffee. Rowan should be meeting him anytime. Jerry had called to let him know that he and Bryan were thirty minutes from landing with the G650. On the trip from Kauai he'd devised a plan for the four of them. They'd fly to Dubai and meet up with Ralph. Jerry and Bryan had OK'd the trip. All they needed was for Rowan to show up.

The two of them would have long hours of flight time to formulate a plan for how to proceed. With what, he wasn't sure. But he'd like to meet Johnny Giacopino for himself and see what the Mafioso could do to influence the President regarding Clifton, Chad, and Bettina. Even if all he could manage was Bettina's release, that would be enough, for now.

Restless, he got up and stalked around the lounge, glancing at his phone. Where the hell was Rowan? Conversation among a group seated at a cluster of chairs caught his attention. He ambled by, hoping to catch the details of their chatter.

A man spoke with a Texas drawl. "That was quite a set of murders last night. Discovery Park no less. You just don't know if you can take your family anywhere anymore."

A woman responded. "Did the police say something about terrorism? I heard that all three men involved were Middle Eastern and that they all died. Apparently one had his throat slit and another was shot in the chest from close range. I didn't hear anything about how the third one died."

Alarmed, he stood still, trying not to picture his friend lying on a table in the county morgue.

Another man chimed in. "The police were cagey about answering questions. I know the FBI was involved, because when I watched the live report, guys wearing FBI jackets were swarming around one of the ambulances."

Relief left him weak-kneed and he sank into a chair. Rowan was alive, or at least he had been the previous evening. But Jerry and Bryan should abort their landing, just in case the airport was being watched. It was impossible to know how much the Bureau knew, especially since they must have Derek in custody. The sniveling shit could have told them all kinds of things.

Jerry answered his call. “Mike, we’re preparing to land, what’s up?”

“If you can, abort and head back to Atlanta. Rowan’s either in the morgue, the hospital, or in custody. I’m going to stick around here and figure out which one it is. And when you get home, you better put the jet under wraps. I’ll explain more when I can.”

“Copy that, brother. Let us know about Rowan. We’re out of here. See ya.”

He stared unseeing around the lounge. What the hell was he supposed to do now? Gathering his thoughts, he made his first decision. He’d drink another cup of coffee. Then he’d call Ralph and Gabriel. After that he’d see if he could figure out what had happened to Rowan.

While he paced along the windows facing the tarmac, nursing his second cup of bitter coffee, he watched a white Gulfstream V taxi in. Ramp agents scurried out to park the jet and chock the wheels, but were waved off by Houston SWAT in full battle regalia. He stepped closer to the windows. The group whose conversation he’d listened in on joined him. The woman sounded excited. “I wonder if they’re bringing in a serious criminal.”

The man next to her replied, “You know, that’s a government jet. By the looks of the guy they just brought out of that Suburban over there, I’d say they’re shipping one off.”

He followed the man’s pointed finger. Dismayed, he watched as four SWAT officers surrounded Rowan while two others held onto his arms. His friend was restrained with a waist chain and cuffs, as well as a chain from his waist to the leg irons he wore. Rowan appeared listless, walking between the two officers with his head down.

The woman chuckled and he wanted to backhand her. "The guy looks drugged. See how they've got him chained up? Do you suppose he was involved in those murders last night? Maybe he's the head of a drug cartel."

Heart-sick, he watched the SWAT team assist Rowan up the steps of the aircraft. Another man trotted up, in a polo shirt and khaki pants. He recognized the face because of the neatly trimmed goatee, and muttered a curse. How had David Harandi managed to get a hold of Rowan?

His next decision made, he left the windows, clutching his phone as desperation set in. They had to do something. Shemal would waste no time in gaining control of Rowan. Once he did, none of them would be able to help their friend.

Rowan closed his eyes as the SWAT agent buckled the seat belt too tight around him and then padlocked the chain between the leg irons to a bolt in the floor of the aircraft. He wondered what the stupid agent thought he'd be able to do even if he could manage to stand up and move around. It was warm inside the plane and he smelled coffee. He'd give anything to have some, or a glass of Jack Daniel's. Surely the FBI had some whiskey tucked away somewhere in the galley.

The last vestiges of the drug left his mouth dry, although his thoughts were becoming more coherent. The pain in his head had dulled, but his arm throbbed worse than before, thanks to detective Matthews' abuse and from being manhandled by the SWAT agents who seemed to enjoy jerking him around. Maybe his old friend turned captor would let him have some water and a handful of Ibuprofen.

When the aircraft door thudded shut, he opened his eyes. David sat across from him, a smug grin on his face. "I've got to admit, seeing you sitting there gives me immense satisfaction. It was a pleasure to inform the President that I've got the man he sent me to catch."

The jet taxied, swayed and turned. The engines revved and cut loose in a roar. Pushed back against the seat, Rowan closed his eyes again and felt the lift as the plane went airborne. Lulled by the steady rumble of the engines, he dozed. Slaps on both cheeks brought him back.

"Wake up, sleepyhead. We've got a couple hours of flight time and you've got a lot of questions to answer. We might as well get started."

The stinging pain on his face ignited immediate hostility. He glared at David. "I don't have anything to say to you."

David's eyes were hard. "I'm not above using enhanced interrogation techniques to make you talk. And I owe you one for the four hours of humiliation I went through courtesy of your impersonation. That was clever."

His sneered. "I enjoyed seeing your pompous ass dragged out of that hotel."

"I'm sure you did. As messages go, I heard the *fuck you* loud and clear. I've got a plan for returning the favor. Just to brighten your day, here's some news for you. Chad Cantor is in the brig at Quantico along with your lovely, pregnant sister. It will be a shame for that kid she's carrying to be raised in foster homes, knowing that his or her father and uncle are traitors. And never knowing his or her mother can't be healthy for a youngster."

"You and I both know that I can't stop you or the Bureau from doing whatever the hell you want to with any of us, whether I talk or not."

"You're right, of course. But I wasn't joking, Rowan. I'll use everything at my disposal to get the truth out of you."

He raised a brow. "You shouldn't forget what happened to Sal Capello."

"Now you've got me scared. Tell me, what would you do if I removed those restraints right now?"

"I'd break your ankle, crush your balls, destroy the joints in your fingers and take out your shoulder. I'd finish by breaking your neck. After that I'd enter the flight deck and remove the first officer. I'd tell the captain where to take me if he wanted to stay alive. Then I'd find the bottle of Jack in the galley and have a nice long drink. When we landed, I'd disappear for good and forget about trying to take out the real traitors."

"That's a great plan. It's not going to happen though. What's this bullshit about the *real traitors?* I'm going to grab some fresh coffee, and then we'll get started on the questions. You're going to answer each one. If I think you're being honest with me, I'll give you a drink of water. You keep it up and do a good job, I'll even tell the doc at the Quantico infirmary to give you some painkillers for that arm."

His mouth was bone dry and his bravado was waning, but he couldn't resist taking a dig. "You are just like the rest of them, aren't you? No qualms about using enhanced interrogation as long as your detainee is restrained and can't fight back. No concern for how people suffer when they're forced to endure your interrogation *methods*. It's all for the country's greater good, right? How did you become such a tool for the CIA?"

A flush crept up David's neck and settled on his cheeks. "All this, and from the man who commits murder without batting an eye. What happened to the FBI special agent who lost his fiancée on 9/11? You turned on your *own country*. You tortured and murdered my uncle. Sa-id loved you, considered you part of the family. Tell me, how did *you* become such a tool for global jihad?"

"*You think I murdered Sa-id?* That's the bullshit here. Muusa Shemal murdered Sa-id. For God's sake, don't you do any real work? Finding out that Shemal killed him took my sources no time."

David stood up, walked to the galley and returned with a mug of steaming coffee and a bottle of water. "You've lived the lies so long you've started to believe them yourself. But I'm only interested in the truth. We're going to start at the beginning. After 9/11, we never connected again. I'm sorry for that. I'm sorry for your loss. Something got twisted in you. What happened?"

He eyed the bottle of water. "You're sorry for my loss? Fuck you. Nothing got twisted. The President was looking for someone like me for black ops. I wanted to kill those bastards before they could kill us. So that's what I did, at the President's request."

David pointed at the bottle of water. Condensation dripped down the sides. "I want the truth, Rowan."

"Goddamn it. That is the truth. Ask the former President. Hell, ask this President. He wanted the same thing – and I delivered."

David sipped coffee. "What changed? Was the money not enough? Did al Qaeda offer you more? When did you start collaborating with our enemies?"

"How can I get through to you? Why can't you even consider that I'm telling you the truth? Nothing changed. I've never collaborated with our enemies. But they started looking for me. That's why Sa-id was murdered."

After a long swallow of coffee, David gave him a sober gaze. "When I was asked to take this assignment, I was almost convinced of your innocence. But you set me up for the murder of Sal Capello. The damage you did to Kyle Matthews and the way you killed seven people, those are things the man I grew up with, was friends with, who built a reputation as a hell of an FBI special agent would *never* do. Those things convinced me you're nothing more than a terrorist."

Weariness overwhelmed him. "Look, you're never going to understand how I operate. But your *assignment* is over. Within a couple days, I'll be gone. Shemal has you and Ainsley duped and hell, the President too."

"Once you're situated in Quantico, unless I personally give the word, absolutely no one will have access to you. Shemal has been instrumental in your capture. Is that why you're determined to smear his good name?"

"For God's sake . . . you think I'm smearing Shemal's good name? You're as blind as Capello. Hell yes, he's been instrumental in my capture. He figured out that I was eliminating his holy warriors, ruining his plans, tracking the funds that CAIR funnels to terrorist organizations around the world. He convinced Ainsley that I was a double agent."

"Rodney Ainsley is not one of my favorite people, but you're practically accusing the Director of the FBI of collaborating with terrorists. That would make him . . ." David scowled. "You're making insane accusations."

He wished he could rub his burning eyes or maybe scratch himself. "I'm done talking. Keep the goddamned water."

David surprised him by grabbing the bottle, twisting off the top and raising it. "I'm not the asshole you think I am. You have to understand that the things you've done . . . the things that have happened, paint a different picture of you. But here, take a drink, I know you need it."

His former friend held the bottle to his lips while he guzzled all the water, choking and coughing when he swallowed too fast. Precious drops ran down his neck. "Thank you."

David looked uneasy. "I am not convinced you're telling me the truth, not by a long shot. Duplicity is a way of life for you. For all I know, you've fooled both Clifton and Chad. And even Ralph Johnston. Why don't you tell me the truth for once? Where is your former boss?"

He met the questioning eyes and thought what the hell. "Dubai."

"That's the kind of bullshit *I'm* talking about."

He sniffed and shifted in the seat while hopelessness settled around him. "You wouldn't know the truth if it bit your ass off. Just remember, I warned you."

CHAPTER THIRTEEN

Indulging melancholy thoughts, Ralph leaned on the patio wall and stared at the vivid pink and orange of the sky as the sun dipped beneath the horizon. The lights of the city far below gleamed in the dusky half-light. He wondered how Chad and Bettina were holding up. It broke his heart to think of them sitting in the brig at Quantico. A bittersweet smile hovered on his lips. He remembered the day Chad brought Bettina to her brother's hospital bed in Sioux Falls. His bachelor-for-life special agent had fallen hard and fast. His smile grew when he thought about Rowan's comment. He could still hear the menacing whisper. *Stay away from my sister*. His smile faltered. God almighty . . .

Someone had used a cell phone to record a prisoner boarding an FBI jet at the Houston airport and posted it on YouTube. The FBI declined to comment, but he'd watched, sick to his stomach, as SWAT agents helped Rowan navigate the air stairs. He'd done that once himself, but he'd taken the restraints off. The helplessness mixed with gratitude he'd seen in his friend's eyes that day still brought a painful lump to his throat.

He rubbed his eyes with the heels of his hands and left the patio. Wanting to obliterate the sad thoughts, he searched the bar at one end of the room and found a bottle of Glenlivet Single Malt Scotch. Marion had gone to check on Janice and Khalil, so he was on his own. A knock on the door startled him. It was probably Khalil. Well good, he'd never enjoyed drinking alone. "Come in."

A stocky man with graying hair and sharp brown eyes stepped into the room waving a cigar. "Mr. Johnston, it's nice to see you're unwinding. It's a long fuckin' flight over here, isn't it?" The man approached, held out a thick hand. "Johnny Giacopino.

I'd like to join you for a drink, if you don't mind. I met your beautiful wife in the hallway."

Ralph shook the strong hand. "It's nice to meet you, sir and please – it's Ralph. We're all grateful to be here. I hope we haven't caused too much inconvenience or distracted you too much from your vacation."

Johnny puffed on the cigar, creating a cloud of fragrant smoke. "If you'll remember, I offered to bring you here. I was hoping your entourage would be larger. It appears that the feds were a step ahead of us."

Ralph held the bottle of Glenlivet over a squat glass and then poured at Johnny's nod. "The feds have been busy. I'm not optimistic about how this is going to turn out."

The Mafioso leaned against the bar and loosened his tie. "Am I correct in deducing that Muusa Shemal is behind all this horse shit?"

Ralph gulped scotch. "Yes. If it weren't for Shemal, none of this would be happening. He has the ear of the Director of the FBI and evidently the President as well. But it's bigger than just Shemal. He is the Muslim Brotherhood's proxy and their goal all along has been to destroy Rowan. They'll see to it that he ends up in Tora Prison, in Egypt. Of course, Rowan hasn't done anything to help his own cause. But that's a dead issue at this point."

"Your boy Rowan and I had a chat in Chicago. I told him he was part of the family. I told him I'd help him. Next thing I know, my crew is pissing up a rope and he's gone. I'd call him on the carpet for that, if I could. Gotta be some kind of a challenge, controlling a man like that."

"Control is never possible. Rowan charts his own course and deals in his own way with whatever obstacles he encounters. The kid's smart as hell, but he's overconfident and reckless."

Johnny opened an ornate cigar box on the bar and pointed. "Help yourself. I've never been a big fan of stating the obvious, but it seems like he's gotten into a situation which requires some outside intervention."

Ralph cut the tip off the cigar, lit it and puffed. He peered through the smoke. "If you'd asked me a few weeks ago, I'd have lectured you about following the rule of law. Circumstances have altered my thoughts since then, but this situation seems cut and dried to me. The President and the entire intelligence community believe Rowan is a terrorist. Almost a year ago, Ainsley had intended to allow Shemal to transport Rowan to Tora prison. He had the President's blessing then and I'm sure he does now. That will be their next step." He stared at the glowing tip of the cigar. "End of story."

The Don shed his black suit jacket and tugged the silver striped tie from around his stout neck. "Nah, Ralphie, nothing is ever cut and dried. Not in my experience. Leverage is the necessary ingredient. We find out what that camel shit eating Shemal values *more* than Rowan Milani and then we've got the advantage."

He looked at the cunning man. "I'm fresh out of ideas. If you've got something in mind, I'm ready to hear it."

Johnny grinned, grabbed the glass of scotch and waved the cigar. "Let's sit down and toss around some ideas. I work better with a sounding board. My connections in this part of the world have given me a few things to consider."

Staring at the bleak, cinder block walls and the steel door with sliders for his hands and feet, Chad wondered how he would survive the ordeal he now faced. He paced the eight-by-eight foot cell while his mind raced. How was Bettina holding up? Would they tell him if something happened to her or to the baby? What would the government do with their baby if Bettina went to prison? His gut tightened. He didn't want their child to grow up and never know them.

No one had come for him and he'd lost track of time. How long had they been in the brig? A guard shoved food through the bottom slider every once in a while, but he couldn't eat. All he could think about was the fierce look in Bettina's eyes, when they'd been separated.

Oh God. She was so much like her brother. If she caused problems, what would the FBI do to her? How could they interrogate a pregnant woman without putting too much stress on the baby? He sat down and put his head in his hands. This was all because of his mistakes. The first time his father hadn't returned his call, they should have left Kauai and flown to South Dakota or Chicago or anywhere.

But he hadn't reacted fast enough. It wasn't like he hadn't seen the warning signs. Still, he *knew* it had something to do with David Harandi. Even Rowan had acknowledged that the guy was resourceful. He raised his head and twisted his shoulders. The tension never ended.

A jarring whistle shattered the silence and he bolted to his feet. A monotone voice instructed him to approach the door. He wiped sweaty palms on the ugly jumpsuit and did as he was told. The sliders opened. He stared at them, then set his jaw, shoved his hands through and positioned his feet. Quick hands placed the restraints on his wrists and ankles. He backed up as the door swung open.

Two sober-faced guards walked him to a room with a table and two chairs. After shoving him down on a cold metal chair, one guard left the interrogation room and the other stood in front of the door. The young man wouldn't make eye contact with him, so he hunched over, staring at his hands and the cold steel circling his wrists.

He couldn't stop thinking about Rowan and the trauma and degradation his friend had endured in this same brig. Would the FBI be as harsh with him as Capello had been with Rowan? Could he endure, the way his friend had and beat the agents at their own game? He already knew the answer. If the Bureau offered him any way to ensure Bettina's freedom, to protect her and their baby, he'd jump at it.

A soft knock on the door caught his attention and he sat up straight. A man wearing khaki pants and a polo shirt entered the room and dismissed the guard with a nod. He recognized him from images Rowan had shown him. The guy moved with a natural grace that reminded him of Rowan, although David didn't have a catch in his stride. But he probably hadn't been stomped on and beaten by CIA thugs the way his friend had.

David slid into the other chair, laid a file folder on the battered table and clasped his hands on top of it. "Hello Chad. My name is David Harandi."

He stared at the man's neatly trimmed fingernails and the sparse black hairs on his efficient looking hands. Would those hands make bruises on his body or would the agent use them to string him up and humiliate him? He raised his head and met the agent's shrewd gaze. "I know who you are, Mr. Harandi."

"Please, call me David. We're going to be spending a fair amount of time together and there is no need for formality." David tapped the file folder with an index finger. "Your background makes for interesting reading. Now that I'm more familiar with your skills, I see your fingerprints all over the operation that kept Rowan free for so long."

Not sure how to respond, not wanting to admit to anything, he fought to keep from squirming. All he cared about was getting Bettina and their baby out of the mess he'd created. But he had to find out if he could bargain for her freedom. "What do you want, Mr. Harandi?" The agent was smart, but he wasn't going to let himself be lulled into cooperating by using the jerk's first name.

"Well, for starters, the password to your laptop would be of great use. FBI special agents are wringing their hands over your ability to penetrate the Bureau's security."

He slouched in the chair. “Breaking my password is kindergarten stuff. If they can’t do that, then they are never going to comprehend my work.”

The eyes that met his were impassive. “Understand this. The Bureau’s people will obtain your password and access your information with or without your assistance. Aren’t you interested in helping Bettina and yourself?”

“How do I know I can trust you? I could share all of my knowledge and give you my expertise and still find myself sitting here or in a federal prison.”

David opened the file folder. “Let me assure you that if you choose not to cooperate with me, you will spend the rest of your life in prison. So, let’s proceed from that understanding. I’m curious about your association with Rowan Milani. Did he coerce you and Ralph Johnston? Were either of you ever in any danger from him? Was Bettina?”

“You are out of your mind if you think that Rowan would *ever* do anything to harm any of us. We helped him because the President and Ainsley turned their backs on him and believed the word of a Muslim Brotherhood operative instead of one of their own. Muusa Shemal knew that Rowan was the one man who could destroy his and the Brotherhood’s plans.”

David replied. “That’s interesting. It appears that you have all rehearsed your story very well. Rowan told me the same thing. So did your father. However, Mr. Shemal has provided proof of Rowan’s subterfuge, along with witnesses. It would seem that you’ve been cleverly deceived.”

Shock and despair gripped him, but he couldn’t let it show. “I know Rowan. If you had him in custody, he wouldn’t tell you squat. And my father doesn’t have any involvement in this.”

“Oh, I don’t know. Rowan might talk to me, if he was under the right kind of duress. You know, injured, in pain, or not thinking clearly because of being drugged. But please, stop with the innocent routine regarding your father.”

The guy was getting to him. "What happened to Rowan? Has he been apprehended?"

"I'll ask the questions in this interview. If you want information, start by providing some to me. Otherwise, I guess you'll just have to wonder what's happened to the people you claim to care about, including Bettina – and your father."

Feeling desperation closing in, he blurted what he was thinking, instantly wishing he could take it back. "I know you've got my father but I don't believe you've got Rowan in custody. If you want me to tell you anything, then let's make a deal. Release Bettina, let her go and I'll give you whatever you want."

David looked at the open file folder. "Your hacking skills are fast becoming legendary. Are you willing to share your knowledge with the Bureau?"

He didn't want to cave, not without the assurance that Bettina would go free. "Before I tell you anything, I want you to release Bettina."

David closed the file folder and stood up. "I'm not in the mood to screw around with you. If you don't want to take me seriously, I'll give you more time to consider your situation and that of your pregnant fiancée. Time moves slowly when you're in a cell, doesn't it? We'll talk again in a few days. Or, maybe I'll concentrate on Bettina and let you sit for a week. Or maybe two, or hell, even a month." David scooped up the file folder and left the room.

The guards led him back to his tiny cell and released him. He sat on the disgusting bed and put his head in his hands. How would he stay sane, isolated from the woman he loved, with no idea of what was happening to her at the hands of David Harandi? Did the jerk really have Rowan in custody? Why would he talk about injuries and pain and drugs, if he didn't have Rowan? If he did, how had it happened and how badly injured was his friend?

He stretched out on the bed as despair overwhelmed him. The agent's comments about his father had only confirmed his suspicions. Was his father being held at Quantico, too? Should he have agreed to work with the FBI special agents? He heaved a sigh. The amateurs at the Bureau would never crack his password. The secrets his laptop held might be the bargaining chip he needed to make sure that Bettina and their unborn baby were released. He didn't believe they'd ever let him go, but if Bettina could raise their son or daughter, it was worth the years it would cost him.

After the fruitless session with Chad, David went to the observation room in the isolation wing of the brig to watch Rowan on the monitor. His prisoner had been processed, taken to the infirmary and then placed in a cell. If possible, he wanted to keep the pressure on and conduct a more in-depth interrogation session than the sparring match he'd let himself be dragged into on the plane. First, though, he wanted to observe the man when he wasn't restrained.

He'd taken the conventional cameras out of the cell and replaced them with two tiny wide focus surveillance units that were almost unnoticeable. So far, Rowan had done little more than pace back and forth in front of the steel door like a restless panther.

Leaning back in the creaky chair, he stroked his goatee. Rowan had acquired a slight limp and rubbed his wrists while he stalked back and forth. He chuckled when Rowan stared directly into one of the cameras and flipped him the bird.

His former friend had always been hotheaded. But the Rowan he knew had also been kindhearted. Now his dark eyes held only the cold calculation of a predator. Rowan's cavalier description of what he'd do if the restraints were removed had convinced him that all vestiges of the kinship they'd once shared were gone.

That knowledge would guide his interrogation. His prisoner needed to understand that he meant business.

He watched Rowan slump down on the edge of the narrow bed. Was that hopelessness he saw in the rounded shoulders? For a moment, Rowan held his head in his hands. Then he punched the thin pillow and stuffed it behind his head before lying flat on his back with his hands clenched at his sides.

He reached for the controls and sharpened the focus on his prisoner's face. While Rowan's left arm remained motionless, he rubbed his right hand across his eyes several times in a quick movement that made him suspicious. Was the badass terrorist wiping away tears? He couldn't get a good enough angle to be sure, but decided there was no better time to dig deeper into Rowan's psyche.

He turned to the guards at the door. "Please bring Milani to Room One. And be careful. He's dangerous and won't hesitate to kill you. Keep a weapon trained on him at all times and be sure he's secured. I'll be along momentarily." The guards nodded and left.

David signaled the guards to wait. He opened the cell door himself and stepped inside. Bettina looked up from the bed where she sat. Dark circles stained the hollows of her eyes and he saw worry etched on her face. "David? Why . . . oh no, are you behind this?" Bettina gestured around the cinderblock cell.

He wished he didn't have to involve her in the mess her brother had created. "Hello Bettina. It's been a long time. I'm sorry this is how we're meeting. Are you doing all right? Did the doctors treat you well?"

She rubbed her arms. "Oh sure, everyone's been peachy. It's nice to be stuck in this miserable, stinky hole when I haven't committed a crime. This is all about getting Chad to confess, isn't it?"

"To a certain extent, yes, it is about securing his cooperation. I'd like nothing more than to release you right now. Unfortunately, your fiancé has not been willing to cooperate with me. I'm hoping you'll be more inclined to help."

"What do you mean by that?"

He leaned against the door. "For starters, did Rowan coerce Chad and Ralph into helping him? Did he threaten them or you and your parents?"

"Are you crazy? Rowan has done everything possible to protect *all* of us. Chad and Ralph helped him because they knew he was not a double agent or a terrorist."

Raising a hand to stroke his goatee, he considered her words. "Rowan's a smart man. Don't you think it's possible he deceived all of you? After all, he spent a lot of time out of the country."

Bettina's eyes narrowed. "When's the last time you even talked to him? Did you ever see him after 9/11? He became a different person after that. The *last* thing my brother would *ever* do is help the people who took Michelle away from him. I know that from the bottom of my heart, no matter how things look to you."

"People high up in our intelligence community would beg to differ. They have access to more than just feelings and loyalty."

"For God's sake, I'm not a fool. I've seen proof that he's innocent."

He shoved away from the door. "What proof is that? Where did it come from?"

For an instant, Bettina looked guilty. "When he was in South Dakota, Danielle and I looked at the records he kept about the terrorists he killed. We never told anyone we'd seen it because we weren't supposed to."

"Was this from a computer file? Where is Danielle now?"

"It was on a flash drive that he'd managed to hide from the CIA agents who almost killed him. Honestly, I don't know where

Danielle is now. The last time I talked to her she was in San Francisco."

"That's interesting. Where is that flash drive now?"

"I have no idea. The FBI's SWAT team took everything from Kauai. Ask them. Or, maybe Rowan still has it. I hope you never catch him, even if it means keeping us here illegally forever."

David tried to soften the blow he knew his words would give her. "Rowan is here now. He's been apprehended. He was injured, but not seriously."

Her dark eyes filled with tears. "Is he going to be all right? He's been hurt so many times. I just can't imagine how his body can keep recovering."

"He killed two men. One of them stabbed him in the arm, but it will heal."

Bettina wiped tears from her cheeks with slim fingers. "David, please . . . you have to believe me. I know my brother. Rowan is not a terrorist. If you have him, you must have the flash drive. Check it out before it's too late and you can no longer help him."

"The murders he's committed would lead me to think otherwise. But believe me, I'll find the flash drive. What do you mean, before it's too late?"

Her lower lip quivered. "Help him before Muusa Shemal takes him away. That's why Rowan left Kauai, to find him and kill him. He's the one who wanted Rowan from the very beginning. Why haven't you talked to Chad or Rowan about this? You are the only one who can stop it."

"Rowan and Chad tried the same thing with me. Muusa Shemal is a respected representative of the Muslim Brotherhood and leads a large mosque in Houston. He alerted the intelligence community to Rowan's terrorist activities. He told me how Rowan killed my Uncle Sa-id. I bet you didn't know that, did you?"

Bettina's eyes were huge. "Rowan would never kill your uncle. He loved him. They spent New Year's together last year. Rowan told me how much fun he had teasing Sa-id about trying to get him to eat Iranian food. Ask him, he'll tell you."

He glanced at his watch. "I've got to leave now. We'll talk soon. I'll look into the things you've told me, I promise."

"What you're doing to us isn't right. You shouldn't be able to keep us here. I want to see Chad. I want to see my brother." Bettina covered her face with her hands.

"What happens next depends on how much cooperation I get from your fiancé and brother." He listened to her soft weeping and watched her for a moment, then left the cell, shuddering at the sound of the deadbolt when he locked the door.

Rowan sat hunched over in the cold metal chair. The guards had come for him while he lay on the bed, lost in memories of Danielle, knowing he'd never see her again. His hands were chained to the table in front of him and his feet were chained to a bolt in the floor. He'd been shivering in the chilly room for what seemed like a long time. His left arm felt swollen and heavy. The doctor in the infirmary had frowned over it and replaced the bloody bandages, but offered no relief from the pain.

A bottle of water sat just out of his reach on the table. That didn't surprise him. David would work every angle to wear down his defenses. Not that it mattered. Shemal would cart him off to Tora Prison soon enough.

He thought about what was coming and tried to tamp down his fear. Sweat dripped down his face and slicked his chest in spite of the cold. David entered the room, slapped a yellow legal pad on the table and slid into a chair. "I just had an interesting conversation with Bettina. It's been a long time since I've seen her. Whoa, what's the matter? Are you feeling all right?"

The phony concern was easy to read. "Just ask your goddamn questions, would you? You don't have a lot of time."

David tapped a pen on the legal pad. "I'm surprised at your lack of interest in your sister, although I guess I shouldn't be. Besides, we have plenty of time. But I'm all for getting started. First question, who are Michael and Gabriel?"

"Archangels, if I remember correctly. Didn't you learn anything in that fancy Catholic school Sa-id sent you to?"

David stroked his goatee. "Derek Norris gave us those names. I know these men are your associates and that they facilitated both of your escapes."

"If you know that, then why the hell are you asking me?"

David laid the pen on the legal pad. "Where are they now?"

A ventilation fan kicked on, sending a cool breeze and the scent of fried food through the room. His stomach growled and his parched mouth watered. "Why don't you ask your dumb fuck informant?"

David picked up the pen, tapped it on the paper again. "Tell me where they are."

He twisted his shoulders but couldn't relieve the tenseness. "I don't know where Mike and Gabriel are. You know better than I do where Chad is and I already told you where to find Ralph."

David laid the pen down. "We aren't going to have another sparring match like we did on the plane. This isn't a game. Give me their location and their last names."

"No." Eyeing the bottle of water, he swallowed, licking his lips without thinking.

David followed his gaze. "Are you thirsty? I can fix that." Something in his adversary's tone made him look up. David raised an arm, twirled an index finger. The door opened and two guards entered. "Let's go."

Anxiety turned to dread as he traversed the hallways between the guards. They came around a corner to a door he remembered. Inside, the smell of chlorine in the damp air brought full-force panic. He tried to slow his breathing. When the guards buckled his knees and laid him on the board, he closed his eyes. Straps tightened across his chest and legs. A heavy cloth was draped over his face.

His body jerked when the water hit the cloth and he gasped, sucked the fabric against his nose and into his mouth while the water poured. He gagged and fought, knowing he'd drown.

The cloth lifted, revealing blurred faces. He groaned and coughed while his chest heaved. David slapped his cheek. "Had enough?"

He blinked through water-filled eyes. "Fuck you."

The soaked cloth swathed his face and he shook his head, desperate to dislodge it. Strong hands cradled his face and the water came again. Involuntary reaction took over and he breathed deep, inhaled water and clawed helplessly with his fingers while his back arched, straining against the straps.

Once more the cloth disappeared, but he couldn't stop choking. David raised his head with unyielding hands. "Only you can end this, Rowan. Tell me where your friends are. What are their last names?"

He coughed and whispered. "South Dakota. Smith and Jones."

Again the cloth covered his face. The water came like a deluge, flooding his nostrils and mouth. He couldn't breathe and he couldn't escape. His hands clutched at the chains around his waist. The straps loosened, the sopping cloth was pulled away and the guards lifted him upright, pounding him on his back.

He took in rasping breaths, vomiting water as the guards dragged him to his feet. They trudged back to the interrogation room and he staggered between them. Secured again in the metal chair, he shivered and coughed. His tormentor surveyed him. "Are you still thirsty?"

"No." He drew a shuddering breath. His chest ached and he coughed again. He hated the weakness in his voice.

"I didn't think so. How'd you like my *fuck you?* Told you I owed you one. Now, give me your associates' last names and tell me where they are."

He lifted his shoulder, cranked his head to the side and wiped his nose on the rough fabric of the jumpsuit. Every breath hurt like hell. His strength was gone. Observing David's smug grin, he closed his eyes. *"Tool."* A resounding whack snapped his head to one side. He groaned at the pain, blinking through tears he couldn't stop from coming.

David stood leaning across the table, face scarlet, hands flat on the surface. "I told you, *this isn't a game.* If you don't answer me, I'll get the guards. We'll keep at it until you provide the information I want. You decide, right now."

He stared at his tormentor. "As far as I know, Gabriel is in San Francisco and the last time I talked to Mike, he was in Houston. Do whatever you want. I sure as hell can't stop you. But that's all I'm telling you."

David gave him a quick nod. "Your choice."

Stark fear had him breathing in painful gasps. He watched the same signal, heard the door, saw the guards. They dragged him down the hallways. Stumbling between them, he could no longer control his breathing. How much could he take? Would they keep it up until he drowned?

In the humid room, David faced him. "You don't have to go through this, Rowan. Just tell me what I need to know. I'll get you something to eat and a shot of painkiller that'll put you out for a few hours."

His knees wobbled and he swallowed hard. "You think I'll sell out my colleagues for a sandwich and a break? You don't know me anymore. If you ever did."

David looked resigned. "Don't say I didn't try. We'll see how you feel in a few minutes."

The guards jerked him forward, buckled his knees, pushed him down on the board and strapped him tight. He closed his eyes and clenched his jaws. The water-soaked cloth covered his face once again. His world shrank to the terrifying water and crushing pain in his chest. He groaned and fought, his body wrenching and straining until he sobbed in utter, humiliated exhaustion and lay quivering, no longer able to resist.

The cloth slid from his face and his head lolled to one side. Shallow, creaking breaths were all the agony in his chest permitted. The guards loosened the straps and lifted him to his feet, but his legs wouldn't support his weight and he fell, face down. He moaned at the biting pain from the cuffs and chain that held his hands at his waist.

David rolled him to his back. "I don't believe this. Get the medics."

He drifted in and out of consciousness and heard the infirmary doctor. "Mr. Harandi, your prisoner needs an intravenous antibiotic for what sounds like the start of a lung infection or possibly pneumonia, and fluids for dehydration. We need to confine him here overnight."

David sounded irritated. "Fine, but do not administer pain medication. And be aware that this is a dangerous man who needs to be restrained at all times. I'll post a guard at the door as well."

Hours later Rowan lay staring at the ceiling. His harsh breaths brought stabbing pain to his lungs. Terror struck when he couldn't catch his breath. Bathed in sweat, he closed his eyes, remembering the other time he'd lain in the same infirmary. No comforting presence embraced him or invited him to ask for help. He knew it wouldn't, not this time.

CHAPTER FOURTEEN

Kyle dug through the box of evidence taken when Milani was arrested. David had called, asking that he search the contents for a flash drive that might have been in Milani's possession. He hadn't been happy about the request. Captain Lavoe had been less than enthused and asked him to copy the flash drive if he found it. The feds always got their way and sometimes that just ticked him off, even though he knew David wasn't throwing his weight around.

He took both guns and the blood encrusted knife, encased in separate plastic bags out of the box and laid them aside. Gazing at the Glock pistols, he snorted. An American made 1911 beat a foreign born pistol every time in his estimation.

When the box was empty, he shined his flashlight inside and found the flash drive, wedged in the bottom seam of the box. He wondered why it hadn't been placed in an evidence bag of its own. At least they'd have a copy of it, on the remote chance that Milani would ever face charges in Houston. One of his guys in IT could access the information on the drive and copy it for him.

Three hours later, he stared at his computer screen in fascination. The IT technician had copied everything from the drive. Part of it appeared to be a database of names. Each name had two listed dates below it. Occasionally they were the same, but more often they were different. The first date was always earlier than the second.

Curious, he jotted half a dozen of the names down and googled each one. All six were radical Islamists and all six were deceased. He tried another six with the same results. Staring at the screen and rubbing his jaw, he thought about his conversation with Milani. He'd been in no mood to fool around with the man who'd done everything *but* kill him. The son of a bitch had hated to talk. Remembering the look in the man's eyes still raised the hair on the back of his neck.

Just for the hell of it, he checked another dozen names. His results were the same, except he couldn't find a few of the people. Some of the dates of death coincided with the second date on Milani's list. He wondered if this could be a list of men Milani had targeted for murder and then recorded the date when he'd accomplished the deed. That offered no hint as to the first date, however. The list could also be men Milani collaborated with in betraying the United States. Maybe they were the names of fellow jihadists he planned to avenge.

Confused, he thought hard. Milani had alleged that Muusa Shemal was the real terrorist. Was he somehow connected to this database of names? What about the two men Milani had murdered the night he'd been apprehended? On a hunch, he found the cell phone number he wanted and dialed. Shemal answered after several rings, sounding hurried. "Yes Detective Matthews, how may I assist you?"

"Mr. Shemal, I wanted to express my regret for the loss of two more of your mosque members at Rowan Milani's hands. I'd also like to record their full names to complete my investigation. Neither of them carried any identification."

"No more of my members were killed by Rowan Milani. I'm afraid I don't know what you are speaking of, and I cannot spare the time to discuss it further."

He wondered how he'd ever entertained the notion that Milani might be telling the truth. It was another anomaly he'd chalk up to having the back of his head smacked on the pavement. "Please accept my apologies, Mr. Shemal. I am sorry to have disturbed you."

"No apology is necessary. I wish you luck in determining the identity of the men Milani killed."

Ending the call, he stared at the list on the computer screen. It was impossible for him to determine what the list might mean, but he was certain it didn't clear Milani of any wrongdoing. He grabbed his phone and dialed again. "Hello David, I've located the flash drive you requested. I'll overnight it to you right away."

"Thanks Kyle. I'd prefer that you give it to the Director of the FBI. He's flying from Houston to D.C. tomorrow. I'd appreciate it if you would personally hand it over to him."

"Not a problem. I'll deliver it myself. I know you're just getting started, but how is the interrogation going so far?"

"Milani is beyond tough. It's possible I took it too far today. The fact that I know him – or knew him – makes it difficult for me to gauge my own reactions. I let him get to me."

"Hang in there. You're just getting started. You'll wear Milani down, I'm certain of that."

David sounded tired. "It's going to take some time. I've got to approach him from a different angle. Maybe you should fly out and offer some Texas assistance."

"I've got a better idea. Bring Milani back here to face some old-fashioned Texas justice. I told him I'd get at a few more details if I ever got a hold of him again."

The Next Day

Patricia shaded her eyes from the sun and tapped her foot while she waited for the phone to connect. "Agent Hancock, you and Agent Talbot need to meet me in Quantico's brig at sixteen-hundred hours today. We'll be ready to transport Milani. Be prompt."

"Yes ma'am. We're ready. We'll be there."

Wanting to keep the agents' gusto for punishing Milani in check, she admonished. "By invitation, the press will be part of this event. This is the administration's opportunity to show the American people that we're on top of the war on terror. Milani must not have a single mark on his face. He must be able to walk and board the jet under his own power. Understood?"

Agent Hancock sounded somewhat subdued. "We'll be gentle."

Satisfied that she'd made her point, she ended the call and threaded her way between the tables in the outdoor dining area of the Hotel Granduca. Muusa and Rodney were waiting at the spot she'd reserved in the far corner, removed from the hustle and bustle of the other diners. The other tables near them were empty except for a lone businessman in a suit, absorbed in his newspaper. She sat and looked from one to the other. "Agents Hancock and Talbot will ensure that the transport proceeds smoothly this afternoon. I've composed a short press release for distribution. We'll get our photo op this time."

Rodney lounged in the chair and sipped coffee. "I've been coordinating with the Washington Bureau Chief. The entire area will be secure. It's just a shame we had to cancel our conference appearance because of your boy scout, Harandi."

Muusa leaned forward, clasping his hands together on the table. "It is imperative that nothing disrupts this public display of victory. We can plan a joint appearance at another conference some other time."

She listened to the palm branches rustling in the early morning breeze before answering Muusa. *"Nothing* will interfere with this event. You have no cause for concern."

The Egyptian man did not look convinced. "You will forgive me, Madam Advisor, but on previous occasions I have heard similar assurances, only to find this clever man plucked from your hands."

"The difference *this time* will be my presence. I will be supervising each move personally. The CIA agents I engaged are most anxious to prove themselves worthy. They understand that in order to receive full payment, they must deliver Milani to Tora

Prison. By the way, they'll be staying on at our CIA station there to ensure that the prisoner remains in good health."

Muusa arched his brows. "Their participation in delivering Rowan Milani to Tora is more than enough to warrant payment of the $250,000.00 that I agreed to. Further involvement is not necessary. My guards are quite capable of handling Milani from that point."

Rodney cemented their position. "Mr. Shemal, I've met with the CIA Director and he concurs that our agents must have access to Milani. He is an American citizen. Any information gleaned from interrogating him will undoubtedly be of great value to our own intelligence agencies. This is a non-negotiable point."

The Egyptian's nostrils flared and for a moment she saw something akin to animosity in his eyes. Then Muusa inclined his head slightly. "Their participation is welcomed. However, you do understand that in order to achieve results, I must have free rein to interrogate Milani in whatever way I deem necessary."

Patricia rushed to appease him. "Mr. Shemal, we are fully cognizant of the fact that without your intervention, we would not have been aware of Milani's collaboration with our enemies. Untold damage could have been done to our national security. We are most grateful. Our only desire is that he remains in shape for interrogation in the United States at a future date."

Rodney came to her aid again. "As you know, the President is particularly pleased that Tora is available. We are confident that Milani's organization will have no ability to touch him in your facility."

"No one will breach Tora's defenses. Milani will not suffer so much that he will be unable to appear in this country for indictment at a future date, if you deem it necessary. Perhaps during the next election, he would be a valuable political asset?"

Patricia replied. "You are very astute, Mr. Shemal. Thank you for ensuring his future availability."

Muusa laid his napkin on the table and checked his watch. "It is my pleasure to assist this administration in any way possible. Regrettably, I am not able to join you for breakfast. Matters at the mosque require my attention. I will meet you at the airport in two hours for our flight to Washington."

Rodney stood as Muusa rose from the table. "Thank you, Mr. Shemal. We remain grateful for your assistance in this matter and look forward to its conclusion. It will be cause for celebration for us all."

Patricia didn't get up, but offered her hand. "I'm disappointed that you can't stay. We'll see you at the airport. I look forward to discussing things in greater depth on the way to Washington."

Muusa took her hand and gave it a light squeeze before letting go. "We will make final arrangements on our flight. Good day, Madam Advisor, Director."

Clifton had always thought of himself as disciplined, a master of self-control. Gazing around the small, windowless room with its dull green walls and gray tiled floor, he fought against a feeling of powerless frustration. The fluorescent lights in the ceiling never went off, but they were dim, creating a feeling of perpetual gloom.

He sat on the folding chair next to the narrow bed with his elbows on his knees, resting his chin in his hands and wondering one more time where he was. The Secret Service agents had put a black hood over his head shortly after leaving the White House gate. David hadn't spoken to him again. Only one time the door to the room had opened and a guard dressed in army fatigues had entered with a pile of his own clothes and a basket of toiletries. He washed up every day in the small sink.

Occasionally a panel lifted in the otherwise solid steel door and a tray of food was shoved through with a bottle of water. Sometimes it was a bologna sandwich. Other times it was soup or toast and a boiled egg. He rubbed his forehead, trying to dispel the pain. No coffee or tea was ever on the tray and he'd suffered with a headache and nausea as his body rebelled at its forced withdrawal from caffeine. Scratching the steadily growing beard, he contemplated his situation again because he couldn't do anything else. With access to his financial records and the illegal search of his home, surely the President and his dogged investigator had brought the full resources of the intelligence apparatus to bear.

He gave up trying to reason through the position he'd been thrust into. His thoughts wanted to escape. They insisted on running wild, so he put his head in his hands and let them. What about Chad and Bettina? If they'd been captured, what would become of their child, his first grandchild? He wondered if the trust he'd set up for Natalie had been frozen. What would happen to her without his guardianship? He raised his head, remembering Patricia's caustic words and the vitriol she couldn't seem to contain. What had made her so bitter and mean-spirited toward him?

He heard the lock scrape and turn in the door and watched in surprise as two stern-faced, armed men entered. They looked like Secret Service agents, and he wondered again where he was being kept. One of the men was lanky, tall and bald, the other stocky and short with medium length hair and sideburns. The stocky agent pointed at the wall. "Mr. Cantor, face the wall and put your hands on your head please."

He obeyed the order. The lanky agent stepped toward him, taking first one arm and then the other and twisting them down, cuffing his hands behind his back. The agent turned him around and placed a black hood over his head. Firm hands grasped his arms and escorted him from the room.

It seemed like they walked him endlessly in circles. He only stumbled a few times, but felt disoriented and claustrophobic beneath the hood. They stopped for a moment, then dragged him a few more steps, only to stop again. His knees sagged against one of the agents as they ascended in an elevator. It stopped and he teetered again when they resumed walking. By the time they stopped again, his heart was pounding.

He heard rattling keys and then they tugged on his arms again. He felt a chill in the air and goose bumps rose on his arms. The agents shoved him into a chair and tugged the hood from his head. He squinted in the sudden light. This room didn't have windows either, but the walls were white and overhead lights blazed. Pain shot through his eyes, exacerbating his headache. The short agent stayed in the room when the tall man left.

The agent gave him an unfriendly stare. "Stay seated, Mr. Cantor."

Squeezing his watering eyes shut against the uncomfortable light, he mumbled, "No problem."

As he sat, with no sense of the amount of time passing, he struggled with an impotent anger. He'd built a successful life as a respected lobbyist and financial investment guru. Now he was being treated like a third world political prisoner in the United States of America. He shifted in the chair. He couldn't relieve the tension in his arms, which were held behind his back at an awkward angle, and he couldn't lean back because of the cuffs that gouged his wrists. While one eye twitched in the irritating brightness, he scowled at the agent. "Do you think you could cuff my hands in front of me? My arms are spasming."

The agent tapped the butt of the black pistol holstered at his side. "I suppose that would be all right."

He wilted in the chair, biting back a sarcastic comment. "I'd appreciate it." The stocky man drew keys from his pants pocket and unlocked one of the cuffs. Rolling his shoulders in relief, he stretched his arms and watched while his wrists were locked together again. He leaned back and crossed one leg over the other, laying his hands in his lap. "Thank you."

The agent returned to his post at the door and didn't answer him. His eyes were no longer sensitive to the light and he looked around the room. An oval table and a few other chairs like his were its only furnishings. At a brisk knock, the agent opened the door, admitting the tall agent, followed by President Whitman. His friend gestured to the taller man. "Bring the coffee in please," and turned to the other agent. "Unlock those cuffs."

The lanky agent left the room and the stocky agent frowned. "Mr. President, I'm not sure that's a good idea."

The President placed his hands on his hips. "I wasn't asking for your opinion, Agent Hawkins."

The short man pulled the keys from his pocket. "Yes sir."

He raised his hands while the agent unlocked the restraints and pulled them off. Rubbing his wrists, he watched as the tall agent appeared with a carafe of coffee and two cups. When he took a deep breath, he caught the aroma of strong French Roast, his favorite.

The President angled his head toward the door. "Thank you, gentlemen. I would appreciate it if you would wait outside. If I need any assistance, I will let you know." The agents looked unhappy, but complied. Whitman poured steaming coffee in both cups. "Clifton, have some coffee with me."

His hand shook and he had to support the bottom of the cup with his other palm. Sipping the stout liquid, he closed his eyes. Nothing could have tasted better. He took another sip and opened his eyes. "Thank you for the coffee."

The President watched him, a frown creasing his face. "I'm sorry for the situation . . . well, about all of this. If the evidence hadn't been so overwhelming, or perhaps if you'd come to me in confidence, I wouldn't have had to authorize the actions that were taken. I felt as though you gave me no other choice."

He sat the cup down on the table. "Gil, since I'm in this . . . *situation*, which I find untenable, let me be blunt. Someone is lying to you."

His friend swallowed coffee and held the cup between both hands. "Go on, I'm listening."

Surprised at the unexpected invitation, he continued. "Rowan Milani is innocent. He is neither double agent nor traitor. Chad came to me early last summer. He told me about how Rowan had discovered disturbing information about Muusa Shemal's travels around the country and his activities in various mosques. He asked me to check into a few things for him. I did."

The President waved a hand. "And, what did you find?"

He studied the earnest face. "This isn't going to make you happy, Gil."

"I haven't heard anything in the last several years that makes me happy. Please, keep talking."

"Rodney Ainsley, Patricia Hennessey, and the now-deceased Sal Capello accepted large sums of money from Shemal in exchange for custody of Rowan Milani. The Muslim Brotherhood wants him. Badly." Swallowing more coffee and marveling at how it clarified his thoughts, he waited, wondering how his friend would respond.

The lines in the President's face seemed to deepen. "Patricia is my most trusted advisor. She's been with me since before I ran for the Senate. What proof can you offer me of this . . . I don't know what to call it . . . this *indiscretion?* And how did you find the proof that Rodney and Patricia accepted money?"

Clifton finished his coffee and poured more. "My sources monitor the financial activities of numerous politicians very closely. Chad has taught me a few things, as well. Gil, you would do well to use his capabilities instead of forcing him to remain in hiding. He's developed software for cell phones that is breathtaking."

"Chad is in custody along with his fiancée. Rowan Milani is as well. It's difficult for me to believe that Patricia and Rodney would collude with a foreign national. Besides that, what did Milani find out about Shemal?"

He hated to think of his son's agile mind forced to succumb to interrogation. "I'm sorry . . . uh, Milani believed that the pattern of travel and Shemal's affiliation with CAIR pointed to him as the head of a long-standing plan to infiltrate and destroy our country from within. The ultimate goal is to dismantle the government of the United States and replace it with a caliphate. He based that on a Muslim Brotherhood memorandum discovered after 9/11, called *The Project.* I believe you're probably more knowledgeable of that than I am."

"Of course, I've read the memorandum. I know my predecessor spoke with Milani about finding the head of that effort to undermine the nation. However, over the years since 9/11, so many moderate Islamic organizations have come to the forefront that I no longer believe that memorandum signals a viable threat. Much more is to be gained by accepting Islam into our culture. CAIR has played a huge role in that. I know Rodney has worked hard to integrate several new training programs at the Bureau. I've backed him strongly on that."

Clifton savored the French Roast and considered the best way to reply. The coffee, combined with his feeling of desperation gave him courage. "I mean no disrespect Gil, but it's possible that you need to rethink your position. Milani is an astute student of radical Islam. Maybe you should set up a meeting and interview him in person."

"I'll take everything you've said under advisement, although you've made what I consider outlandish accusations. I've always valued your friendship and have depended more than once on your honesty. However, I must continue your detention, until some of these *things* can be ascertained. Is there anything I can do to make it more bearable?"

He scraped his fingers through his bristling whiskers. "Coffee would be a welcome addition to the menu. I'd appreciate a razor, too. You can reassure your ultra-watchful agents that I'm not interested in committing suicide. And I'd love to see a newspaper now and then."

Whitman stood up. "Consider it done. We'll talk again soon." His friend surveyed him gravely before leaving the room.

Clifton sat, disconsolate, waiting for his keepers. Soon, the agents returned with the cuffs and hood. Loathing his helplessness, he held out his hands and closed his eyes. He abhorred the sound of the cuffs locking around his wrists and the stifling hood sliding over his head. An involuntary shudder rippled through him when he realized how vulnerable he'd made himself. If the President chose to investigate and asked Patricia or Rodney the wrong questions, what would happen to him . . . or to Chad?

Michael lounged outside the front entrance of the Hotel Granduca, waiting for the cab the bellhop had arranged for him. He watched a black Cadillac limousine pull up and glide to a stop. Muusa Shemal strode past him as a uniform clad driver scrambled to open the back door. His hand went instinctively to the holstered 1911 at his side beneath the suit jacket. He gazed longingly at the heavy body climbing into the limo.

But he could help Rowan more in the long run by staying free. He'd overheard enough of the conversation between Shemal, Ainsley, and the woman to know that his next destination was Washington, D.C. Whether he could do anything to prevent them from hauling Rowan out of Quantico was debatable, but he could certainly keep tabs on their movements.

He tipped the bellhop and climbed in the cab. "George Bush Intercontinental Airport, please." The vehicle accelerated into traffic and he stared out the window, pondering the bits and pieces of the conversation he'd overheard. Shemal referred to the woman as *Madam Advisor*. She had to be Patricia Hennessey, the woman Chad had talked about. From listening, he'd deduced that she wielded significant power and had been operating behind the scenes in all the shit going on with Rowan from the beginning.

Rowan had never mentioned her in connection with Shemal. Throughout the entire operation, he and Gabriel had taken pride in being a step ahead of the FBI, CIA, and Shemal. Of course, that had gone down the toilet when his damned stubborn friend had taken off on his own, but still . . . He hated being blindsided, and that's exactly what had happened. And it figured that it would be some woman with her own version of a hard-on for Rowan.

What the hell had Rowan done to piss this bitch off to the extent that she'd react so viciously? He knew from long experience that Rowan was capable of damn near anything when it came to women. He thought about Marta. His friend had paid a dear price for ignoring Shemal's whore. They'd been blindsided by her as well.

The cab driver glanced at him in the rearview mirror. "Which airline?"

He made a quick decision. "Private flight, Atlantic Aviation please."

The cabbie nodded. "OK."

Gathering his thoughts, he dug his phone out of the suit coat pocket. He punched a contact and waited to hear the gruff voice. "Hello, Ralph. How are things in Dubai? Has Marion spent all your money at the Mall of the Emirates yet?"

"God almighty, she's doing her best. What's going on, Michael? I was planning to call you. Johnny's putting something together on Rowan's behalf."

The cab exited onto the approach to the airport. "Did you know that the President's advisor was involved with Muusa Shemal from the start? From what I overheard, she's the one who hired those first two bastards who damn near killed Rowan."

"Sweet Jesus, Patricia . . . That broad has been stuck like glue to the President since back in the day. I always thought she smelled power and got her hooks into the quickest ride. God only knows what she has against Rowan."

"It's hard to say. With Rowan, you just never know. Look, I've got to go, but I'll be in touch soon. I'm looking forward to hearing what Johnny has in mind." The cab dropped him at Atlantic Aviation. He walked around the customer service area, the same way he'd done the day the FBI took Rowan. As he'd thought, the Bureau's Gulfstream V sat on the tarmac. He made a reservation on a United flight leaving at 12:56 p.m. That would put him in Atlanta at 4:01 p.m.

Wondering whether he should have taken the 10:19 a.m. flight direct to D.C. in order to stay ahead of Ainsley and Hennessey, he grabbed coffee and a newspaper. He found a chair and pretended to read the paper while he tugged on the collar of the dress shirt and loosened his tie. Blending in at the Granduca had been more important than comfort and he always felt better about riding in First Class when he looked the part of a legitimate businessman.

A scenario began to take form in his mind and he dug his phone out again, punched a different contact and waited, tapping impatient fingers on the arm of the chair. "Que pasa, Amigo?" Children's voices piping up in the background made him feel guilty.

Gabriel sounded happy. "Hola, Amigo. Sì que pasa? Where are you?"

Thinking about Rowan again, he shoved the guilt aside. "I'm in Houston, about to catch a flight to Atlanta. How's the fam? Happy to have you around, I bet."

"That's not why you called, is it? Come on, Michael."

When Gabriel called him "Michael" instead of Amigo, his canny friend was about to tell him how wrong he was about something. "Rowan's headed for Tora Prison, today. And I . . ."

His colleague interrupted him. "Holy Mother of God, why are you flying to Atlanta and why didn't you tell me about this before now?"

"I only found out a couple hours ago. I have an idea, but all my equipment is in one of Jerry and Bryan's hangars. It's a simple op and I need a spotter. Interested?"

"A simple op, Amigo? Aren't they all? Like you could find a better spotter. What's your *idea?"*

He glanced toward the door and saw Ainsley, Hennessey and Shemal. They crossed the customer service lounge without stopping. He stared after them. "Fuck me, they're here."

"Michael, what's going on?"

Twisting in the chair, he watched the threesome board the FBI's Gulfstream V. "Shemal's leaving on the Bureau's jet with Ainsley and . . . Never mind, I need to go. How soon can you meet me in Atlanta?"

"I can be there sometime late this afternoon. Is that soon enough?"

He flung the newspaper down and stood up. "It'll do. Call me when you land. See you soon." Outside, heading toward the passenger terminal, he saw the Bureau's jet taxi toward the runway. He wasn't going to make it to Washington in time to help his friend, but he would take a lot of pleasure in finishing some of what Rowan had started.

Derek took a deep breath and opened the front door. It felt great to be home. He stepped inside and shivered. The air felt chilly and the oak dining room table Danielle loved so much was covered with a fine layer of dust. The place smelled like the windows hadn't been opened for way too long, so he walked through the house opening all of them a crack. Wandering into the kitchen, he unlocked the patio door and flung it open, half expecting Danielle's Rottweiler Shasta to come bounding up from the pine-shaded, snowy backyard.

At least he didn't have to worry about taking care of her dog. He turned to check the counter for the bottle of Bacardi he'd left there over six months ago and stopped. The day Michael picked him up they'd waited for an hour until a woman arrived to pick up Shasta. Michael scared him almost as much as Rowan and the man had been impatient, pacing through the house and looking out the windows until the woman pulled up in a big, four-door pickup.

He dug the new phone the FBI had given him from his pocket. Before he started on the Bacardi and Coke to celebrate, he wanted to call Special Agent Winters. The FBI agent had arranged everything for him and he wanted to do whatever he could to help him find Rowan's friends.

The special agent answered right away. "Derek, is everything all right?"

This guy was nothing like Rowan. "Uh, sure. Everything's fine. I just remembered something else."

"That's great. What is it?"

He hoped it was something they could use. "Last year when Michael picked me up, his mother was here. She told me her name was Georgia. She lives on some West River ranch. I heard Chad and Michael talking one time in Kauai about Bettina needing a doctor and how his parents run a medical clinic, somewhere close to one of the Indian reservations. But I still don't know Michael's last name, sorry."

"Don't worry about that. This is great news. We'll run with it and see what we can find in western South Dakota. Thanks, Derek. If you think of anything else, give me a call."

After filling a glass with Bacardi and a can of Coke he found in the fridge, he went to the living room and settled down on the sofa. He took a long swallow and thought about how much fun he and Danielle used to have as housemates. The house felt empty without her. He drained the glass, trudged to the kitchen to make another drink and went back to the sofa.

Stretching out with his feet on the coffee table, he laughed out loud. *He wasn't a prisoner anymore.* Chad couldn't order him around and Rowan wasn't there to intimidate him. He massaged his neck. Rowan couldn't kill him from a prison cell. The jerk had ruined everything for him, but now, he had his life back, except for one thing. He gulped more rum and Coke, sat the glass on the coffee table and wiped his mouth.

Now that everything was back on track, he'd make his move. He'd wanted this for way too many years and thought he'd missed his chance. Maybe someday the jerk would know that in the end, he'd won. He found Danielle's number in his new phone and frowned at it. The FBI guys had tried everything they knew to trace the phone numbers he gave them, but nothing worked. That freaking genius Chad had somehow made it impossible.

He punched the number in and waited. She answered after a bunch of rings. "Derek? Where are you?"

The boozy haze made it easier to tell her what he'd wanted to for so many years. "Hi Dani. Listen, I'm in Sioux Falls, at the house. Got my job back at the 'port and everything. I thought . . . uh, you know, we've been together for so long. And, well you know, we've been through a lot. It's time for me to tell you that, uh, I'm in love with you. Ever since we first met. And uh, I was just hoping you could come back." She didn't say anything and he couldn't tell if she was still there. "Dani, did I lose you?"

Danielle's voice was so soft he had to concentrate hard to hear her. "Oh Derek. The last place in the world where I want to be is back in Sioux Falls, with you."

He fiddled with the glass and drank more, not sure he'd heard what she said. "I know it's probably a surprise. I was just sitting here in the living room, remembering how much fun we used to have. It would make everything perfect if you were here. Maybe you could get your old job back with Legacy. We could be together, like I've always dreamed about."

Her voice was louder. "Oh my God. Wow. Rowan told me over and over that you were in love with me and I never believed him. How could I have been so blind?"

Why did she have to bring *him* up? "What? How did he know? See, I couldn't *tell* you. I never thought I was good enough for you, until I made supervisor. Then I was going to talk to you, but *he* came and ruined everything for us."

Danielle's voice softened again. "I don't know how he knew, but it used to bug him, a lot. He even told me I belonged with you, when he left."

"Rowan said that?"

"Yes, he did. I think he never trusted me, even though I tried so many times to tell him that I didn't love you."

"How, I mean really, how could the totally badass Rowan Milani be worried about me? Shit. For once I agree with him. You do belong with me. He didn't deserve you."

"Derek, you were my best friend for so long. It was great sharing the house. But you're living in a dream world. I don't love you *that way.* I never did. I'm sorry. The last thing I want to do is hurt you. And I know you hate Rowan, but there's no one else for me but him." Her voice broke. "Even though I'll never see him again."

His face scrunched up. It felt like she'd punched him in the gut. "Dani, that's not right. He's gone for good, but I'm here for you, like I always have been."

"I know. But I can't . . . I don't want to *ever* be in the airport or the house again. The only thing I can do is move on."

He heard the misery in her voice, but couldn't get past his own pain. "Don't do this to me, Dani. It won't ever be the same without you. I've waited so long. Just give me a chance. We make a great team, remember? Everybody from the 'port always wanted to hang with us."

"Oh sure, party every night, because it's happy hour somewhere, right? I can't do that anymore. You can buy the house from me and have parties with everybody from the *'port.* I don't care. I just don't want to deal with it."

Somehow, Rowan had managed to screw him over from a prison cell. Pushing himself up off the sofa, he wobbled back and forth before heading to the kitchen for more Bacardi. "I guess it's over then, huh?"

Danielle's voice was muffled and it took him a second to figure out she was talking to someone else. Then she came back. "I've got to get going. Um, sorry, again. Thanks for calling, take care. Bye, Derek."

The phone went silent. He stared at it. She'd shafted him, for the creepy jerk who'd killed one of their best friends. "I hope you rot, wherever you are." Back in the kitchen, he emptied the bottle of Bacardi in his glass and looked at the clock. Maybe some of the guys would come over after work. They could order pizza and drink all night.

CHAPTER FIFTEEN

Rowan lay down on his bed in the cinderblock cell and raised a hand to cover his eyes. The lights in the ceiling stayed on 24/7. That was all right with him. He didn't want to sleep. In the infirmary, his body had given in to the exhaustion and the pain. He'd drifted off, only to feel the water and the tight straps. Over and over he'd woken, sweating and terrified, certain he was drowning.

His body tensed when he heard keys in the lock and he watched the door with dread. It opened and David came into the cell carrying a plastic wrapped sandwich and coffee in a paper cup. A guard carrying handcuffs followed. His stomach growled and his mouth watered. He turned his head away.

He started at a touch on his shoulder and turned to stare into his former friend's concerned brown eyes. "For God's sake, don't you get it? I can't stop you from fucking with me, but I'm never going to give up my friends . . . or tell you their names."

"I stepped way over the line yesterday. I never should have water boarded you. If I was still in the CIA, I'd probably be prosecuted."

He laid his hand back over his eyes. "Well then, aren't you the luckiest son of a bitch alive."

"Look, I'm sorry. We'll forego the interrogation room today and talk in here. Simple cuffs, that's it. This sandwich and coffee is for you. I've got some pain meds in my pocket. Come on. Sit up."

Knowing he didn't have a choice, he let his arm flop down at his side and winced as he swung his feet to the floor and pushed himself upright. "You remember Janice, my mother, don't you? You sound just like her. Hell, if you're sorry, then everything's fine. I mean, what the fuck? It was just a little water boarding. Nothing to get all bent out of shape about."

The guard stepped in front of him. "Stand up and move to the wall, please."

David gestured at the guard. "Just cuff him. It's all right."

The guard looked uneasy. "Sir, you warned us about how dangerous this prisoner is and that we need to exercise caution. I need to cuff his hands behind his back."

"Thank you for the input. I appreciate your concern, but I said, it's all right."

The guard didn't move. "Sir, if you don't want his hands behind his back, then we need to take him to the interrogation room so that I can restrain him. This is unsafe and goes against procedure."

David looked impatient. "Your concern is noted. I'll take responsibility in this instance."

The guard locked the cuffs on his wrists. "Yes sir."

Rowan watched the guard leave. David spoke as the door closed. "I can't undo what's been done. The President gave me carte blanche, told me to do whatever it took to get to the truth. Finding your cohorts in order to cut off whatever plans you've made is where I chose to start. You're such an arrogant prick, I got carried away."

He stared at the cold metal cuffs and fought a surge of rage, tried to tamp it down. If he reacted, he'd only be mistreated again and he wasn't sure how much more he could take. "Oh, I see, it was my fault. What's next on your list of *carte blanche?"*

David held out the sandwich. "Have something to eat. It's peanut butter and jelly, which if I remember correctly, is your favorite. The coffee isn't Starbucks, but it'll have to do. I've got some different questions for you today."

Suspicious of his captor's changed attitude, he eyed the sandwich. His mouth watered again. His arm throbbed and his entire body ached from struggling against the previous day's abuse. "OK."

While he wolfed down the sandwich and held the coffee between his knees, David pulled a bottle of pills from his shirt pocket, shook out three and held out his hand. "Take these and then we'll talk."

"OK." He downed the pills with lukewarm coffee.

David strode back and forth in the limited space. "Bettina told me about a flash drive she saw. She said it proves your innocence. Detective Matthews found a flash drive among the evidence collected when you were arrested in Houston. I'll have it today, as soon as Rodney Ainsley arrives."

His heart pounded and he immediately started sweating. "It's a list, of jihadists I eliminated at the President's request, but you'll never see that flash drive. Who else is arriving with Ainsley? And when?"

"I talked to Ainsley this morning. It shouldn't be too long before they arrive. Patricia Hennessey and Muusa Shemal are traveling with him. What are you talking about? Of course I'll see the flash drive. I'll ask the President to verify the names. If it checks out, I may be forced to revise my thoughts on you and this entire investigation."

The rage intensified. He was so goddamned helpless. He was powerless to stop them. "It's too late now, no matter what you check out. I tried to tell you."

A disembodied voice crackled into the cell. "Mr. Harandi, you have an urgent call on the secure line. You can pick it up wherever you'd like."

David shot him a puzzled look. "That's never happened. Let me take care of this and I'll be right back."

He watched David leave, heard him lock the door. The only sound was his harsh breathing. He'd failed. He hadn't ended the threat or taken out the major players. And now, it was too late.

* * *

Michael wiped sweat off his forehead. The hangar was humid, the air stagnant and smelling of oily grime. “Listen Gabriel, I know. We’re limited in what we can do. But from what Ralph told me, that woman may have been pulling the strings from the beginning of this whole mess.”

Gabriel kept sorting through the boxes and suitcases Michael had hurriedly shipped from Kauai to Business Jet Express, Jerry and Bryan’s base on the private side of Atlanta’s Hartsfield-Jackson International Airport. “You didn’t ask for a spotter because you think we’re limited in what we can do.”

Michael saw the box of ammo he’d been searching for and set it aside. “You’re a smart man. When Jerry and Bryan finish the trip they’re on, we’ll head for D.C. What I meant is that we’re limited in what we can do for Rowan at this stage. They’ll be guarding him better than Fort Knox in preparation for the transfer to Tora. The intelligence community and the Administration are not going to risk the embarrassment of letting him escape a third time. But we can’t stop trying. We’ve got to figure out a way to get him out of this. Maybe our new friend Johnny is the key. Ralph said he was planning something on Rowan’s behalf.”

“He’s obviously got a lot of resources. But right now, I want to know about the *simple op* I lied to Sherie about before I left.”

“It is simple. We’re going to finish what Rowan started. Ainsley was next on his list. If the President’s advisor – Patricia Hennessey, has been orchestrating things with Shemal, we’ll take her out as well. It’s the least we can do.”

Gabriel stared at him, wide-eyed. “You want to take out the Director of the FBI and the President’s advisor? In Washington, D.C.? Holy Mother of God. If Sherie divorces me before I’m executed, it’s on you.”

Michael saw real misgiving in his friend’s expressive eyes. “I need to know right now if you’re with me. When we started this operation, you and I agreed that in addition to keeping Rowan out of harm's way, we would help him take out whoever was responsible for collaborating with the real enemies of our country."

Gabriel made the sign of the cross. "Si, Amigo. I haven't forgotten."

"Good. Look, we've been taking care of risky business for this country for a damn long time. I'm not quitting and I'm not surrendering. Ainsley and Hennessey are committing treason by collaborating with Shemal. They're handing Rowan over – they're renditioning him to Egypt. No one else is ever going to make them accountable. They'll get away *scot-free* and Rowan will be out of reach forever. Whatever it takes, I'm going to finish this. I gotta ask you one more time, Amigo. Are you with me?"

The expressive eyes turned hard. "I'm here. Isn't that answer enough?"

He hefted his M110 sniper rifle. "It is. All right, I think we're about done here. We can ship most of this stuff to Dubai. I'm sending everything else to Pierre. Asal can pick it up and store it for me. When we're done with this op, I'm thinking we may need to back off for a while. We'll need time to get organized and coordinate with Johnny and Ralph. I can't think of a better place to make plans than with my woman."

"Sounds good to me. I hope I make it back to San Diego."

The kcy turned in the lock and Rowan's body went rigid. The door opened and the Director of the FBI strode into the cell and closed the door. Rodney paced back and forth, slapping his fist into his palm. "I've planned for this moment ever since you managed to escape from Quantico."

He watched warily, wondering why the Director hadn't brought guards along. Was Shemal waiting or watching? And where was David? Rodney gave him a baleful look. "You damn near ruined my career, not to mention the embarrassment you've caused the Bureau and the entire country."

The rage boiled over. Ainsley's career and reputation had been ruined by him? "You brought all that on yourself, when you decided to believe Shemal's lies about me."

The Director laughed. "You piece of shit. You fooled Johnston and Cantor, got them to betray their country too, but you've never fooled me. And now we're going to have a private interrogation session, just you and me."

He couldn't believe Rodney was arrogant enough to think he'd talk. "Go fuck yourself. I'm not answering any more questions."

Rodney stopped in front of him. "I'm not talking about that kind of interrogation." The man's fist was a blur, smashed into his jaw and sent him sideways onto the floor.

He landed on his injured arm and laid there, stunned. The Director kicked him in the gut, taking his breath away. He saw the foot coming toward his face and managed to fling up his hands, tangling his fingers in the pant leg. When he heaved his body over, Rodney's leg came with him. The rest of the gangly man did too, staggering over the top of him and crashing down.

The pant leg slipped through his fingers as Rodney scrambled to his feet. The man stood over him. "You raghead son of a bitch, I'm going to teach you a lesson you'll never forget."

He couldn't take any more pain. Adrenaline and rage gave him strength he didn't know he had. When the Director bent low to grab the collar of his jump suit, he rammed the heels of his hands into his opponent's throat. Rodney doubled over, gagging and grasping his throat with both hands. He took advantage of the distraction and raised his foot, kicking the inside of his adversary's knee, bringing him twisting down on top of him.

While Rodney screamed obscenities, Rowan gritted his teeth and forced his throbbing left forearm under the squirming man's neck. His reach was limited by the cuffs, but he pushed hard against Rodney's throat with his left wrist and dug into the scraggly hair and scalp with his right hand. Rodney choked but fought hard, bashing his head with bony knuckles and pounding his shins with sharp heels. He kept the pressure on while his arms shook and the cuffs scraped the skin off his wrists.

Rodney kept slapping at his face, but the flailing heels bounced on his legs with less power. It was the opportunity he needed. Shoving his left fist against his opponent's jaw, flattening his right palm against his temple, he twisted Rodney's head as hard and fast as he could. The satisfying crunch and snap came, like he knew it would. Then the heaving body went still.

Exhausted, he untangled his arms, shoved Rodney's body off of him and lay there, taking shallow, groaning breaths. Now they'd keep him in Quantico and he'd probably be executed. But by God, he'd taken out one of the real traitors. He heard a key in the lock again and turned his head, hoping to see David instead of guards. The door opened and he swallowed hard. The imposing bulk of CIA agents Seth Hancock and Lucien Talbot filled the doorway. The two men carried chains and restraints. They grinned at him until they saw Rodney's body lying beside him.

Seth tossed the clanking chains to Lucien. "Get him off the floor and restrain him. I'll check on Ainsley."

Behind them, Rowan saw pointy-toed shoes and muscular, nylon clad legs. He blinked and followed the legs higher until they disappeared under a narrow skirt. Above that, staring down with a horrified look was a woman who despised him. "What the hell have you done? Rodney, are you all right? I knew he shouldn't have come in here alone."

Lucien reached down, wrapped one massive hand around his injured arm, lifted him straight up from the floor with barely a grunt and slammed him against the wall. His head smacked the cinder-block surface. His chest ached and burned and he moaned with every breath. Lucien pressed a knee against his legs and forced his arms up. While he grimaced at the pain, the blonde agent padlocked the chain around his waist and locked his cuffed wrists to the chain.

Seth crouched next to Rodney's body and twisted around to give him a disbelieving look. "You killed him."

Patricia wailed. *"No, no, no.* He's got to be unconscious. Call the medics. We've got to start CPR." She fell to her knees and pushed on the prone chest. He heard the anguish in her voice. "You're wrong. You've got to be wrong."

The adrenaline rush was long gone and he wanted to slide down the wall, but Lucien kept him pinned. The agent stared, outrage displacing the usual cruelty in his brown eyes. "You killed the Director of the FBI."

Seth put an arm around Patricia. "He's gone, Madam Advisor. We need to move Milani *now.* When this goes public, the Bureau will take over. Shemal will be screwed and so will we."

Seth stood up and helped Patricia to her feet before turning toward him. Grabbing the leg irons from Lucien, the big man squatted beside him. The cold metal closed around his ankles. The two men who'd permanently damaged his body, whose faces he still saw in his nightmares held all the power. Again. Seth stood up. "If Shemal wasn't waiting, I'd finish the job we started in Sioux Falls."

The rage stirred again, deep inside. He glared into the pig-like eyes beneath the jutting forehead. "Allahu Akbar, motherfucker."

Lucien yanked him away from the wall by one arm. "You never learn, do you? Stupid raghead." The huge fist drew back, the muscles in the thick arm bulging.

Patricia slapped her hand on Lucien's wrist. "Stop, he's already got a cut on his face and Shemal insisted that he be unmarked." She clawed hair out of her face. "But this won't show."

He saw the pointy-toed shoe coming. She kicked him squarely in the testicles and he dropped. Lucien let go of his arm and he writhed on the floor, choking and gagging. She kept kicking him, her sharp-toed shoe stabbing his legs and kidneys. The fierce agony in his groin spread into his gut and he curled up, unable to catch his breath.

David burst into the tiny cell. "What the hell is going on? Patricia, what are you doing? Who are these men? Rodney? Rowan, are you all right? Good God, what happened in here?"

Patricia shrieked. "This *animal* killed Rodney. My agents are taking him. You need to help me. Lucien, get him up. Get him out of my sight."

Lucien hoisted him to his feet, but his knees buckled. David gripped an arm and he sagged between the two men, feeling like someone was trying to hack their way out of his balls with a knife.

David's face was brick red. "He's my prisoner and he's not going anywhere. How the *hell* did this happen? I want answers right now."

Patricia flung her arms in the air. "Rodney is *dead.* This piece of shit is no longer your prisoner. Lucien, Seth, take him. We'll deal with . . . we'll take care of Rodney. Oh God, I have to cancel the press conference. Don't say anything to the press, just get him on the plane."

Rowan squinted up at the Neanderthal agent while the stabbing agony continued. "You're a pussy. I'd slice her fucking throat wide open and watch her bleed out before I'd take orders from her."

The enormous man ripped him out of David's grasp and put the massive fist intended for his face in his solar plexus instead. Bent double, the breath driven forcibly from his lungs, he fell against the wall and stayed there, groaning and choking.

David went apoplectic. *"That's enough. This shit ends right now."*

Patricia ignored the outrage in David's voice. "Don't get in my way. This traitor is going to Tora Prison in Cairo. My CIA agents are transporting him."

David grabbed his arm again and forced his body upright. "Tora? Cairo? Have you lost your mind? If he killed the Director of the FBI, he's staying right here."

Patricia stalked to the door and swung around, crossing her arms. "The President authorized this transfer. The aircraft and crew are waiting. Let him go or I'll have you detained, right here in this cell."

David scoffed. "I'd like to see you try. I'm calling the President right now."

Rowan leaned against his former friend and mumbled. "It's too late. Ask Chad . . . call Mike."

Lucien yanked him away and Seth latched onto his sore arm. He caught David's angry, bewildered gaze for an instant, then the agents jerked him around and dragged him out the door.

It was quiet on the jet – *his* jet. He would leave no more tasks to the kafir nation's useless intelligence services. Muusa sipped fragrant Jasmine tea and waited, thinking about what procuring his prize had cost. The Brotherhood's resources were endless, but capturing the Jinn had cost him, personally, more than he'd expected. He pictured his habibti, Marta, with her soft white skin. He'd never find another so skilled at satisfying him.

He swallowed more tea and ran through their names. Mohammad, Amir, Firouz, Asad, and countless others. The Jinn was responsible for many deaths, either by his own hand or by making the American President aware of his warriors, so that drones could take their lives. Now, though, the bloody sacrifices would be avenged.

The challenges had not defeated him, nor had the losses he'd suffered. Allah had rewarded him at last. The Jinn belonged to him now, to do with as he chose. It would take time, but he and the Brothers were patient. His lips curled. Forbearance was but one trait that made his people superior to the foolish Americans.

The tea grew cold and he sat the cup aside. The Americans clamored for immediate gratification like spoiled children. Allah had seen to it that the callow nation had the attention span of children as well. In a short time the upheaval caused by the country's supposed traitor murdering the Director of the FBI would die away.

America would forget. Then, Rowan Milani's true suffering would begin. It would not end until all the blood that cried from the ground was satisfied. It would not end until Allah chose the day of the man's death.

The sound of a vehicle pulling up and doors slamming ended his reverie. Craning his neck and peering out the window, he saw the CIA agents pull his captive from the black Suburban. Pleasure filled his soul as he watched their slow progress to the stairs of the jet. He turned away and folded his hands in his lap. Now he would take possession of what was rightfully his.

He heard the clang of chains and labored breathing coming closer. The muscular blonde agent moved past him and then, his prize half fell into the seat facing him. Snapping his fingers, he dismissed the big men. "Leave us. Seat yourselves in the front and tell my pilots we must leave immediately."

The two agents moved back up the aisle. His prize looked disheveled. Sweat darkened the orange jumpsuit beneath Milani's arm pits and across his heaving chest, telling him that the man was in pain. But only malevolent hubris radiated from the dark eyes. He relished the thought of how he would humble Rowan Milani before Allah.

His flight crew wasted no time. The Lear Jet rose into the air with the muted roar of powerful engines. He unbuttoned his suit coat. It was time to make himself more comfortable for the long flight. Perhaps he would dine on succulent lamb. Then he would retire, in order to be well-rested. Before arriving, he would cleanse his body and choose appropriate adornment for his triumphal arrival in Cairo.

Watching closely, he saw a glimmer of fear cross the otherwise inscrutable face and observed how his captive's throat convulsed. Fear was appropriate. "Preparations for celebration are underway in Egypt. A fitting home awaits you in Tora. I will see that you have a long life there."

His prize leaned to one side and didn't seem to have the strength to sit up straight. But Milani's dark eyes swiveled to meet his. "You ended my life a year ago. One day, I will end yours."

He crossed one leg over the other. "Typical American braggadocio."

Rowan bent low to wipe his nose on his hands, then raised his head and sniffed. "I'm not bragging. I'm giving you fair warning."

His good humor faded and the heat of anger rose. "You speak bold threats for one who sits before me beaten and trussed in chains. Allah would have you learn true humility at my hand."

Rowan sneered. "Fuck you. Fuck Allah."

The deliberate blasphemy further ignited his outrage. Twinges of pain crossed his chest. He began to understand why the CIA agents had not been able to resist assaulting the man. He pulled the loaded syringe he had prepared earlier from his suit pocket. "I will administer the same drug my holy warriors used before you murdered them. Perhaps while you are unconscious, I will sever your tongue. Or remove what every man cherishes above all else."

Rowan gave him a derisive look. "No, you won't. You don't have the balls. I'm not just *your* prize, jerk wad. The Brotherhood wants to pass me around, so that everybody can have a piece. You have to obey your masters."

His nostrils flared and his hands shook. How did the Jinn know the Brotherhood's plans? He longed for the moment when the proud man began to learn true humility. His snapping fingers brought the black-haired agent to his side. "Yes, Mr. Shemal?"

He gestured at his captive. "Make his arm ready."

The agent nodded and knelt next to Rowan, covered the man's bloody, cuffed wrist with one hand, grasped his elbow with the other and twisted his arm flat. "Is this what you need, sir?"

Noting Milani's clenched fists and grunt of pain, he nodded. He trailed his finger along the vein he wanted, inserted the needle and injected the contents of the syringe into the Jinn's circulatory system while staring at his unrepentant face.

He shed his suit coat and retook his seat. Rowan's fists relaxed, his eyes closed and his head tipped forward. Muusa took a deep breath and let it out slowly, savoring one more moment of victory over his enemy.

Chad looked up as the interrogation room door flew open and David strode in. The look on the other man's face sent his heart rate spiraling. His palms started sweating, but he couldn't wipe them on the jump suit because they were cuffed and chained to the table. If something had happened to Bettina . . .

David sat in the chair across from his, smacked a notepad and pen on the table and shoved them toward him. "I need your help. Rowan has a colleague named Michael. I need his phone number. Write it down for me. I don't want you to say it."

"You know I can't give you that number."

"Look, Rowan's on his way to Tora Prison, with Muusa Shemal and his CIA handlers. Before they hauled him off, he broke Rodney Ainsley's neck. He managed to tell me that I needed to talk to you. He told me to ask you for Michael's phone number."

Torn between shock and dismay, he stared. "So you did have Rowan in custody . . . how could he kill Ainsley? Oh God . . . and now Shemal has him?"

David tapped an impatient finger on the table. "Look, I'm sorry, but I need that number. This entire shit show has taken a turn I never expected. What I thought was truth now appears to be fiction. I've learned more in twenty minutes with your fiancée than I did in a couple hours of enhanced interrogation with Rowan."

He jerked his head up. "What? With Bettina? What did you do to her?"

David laughed, but sounded bitter. "I didn't *do* anything to her. We talked. She told me about a flash drive that would prove Rowan's innocence."

"How did she . . . I don't believe it. She and Danielle. I never knew she'd sneak around like that."

David rubbed his goatee vigorously. "You need to remember who she's related to. You might also want to think twice about leaving her in a room with someone she doesn't like. *Anything* could happen. Now, give me the number and tell me what to expect from Michael."

He folded his hands. "I'll give you the number, but I want one thing first."

"Last time I checked, you were not in a position to bargain."

It was his turn to laugh. "Neither are you, apparently."

David threw up his hands. "All right. You want a visit with your fiancée?"

"Rowan told me you were a smart guy and not to underestimate what you'd do. Yes, take me to wherever she is and I'll give you more than Mike's phone number. Now that Rowan's in Shemal's hands, you have to let me help you. For his sake."

* * *

The President finished his dinner with the First Lady and retired to his private office in the living quarters of the White House. A Secret Service agent approached. “Mr. President, Ms. Hennessey says it is most urgent that she see you. She says it cannot wait.”

“All right, tell her I’ll meet her in the West Wing in ten minutes.”

“Yes sir.”

When she arrived at the West Wing office, Patricia stood in the middle of the room, wringing her hands. Her eyes were bloodshot, her hair in disarray. He’d never seen her so distraught. “Patricia, what is it?”

She sank into one of the overstuffed chairs. “Sir, Rodney is dead. Milani killed him.”

Shocked, he sank down in the adjacent chair. “When did this happen and *how?*”

Patricia covered her face for a moment and then gave him a bitter look. “Rodney wanted to interrogate Milani privately. He insisted we give him ten minutes alone. Milani overpowered him and we found him on the floor of the cell with his neck broken.”

The President stared, aghast. “We need to investigate this thoroughly and see that justice is done. Cancel the transport to Tora. Also, I want to see the surveillance recording from that cell as soon as possible.”

“Milani is already en route to Tora. My agents transported him immediately. Mr. Shemal has been patient . . . he’s paid . . . he’s worked with us, helped us capture Milani. I wasn’t going to disappoint him again.”

Patricia had just unintentionally confirmed what he’d had an aide delve into after his last conversation with Clifton. “In what manner and to who has Mr. Shemal made payment?”

“I said . . . what I meant is that he’s used his own resources to search for Milani and he’s paid dearly, in assisting us.”

The President watched Patricia’s face. Her lips formed a thin line. She wouldn’t meet his eyes. “We’ll come back to that in a moment. You will contact Shemal *now* and get that aircraft turned around. Milani is an American citizen and he's murdered one of the highest law enforcement officials in the country. That changes everything. I don't care how much Shemal has invested, Milani must be returned. The CIA agents on board can facilitate his return to Quantico."

"Sir, we cannot afford the loss of goodwill with our Egyptian allies. The Muslim Brotherhood, represented by Mr. Shemal has contributed too much. We must not lose their trust."

The President stood up. "We support our Egyptian allies with billions of dollars every year. If we choose to prosecute one of our own citizens in our own country, that is our sovereign choice. Perhaps Mr. Shemal and the Brotherhood should concern themselves with not losing *our* goodwill."

Patricia looked up at him and touched her straggling hair. "Mr. Shemal has saved this administration from untold damage by Milani's treasonous actions. We owe him."

He faced her, hands on hips. "This conversation is over. You are mistaking me for someone with whom you can argue or negotiate. Contact Shemal and your CIA agents on board. Inform them that I intend for Milani to be transported back to Quantico – *immediately.*"

"Mr. President, I can't do that. You're making a mistake."

He interrupted her. "Madam Advisor, you're relieved. I no longer require your services. The Secret Service will escort you from the premises. I will forward the contents of your office to your home address."

Her chest heaved as she stood up. "You . . . sir, you don't mean that. I have made this administration my life. I've helped you the whole way. You owe your success . . . it's all because of *me.*"

The President walked to his desk and pressed a button on the phone. "I need a Secret Service escort, please. Yes, right away. Thank you."

Patricia teetered back and forth. "Sir, please, you can't take this away from me. You owe me," she whispered.

After a gentle knock, the door opened, admitting two agents. Whitman gestured toward Patricia. "Please escort Ms. Hennessey to her home and see that she's settled." The agents grasped her by the elbows and Patricia went with them, eyes glazed with tears. He nodded at the two men. "Thank you."

When she was gone, he sat at the desk and pulled his personal cell from his pocket. He punched the contact he wanted. "David. I need to see you now. I'll send a car. Bring the video of Milani and Ainsley. I want to know exactly what happened before the media gets a hold of the story." He ended the call and folded his hands together on the desk.

Making another decision, he pressed the button on the phone again. "Bring Clifton Cantor here, right away. Thank you." He leaned back in the chair. One way or another, he would get to the truth. He pressed the button one more time. "We have a problem. I need to contact an aircraft bound for Egypt."

CHAPTER SIXTEEN

Michael stared out the second story window of the hotel room he and Gabriel had settled into. His phone vibrated in his shirt pocket and he dug it out. The number was one he didn't recognize. "Identify yourself."

A low-key voice with a subtle accent answered. "This is David Harandi. Is this Michael?"

Surprise left him speechless and the voice became urgent. "Rowan told me I needed to call you. Chad Cantor gave me your number. Some information has come to light that changes the focus of my investigation."

Gabriel joined him at the window. He laid a finger on his lips and put the phone on speaker. "Convince me that you've been with Chad and Rowan. Maybe after that, I'll talk."

The phone sounded like it was being passed around. Chad spoke, sounding strained. "Mike, it's me. I'm in the brig at Quantico. I gave David your number. Bettina told him about Rowan's flash drive with all his kills on it. You've got details about past operations with Rowan that I don't have. And Mike, Rowan killed Ainsley before Shemal took him."

He muttered, "Fuck me."

Gabriel looked alarmed. "Holy Mother . . ."

David came back. "Is that sufficient? What I'd like more than anything is to meet with you. I give you my word that it's not a trick. I won't attempt to bring you in. No one knows I'm contacting you."

He gave Gabriel a questioning look. "Let's have a phone conversation first. What exactly did Rowan want you to contact me about?"

David sounded rushed. "This is risky for me too and I don't have much time. I need details about what's on the flash drive for one thing. I thought I'd have access to it myself, but that didn't happen. Rowan told me his sources figured out things about Shemal. If I'm going to sort this out, I need that information. Will you meet with me or not?"

Gabriel met his eyes and whispered. "Do it, Amigo."

Michael gazed across the street at the entrance to Quantico Marine Base. "Yes, I'll meet with you."

David sounded relieved. "How long will it take you to get to Washington? Or, can I fly somewhere to meet you?"

"I'll meet with you in twenty-four hours, in the sauna at the Sleep Inn, by the main gate of Quantico. Come naked."

The video recording ended with medics placing Rodney's body on a gurney and removing it from the cell while he and Patricia watched. The glow of the laptop screen revealed the deepening concern in President Whitman's face. David cleared his throat. "I'm sorry I couldn't stop them from taking Milani, sir. The agents were armed, and I am certain they would have obeyed Patricia, had she instructed them to detain me. I thought it would be more productive to remain free."

Whitman turned toward him. "You made the correct decision. After talking with Patricia this evening, it's obvious to me that she would have stopped at nothing to place Milani in Shemal's hands."

"Thank you sir. Are the agents on their way to Quantico with Milani now?"

The Commander in Chief looked grave. "The aircraft ignored our instructions. Did you know Milani was transported on an Egyptian aircraft operated by Muusa Shemal instead of our jet? The CIA agents' phones went to voice mail. I chose not to intercept the jet and risk an international incident with Egypt. I'll have more leverage if I approach the situation through other channels."

Looking up at a quiet knock, David was surprised when two Secret Service agents escorted a hooded and handcuffed man with a lanky frame into the office. They sat him firmly in an adjacent chair and lifted the black hood. The taller, bald agent removed the cuffs. Clifton rubbed his face with both hands and smoothed his hair.

The President observed Clifton for a moment. "It's going to be a long night. We've got a lot of rethinking to do and Clifton has information that I believe will be enlightening."

David settled deeper into his chair and cracked his knuckles. "Getting at the truth when it's being purposely obscured is an arduous process. However, the *truth* is what you and I have been after since the beginning, correct?"

Whitman's look turned quizzical. "Of course. Are you questioning that?"

He contemplated the lean face, knowing he was treading on dangerous ground. "It seems that although Milani's counter-terror exploits were conducted at your specific instruction, you were quick to condemn him. In addition, you made no active effort to determine whether or not you were being lied to by your closest advisors."

Clifton blinked at him. "You've got even bigger balls than I gave you credit for, Mr. Harandi. Be careful. Look where your help put me."

The President looked from him to Clifton and back. "At the outset, I placed Milani in Ralph Johnston's custody. All the while, I received a continuous stream of intelligence reports from Rodney and Patricia, both well vetted and trusted members of my administration. Those reports confirmed that while Milani was supposedly acting on the country's behalf, he was actually undermining and betraying the country."

David massaged his jaw. "But you allowed Rodney special access to you, instead of funneling his input through the Director of National Intelligence. And you courted Muusa Shemal, to the point of personally authorizing an American citizen to be renditioned to Egypt. Why would that be preferable to Quantico or Gitmo? I could have interrogated Milani effectively in either place to find the truth. If, as you say, that is what you were seeking."

The President's face hardened. "The reason the Director of National Intelligence was never briefed is because Milani's operations were known and authorized exclusively by *me*. For all practical purposes, he didn't exist. My predecessor called him our *ghost agent.* Patricia entered the loop by accident and she brought Rodney along. Things proceeded from there. But get to your point. What are you hinting at?"

David eyed the President. "Sir, I don't intend to hint at anything. I'm a simple man. The machinations of politics and power are out of my purview. You can give me an assignment, point me in a direction and I'll go until I get the answers."

Whitman threw up his hands. "We've got a lot of ground to cover, so please make your point."

"Mr. President, I believe political expediency has driven this entire debacle. Rather than risk Milani's exploits coming to light and damaging your presidency or our country's standing in the world, you let him become a scapegoat."

Clifton leaned forward, hands clasped together. "He's right, isn't he, Gil?"

The Commander in Chief looked uncomfortable. "The situation surrounding Milani is complex. I've had to consider more than just his guilt or innocence. I suppose the most uncomplicated answer, for a simple man such as yourself, is yes."

As the last vestiges of the respect he'd held for Gilford Whitman crumbled, anger and disgust took hold. He gestured at Clifton and drove home his point. "So, while you've remained above the fray, shielded from any complicity, innocent people have been detained or forced into hiding. Their lives and careers have been destroyed because they possessed the courage to stand by their falsely accused colleague. And your gutless, political decision keeps bearing fruit, doesn't it? The Director of the FBI is dead. A CIA agent is dead. Numerous others are dead as well. It's likely Milani will join them."

Both Clifton and the President stared at him. Neither man seemed inclined to speak. He'd overstepped his bounds, but he didn't care. He wasn't finished. He met the President's dispassionate gaze. "Sir, you've deceived me from the outset. You planned all along to send Milani to Egypt with CIA handlers. I trust that decision was based on political concerns as well. You'll understand, I'm certain, why I must tender my resignation from this *assignment.*"

Clifton became animated. "Gil, it's gratifying to hear another, independent source confirm much of what I've known. It is unfortunate that Patricia and Rodney lied to you. Don't let him resign. You need an uncompromising voice of truth, now more than ever."

The President folded his hands on the desktop, looking weary. "Earlier tonight I dismissed Patricia from her position, after twenty years of being my closest advisor. I followed your counsel, Clifton. You were right. Both Patricia and Rodney have received substantial sums of money recently. It's been cleverly disbursed, of course."

David raised a brow. "Chad gave me that same information today. He also informed me that the CIA handlers Patricia hired had been paid $250,000.00 *apiece* to deliver Milani to Shemal."

The Commander in Chief bent his head for a moment and then met David's eyes. "I do *not* accept your resignation. Clifton is right. I need the unvarnished truth, wherever it leads. Regarding Milani, what started as a black op so clandestine that only I and the previous President knew about it blew up when Muusa Shemal . . ."

David watched as the President's eyes narrowed and the muscles in his jaw tightened. "We need to investigate Shemal's connections. If not for his involvement, Milani would never have come under suspicion."

Clifton responded. "Although I agree that it is necessary, isn't it a bit late to begin an investigation of Mr. Shemal's connections? But since you've managed to veer into the truth, may I go home now? And will you please release my son and his fiancée?"

The President looked grim. "Patricia assured me of Shemal's integrity from the outset. Until we have rock solid proof of his wrongdoing, the release of *anyone* will be jumped on by the media. Let's not forget, Milani did murder the Director of the FBI. The intelligence community and the entire country will expect justice. He'll still face charges here. You're a different story, Clifton. Your detention is officially over. I'm sure it isn't adequate, but I apologize. I would appreciate your continued involvement in this matter."

David frowned. "Mr. President, you saw the video. Milani's life was in danger. He acted in self-defense. In the same situation, I would have eliminated the threat to my life in much the same way he did."

Clifton crossed one leg over the other. "I'll stay involved in order to help you find the truth and exonerate my son. But Gil, none of this is going to matter if Milani is dead. Getting him back to the U.S. is paramount."

The President nodded decisively. "I'll do everything I can to guarantee Milani's return. Now, I want a complete briefing on every scrap of information either of you have on Shemal and this entire debacle. Let's get started."

* * *

The Next Day

Helen Evans stood behind her husband, hands planted on his shoulders while he sat across the table from FBI Special Agents Miller and Jones. She didn't know how hard she was squeezing until Charlie gently peeled her hands away. She slid into the chair next to him and looked at the two men. "We've heard from Danielle."

Special Agent Jones was blonde and the older of the two agents. "That's great news. Did she let you know where she's been or where she is now?"

Charlie patted her hand, then turned to face the special agents. "Helen can tell you all about it. She spoke to Danielle longer than I did."

Special Agent Jones opened a black leather portfolio and pulled a pen from his shirt pocket. "Talk to me, Helen. Tell me what you remember of the conversation."

She didn't know where to start. "Dani called yesterday morning. I thought she sounded good, maybe a bit lonely. She didn't tell us where she is, but she wants to come home."

The special agent quit writing and gave her a quizzical look. "We've discussed how to converse with her in the event of a call. Did you get a feeling as to whether she is under duress or being coached in what to say? You made sure not to mention that the FBI has been searching for her, correct?"

Charlie stirred and she looked at him. "Go ahead, dear. Did you think of something she said?"

Her husband ran a hand through the thick, dark red hair that had started graying at the temples. "We only talked for a few minutes, but I felt she was being careful about what she said, like maybe she wasn't alone. Also, given the fact that she was associated with a domestic terrorist, I'd have to think she would assume that the FBI was searching for her."

Helen focused on Jones. "I didn't say a word about the FBI. Dani didn't sound like she was afraid or being held against her will. She apologized over and over for being out of touch and said it was a long story. Then she sounded sad and said she missed us and wanted to come home and start over."

Special Agent Jones tapped his pen on the legal pad. "It's likely that your daughter is still with Milani's associates. It's interesting that she talked about starting over. However, given the circumstances . . ."

Special Agent Jones glanced at his dark haired companion, who'd sat so quietly that Helen had almost forgotten he was there. She wondered what details the agents weren't giving them. "If she wants to come home and is apparently free to do that, it doesn't matter who she's with now, does it?"

Miller looked at Charlie and then her. "That's true. The most important thing is reuniting you two with your daughter. We'd like to debrief her, but the Bureau has no interest in or need to detain her. Her freedom was secured by Milani last year."

His words assuaged her doubts. "Thank you. The fact that he surrendered on her behalf convinced me that she was never in any real danger when she was with him. I'm ready to call her back. It's been hard to wait until you could get here."

Special Agent Jones looked sympathetic. "This has been a long road for you two. Let's hope we can bring it to an end soon. Go ahead and call. Just be yourself, happy and excited to have your daughter coming home."

She looked at Charlie. He was grinning at her, laugh lines crinkling around the slate blue eyes he'd passed on to Danielle. Grabbing her iPhone with shaky fingers, she took a deep breath and tapped the contact.

Danielle answered right away. "Mom? Thanks so much for calling back. I bought a ticket for a flight, but it'll be a few days before I can leave. Thanks for letting me move in. But it won't be forever, of course. Just long enough for me to figure out what to do with my life."

Hearing the simple happiness in her daughter's voice brought tears to her eyes. If only she could hug her. She jumped in when Danielle took a breath. "We're excited too, darling. Your father and I talked about it. You can take over the entire lower level and stay with us as long as you want. Don't worry, we'll work it out. When will you arrive? Can you give me the flight info?"

Her talkative daughter became reticent. "Um, if it's OK, I'll just call you the night before I leave, and again when I land."

Helen glanced at Special Agent Miller before answering. "That sounds fine. We can't wait to see you. I'm looking forward to doing some of the things we used to before, when you lived in Seattle. It's been so long, Dani. Oh, I've been dying to ask – any chance of a visit from that amazing man you told us about last spring?"

She'd been trying so hard to be upbeat and keep her tone light, that the whole conversation felt stilted. When Danielle answered, she winced at the raw pain in her voice. "Oh Mom, he's not here. Like I said, it's a long story. One I'm trying to put behind me."

"Hang in there, kiddo. Stay busy and before you know it, we'll be watching the fish mongers, trying to decide between swordfish steaks or king salmon filets for dinner."

Danielle laughed, but the earlier happiness was gone. "I can't wait. I'm dying to see you both."

Helen felt guilty about her subterfuge. "Stay in touch and let us know the details when you can. Take care, Dani. We love you."

Her daughter whispered and Helen wondered whether she was crying or if someone had come into earshot. "Bye Mom, I love you too. See you soon."

She stared at the ceiling for a moment, realizing that she'd been tense and rigid for the entire call. Leaning forward, she rubbed her forehead and looked from Charlie to the two agents. "It breaks my heart to *deceive* her. She sounded so sad. This was a lot harder than the first time we talked. Special Agent Jones, are you sure the FBI isn't going to want to take our daughter in for questioning?"

Jones looked pleased. "Helen, you handled the conversation like a pro. You have my word. Danielle is free to live her life as she chooses."

Unable to shake the guilty sadness, she gave Jones and Miller a sober look. "I handled the conversation like a mother. The only thing I care about is our daughter returning safely to us."

Special Agent Miller replied. "No one is going to prevent that from happening. We'll meet her in the airport and debrief her. Then she'll be free to go home with the two of you and move on with her life."

David grasped the door handle and pulled. A wave of dry, wood-scented heat inundated him. Inside the sauna, along the back wall sat a lean, muscular black-haired man wearing nothing but a towel draped over his lap. One hand rested beneath the towel. The other held a smart phone. He met the man's appraising stare. "Michael, I presume? I'm David Harandi. Thank you for agreeing to meet with me."

The hand emerged from beneath the towel, gripping a forty-five caliber 1911 pistol. "The only reason we're having this meeting is because Rowan told you to contact me."

He touched the towel wrapped around his waist. "Fair enough. As you can see, I have nothing to hide."

Michael wiped at a line of sweat on his face. "What kind of operational information do you need?"

"I need to know how Rowan put together information on Shemal showing that he's part of a terrorist organization."

"Why didn't you ask Rowan about that?"

Sweat formed on David's forehead. "My interrogation sessions were supposed to focus on taking down his organization and finding two key players – Michael and Gabriel. We'd barely gotten started with the process. He flat-out refused to divulge any information, until just before the CIA agents took him away."

"That sounds like Rowan. I'm sure you made it as difficult for him as possible."

He eyed the 1911. "I did my job. As I said on the phone, I want details about what's on the flash drive. Why was he betrayed? And how? I need to sort things out if I'm going to proceed."

Michael rested the gun on one knee. "My source can give you pertinent data about Shemal and the Brotherhood's plans. I can tell you why and how Rowan was betrayed in the first place, and then we'll make a call. After that, we'll talk about the flash drive."

David raised both hands. "Start talking. I'm listening."

"We started running ops about a year after 9/11. After Rowan read *The Project,* he spent most of his spare time searching for the Brotherhood's leader in this country, the tip of the spear, you might say."

"Is that how he came across Shemal?"

"You're smarter than you look. What we didn't know was that Shemal had been tasked by the Brotherhood to figure out who kept killing their holy warriors, diverting their precious funds and screwing up their plans."

Shifting on the hard wooden bench, David began to realize how badly he'd misjudged his former friend. "So, Shemal must have deduced that Rowan was the one. Do you know how that happened?"

"Yes, I know exactly how that happened. Rowan had a network of sources, people with access to information, who loved the United Sates and wanted to serve the country in some capacity. Some of them were even long-time friends."

Feeling sick to his stomach, he rubbed his sweaty forehead. "Please continue."

Michael arched a brow. "All right. Shemal had this one particular source abducted. He tortured him brutally. Over a week's time he cut off his hand and mutilated his body, until the source gave up Rowan's name. Once Shemal had that information, it wasn't difficult for him to find willing accomplices to testify to the fact that Rowan was a double agent."

Sadness engulfed him. "Who was the source?"

The blue eyes were cold. "Oh, I think you already know."

Janice stared heartbroken at the television. A shredded tissue lay in her lap. How many times must she watch as her only son was taken away? And this time, she knew in her heart that he would never return. Seeing his bleeding face, she touched her cheek. If only she could help him. Her eyes filled with tears when the two big men jerked on his arms. He looked so helpless.

She shut off the TV, pulled more tissues from the box and wept quietly. Rowan would never know how much she cared for him, how she longed and prayed for a happy life for him and Danielle. He was too full of bitterness. It had born ugly fruit in his life and in all their lives. Her precious Bettina, carrying their first grandchild had paid a price for Rowan's thirst for revenge. Now it would take him away from them forever.

A gentle touch on her shoulder had her looking up, expecting Khalil or maybe Marion. She was surprised to see the man who had so graciously offered his home to all of them. He looked disturbed. "Mrs. Milani, why are you sitting all alone in here crying? It's never good to mourn alone. Let me get you a drink and you can tell me what's on your mind."

How could she explain to a stranger how she was feeling? Before she could tell him no, he had poured two glasses of whiskey from a decanter and sat down on a chair next to the sofa where she was huddled. She took the glass of amber liquid. “Thank you, Mr. Giacopino and please, my name is Janice.” Not knowing what else to say, she lifted the glass. The fumes made her cough, but she sipped and swallowed.

He watched her and then took a gulp from his glass. “Ah, that’s good for whatever ails a person. Or so my mother used to say, may God rest her soul. You come from an old Italian family in Chicago.”

It was a statement, not a question, and she wondered what he knew about her family. She took a deeper swallow of whiskey and felt it burn all the way down. Her insides began to relax. “Yes, my entire family still lives in Chicago. When I married Khalil, we moved to California where he was attending college.”

“And raised a couple of good lookin’, smart kids. One of whom has caused you considerable heartache, by the looks of things.”

Fresh tears brimmed in her eyes. Wiping them with the tissue, she drank more whiskey, surprised to see that she had emptied the glass. “Rowan was always a passionate, strong-willed boy and he grew into a man with such courage. But now . . .”

He patted her knee and poured more whiskey for her. “Let me tell you a secret, Janice. Things aren’t always what they seem. I’m going to make you a promise today and I don’t want you to forget it. You with me?”

She downed more whiskey and nodded. “I’ll do my best.”

Johnny held his glass in both hands and looked smug. “I’ve got a plan being organized as we speak. It’s one of those deals that take a little time and finesse to put together, if you know what I mean. I figured out something about that son of a . . . that *man* who has your son.”

She sipped more of the pungent liquid, wondering what in the world he was talking about. “I see.”

He raised his glass and clanked it against hers. "I came across the one thing more important to him than Rowan. And that's called leverage. Once everything is in place, we'll knock him upside the head until he doesn't want your son anymore."

Fear clutched at her heart. "Oh dear Lord. If he doesn't want him, he might kill him."

"That will not happen. Trust me, when it's all said and done, he'll hand Rowan back to us, alive and well."

She finished her second glass of whiskey. "Mr. Giacopino, I hope with all my heart that you are right. I will pray for your plan."

He winked at her. "You do that."

The voices echoed in his head. *Stand up! Move! Step down. Worthless piece of shit. Fucking dog.* Rough hands slapped, punched and shoved him. Rowan opened his eyes and stared up at the bleak ceiling. The cold from the tiled floor seeped into his body through thin material and his teeth chattered. His injured arm felt hot and swollen. Using his right hand, he lifted it and winced.

Distant voices hollering in Arabic wafted through the barred window, along with the stench of shit and rotting garbage. Something scuttled across his bare foot and his leg twitched. He held his weakened left hand with his right and closed his eyes, trying to take stock of his body. It was all pain. Each breath, every movement. He closed his eyes as consciousness ebbed away.

His moans woke him and he tried to swallow but his mouth was too dry. He tongue felt thick. He still lay flat, but his body had numbed and he didn't want to move . . . didn't think he could. From the corner of his eye he saw a door. It looked like it was made of iron, with some kind of narrow window, but he couldn't be sure from where he lay on the floor. What would happen to him? Shemal would never let him go. He was lost. So lost.

He woke again to the sound of the door sliding open. Terror gripped him and he watched two men enter. They stood over him. One kicked his side and spoke in Arabic. “Get up, useless dog.” But he couldn’t move. Sweat stood on his forehead and he took ragged breaths. The guards reached down, grabbed his arms and pulled him to his feet. His stood trembling between them.

When his knees buckled, they cursed, dragged him back up and leaned him against the wall. One got in his face. He smelled fetid breath and saw brown, crooked teeth. “You will stand up and walk with us, worthless American dog.”

The tubby man glared at him and spat on the floor. “You will rot here. You are worse than a dog.” The man spat again. “Useless bastard. American shit.”

The tall guard poked him in the chest. “He is American and cannot know what you say. Come on, we need to get going. We’ll have to help him walk.” The guard pulled a black hood over his head. They cuffed his wrists behind his back and shackled his feet.

Each one gripped an arm and Rowan stumbled blindly between them, half falling and stubbing his toes. The hood stank like dried saliva and he couldn’t keep from sucking it into his mouth with every tortured breath. Finally, they shoved him onto the floor of some kind of vehicle. The heat and roar of the motor vibrated in his chest. He lay sweating, inhaling exhaust fumes, his body listing from side to side as the vehicle stopped and started and careened around corners.

He was barely conscious when they pulled him from the vehicle. His body felt wooden. They shoved him into a metal chair and yanked the hood from his head. He closed his eyes against the bright lights.

Drawing a shuddering breath, he smelled disinfectant and remembered. They were taking him to see a doctor. His head dipped and his thoughts scattered. The doctor would fix his wrists and his shoulder. Seth had stomped on his foot and the doctor would fix that, too. But he still limped. He saw the kind doctor who'd tried so hard to make everything right. A stinging slap to the cheek and a gruff voice brought him back to reality. "Wake up."

His eyes flew open. He wasn't in Sioux Falls. No one here wanted to help him. A man in a white coat with a stethoscope around his neck stood in front of him. He had serious brown eyes, a neatly trimmed beard and spoke accented English. "I am your doctor. You will sit quietly or these men will beat you."

The guards stood on either side while the doctor shoved a thermometer in his mouth and unbuttoned the thin garment he wore. The stethoscope was cold against his chest. The doctor took his pulse and blood pressure, and examined his injured arm.

After jotting notes on a clipboard, the doctor looked at the guards and spoke in Arabic. "He must have medicine, in order to make him fit for what Master Shemal desires. Put him in a bed. I will send nurses with instructions."

None of them knew he could understand. The doctor grasped his whiskered chin with one hand, tipped his head up and switched to English. "You will eat and drink what is provided. You will take the medicine from our nurses, although it pains me to treat an unclean dog like you."

The doctor let go of his chin and his head bobbed on his chest. He wished they'd let him die. But they would keep him alive and do whatever they wanted to him, until he'd atoned for all the holy warriors he'd killed. Until they'd exhausted their imaginations and there was nothing left of his body or his mind.

Ralph stared at his phone. Michael had filled him in on the latest news. He thought about Rodney Ainsley. That the sneaky bastard had *literally* met his end at Rowan's hands boggled his mind. But thinking of Rowan in Shemal's hands left him beyond sad. He'd never felt so heavy-hearted.

Everything they'd worked so hard and sacrificed so much to prevent had happened anyway. In the end it appeared that too many things had been stacked against them. How could they have known that Patricia had collaborated with Shemal – from the *beginning?*

Disconsolate, he sank into a lounge chair on the patio. The phone rang in his hand and he damn near dropped it. Surprised at the ID, he punched talk. "Is this Clifton Cantor?"

"Ralph, it's good to hear your voice. I'm glad you're safe."

He stared at the bustling city spread out far below him. "It's good to hear from you, too. Last I knew you were being detained in an undisclosed location."

"I was just released, thank God. I had to get a hold of you. The President is coming around. He fired Patricia and is working behind the scenes to bring Rowan back from Egypt."

"That's the best news I've heard in a long time. But it's hard to believe Shemal will just let Rowan leave."

Clifton's tone became urgent. "That's why I called. It's time for you to reach out, bank on that long-time friendship with the President. Hammer home the truth about this whole mess. Keep him motivated."

"I've been mulling that over and wondering if now's the time. Before, he had Rodney and Patricia whispering in his ear."

"You have no idea the animus that woman harbors. She's unhinged. Probably worse now, since the President relieved her of her position. I need to go, but I'll stay in touch and keep you informed of what's going on here."

"Thanks. I'll do the samc." Ralph heaved a sigh. It was time. If there was anything he could do to help Rowan, he had to try. He punched number one on speed dial, remembering the last time he'd called. The White House operator answered and he used the same words. "Get me the President. Tell him it's Ralph Johnston, calling about Rowan Milani."

Pacing back and forth, waiting for the President, his thoughts rambled. He wondered if all of them might be able to go home eventually. He'd given up on that, figured Dubai was as good a place as any to retire. He'd take the taste of freedom in the desert over a Quantico cell any day. The phone clicked and the operator said, "You have the President."

He belatedly remembered the time difference. "Good morning, Mr. President."

The Commander in Chief sounded like the man he'd always known. "Ralph, I'm delighted that you called, though I am surprised as well. You're a hard man to find. Or, let me put it this way. You're a hard man to catch."

The turn of phrase made him uneasy. "Gil, many times I've wished we could talk. But, with certain events that have transpired, I knew I couldn't wait any longer."

"I presume you're talking about the death of your former boss and the *resignation* of my advisor. If I asked, would you tell me how you know about those *certain events* before they've been released to the media?"

"Well sir, I'd be hard pressed to divulge that information, which is why it's better that I stay indisposed for the present time. But that isn't the reason I called. It's imperative that you do everything possible to retrieve Rowan Milani from Muusa Shemal and the Muslim Brotherhood."

The President didn't miss a beat. "I couldn't agree more. Milani must be renditioned back here, to face justice for the murder of Rodney Ainsley. I've been speaking with the Egyptian president and he assures me that Milani will be returned. To put it bluntly, the Egyptian government needs our financial assistance. It's just a matter of handling things diplomatically with Shemal."

Ralph ran his hand along the top of the wrought iron patio rail. "Have you learned more about Shemal's motivations?"

"Yes. I've learned that much of what I've accepted as fact has instead been well-crafted lies. I'd planned to speak in person with Milani about Shemal, but before I had the chance, he murdered Ainsley. That puts him in an entirely different position. Once he's returned, he will be tried for murder. It's possible he'll face a military tribunal."

He gripped the rail, trying to forestall the panic building in his chest. "Gil, what do you mean? Rowan is an American citizen, with civil rights. He is entitled to due process. Why would he face a military tribunal?"

"Milani was declared an enemy combatant. Rescinding that, after what he's done, regardless of his prior innocence may not be in the best interests of the country. Politically speaking, he's an albatross around my neck. Sometimes it's best to let this type of problem resolve itself in the most expedient way possible."

At the President's callous words, Ralph sank back down in the lounge chair. Fierce anger lit a fire in his belly. If there was one thing he'd learned from that cunning bastard Ainsley, it was how to play Washington's fucked up games, and *win*. "Yes sir, I understand that completely. You might say Milani made his own bed."

"That's exactly what he's done. Once the firestorm has died down, I'll do everything in my power to ensure that you and Chad Cantor are absolved of any wrongdoing."

"Thank you, sir. I believe I can speak for Chad, as well as Marion and myself when I say that we are most grateful for your assistance. We'd like nothing better than to put this entire mess behind us." He'd said the same thing to Ainsley, nearly verbatim, almost a year earlier. He wished the circumstances were the same as that time.

The President's tone became brisk. "That goes for me as well. I may need your input in the coming days. I hope you'll stay in touch."

He resisted the urge to tell the leader of the free world where he could stick his input. "I certainly will, Mr. President. You have a good day."

Ralph ended the call and dialed another. McKenzie answered right away. "Hello. Is this who I think it is?"

"Jack, things are looking grim from my end. I don't trust the President at all. I guess I never realized his penchant for talking out of both sides of his mouth."

"Where have you been for the last few years? Oh, never mind. You've been busy. Whitman is a typical politician. How is it that you never saw that?"

The truth in his friend's words stung. "Hell, maybe I am an idiot. I thought friendship meant something. So I was wrong. Have you gotten anywhere?"

"Like I told you before, the Muslim Brotherhood is very much in vogue right now in the District. Your buddy Milani didn't help himself by murdering the Director of the FBI. I'm not supposed to know that yet, but I do have sources in the White House. It would help if there was someone in your camp that I could talk to in person."

"You're in luck. Clifton Cantor was detained by the President and has just been released. He has connections everywhere. Give him a call and set something up."

"Excellent, Ralph. I'll do that. You take care now, wherever you are."

Ralph stared at the city below, a few lights coming on as the sun sank lower. "Don't you worry, Jack. I'll take very good care. You do the same."

CHAPTER SEVENTEEN

A Week Later

Rowan gulped the last of the lentil soup and let the bowl fall to his lap. It clattered against the long chains that connected his cuffed wrists to the bed. He felt better and wished to God that he didn't. The nurses had been faithfully giving him drugs for pain and antibiotics for his arm and lungs. But they hated him. They talked about him in Arabic, telling each other how they'd murder him if they could. He debated every day whether or not to incite them to try.

Despair rolled through him. The doctor had been instructed to make him well so that Shemal could torture him. He gazed at his bandaged wrists beneath the metal cuffs. Once he was whole, it would start. And day by day his body betrayed him by healing. Anticipating the horror left him shaking and sweating through the night, until the nurses had to drug him, slowing his mind and forcing his body to rest.

He looked up when the doctor came through the door with a nurse following obediently behind him. She sat a tray of medical supplies on the bed and averted her eyes while the doctor spoke. "I must treat your arm now, worthless dog. Today you return to your master's care and I am done with you."

His heart rate increased. When the doctor picked up a scalpel from the tray on the bed he forced himself to breathe evenly. The doctor lifted his arm and cut off the bandage, muttering in Arabic. He clenched his jaws when his arm was jerked upward so the physician could see the stitches on the backside above his elbow.

Still muttering, the doctor placed the scalpel down on the bed and leaned close to examine the wound. The nurse was busy gathering bandages and tape from the tray. Rowan grabbed the scalpel and sliced across the doctor's neck, saw the bright red froth of blood before the man let out a garbled scream, staggered backward and pitched over on the floor in the doorway. He'd wanted to drag the scalpel all the way around the doctor's neck to inflict as much damage as he could, but the chain limited his reach. That he'd hit the fucker's artery at all had been pure luck.

The nurse yelled for help. He heard the doctor moaning. Closing his eyes, he tried to calm his breathing. He was panting like the dog they told him he was. Now, they would have to kill him. The guards would come. They'd execute him and Shemal wouldn't have him. He'd made the right choice. His only choice.

He heard running footsteps and men yelling. Women shrieked from the hallway. But when he heard barked orders in English, to clear the way, he opened his eyes and watched the door. The two CIA agents sidled into the room, stepped over the doctor and stood on either side of the bed. Seth and Lucien towered over him while he sat helpless, sweat dripping down the sides of his face. His effort had been for nothing. The two thugs would make sure that Shemal kept his prize.

Seth faced him. "You're unbelievable. Maybe we should toss you to the crowd in the hallway outside your door."

He glared at the close-set eyes. "Do it."

Lucien produced a set of keys and unlocked the chains that secured him to the bed. "Not a chance."

Seth pulled a set of handcuffs from his pants pocket before unlocking the cuffs on his wrists. The former Marine wrapped a massive hand around his shoulder and pushed his body forward, then wrenched his swollen arm behind his back. Lucien twisted his other arm backward to meet it. The cuffs locked tight around his wrists, another way for the agents to torment him.

Lucien shoved him back against the bed and patted his cheek. "They should never have let you have your hands. Dumb ragheads."

Seth grabbed his tender arm and dragged him off the bed. "Speaking of which, let's go *raghead.* Your master wants to see you. He's not going to be pleased. Maybe he'll cut off your hands to stop the crazy shit you cause wherever you go."

Seth dug strong fingers into his arm. He gritted his teeth at the pain while helpless rage burned in his chest. Lucien smacked him on the back of the head. The two agents manhandled him and he could do nothing to stop them.

The three of them had to move single file through the doorway to avoid the pool of blood where the doctor lay. When the crowd shouted Arabic curses and insults, spitting and shaking their fists, some of them throwing their shoes, the agents pulled their weapons. The wall of flesh parted and they walked into the milling crowd jammed into the hospital hallway.

He saw wild eyes and screaming mouths, felt the anger in the fists on his back and the feet that kicked him. The frustrated crowd knew who he belonged to. Their anger was matched only by their fear of Muusa and the Brotherhood. No one dared take Muusa's prize. He hadn't thought of that before attacking the doctor. Hopelessness settled around him as they exited the hospital.

Michael sat cross-legged in the dry grass beneath the copse of trees they'd chosen. Assembling his rifle before an operation sharpened his mind and gave him the simple pleasure of handling a precision weapon. Gabriel stood motionless to one side, staring down the hill at the collection of headstones. After conducting their own recon of the rural Virginia cemetery where Rodney Ainsley had been buried, they'd decided it was the best spot to carry out the op.

Wriggling flat in the debris, he squinted into the scope of his M110 semi-auto sniper rifle. Adjusting the scope, he picked out the newest headstone and brought the flowing script into crisp focus. *Rodney Eugene Ainsley.* Who gave a kid a name like that?

With Gabriel's help, he had penned a note to Patricia, offering indisputable proof of the identity of Rowan's colleagues, including their names, location and how she could arrange for their capture. It stated clearly that the proprietor of the information would provide an envelope containing all the documentation she needed. But she must come alone to Rodney's gravesite to collect it. If Patricia had taken their bait, she would be arriving in a few minutes. He began the process of slowing his heart rate while conducting the mental checklist he followed before each shoot. Gabriel hunkered down beside him. "Three clicks left and two clicks up."

"Three clicks left and two clicks up." He made the adjustments and looked up. From their vantage point on top of the hill he saw a silver Porsche 911, glinting in the mid-afternoon sunlight, as it approached on the curving road. It slowed and turned into the cemetery, navigating the narrow paved road to the Ainsley family plot.

Gabriel shifted on the cold ground and made the sign of the cross. "The mark is here."

The car door opened and he recognized Patricia's strawberry blonde hair. "All right, it's a go."

His colleague stared through binoculars. "I've got the mark at 625 yards."

Focused on each heartbeat, he took slow, deep breaths and didn't answer. He followed the woman's movements, observing while she bent low to pick up the brown manila envelope they'd deposited on the FBI Director's grave. Watching while she opened it, he placed his finger on the trigger and waited. Patricia held the papers in both hands and let the envelope drop to the ground. After a few moments she reached down to retrieve it and tucked the fake documentation back inside. He took another breath and held it. She lifted her head and he found the spot he wanted, just behind her ear.

Gabriel spoke quietly, with conviction. “Send it.” He pressed the trigger, heard the muted bang. His colleague scrambled up and retrieved the shell casing, muttering in Spanish.

Michael disassembled the rifle with skilled fingers and packed it in its case. “That was a good, clean op. Great job on the spotting.”

His friend made the sign of the cross again. “You’re welcome. Excellent shooting.”

Gazing down the hill, he saw the crumpled body. The red jacket seemed fitting. He turned away. “Thank you. Now let’s get the hell out of here. We’ve got a plane to catch.”

Muusa strode back and forth in the dank cell, waiting for his agents to return with his prize. He’d needed the time while Milani was in the hospital to attend to matters at Al Azhar Mosque and University, where he worshipped and taught while he was in his native land. But also, he wanted the Jinn to be well, in order to withstand his ministrations. He must guard against the day when the Americans wanted their *traitor* back.

Now, at last, it was time to begin. It would please Allah for him to teach his prize the true meaning of humility. The process would be sweet and he would not allow its completion for some time. He remembered the hubris in the Jinn’s eyes and the man’s jeering promise to kill him. He would find pleasure in breaking the spirit of one so brash.

The door to the cell opened and the two agents entered with Milani between them. He angled his head, but the men did not leave. Seth held Milani by the arm. “This worthless piece of shit killed the doctor you assigned to treat him.”

Immediate fury rose in his chest, bringing back the tightening bands of agony. Everyone who came within reach of the Jinn had died and now the cursed man had come to blight his homeland. "Leave us."

The agents nodded and left, sliding the door closed behind them. Milani watched him. He saw wariness, even resignation in the man's eyes, but not the fear he had been expecting. It was fear that he required if the proud man was to be humbled. He took careful breaths and the painful tightening in his chest subsided. He dabbed at the sweat on his forehead and walked a slow circle around his prize before stopping in front of him. "You will kneel." Milani locked eyes with him, but did not move.

He stepped quickly and kicked the back of his prisoner's knees, sending him to the stained concrete on his belly. Placing his foot on Milani's back, above the cuffed wrists, he pressed down until the man grunted and coughed. "As I told you, it is Allah's will that you learn humility. This is your first lesson." Removing his foot, he reached down, grasped the cuffed wrists and hauled Milani to his knees.

Blood leaked from beneath the stitches of the man's wounded arm. Dirt clung to his ragged beard. Hatred filled Milani's eyes, but there was a glimmer of something else; dread perhaps. How he relished the task of making this man feel true terror. "Do you begin to fear me now, clever Jinn?"

Milani spat on the floor, but did not answer. Muusa pulled a dagger from the scabbard at his side and saw the almost imperceptible twitch in the muscles of Rowan's bearded face. Lifting the whiskered chin with the tip of the dagger, he turned it, enough to anchor the knife in flesh.

He saw Milani's throat convulse. "Your body answers whether or not you choose to speak. Tell me, Jinn, what is your body saying?"

His prize stared at him, but still would not speak. He pulled the dagger away from Milani's chin and laid the razor sharp edge next to his mouth. "Speak or by Allah I will cut out your tongue so that you can never speak again."

Sweat ran in rivulets down Milani's face and neck. A trace of the submission he sought appeared and vanished in the cold, black eyes. "You are the one who is afraid."

He threw back his head and laughed. "You believe that I fear you?" Before his prize could answer, he sliced with the dagger, producing a thin, red line below the man's cheek bone. "Answer me, worthless dog."

Milani's chest rose and fell in quick breaths. "Yes."

Puzzled, he watched as a tiny river of blood from the cut on Milani's cheek mingled with his dripping sweat. "Why would you think such a thing?" Again he sliced flesh, this time where collar bone met shoulder muscle. "You will answer me."

Milani winced, but he heard menace in the quiet voice. "If you are not afraid, remove the cuffs and free my hands."

He stepped back and observed his prize. The utter hubris of the man who kneeled before him was astonishing. Never had he found such boldness in a helpless opponent. "You have committed acts of evil against my people around the globe. You will never use your hands again."

Milani smirked. "Coward."

Anger consumed him and he brandished the dagger, shredding the thin prison garment with a swipe across Milani's belly. The provocative man doubled over and Muusa feared he'd gone too far. He hollered. "Guards, come now."

The door opened and his two chosen warriors stepped inside. Furious with both himself and Milani, he gestured at his prize, hunched over on the dirty floor. "Take him away. Do what you will with him but *do not* cause permanent damage to his body. Control yourselves or I will do to you what you do to him."

The two men nodded, gripped Milani's arms and lifted him to his feet. The bleeding man glared at him. "You need cuffs, chains and these bastards to do your work. No matter what you do to me, you will always be the coward. "

Engulfed in righteous fury, he raised the dagger, intending to pierce the heart of the vile man. Before he could sink his dagger into the Jinn's flesh, the taller guard slapped Milani across the face. "Master, do not let this American dog taunt you. Let us show him what Allah has planned. You have more important matters to attend to."

The agony in his chest returned and he struggled for breath. "Yes, take him away."

Shemal's guards were almost gentle while they removed the cuffs and shackles. Rowan lay blindfolded with his face pressed into a dirt floor. The two men had taken him from the session with Shemal. Now they tied his hands and feet together behind his back with a coarse rope.

Their conversation struck terror in his heart. "The rope is strong, but will it hold his weight? He is a big dog."

The other guard was confident. "This rope will hold. It's been tested before."

His breath came in heaving gasps when the ropes tightened on his wrists and ankles and his arms and legs were pulled taut. Stabbing agony invaded his left arm. He heard the guards grunting as his body rose and hung suspended a few inches above the floor. Their clomping footsteps receded and the door closed.

The pain overwhelmed him. The weight of his body pulled and twisted the muscles in his shoulders, arms and legs. It felt like his spine was breaking in half. He gritted his teeth and clenched his fists as his body swayed. Gasping, struggling to breathe, he hung there, his face contorted in agony.

He couldn't hold out. Tears streamed beneath the blindfold. He tried to beg for relief, but the anguish obliterated his thoughts and only mumbled groans came through his cracked, trembling lips. The door opened, he heard footsteps, and then his body dropped to the floor. Dirt filled his mouth and nose. He inhaled it, choking and coughing. He waited for them to untie his hands and feet, but instead he heard the rope stretch. The two men raised his body off the ground again and his agony continued, until his hands and feet were numb.

The guards seemed to know what he was feeling. They again dumped him in the dirt. When he heard the rope tighten, his body shook. "No, no . . ." The guards ignored his plea and hoisted his body up once more and left. Blood ran down his left arm as the stitches pulled free. Moaning, drooling, mindless with pain, he hung there, helpless.

The guards returned and lowered his body to the dirt. He lay gasping and shaking, waiting for the torture to begin again. The two men argued in Arabic. "He deserves more."

The other one disagreed. "Don't you remember what the Master said? If we damage his body, he will make us endure the same punishment."

"Yes, I remember. You are correct." The guard loosened the ropes and pulled them away. His arms flopped against his sides and his legs lay lifeless. He groaned when they pulled his arms back and cuffed his wrists together. The shackles closed around his raw ankles and then the guards dragged and pulled him to his feet.

He stood swaying between them. One of the men ripped the blindfold off his face and he gazed dully at his torturers. The taller guard, with the brown teeth, spoke. "He is not so full of foolish words now."

The short, fat guard sniffed. "No, he is not. I can't tell if he pissed himself or is covered with sweat. Either way, he stinks like a donkey. Now we must clean him up and treat the wound on his arm or the Master will be angry."

They jerked on his arms. He took tentative, painful steps between them and they left the stinking, filthy torture room.

* * *

The President's office in the West Wing had become the preferred meeting place to discuss the stream of never-ending disasters. First Rodney and now Patricia. David observed the President he no longer trusted. "Sir, the Roanoke County Sheriff has nothing on Patricia's death. They have conducted an extensive search of the area, but found no shell casings, no unusual visitors – nothing. The cemetery was in a rural area, as you know."

President Whitman looked as though he'd aged years since the debacle surrounding Rowan began unraveling. "The FBI will conduct its own investigation. Acting Director Berenger will be thorough in her approach, believe me."

"I have no doubt of that. What's the status of Milani's return?"

The President gave him an incredulous look. "You won't believe this. Milani murdered a doctor in the hospital where he was taken for an exam. The Egyptians are balking, insisting that he must now stand trial in their court."

He sat slack-jawed at the news. "Do they have any proof?"

"Apparently a nurse was in the room at the time and witnessed the attack. Agent Hancock confirmed that he and Agent Talbot saw the doctor's body on the floor. The scalpel Milani used has his prints on it. As far as the Egyptians are concerned, that's all the evidence they need. He won't be returning to the United States anytime soon, if ever."

The President's words made him uneasy. "Sir, they may change their tune once things calm down. Our foreign aid dollars are important to them, after all. I wouldn't consider this matter closed."

President Whitman shrugged. "I'm inclined to let them have him. The media has shifted focus from Rodney's death to Patricia's. The fact that she was killed by a sniper has captured their collective imagination. The country is losing interest in Milani as well."

The more he learned about Whitman, the more he realized that the man was nothing but a cynical politician. He and Patricia had been a perfect match. “Out of sight, out of mind, would you say, sir?”

“You’re catching on. My main consideration is how this affects my administration. Ralph Johnston actually called me. He touted Milani’s innocence, of course. I assured him that I’d do everything in my power to absolve both him and Chad Cantor of their connection to Milani. However, looking toward the future, I believe we’ve got to rethink that. For many years I’ve considered Ralph to be a good friend. But after talking with him and considering how his actions over the past year contributed to this entire debacle, I’m afraid he’s no longer trustworthy.”

“As a matter of fact, I want you to refocus your efforts on locating Ralph Johnston and bringing him in. Chad Cantor must know where he is. Put the pressure on him. If this mess with Milani gets out and blows up in the next election cycle, I want to present both Johnston and Cantor to the country and assure the people that my administration has taken care of the problem.”

The President’s political calculations and the cold dismissal of Ralph Johnston disturbed him. “If I understand correctly, you have no intention of making public the fact that Milani was not a traitor.”

“Certainly not. Use your head. He operated at my discretion. That his exploits were directed by me can never be divulged. Especially not now, after he murdered Ainsley. Johnston and Cantor chose to protect him. If they pay a price for that on behalf of our nation, then so be it. I’d like you to keep a close eye on Clifton as well. I’m beginning to think I acted impulsively in releasing him. He’s another long-time friend whose loyalty I’ve begun to doubt. In addition to that, he’s an influential man and it’s possible he’d be listened to if he decided to speak out on his son’s behalf.”

David managed to hide his alarm at the President's abrupt attitude shift regarding his closest friends. How much longer could he remain on the good side of the Commander in Chief, and what would happen to him if he strayed too far in one direction or another? "You're right, of course. I've been thinking about a measure you may want to consider. Bettina Milani is pregnant. I've interrogated her extensively. She's been forthcoming and helpful. Chad and Rowan sheltered her from any real knowledge of what they were up to, so she doesn't know much. If you would consider releasing her . . ."

The President interrupted him, responding enthusiastically. "That's an excellent point. We can use her to gain Chad's cooperation. If he'll give up Johnston's location, I'll release her."

He spoke carefully, not wanting to create more paranoia in the President's mind. "Well sir, not to steal your thunder, but I've hammered on that consistently with Chad. It's my belief that he does not know where Ralph Johnston is hiding. I've told him over and over that if he reveals the location of his colleagues, then Bettina can go free. The issue with Chad aside, considering what's best for your image, if you magnanimously offered to release her, I believe you'd be favorably perceived. It would play well during the election cycle and prevent the other side from portraying you as cold-hearted."

The President looked pleased. "You've got a knack for this. I believe the word you're looking for is balance. We allow Ms. Milani to be released, which shows that we're not hard-core hawks. I like it. Start the process. I'll approve it. But don't tell Chad. Let him think she's still incarcerated. Think of it as one more lever in your interrogation of him."

"Thank you, sir. It's a humane gesture on your part. I will be sure that Chad has no knowledge of her release. Starting immediately, I'll focus on his frame of mind and make sure that we have more fruitful interrogation going forward."

Whitman's use of the word *we* made him uncomfortable. He wondered if the President considered him to be Patricia's de facto replacement. He would never condone *any* of the options the President considered as routine in protecting his administration. It was time for him to withdraw. But he had to be careful.

The same Patriot Act and National Defense Authorization Act provisions that had been used against Clifton could be used against him. He'd have to craft a plan and prepare his resources. If he decided to leave, no one could know where or how. It was entirely possible that the people he'd expended so much time pursuing would become his allies. If they'd have him.

CHAPTER EIGHTEEN

The Next Day

Johnny sat down on the sofa and looked at Ralph. Although the two of them had existed on opposite ends of the spectrum as far as the law was concerned, their thought processes were similar. He'd sensed a warrior kinship with the former SEAL. It was fun to have someone besides Gino to bounce ideas off of.

They'd met again for drinks in his study in the condo. He picked up his phone. "I'm ready to make the call. You got any words of wisdom for me?"

Ralph replied. "You need to remember that Shemal isn't going to believe you. He'll call your bluff. You need to be certain everything is in place for immediate – and I mean *immediate* response. That's the only thing he'll respect."

Grabbing the scrap of paper lying next to him, he thought about the value of having contacts in diverse places. Squinting at the number, he punched it into his phone and hit send. Now, would the son of a bitch pick up? The voice that answered was low, cultured and intelligent. "Hello, you have reached Professor Shemal. How may I assist you?"

The number he'd dialed was for the terrorist's personal cell phone. Who would have thought that he would be so formal? "Mr. Shemal, you need to do exactly what I'm going to tell you to do."

"Who is calling? Speak quickly or I will hang up."

"Who I am is none of your fucking business. Here's what I want. Agree to bring Rowan Milani, alive and in good condition, to Cairo International Airport, to the executive FBO adjacent to Hall Four at fourteen hundred hours tomorrow or there will be terrible consequences for you."

"You cannot threaten me. The President of the United States has agreed that Milani will remain in Egypt to stand trial for murder. My answer must be no."

Johnny looked at Ralph's expectant face and winked. "Our respective governments have nothing to do with what I'm telling you to do. This is between you and me. I damn sure *can* threaten you and I am doing so now." The line went dead. He pulled the phone away from his ear. "The camel turd hung up. I'll be damned. You were right."

Ralph heaved a sigh. "It's time for step two."

Johnny punched the contact he wanted and waited for his crew leader to answer. "Roberto, is everything set?"

"Whenever you're ready, boss. Give the word and it's done. Ricci double-checked everything last night."

"Good. We're not waiting for fourteen hundred hours tomorrow. Do it, right now."

David left his town house and checked his watch. He had an hour before Clifton expected him. It was a drizzly, cold afternoon in Washington. A gust of wind rattled the bare tree branches along the sidewalk. He zipped up his jacket and shivered as he headed for his car, wishing he'd parked it in the garage.

Reaching the Mercedes, he slid inside and turned the heat on high. The wipers swished across the windshield intermittently, keeping it clear as he drove in sluggish traffic across the city. He tried to organize his swirling thoughts. Things would move quickly once he put everything in motion and he couldn't have any loose ends. If he wanted to stay in Washington, his involvement needed to be untraceable. Otherwise, he'd be in a cell next to Chad.

He arrived at Clifton's office with minutes to spare. Clifton greeted him with a sardonic look. "I don't suppose another *legal* search of my home is taking place as we speak?"

"I'm not sure there's an adequate apology for what you have been through."

Clifton gestured to a pair of genteel arm chairs. "Please, sit down. Let's move on. You can buy me dinner sometime, how's that? I am concerned about why you wanted to meet. You sounded cryptic on the phone."

While he thought about how to start, he let his gaze wander around the room. A large window with blinds and ornate curtains commandeered one wall. An elegant grandfather clock stood against the adjacent wall. Clifton looked alert behind a massive, antique desk. "Since I'm the only remaining member of the team tasked with capturing Rowan, the President has sought my counsel more and more. I hadn't realized the extent to which he'd go to protect his administration. I have managed to convince him to release Bettina Milani. But there is something I need to warn you about."

Clifton regarded him with raised brows. "What?"

"The President is thinking about the next election cycle and wants to use Chad and Ralph to demonstrate how his administration cleared up the domestic terrorism issue that came to light because of Rowan. He's concerned that you will speak up and he told me that he'd consider detaining you again to prevent that."

"I see. When will Bettina be released?"

"The President signed off on it, so it's up to me. My preference would be to send her along with you to wherever her parents and Ralph are located."

"I can arrange that. Give me twenty-four hours. I should tell you, I've been approached by an investigative reporter, supposedly on Rowan's behalf. It's a shame I won't be able to meet with him now."

"That's interesting. Maybe I can talk with him, if you wouldn't mind giving me his name and number. I don't suppose you'd care to tell me the details of your flight or where you're going?"

"You'd be right. Although, for a man in your position, gaining access to tracking data on a private flight should be easy. You could always ask Chad for his help. Or, you could ask him to remove any trace of the flight. I would, however, be glad to pass along the reporter's info. His name is Jack McKenzie. Ralph Johnston referred him to me. I'd wager that he'd be interested in talking to you as well."

David hesitated for a moment and decided to share his thoughts. "I'm thinking that at some point I may want to join you. Not yet, but I've received a thorough education on what happens to those who interfere with the political designs of this President."

Clifton reached for a pen and notepaper. "Here's McKenzie's contact information and another number you may want at some point. If you need quick access to a safe location, tell this person that I told you to call."

He stood up and took the paper, stuffed it in his pocket and held out his hand. "Thanks for seeing me. Let me know what time to meet you with Bettina."

Clifton stood and shook his hand. "Take good care, David. I'll call you as soon as I have the details."

Johnny stood at one of the windows in his office, over a hundred stories above Dubai. The choices he'd made offered privileges he'd never taken for granted. Injustice grated on him, which was why he both embraced and enforced his own code so severely. The courts and the country had been corrupted by greedy politicians whose only interest was power, gained and kept, regardless of the cost. The end always justified the means for people like that.

He marveled at how the apparently simple decision to help Clifton with the problem of Sal Capello had evolved into providing safe haven for the small group of people. And now, he'd add Clifton and another Milani. Soon, he'd bring his wife. The course he'd chosen with Shemal was just and deserved. But it brought the possibility, until Shemal was dead, of his being exposed.

In that event, he needed to have fluid resources and be ready to move at a moment's notice. His Middle Eastern friends had assisted in his endeavors so far, but if others of a more radical Islamic persuasion discovered what he had done and was planning to do, they would want vengeance. He'd always enjoyed playing the game and he had no qualms about stacking whatever deck he was playing in his favor. This would be no different; he just needed to prepare.

The transfer of funds had been initiated and would take twenty-four hours to complete. Then the entire bulk of his resources would be hidden from both U.S. and Middle Eastern hands. The exercise invigorated him, kept him feeling young. His next goal was securing Milani's release. Once he'd accomplished that, maybe he'd drag his wife on a real vacation. Or, leave her to shop in Dubai with the other women and take the men on a safari.

His phone rang, as he'd expected it would. "Hello Mr. President. Thank you for returning my call."

The former President, whom he considered a close friend, sounded chipper. "Johnny, how the hell are you?"

He sat down at his desk. "Doing damn fine sir, and you?"

The crafty politician didn't waste time. "You didn't call to ask me how I'm doing. What's going on and what do you need?"

"Your ghost agent, who goes by the name of Rowan Milani, is on my mind."

Silence greeted his words and he wondered for a moment if his friend had hung up. "Well, you've got my attention, but you must know that there is absolutely nothing I can do to help a man who has betrayed his country."

Nabbing the bottle of Glenlivet, he poured some into a crystal tumbler and took a hefty swallow. "If you've got the time, I'd like to enlighten you to the facts of Milani's situation. And then, I'd like the kind of help that only you can provide."

The Next Day

Chad waited, hunched over in the uncomfortable chair. His hands were cuffed and anchored to the table. He looked up when the door opened. Bettina stepped inside with David Harandi. She wasn't handcuffed, and she was wearing the same t-shirt and jeans she'd had on the day the FBI found them on Kauai. David held her upper arm, provoking his immediate anger. No one else had any business touching her. "What are you doing?"

David spoke calmly. "The President has authorized Bettina's release. I'm giving the two of you a few minutes together before I escort her out."

Relief coupled with dismay and left him floundering. Knowing she was close by had been a comfort to him. "Are you sure? She can go?"

Bettina pulled away from David, rushed to him and put her arms around him. "I don't want to go. Not without you. But he won't let me stay."

Her touch, the warmth of her body, choked him up. "Sweetheart, it's OK. It's better for you and for the baby, if you go. You can be with your parents, with Ralph and Marion, and get the medical attention you and the baby need. I want you to go."

David sat down across from them. "I've made arrangements with your father. We're meeting him in two hours."

He stared at the cuffs and the chain, holding him at the table, helpless and humiliated. Meeting David's gaze, he raised his hands. "I want . . . I need a few minutes alone with my fiancée. Please. Without the cuffs."

David unlocked the cuffs from the table. "I know that you are a Second Degree Black Belt. This is as good as it's going to get."

He looked at his captor with loathing. "You think I'd risk her freedom for a hopeless escape attempt from Quantico? I'm not stupid."

Bettina rubbed his shoulders. "Please just leave us alone for a few minutes."

David stood. "You can't be left unsupervised, but I'll wait at the door. Take it or leave it."

Instead of answering, he turned his back. He pulled Bettina onto his lap, raised his arms and encircled her. Burying his head in her hair, he focused on her scent and the feel of her body in his arms. The knowledge that it might be years before he would see or touch her again terrified him. He held her tight. "It'll be OK, sweetheart. It's for the best and it won't be forever. My dad will make sure you're taken care of."

Bettina sniffed and stayed pressed against him, murmuring into his chest. "I hate this so much. I miss you. I don't want to do this without you. Last night, I felt the baby move for the first time. You should have been there. You deserve to be there."

Her words shook his composure, but he had to hang on for her sake. "Oh, sweetheart. I'm sorry. I wish I could have been with you. Maybe I can feel him moving now."

She straightened up and grasped his cuffed hands, placing them gently on her abdomen. "Him? Feel that? He's swimming around, he must know it's his papa."

Her jeans were unbuttoned and half-way unzipped, letting him explore the smooth skin he loved. He scrunched his eyes closed and concentrated on the feel of her belly, surprised at how much it had grown. Something rippled beneath one hand, so gentle and fleeting, he wondered if he'd imagined it. Then it fluttered against his hand again and he knew it was real. How could he let her go? He had to be there with her, with this new person they'd created. But he couldn't.

He left his hands on her belly, but the baby didn't move again. Bettina leaned against him and for a few seconds everything felt right. Then he heard David stirring, felt the cuffs on his wrists. Panic gripped him. He breathed deeply, trying to banish the desperate urge to act, to do something – *anything* – to stay with her.

Bettina put her hands over his. "I love you so much. I promise to record everything that happens. I'll write it all down, I'll take pictures and make videos every day, and keep it all for you. When this is over, we'll relive it, together."

God, he couldn't believe how strong she was. In the end, she had more courage, more guts than he did. His lips quivered. He laid his chin on her shoulder as heaving sobs shook his body. He forced himself to stop. His voice wobbled. "Oh, sweetheart, I'm so sorry. I love you, too. Please be careful. I'll do anything I can to get out of here."

David approached them. "All right, you've got to wrap it up so we can get going."

Bettina turned inside the circle of his arms and put her hands on either side of his face. She wiped the tears off his cheeks with her thumbs. "Let's stand up, so you can kiss me properly."

"OK, sweetheart." They stood and he put his arms around her as best he could. She held onto him so tight he didn't think he could breathe. Then she reached up and drew his head down. He closed his eyes, lost himself in the softness of her mouth and clung to the kiss until David opened the door and two guards entered the room. Bettina slid from beneath his arms. It was over, their time was up. The guards grasped his arms and tugged.

David produced handcuffs, restrained Bettina and gripped her upper arm. Fierce anger engulfed him. He yanked his arms away from the guards, surprising them. Both men pulled their weapons. David held onto Bettina and raised a hand. "Whoa, everyone take it easy. Chad, sit down in the chair, right now. Guards, holster your weapons. *Now.*"

He sat, glowering at David while one of the guards locked the cuffs to the table. "Why is she restrained? You said she'd been released. Why can't you keep your hands off her? You don't have any right to touch her."

David let go of Bettina and pointed at him. "You need to calm down. I'm following protocol. I've learned the hard way what happens when I don't. I won't touch her again. I promise. Now, you're going to stay right here until I get back." David gestured at the guards. One of you stay in here, one of you wait outside the door. Keep a close eye on him."

Chad focused on Bettina. "I love you sweetheart." One guard stood next to the door and the other one opened it. David motioned for Bettina to leave.

She blew him a kiss. "I love you Chad. Good-bye . . . for now." Then she was gone. The guard closed the door and stood in front of it. Chad slouched in the chair and stared at his hands. The anger dissipated. Loneliness rolled over him in waves.

Her body rigid, Bettina sat in the front seat of David's Mercedes. He slid into the driver's seat and flourished a key. She held out her hands and watched while he unlocked the cuffs and pulled them away. She stared at him while she rubbed her wrists. "You're a jerk, you know? Why did you have to do that in front of him? Couldn't you see how this whole thing was killing him? Would it have hurt to wait until we were out of the room before you handcuffed me? Or did you think I was going to bolt off down the hallway and embarrass you?"

David opened his mouth, closed it and punched the Start/Stop button on the dash. "I was only doing my job the way it's supposed to be done."

She rolled her eyes. "Whatever. Did you have to leave him sitting in that horrible interrogation room, cuffed to the table for hours, with a guard staring at him? Do you have to be so deliberately cruel?"

The car took off with a jerk. David snapped the turn signal on and sped into traffic outside the front gate of Quantico. "I couldn't predict or control Chad's emotional state or yours, so I took every precaution. That's not being cruel. He was overwrought. This way he'll cool off. By the time I get back, he'll be calm. Unlike your brother."

The mention of Rowan piqued her interest. "What do you mean?"

He passed a car before giving her a dark glance. "If I hadn't been kind to him, if I'd taken him to the interrogation room and kept him restrained to the table, Rodney Ainsley would still be alive today and Patricia Hennessey probably would be, too. And Rowan would most likely be here instead of in Tora prison."

She drew a sharp breath. "Rowan's gone? He's in Tora . . . oh no. Shemal has him? Oh God."

David gripped the wheel. "That's right. Like I said, sometimes I learn things the hard way. But I don't repeat my mistakes. Unlike your brother."

Worry for Rowan left her clutching her hands together, but Harandi's comments rankled. "What's with you and Rowan? You don't know anything about him. Just because he did things . . . pursued things the way you disapprove of doesn't mean he made mistakes. What's wrong with you anyway? You used to be like a big brother to me. Being a CIA agent changed you. Now, you're just . . . just a *tool.*"

To her utter surprise, David laughed and for a moment he looked lighthearted. "You are so much like Rowan. I wonder if Chad has any idea what he is in for. You are one tough lady. I swear, your kid is going to be something else. It's scary as hell to think about."

"What difference does it make whether Chad has any idea of *anything?* Stop talking about our child. For God's sake, David, give me a break, would you? It may be years before I see him again, if I ever do. You don't know anything about me. So please, just shut up and drive. Just take me to wherever I have to go."

David gave her a curt nod and kept his lips clamped together. She stared at the bleak scenery of early spring and shivered. David glanced at her and turned up the heat. A jacket would have been nice, but at least she wasn't itching from the disgusting Quantico brig jumpsuit. She leaned back and closed her eyes. Chad's agonized face was all she could see.

When David touched her shoulder, she jumped. An overhead green and white sign said they were nearing Thurgood Marshall Airport. They'd driven to Baltimore? She stretched and yawned. How could she have fallen asleep? "Are we almost there? I need to use a restroom, if you don't mind."

He didn't look at her. "We'll be there in five minutes. I think you'll make it. I need to drop you off and get back to Quantico. Any words you'd like me to convey to Chad?"

"I told him what he needed to know. He's a good man and so smart. He could help you, if you'd let him."

David didn't answer. They pulled up and parked in front of a two-story glass and concrete building. A sign in front said something about private flight services. She saw a tall, lanky man lounging near the curb. He looked so familiar. When he smiled and waved, a hard lump formed in her throat. He hurried to the car and opened her door. She looked up, into kind, blue eyes and grasped his outstretched hand. "You must be Chad's father. I'm Bettina. It's nice to finally meet you."

The man helped her out of the car and drew her into a hug. When he stepped back, she saw tears in his eyes. "Bettina, I'm Clifton. I've heard so much about you. I've looked forward to meeting you since the first time Chad told me about you."

David came around the car with a plastic packet and gave it to her. "Here are your identification documents from the house on Kauai that were confiscated by the FBI. Take good care of yourself. And don't worry, I'll make sure that Chad is OK. You may not believe me, but I want things to work out for all of you – including Rowan."

She clutched the packet in one hand and touched David's arm as he turned to go. "Thank you."

David gave her a brief nod and looked at Clifton. "Good luck. Safe travels, wherever you're off to. I've got your cell number and you've got mine. Stay in touch. I'll let you know if anything changes."

Clifton put an arm around her shoulders. "We'll be fine. Keep a sharp eye and don't lose those numbers I gave you, especially the second one."

David spoke before heading back to the Mercedes. "I won't."

Clifton guided her toward the building as a jet rumbled overhead. "Let's go. We've got a long flight and plenty of time to get acquainted. I hope you don't mind, I took the liberty of purchasing a few items of clothing for you. Once we're in Dubai, you can go shopping with Marion and Janice, but this will get you started."

A wall of grief slammed into her. She wobbled, felt Clifton's arm tighten. "Dubai? Oh God, that's half-way around the world. I'm not sure I can do that. It's so far away from Chad. If anything happens to him . . . I won't be there."

Clifton stopped walking and gave her a sober look. "I know this isn't easy. I feel the same way, leaving Natalie and Chad. But I'm convinced that we'll be better able to help Chad and Rowan from Dubai. And we'll be free from the reach of the government. Can you trust me on this? We can lean on each other. God knows I could use a family right now."

The lump in her throat made talking impossible. Clifton opened the glass door and they stepped into a bustling, airy room. He led her across the expanse, conferred with the reps at the counter and then led her back outside. A gleaming blue and white jet stood on the tarmac, engines roaring.

Hours later, lying back in her seat, she watched the man who reminded her so much of Chad. Clifton had done his best to keep her mind occupied. He'd regaled her with stories until his voice became hoarse. Then the flight attendant had brought them dinner. Now Chad's father sat with a glass of wine, staring out the window. The loneliness crept back. She placed her hands on her belly and closed her eyes.

David sat in his living room, wishing he could excise the good-bye he'd witnessed between Chad and Bettina from his mind. The bottle of Hennessey X.O. next to the sofa was almost gone. He poured the remainder into a snifter and turned on the TV. A news reporter stood in front of the smoking wreckage of what used to be the House of Allah Mosque in Houston.

Shocked at the destruction and thankful for the diversion, he grabbed his phone and punched Kyle's number. The homicide detective answered immediately. "Hello David. How are things going in D.C.?"

"By the looks of what I'm watching right now, probably better than in Houston. I'm sure you're probably neck deep in the investigation, so I won't keep you long. Since this was Shemal's base of operations, I was interested in what you could tell me about what happened."

"The investigation is in the initial phase, of course. So far we know that it was a professional job. By that I mean, whoever did this had extensive knowledge of explosives and construction."

"Good God. In other words, this wasn't some amateur with fertilizer and diesel fuel."

"Absolutely not. No group has stepped forward to claim responsibility. We've started interviews. Initial reports had approximately sixty-five men in the mosque when the explosions started. So far we've got thirteen dead and damn near everyone else with some kind of injury, many of them serious."

David swallowed more cognac. "That's a hell of a mess."

"You're not kidding. Say, I've been meaning to call you. I asked Shemal about the two men Milani killed the night he was apprehended. He said they were not connected to the mosque. I checked into that with a few contacts I've got here and there. Besides that, I couldn't stop thinking about what Milani told me."

He prodded the detective. "Yes? Did they turn out to be connected to the mosque?"

"As a matter of fact, they were part of a group of Iranian men Shemal recruited last fall to work on *web-related issues.* How's that for a vague explanation?"

David snorted. "Sounds like a winner to me. When you've got some time, I'll fill you in on what I've learned. Puts a whole different spin on most of what's happened with Milani."

"Did you learn anything of value from the flash drive?"

"What with everything that has happened in the last forty-eight hours, I totally forgot about that. Sorry. That's the long answer; the short answer is *no*. Rodney never had a chance to give it to me. However, I did learn more about it from one of Rowan's colleagues."

"Well, that sounds intriguing. When things settle down a bit here, I'd like to discuss what you found out. I can help you out with the flash drive. I made a copy, just in case Milani could ever be extradited back here. I'll overnight it to you."

"I appreciate that. Although at this juncture, I'm not sure if it will help, but it may be of value later. I'm thinking that it would be in my best interests for someone that I trust, outside of Washington, to know what I've learned."

Kyle yawned. “Now you sound paranoid. Hey look, I need to get going. I promised Erin and the boys I’d try to be home early tonight. I’m not doing too well with that.”

“That’s OK. Take good care of yourself. Thanks for giving me the scoop, and for sending the flash drive.” He ended the call and finished the cognac. Talking to Kyle had sparked even more questions.

He stared at the empty snifter, thinking he needed something stronger than cognac if he was going to get any rest. Conflicting emotions over the lover he’d lost and the woman he’d come to despise had deprived him of sleep for the last several nights. He slid lower in the recliner. Trying to figure out if he should be mourning took time he didn’t have. And maybe that was an answer in itself.

Besides, other more pressing tasks required his attention. Such as making sure that the President had no reason to suspect he was anything but loyal, and arranging an exit from the country should the need arise. He remembered Patricia’s threat about tying him to the bogus terror-related activities of Sa-id. He’d dismissed it, but wondered if she’d ever mentioned anything about it to the President.

Setting the glass next to the empty bottle, he hunkered down and closed his eyes. If he’d had any clue of the complexity surrounding his old friend Rowan, he’d have told Patricia and the President to shove the assignment up their collective asses. One thing was certain though: He had no intention of ending up in a cell in Quantico or anywhere else.

CHAPTER NINETEEN

Muusa put his head in his hands. He couldn't escape the images of his beloved mosque. The charred walls, the ruined treasures from his homeland, and his faithful holy warriors, slaughtered while they studied the Qur'an and prepared for jihad wrapped the tightening bands of agony around his chest. The Imam had called, telling him the names of the dead. Those who had perpetrated this evil act would pay. No one destroyed a house of worship without reprisal. The Jinn would give him their identity.

He stood up and walked restlessly around the shaded area, his shoes scraping the stone walkway. Al Azhar mosque and University was where he sought refuge during visits to Cairo. Away from the stench of Tora and bustling with students, many whom he still taught, it filled his soul with pleasure. The courtyard garden, adjacent to some of the university buildings brought him Allah's peace as nowhere else on earth. Except for this day, when his mind could focus only on the tragedy in Houston.

Returning to his seat at one of the benches beneath a Sycamore tree, he took slow breaths and waited for the agony in his chest to cease. He withdrew his phone from the pocket of his tunic and dialed the number. The kafir Americans would never find who had perpetrated the evil on the House of Allah. The shayton who had called him, demanding that he release his prize, had committed this abominable deed.

He waited, sweating as the spasms in his chest returned. The arrogant voice didn't bother with civility. "Can you live with the consequences of your refusal to do as you're told? You deliver Milani alive and well, or I promise you more of the same. I'm a man of my word. What is your decision?"

Savage anger constricted his chest even more. He wasn't sure he could answer. He stifled a moan and clutched the edge of the bench. "You will not dictate terms to me. Allah will exact payment for your evil works."

The shayton mocked him. "I can dictate whatever the hell I want, and this is what I am dictating to you right now: You will bring Milani to the airport, where I told you, or you can expect more of the same. It's a simple choice."

He raised his fist and shook it. "Rowan Milani belongs to me. I will *never* do what you ask. Who are you that you think you can destroy Allah's sacred buildings and murder his holy warriors?"

"You have twenty-four hours to call me back. If you choose not to, then you will face the consequences." The connection ended.

Shrieking in rage, he clutched at his chest. His phone dropped to the ground. He closed his eyes, willing the pain to leave him. Rowan Milani was his. No one could make him give up what had cost him so much to obtain. He must consult with the Brothers. Rowan Milani could never be relinquished.

Danielle stepped out of the jet way and into the gate area in SeaTac. Her heart sank when she saw two men in suits approaching as she headed for the concourse. They had to be from the FBI. She'd seen Ralph, Chad and Rowan with that same detached, forbidding look on their faces. One of the men stepped ahead of the other. He looked older and had short blonde hair and light blue eyes. The other one looked younger, and had black hair and brown eyes.

The blonde agent spoke. "Excuse me, Ms. Stratton is it? Or are you going by Mrs. Hawthorne?"

The question caught her totally off-guard and she stood facing the two special agents, not sure how she should respond. The younger agent held out a hand. "I'm Special Agent Miller. This is

Special Agent Jones. We'd like to talk with you for a few minutes before you meet your parents."

She shook the proffered hand. Had her parents agreed to this? Had they been cooperating with the FBI? Had these two men been listening when she chatted with her parents? "Um, I'd like to call my parents and let them know I'm here."

Special Agent Miller gave her an affable smile. "Go right ahead. We're going to escort you to a conference room on the lower level where we can talk privately. You can call your parents while we walk. I'll take your bag for you."

Walking between the two men, she felt helpless, trapped and betrayed. Would she end up in a cell again? Her mother answered on the first ring. "Dani, are you in the airport? We parked, since we weren't sure when you'd arrive. We're at the Starbucks in the main terminal. Just tell us where you'd like us to meet you."

The excitement she'd felt at coming home to people who loved her, to people she trusted, was gone. "Hi Mom. I'm with Special Agents Miller and Jones, as I'm sure you already know. I have to talk to them before I can meet you. I'll call you later, if they let me." She ended the call before her mother could respond.

They rode the train to the main terminal, where the two agents led her down a hallway to a conference room. Inside, Jones motioned her to sit at a rectangular table. Facing them, she wanted to appear confident and unafraid, so she sat up straight and folded her hands in front of her.

Special Agent Jones opened a black leather portfolio and pulled a pen from an inside pocket of his suit jacket. "Ms. Stratton, or Mrs. Hawthorne, which name do you prefer? Or would it be more appropriate to call you Mrs. Milani?"

The question hurt. She'd thought about being Mrs. Milani more than they would ever know. One thing she'd learned the previous summer was never to offer more information than necessary. "My name is Danielle Stratton."

Special Agent Jones jotted a note before looking up. "Where have you been keeping yourself since you were released in Sioux Falls last July?"

She thought they must already know the answers. Everything was a game and she didn't trust them to let her go. If they could catch her in a lie and trip her up, they could keep her as long as they wanted. "When Special Agent Hawkins released me, he said I was free to go, no strings attached. He said the FBI had determined that my connection with Rowan Milani was innocuous. So, what difference does it make where I've been?"

Special Agent Jones smiled, but his eyes were icy. "We understand that Rowan Milani has quite an extensive network. It was our hope that you may be able to shed some light on who these people are."

"The only people associated with Rowan that I met were Chad Cantor and Ralph Johnston. You have Rowan in custody now. Why don't you ask him about his network?"

Special Agent Miller stood up. "Ms. Stratton, when Rowan Milani was apprehended, his cell phone had an open connection. The ID said *Danielle.* We know he called you. If you want to go home to your family this evening, stop with the innocent routine and answer our questions."

"I am innocent. Yes, I spoke with Rowan. We spoke often, although we weren't together. Rowan is an honorable man. He felt bad that I'd been caught up in his mess. Because of that and to protect me from further harassment by the FBI, he offered me a fake identity, a checking account and a place to stay in San Francisco. I don't know how he managed to do those things, but I needed to start a new life and would have been a fool to turn him down. That's the truth. It's all I know. Since I was freed with no strings attached, I'd like to leave now. Or do I need to call an attorney?"

Miller and Jones exchanged glances. Jones closed the portfolio and tucked the pen back inside his suit jacket. “All right, Ms. Stratton. You’re free to go. Thank you for your time.”

Surprised and relieved, she looked from one agent to the other and stood up. “Thank you. I hope I never see either of you again.” She left before they could think of anything else to ask her. Feeling desolate, she took the escalator up to the main terminal and headed for Starbucks.

Her father spotted her first and rushed to greet her with a hug. He pulled away and held her at arm’s length. “It’s so good to see you, Danielle. You look great.”

Her mother was right behind him, looking guilty. “Oh Dani, I can’t believe you’re here. I hope you’ll let me explain about the FBI. Let’s get your luggage and head home.”

She grabbed the handle of her carryon, ignoring her mother’s words. “This is everything. We can leave right now.”

Her father patted her back. “Let’s get you settled. Then you and your mother can go get whatever you need. I’ll cook dinner. How does that sound?”

Their happiness should have comforted her. But she couldn’t get past feeling her trust had been broken. “That sounds fine.”

Her mother gave her a quick hug. “Let’s go home. I’m anxious to see how you like what we’ve done with the lower level. It can be your own private apartment for as long as you need.”

Two hours later, she was relaxing by herself on the double bed in the bedroom her mother had prepared. She lay there in the semi-darkness, staring at the ceiling. Talking about Rowan with the FBI agents had filled her with an intense longing. She missed him so much. Now that he was in custody, she would probably never see him again. But she couldn’t help wondering what was happening to him.

In her hand she clutched an oversized coin. On one side, the Twin Towers of the World Trade Center were etched in gold. On the reverse side, in flowing script were the words: *We will never forget. 9/11/01.* Almost a year earlier, she'd given it to Rowan, while he lay recuperating in the hospital in Sioux Falls.

She'd found it lying on the coffee table in the living room at the estate in Kauai. Rubbing the coin, she wondered if he'd forgotten it or left it on purpose. It had meant so much to him, or at least that's what he'd told her. Now it was her one remaining connection to the only man she would ever love.

Rowan sat on a chair in the cement walled room. His hands were cuffed behind his back, attached by a chain to the shackles above his bare feet. Shemal strode in circles around him. The depravity emanating from the man's thickset body was palpable. Every time the bastard touched him, his hands clenched into sweaty fists. He'd never wanted, never *lusted* to kill someone as much as he wished for the opportunity to murder the man who controlled every tormented moment of his existence.

Shemal enjoyed toying with him. At first Rowan had been able to curb his body's reactions to the foul man, but not anymore. His weakened mind could no longer control his breathing when the knife cut into his skin and he was helpless to stop the copious amount of sweat his body produced. It soaked his hair, ran down his face and covered his body. The thin cotton prison uniform was drenched.

Shemal's hand slithered into his hair and wrenched his head back. He clamped his jaws shut, stifling a groan. The cold edge of the knife touched the side of his throat and he swallowed instinctively. The almost playful lilt in Shemal's voice raised goose bumps on his arms and legs. "Your carotid artery is laid bare. Shall I open it, the way you opened the throat of my habibti Marta?" The hand twined more tightly in his hair and jerked on his head. "You will answer each time I speak to you, worthless American dog."

The knife traced a line back and forth across his neck. He couldn't stop himself from swallowing again. "You don't want to kill me."

"You do not know what I want." The knife slid from his throat to his chest and twisted in a quick slash. His body jerked. The hand disengaged from his hair and he looked down, saw red blossoming on the sweat stained garment. The coppery scent of blood mingled with the sour stench of sweat.

His tormentor stood in front of him. "The President of Egypt has spoken with your President. He promised to return you to the United States to face trial for killing the kafir Ainsley. But now you face charges here for murdering the doctor who cared for you and made you well. We will not return what belongs to the Brotherhood. Do you remember from your study of Islam, that war is deception?" The knife slashed again, across his thigh. "Answer, dog."

His thigh burned and so did the wound on his chest. They joined the collection of nicks and gashes that Shemal reveled in carving on his body. So far, they were only surface wounds. He was terrified of what the barbaric man would do to him if he didn't answer the questions. "Yes, Allah's holy warriors excel at lying."

Shemal grasped his beard and wrenched his head up. His eyes glowed with enmity. "Now you will tell me who set the explosives that destroyed the House of Allah in Houston. Who is it that is threatening me with more destruction?"

Dumbfounded at the question, Rowan stared into the maniacal face. The knife flashed and he felt the sting on his neck. "I don't know."

The thick fingers dug deeper into his beard and took hold of his chin, but he felt the knife between his legs. He sucked in a quick breath. Shemal yanked painfully on his beard. “Tell me the truth or I will neuter you like I would a dog.”

He could only think of one man capable of the bombing, and that man could take care of himself. “Johnny Giacopino. He’s a mafia boss in Chicago. He . . . he helped me kill Capello.”

Shemal let go of his chin and stepped back, giving him a triumphant look. *“You* are the coward.”

His head drooped. “Yes. I am a coward.”

Shemal drew close again and raised his chin with the tip of the knife. “The Brotherhood has formulated a plan to deceive the man who destroyed the House of Allah. As you understand, war is deceit. Today as the world watches, you will die.” Shemal swung his head toward the door and hollered. “Guards, it is time.”

A group of bearded men entered the room. One of them pulled a black hood over Rowan’s head. He heard the sound of the chains being unlocked. Heavy hands grabbed him and lifted him to his feet. The men hurried him along with them and he couldn’t keep up. When he tripped, they dragged him until he regained his footing. The hands jerked him to a stop and forced him to his knees. He felt bodies on either side of him. Someone straddled his legs from behind, their knees grinding into his back.

The hood lifted. The men holding onto him wore white tunics and pants. Their heads were obscured by green masks. Only hate-filled eyes and leering mouths showed through slits in the fabric. Others scurried back and forth, chattering excitedly in Arabic. He swayed from side to side and would have toppled over if not for the rough hands that held him upright.

Bright lights switched on and he closed his eyes. The men shook him and he heard Shemal’s voice. “Open your eyes, clever Jinn. Allah requires your worthless soul.” A hand gripped the top of his head and forced it forward. “Look into the camera. We will record your death at my hand. You will have no blindfold to hide your terror.”

Understanding gelled in his mind. His pulse ticked wildly in his neck and thundered in his ears. Shemal had deceived him. The hand yanked his head back. He saw the curved dagger descend and felt it against his neck while a masked face grinned down at him. "The world will see that we do not negotiate with the infidels."

The group of men began chanting "Death to America," interspersed with shouts of "Allahu Akbar." The heavy hand forced him to stare into the lights and camera. His chest heaved and he tried to think. He needed more time. He felt light-headed, dizzy. The room swirled. The men cackled and shrieked, "Allahu Akbar," over and over. He closed his eyes. Horrific pain engulfed his head. And then he was tumbling, falling endlessly into silent, empty darkness.

CHAPTER TWENTY

Two Days Later

David trudged along the hall toward the interrogation room where Chad was waiting. Every day he'd worked with Rowan's friend. The man had been forthcoming, painting a detailed picture of the betrayal perpetrated on Rowan by the country's intelligence community. The list of people who had willingly accepted Muusa's lies astounded him. But then, why should it? He'd bought the entire deception as well.

The former special agent's information had bolstered the data he'd gotten from Michael's source. The mystery woman had gotten him into secretive jihadist forums and online chats he'd never known existed, even with his CIA contacts. The access would be a continuing treasure trove of intelligence. He'd give anything to know *her* identity. She'd also verified for him, once and for all that Shemal had killed Sa-id. He'd seen the archived file from the jihadist forum and read the gloating terrorist's own words.

Standing in front of the door, he took a deep breath and let it out slowly. While interrogating Chad, he'd come to understand the special friendship between Ralph, Chad and Rowan. He'd learned about the depth of commitment Michael, Rowan and Gabriel, whom he hadn't met, held for each other. And he'd discovered that Chad Cantor was a *good* man. A brilliant man, whose talents the Bureau had wasted.

Squaring his shoulders for the unpleasant task before him, he opened the door. Chad sat with his hands folded, cuffed to the table. He noted the dark circles beneath the intelligent eyes and that the boyish face looked drawn. And now, he would make the ordeal of confinement even worse. He slid into his chair and faced the younger man. “Good morning.”

Chad gave him a longsuffering look. “I’ve given you everything I can. I’m interested in making a deal. I’ll give the Bureau the software programs I wrote to reprogram our cell phone Sim cards to make our calls untraceable. I’ll teach it to the dummies in IT. I’ll train the Bureau’s hackers how to breach any security system. But I want guarantees for Ralph and me.”

Surveying the earnest face, he felt guilty. The President had made it clear that Chad Cantor was going nowhere. “We can talk about that later. I’ve got some news to share with you this morning. I don’t know quite how to put this. Rowan is gone.”

Chad straightened in his chair. “What do you mean, gone?”

He didn’t know how to ease the blow and didn’t want to dispirit his prisoner even more, but he forged ahead, wanting to get it over with. “I’m sorry. I wish I didn’t have to tell you this. Rowan is dead.”

“What? But you told me he was supposed to be put on trial.”

He watched as sorrow overtook the shock in Chad’s face. “I know. The Egyptian President told us that.” He stopped, not wanting to go on.

Chad hunched over in the chair. Tears brimmed in his eyes. “How do you know he’s dead?”

“A video was sent to every television network and cable news channel. Not one of them would play it, so they posted it on YouTube. It’s gone viral. Some radical group that was angry over the doctor Rowan killed and opposed to any U.S. involvement in Egypt got a hold of him. I’m so sorry. They beheaded him.”

“Have you seen the video?”

His eye twitched and he rubbed at it viciously. “Yes, unfortunately I have.”

Chad’s lower lip trembled. “I need to see it.”

“You don’t have to watch it. I don’t recommend it.”

Chad laid his head on white knuckled fists for a long moment, then sat up and looked at him. "Uh, I can't answer any questions today. I need . . . uh, please . . . take me back to my cell."

"Sure. We'll give it a rest for a few days. I'll get the guards." He stood up. The injustice of Chad's incarceration grated on him and he didn't know where to turn. He thought about Michael and wondered if Rowan's hardnosed colleague would help him. The door closed, but he heard Chad saying something and stepped back into the room. "What did you want?"

Chad's eyes were red-rimmed, his face grim. "I do want to see the video. Can you arrange that?"

"Are you sure that's a good idea? I haven't been able to sleep or eat since I saw it. It's *ugly.*"

"No, you don't understand. Rowan was a prize for Shemal and the Brotherhood. They wouldn't just let him be taken and killed by some ragtag bunch of crazies."

"The video looked genuine to me. If you're sure you want to see it, I'll bring my laptop in right now."

Chad closed his eyes. "Please."

Danielle tugged off the rain dampened jacket and laid it over a chair to dry. She looked around the lower level family room. It was starting to feel like home. When her phone rang, she answered right away. "Hi Angelo. Sorry I hadn't called. I'm starting to settle in here. You were right. It's good to be with family. And would you believe – next week I start a new job with Boeing. It's great to have a fresh start and I even . . ."

Angelo interrupted her. "Danielle, I am so sorry. I have some news. You deserve to hear it in person, not by phone. I wanted to call before you saw something on the news or online. I just heard it myself. Are you with your parents right now?"

Fear squeezed her heart. "No, they're upstairs. What happened?"

Angelo was firm. "You must not be alone. Promise me you will go be with your parents after we talk."

Her breath caught in her throat. "All right. Please, tell me what happened."

She'd never heard such agony in Angelo's voice. "Rowan has been killed."

She closed her eyes. It couldn't be true. Not *Rowan*. She saw his face – the reckless grin and his eyes, so full of desire. Whenever they kissed, she could feel the smile in his lips when they touched hers. She slumped down on the sofa. He was dead? He couldn't be dead.

Angelo's voice intruded. "Danielle? Are you there? Please answer me."

She'd forgotten that the phone was still against her ear. "How could he be killed at Quantico? I thought that with Sal Capello gone, they wouldn't hurt him like before. I never imagined . . ."

"They moved him secretly, to a prison the CIA uses in Egypt. That's where he was killed."

His words filled her with anguish. "Oh no. I remember. He told me about Tora. Oh my God. He was so frightened of being taken there."

"Danielle, you need to find your parents. It is important that you be with them, so that you are not dealing with this alone. Are you all right?"

Didn't he know? She would never, ever again be *all right*. She switched the phone off. Sobs shook her body. The pain in her heart left her gasping. She drew her knees to her chest and wrapped her arms around them. Burying her head, she wept until she was exhausted. Tears soaked her face and her eyes burned. She curled up on her side and whispered, "Oh God. Rowan, how can you be gone? You can't be gone. I love you. I miss you so much."

* * *

A Week Later

Michael tossed his phone to the bedside table and scratched the stubble on his jaw. “I don’t believe this.”

Asal stirred beside him in their bed and traced lazy circles on his chest with her fingers. “What’s the matter, Mikey? It’s too early in the morning for trouble.”

He grabbed her fingers and kissed them. “That was my mother. Two FBI agents were snooping around their clinic on the rez and out at the ranch. They interviewed her and my father. Asked all kinds of questions about a son named *Michael,* wanting to know where he’s been for the past ten fucking years. The agents wondered why the record ends after he left the Army Rangers. I can only think of one way that they got a line on my parents.”

Asal sat up next to him, her black hair tousled. “What did Georgia and Frank say to them?”

“My father told them they hadn’t heard anything from me in about a year and that they assumed I was on some kind of long-running clandestine operation.”

She sidled closer. “What are you going to do?”

Michael wrapped an arm around her shoulders. “I can’t stay in Pierre. If they somehow made the connection to South Dakota and know about the ranch and have my last name, it’s only a matter of time before they make other connections.”

“If they know about your service as a Ranger, they surely know you were a sniper. They can find out who you worked with. Gabriel may be in trouble. You both may be in trouble if the President’s investigator is notified.”

Smoothing hair off her face, he turned her head so he could kiss her. Enjoying the sensuous lips, he tugged the sheet down and caressed her breast, wishing they had more time. He pulled away from her mouth reluctantly. “Yeah, I need to make a few calls. Then I need to leave. You want to come with me this time?

I know you didn't come to Kauai because of Rowan, but that's not a problem now."

Asal pushed away, her hands on his chest. "What do you mean? Why do you think Rowan had anything to do with me deciding not to come to Kauai with you?"

Remorse overwhelmed him as he thought about his friend. "Never mind. One time, after too much whiskey, Rowan confirmed something for me, that's all."

She arched her sculpted brows. "I can only imagine what either one of you might have thought or *said* after too much whiskey. With Rowan, that was a normal occurrence. Besides that, you had your hands full when you went to Kauai. You didn't need any other distractions."

He saw the heat coloring her cheeks. "I know you and Rowan had a thing, years ago. I didn't hold it against him. God knows you're irresistible. Eventually, I forgave you for preferring a guy like him over me. At least you corrected your mistake."

Asal punched him lightly on the shoulder. "You are nearly as egotistical as Rowan was. That was seven or eight years ago. And, for your information, the *thing* lasted one week. It didn't take a genius to figure out that Rowan couldn't care less about whatever woman he happened to be with. That's one of the differences between the two of you."

Memories of Rowan flooded his mind. "It doesn't matter now. What I want to know is whether you'll come with me this time. It might be better for you, in case the feds keep connecting the dots."

Asal put her hand on his cheek. "Mikey, I know you think you should have been able to prevent what happened. But you can't be omnipresent. Rowan knew that."

Embarrassing tears brimmed and spilled over, surprising him. "I know."

She wiped the errant tears from his cheeks. "Yes, I'll come with you. Where are you planning to go?"

"First I need to make a quick stop in Sioux Falls. Then we'll get Jerry and Bryan to fly us to Dubai. I've got to make those calls. You better start packing."

Two Days Later

Gabriel wandered along the second floor walkway of the Plaza Mayor Mall, waiting for Sherie. His head ached and his stomach rolled. The hangover plaguing him was one of the worst he'd ever had. He raised his sunglasses long enough to massage his eyes. When they returned to the villa, he planned to work on tomorrow's hangover. This time, he would drink Jack Daniel's single barrel whiskey in honor of his fallen brother.

He made the sign of the cross. Ever since Michael had called him with the news, he had been consumed with guilt. Nothing alleviated it. He loved his wife and his children but Rowan had been – he *always* would be – his blood brother.

No one understood the bond, the solidarity between him, Michael and their stubborn amigo. He should have been with Rowan in Houston. But he'd lost sight of the goal. All he'd been able to see was his friend's obsession. And now, Rowan was gone forever.

Looking up, he saw Sherie walking toward him, laden with an assortment of shopping bags. Even though she had not said anything, he knew she felt relieved that the hombre, as she called Rowan, no longer threatened to take him away from her and their children. She reached him, looking sexy in the sleeveless white sundress and sandals, her luxurious hair floating around her shoulders. He leaned close and inhaled the sweet spiciness of her perfume. "Did you find what you were looking for?"

Sherie held up the bags for his inspection. "It's a start. We left so much behind. I'll be catching up for a while."

Thinking about the suitcases and boxes he'd crammed into the SUV before they left for Mexico, he took the bags from her and decided not to comment. "You have all the time you need. When do we pick up the Sophia and Jamie from your parents?"

"I arranged a surprise. Grandma and Grandpa are going to keep them overnight. We can have dinner, go to the cinema or if you prefer, we can have a quiet evening to ourselves in the villa."

His first thought was that he'd prefer to spend the evening drinking alone, mourning his friend and numbing the pain in his heart. But Sherie looked so pleased with herself that he couldn't bear to hurt her. Summoning phony lightheartedness, he held up the bags. "Holy Mother of God, you offer me an evening alone with my lover? My choice is made. Let's get going."

Sherie fell in step with him as they walked through the mall. "Do you think you can be content here in Leŏn someday? It's different, for me too, even though I spent summers here with my grandparents until I was in high school."

He couldn't tell her that being forced to choose exile in order to avoid federal prosecution was eating away at his spirit. So, he said what he knew she would like to hear. "As long as I am with you and our children, I will be content anywhere."

Sherie rubbed his back as they rode the escalator to the ground level of the mall. "My grandfather would love it if you took a position in the company. My father and uncles are nearing retirement age and you could bring a fresh perspective."

It took all his skill at deception to cover his dismay. "I am honored that they think so highly of me."

"It makes me happy to be here. I loved San Diego, but it is good to be near family."

The sourness in his stomach matched his attitude. He would not work for a bus company, even if it was the largest in Mexico. "If you are happy, then I am, too."

Sherie tucked her arm into his as they headed toward the exit. “Having you here with me, and with Jamie and Sophia means more to me than anything else.”

“Me too.” For the first time in their thirteen years of marriage, the family obligation grated. Maybe he’d been too independent for too many years. Much as he loved his family, he found himself longing for the opportunity to leave, to be part of another secret op with the men he called his brothers. But that would never happen again. Now, too late, he realized that his heart was divided. He would never be content with a nine-to-five job and quiet home life. That realization made him anxious to return to their brand new home and crack open a bottle of Don Real . . . and then the whiskey.

Muusa watched his students file out of the classroom. It had been a productive day of teaching. Now he would meet with other members of the faculty for dinner. He would regale his colleagues with the personal phone call he had received from the President of the United States. His fellow professors would rejoice with him in the victory Allah had given them.

The weak dog had called to express his deep regret over the loss of Rowan Milani to rebel forces, but also conveyed his relief at the closure of a sordid chapter of betrayal and retribution. The President had offered his condolences over the losses suffered in the destruction of the House of Allah as well. Of course, inept American law enforcement had no leads as to the perpetrators. He had chosen not to reveal the name of the man who had committed the horrific crime. The Brotherhood would deal with Johnny Giacopino in its own way, at an appropriate time.

He stepped into the vast, sunlit courtyard in the center of Al Azhar mosque. He heard a rumble that sounded like distant thunder and raised his head to the cloudless sky. A series of explosions rocked the courtyard and threw him to the ground as screams punctuated the quiet of late afternoon. Slabs of the ancient walls blew hundreds of feet in the air and began falling like deadly missiles. He scrambled to his feet and began running. Pieces of stone pelted him and a chunk the size of a melon banged the side of his head, driving him to his knees.

He swayed back and forth while waves of dizziness rolled over him. Many others had fallen. Blood stained the once pristine white marble and it was littered with debris. He couldn't make sense of what was happening around him. As he sat, hands on his thighs, fighting the pain, he remembered the words of the shayton on the phone. The man had promised more destruction.

But he and the Brothers had shown the entire world that Rowan Milani was dead. He rose to his feet and wiped dripping blood from his face. Still dizzy, he staggered across the marred stone surface, amid shouts for help and groans of pain. He must meet with the Brothers. They would find the shayton and destroy him. "Allahu Akbar . . . it will be so."

Asal spotted her prey at the bar as soon as she stepped inside what the airline people had called *The Crow Bar*. She sniffed at the scent of stale cigarette smoke that still lingered from the days when it was legal to smoke in South Dakota bars. Derek sat alone on a stool, wearing a hooded sweatshirt and jeans. A battered ball cap was shoved low on his head. Seducing him would be child's play.

She sidled onto a stool at the opposite end of the bar and took off her jacket. The white sweater, tight jeans and tall, black boots were much too classy for this establishment. Flinging her hair over her shoulder, she caught Derek's eye.

The bartender stood in front of her, beer belly protruding above his pants. "You must be new in town. What can I get you, sexy lady?"

The repugnant man made her long for the days when she worked real covert ops with Michael, Gabriel and Rowan, in her native Iran and other spots in the Middle East. She missed the challenge. This was just a simple game. Gazing at him from under long lashes, she allowed her accent to come through. She would honor Rowan, as well. "I would like a shot of Jack Daniel's single barrel whiskey, please. You may leave the bottle on the bar. It's possible my new friend down there may join me."

The bartender whistled. "Hot damn, a woman after my own heart. Hey Derek, I think someone just bought you a drink."

Derek wandered toward her, removed the ball cap and ran his fingers through his rusty brown hair before clambering onto the stool next to hers. "My name's Derek. What's yours?"

She parted her lips just long enough to focus his attention on her mouth. "Names are so unimportant, don't you think? It's what's in a man or woman's heart that I value."

The boorish fool waved at the bartender. "Oh yeah, what she said. Gary, how about another glass over here? I could use some Jack."

The fat man smacked two shot glasses on the bar. She poured for both of them and raised her glass. "To absent friends and new ones as well."

A tedious hour later, she helped him up the snowy front steps of the house he told her he used to share with a woman he had loved and lost to a jerk who'd almost killed him. After he poured a Bacardi and Coke, he went to the bathroom. She tapped the small envelope of white powder in his drink and swirled it with her finger.

Enduring another thirty minutes of his company while he guzzled the drink, she made her move. Stretching suggestively, she yawned and patted her mouth. He was so easy to lead, so gullible. While he lay naked on his back in the double bed, she straddled him and pulled off her sweater. He was mesmerized. "Oh man, you're so pretty."

His words slurred. When he tried to raise his hand, it fell back at his side. The drug had done its job. He would be lucid, but he would not be able to move. Reaching into the back pocket of her jeans, she pulled the Karambit. Sadness tugged at her heart. She would have loved sharing this with Rowan.

Derek's eyes widened when she held the knife in front of her. "Where did you get that?"

She caressed his cheek with the curved blade. "My friend Rowan Milani gave it to me, a long time ago. We were on a clandestine operation in Turkey, near the border with Iran."

She could tell he was trying to move. It pleased her to see terror invade his eyes. "Oh no, no. This can't be happening. How can you be one of *them?* Why pick on me?"

Losing patience, she grabbed his wrist and sliced efficiently. "You brought this on yourself. If you had only kept your mouth shut, your life could have continued. But you chose to tell the FBI about the people who kept you safe, who gave you a home."

He breathed in heaving gasps. "I only did what was right. They deserved everything. It was like a prison for me there. No one cared. I was all alone."

She raised his other arm and cut his wrist. His blood leaked steadily, but she wasn't quite finished. "If not for Rowan's largesse, the CIA would have taken you into custody. Who knows what they may have done with you."

His eyes focused for a moment. "Rowan Milani ruined my life. He took everything away from me. When I saw the video of him being beheaded, I celebrated." He grinned up at her.

She wanted to slap the grin away. Instead she hooked the tip of the knife just below his ear and drew it straight and deep across his neck. Dark blood flowed and wasted breath bubbled from his severed trachea. A spray of bright red blood from his carotid artery spattered her chest and face.

She wiped the knife on the sheet and found the bathroom. While washing the blood from her chest and face, she thought about the misery the stupid man had caused. She pulled her sweater on and left him lying on the bed. Then she went downstairs to wait for Michael to pick her up. He wouldn't be long.

Angelo opened the door of his tiny apartment and stepped back. "Michael? Please, come in. This is quite a surprise. What in the world brings you to Sioux Falls?"

Michael stepped into the tiny combination living room and kitchen. "I'm here to make a request. We don't have a lot of time. I'm not in the mood for anything but a quick *yes*, just so you know."

Angelo waved an arm at his worn sofa. "Sit down, please, and tell me what I'm getting into this time."

Perched on the edge of the sofa, Michael laced his hands together and gave him a sober look. "Derek has been chattering to the FBI like the little shit monkey he is. My parents have come under scrutiny. Gabriel has taken his family to Mexico. I just talked with Jerry and Bryan. The FBI has all but shut them down. The only way the Bureau could get any of this information is from Derek."

"It's only a matter of time, then, before they find me."

"That's right. And there's no reason for you to spend the rest of your life detained for agreeing to move to Kauai to help us."

"Give me a second. I'll be right back." While Michael waited, he went to his bedroom and grabbed the carryon he'd packed earlier.

Michael looked surprised. "How did you know?"

Moving to the kitchen counter, he poured coffee into the Starbuck's to-go mug Rowan had left in the study at the estate house. He unplugged the coffee pot. "Just a hunch. I talked to Ralph and he told me about Derek being left behind with Chad and Bettina. He is a bitter, wounded man. Those types are usually anxious to get even, any way they can."

Michael stood up. "You nailed it. Let's get going. We need to pick up a friend who's taking care of a few details. Then we've got to head for Omaha. Johnny Giacopino is sending his jet from Chicago. I'm tellin' you, I don't know what we'd do without him."

Angelo slurped coffee and grabbed his jacket. "Where are we going?"

Michael smiled. "Someplace where you won't need that jacket."

Agonizing consciousness returned. He heard ragged, groaning breaths and realized they were his. His hands formed shaky fists, but he had no strength. His shoulders burned and jagged pains radiated from his back and traveled down his legs.

He heard footsteps, opened his eyes in the inky darkness and tried to lift his head. His body shook and his heart rate skyrocketed. The guards must be coming. He couldn't escape, couldn't stop them. They'd haul him back to the vile, stinking room. Or they'd take him to Muusa . . . and his dagger.

He remembered the foul man's triumphant words. *The Brotherhood has formulated a plan to deceive the man who destroyed the House of Allah. As you understand, war is deceit. Today as the world watches, you will die.* Muusa and the Brotherhood would see to it that he suffered for as long as his body was able to breathe. The guards could do whatever they wanted with him. No one would stop them. No one would know.

The pain burned through his mind like a wild fire. It destroyed everything . . . the illusion of justice he'd clung to and the pride that had driven him. He closed his eyes to face what the agony revealed, wishing he didn't have to. But it was no use. His fragmented thoughts tumbled one over another. He saw his sweet, young Michelle and the burning Twin Towers, heard Ralph's gruff, comforting voice. Then he was with Gabriel and Michael.

They killed all the holy warriors and flew away in a plane with Jerry and Bryan at the controls. He laughed and drank Jack Daniel's. His throat closed. He could taste the whiskey and smell it over the stench that permeated the cell.

He saw the love in Chad's eyes for Bettina. His parents' faces swam into his mind. His father, always patient and kind. And his mother, so determined to find forgiveness from him. But he'd been hard-hearted.

Angelo's gentle voice whispered that he'd gone off-course. But he hadn't wanted to hear it. The psychiatrist's features dissolved, to be replaced by Danielle's sad face. He'd known deep inside that she loved him and would stay with him, no matter what. But he'd sent her away.

Hot tears leaked down his face. Lying alone in the filth, he wept. If only he could go back. He'd be a different man. But it was too late. He was always . . . too late. Reality was the cold, stinking cell and the unrelenting pain and humiliation. It would never end, until Muusa and the Brotherhood let him die.

He heard footsteps again, close by. Something brushed his face. Muusa or the guards must have returned, even though he hadn't heard the cell door open. He waited, heart pounding, for rough hands to wrench him to his feet and take him away, for the agony to begin again. Nothing happened.

He twisted his head and opened his eyes, saw sandaled feet. A person knelt beside him, wearing a robe that seemed to glow with brilliant white light and radiant colors at the same time . . . colors he'd never seen before. He blinked. The shimmering brightness didn't hurt his eyes; it warmed his body and permeated his soul. The figure reached out, wiped the tears from his face. The pain left his body.

The kneeling figure spoke, inside his mind. *Rowan.* He recognized the voice. It whispered unfathomable kindness – to him. Fresh tears blurred his vision. He didn't deserve what he sensed was being offered. He couldn't make out any features, but in his mind's eye, he saw the tender smile. The hand that had wiped away his tears gently closed his eyes. As he drifted into pain free unconsciousness, he heard the voice, one last time. *Redemption is yours, if you choose it.*

* * *

Hey Toots!

Hope I get to meet you sometime soon.

Stay locked & loaded & enjoy the story.

Mary Y

Mary Yungeberg

Picture by Julia Wollman

Mary has been an avid writer all her life. After numerous freelance articles published in a variety of magazines, along with several careers, she chucked her "real world" job to pursue her dream of writing thrillers. CONSUMMATE BETRAYAL, published in 2012 was the first in the Rowan Milani Chronicles. UNHOLY RETRIBUTION is the sequel. Both books are available in print and digital formats.

Mary is passionate about inspiring women to live with purpose and pursue their dreams. She is a strong believer in empowering women to defend themselves. She loves the sport of shooting and capably handles her two Glock pistols. When she's not at the shooting range or working on the next installment of the Rowan Milani Chronicles, you may find her burning up the pavement in her black Mustang convertible.

She lives in eastern South Dakota with her husband and Lucy, an intemperate Rat Terrier who runs their household.

For more information about the Rowan Milani Chronicles, visit Mary's website: MaryYungeberg.com.

Made in the USA
Charleston, SC
14 March 2014